GEN Z
CROSSING

GEN Z
CROSSING

GARY A JAMES

GEN Z CROSSING

This is a work of fiction. All of the characters, names, incidents, organizations, and dialogue in this novel are either the products of the author's imagination or are used fictitiously.

iUniverse books may be ordered through booksellers or by contacting:

iUniverse
1663 Liberty Drive
Bloomington, IN 47403
www.iuniverse.com
1-800-Authors (1-800-288-4677)

Because of the dynamic nature of the Internet, any web addresses or links contained in this book may have changed since publication and may no longer be valid. The views expressed in this work are solely those of the author and do not necessarily reflect the views of the publisher, and the publisher hereby disclaims any responsibility for them.

Any people depicted in stock imagery provided by Getty Images are models, and such images are being used for illustrative purposes only. Certain stock imagery © Getty Images.

ISBN: 978-1-5320-9013-4 (sc)
ISBN: 978-1-5320-9012-7 (e)

Library of Congress Control Number: 2020909174

Print information available on the last page.

iUniverse rev. date: 05/28/2020

Dedication

*For the children and youth of Rhema
KidsWorld, both past and present.
May this work of fiction fall into your hands one day, and
may it inspire you to reach for your limitless potential.*

Contents

The Philosophy of

On Monday, January 14th, the spring semester began. Students flooded the campus for the first time since the Christmas holidays. Some students, on arrival, began their search for classrooms, while others, for their classmates. Then some were setting foot on the campus grounds for the first time. Inside the buildings, these newer students walked almost aimlessly through the halls in search of important facilities. They would have fared better had they been bold enough to stop and ask, but they did not. This added to the deluge, as members of the faculty moved through hallways, trying to dodge student bodies as they walked towards their classrooms.

Madison Chambers had already found his friends. Madison and his friends were in their first year of college. They had completed the fall semester, and the winter semester was already planned. All four classes had been selected, all books already purchased, he even knew the room numbers in which the lectures were to be held. Madison already knew. He had to know. He would have been dissatisfied had he not known where everything was.

"I found out who's teaching Philosophy of Science Ontology Part 2," said Oden.

"Are you just finding that out?" queried Madison. "By now, that's old news. Professor Clarke decided to not teach this semester because of his book tour."

"Well, I'm just finding that out," countered Oden. "And by the way, when did you first hear of this change?"

"Oh, this happened back in November."

"November? And you expect me to find that out on the day it happens?" barked Oden. "November has long passed, you know?"

"Not according to my standards," said Oden.

"I've been wondering about your standards, Oden," said Madison.

Madison and Oden are good friends and have known each other going as far back as the eighth grade. Both are of Caribbean descent. Their peers would often compare the two as night and day because of their dispositions: one is more on top of everything when it came to time and what needed to be known. At the same time, the other is more passive and disorderly. This difference had often been the seed of conflict. Though Madison never took the differences between himself and Oden personally, he had often been annoyed by Oden's sluggish attitude towards quizzes, tests, and assignments given by the professors. While Madison would get things done early, Oden would wait until the last minute to turn his work in. This annoyed Madison, mainly because they were often studying partners. Oden, on the other hand, had his qualms about Madison's in-class practices. Being the one to always inquire, Madison would often hold the class up with his knack for fielding the professor with questions on earlier points. Oden would rather the professor move on to the next points.

"I wonder if you've taken the time to read Professor Johnson's syllabus," said Madison.

"It shouldn't be much different from Professor Clarke's syllabus," said Oden.

"Their teaching styles are different. And more than that, Professor Johnson is not like any other professor. I'll even say that he makes the classes more challenging."

"I think you're the one who makes classes more challenging," quipped Oden.

"How do I make classes more challenging?" asked Madison.

"That is too easy. By the way you stall the professors with your questions. You could at least wait for class to be over . . . but no. So many follow-up questions. So many things the professor has to share in one session alone. It's because of your inquiring mind that he has to either extend a lesson or push it to the next day. This is what you always did back in grade school, and the teachers were always annoyed."

"There is nothing wrong with raising questions," countered Madison. "In fact, this is what professors should be encouraging. This is how people learn."

"Oh, I learn during sessions because I'm listening. I'm wondering if you are. The others get it. That is why their hands aren't going up all the time."

"I don't know what kind of teacher or student would not expect a Q and A in a classroom."

"I know this prof's temperament," said Oden, "that he can lose his patience easily. He's been known to throw students out, and even fail them. That is Professor Johnson."

Ted Johnson walked from the teacher's lounge towards the lecture hall with a binder in one hand and a coffee mug in the other. The cup was three-quarters full of hot black coffee. Ted watched the cup intermittingly while looking out for the odd clumsy student who could bump into him at any moment. The walk took Ted from the second to the first level. He decided to take the stairway, believing that there would be less traffic to deal with. Ted walked the busied hall, meandering his way through the couple hundred feet between himself and the lecture hall. And, sure enough, an unknown student came towards him while looking sideways. Ted tried to avoid this youth but couldn't. His coffee-carrying hand was bumped, and a quarter of the contents spilled onto Ted's left pant leg and shoe, causing a stinging sensation. The youth got the worst of it because coffee spilled on his shirt, pants, shoes, and books.

"Why don't you watch where you're going?" snapped Ted.

"I'm sorry!" cried the student.

"Look, you got coffee on yourself. Go on . . . get! And clean yourself up." Ted looked down at his pant leg and shoe and saw the stains that were enough to grieve him.

Ted continued his walk to the lecture hall. Another student approached him, one he'd never seen before. She appeared to be new to the campus. "Excuse me, professor, I'm looking for . . ."

"Information booth is down the hall. They'll be glad to answer your question." And Ted walked on.

Ted walked into the already full lecture room, which had some sixty to eighty-five students sitting in wait. A few hushed interactions between students filled the room. They went silent the moment they saw the professor walk in. Ted placed the coffee cup on the desk facing the room before walking to the lectern. He looked up at the sea of faces; they also looked at him.

"As I look at this sea of faces, I am unaware of the thoughts going through your heads. Irrespective of the thoughts in question, I am hoping that you all know why you are here. If you don't, then you are in trouble. If this is the case, then I suggest you drop this class and don't come back. And if you do know why you're here, then welcome to the next level of the Philosophy of Science Ontology. If you think that most of your learning will be done in this hall, then you have another thing coming. This class is supposed to challenge you, not just inform you, meaning that most of what you'll be doing will be in the libraries, in your dorm, at home, or wherever you'll be doing research. Ask me what you will . . ."

Madison sat in the middle of the second row from the front. Madison had always opted for the middle of the second row. It brought him close enough to the professor to hear and become acquainted with the lesson points. It was close enough. Meanwhile, it was not so close that he would find the professor talking over him. When he heard, "Ask me what you will . . ." it thrilled him.

Oden sat in the second-to-last row from the top, at the far right. Oden always chose this spot. It allowed him to catch what the professor said while keeping himself out of the spotlight and away from the professor's attention. It also allowed Oden to slip out of the class, unnoticed, to use the restroom. And before class began, he could eye the hotties that walked through the entrance—and he had seen several. Oden heard, "Ask me what you will . . ." and knew that there was more to be said by the professor.

"but don't expect me to bear with you throughout class time or the semester. Most of what you'll learn will be on your own time. My job is to teach you how to learn in your own time. Yes, there's a way to learn and a way not to learn. You learn by testing things, whether these are ideas that are to be further understood and judged or objects that can be observed, measured, or weighed. If these ideas or objects wreak of myth and legend, then they are to be disregarded."

The first hand went up. It was Madison's. Ted pointed to Madison, giving him the okay to ask his question. "Professor, I believe the entire class understands what you mean by 'myth and legend.' I'm not religious, either. But how does one's worldview affect or hamper his research or even success in this class?"

Oden looked down at Madison with an impish smirk, believing that what he had expected in Madison was beginning to happen.

Ted looked pensively at Madison for a moment. Ted understood where he was going with this question. He then turned his attention to the class. "Okay, I would like to see the hands of all who are religious. Anyone with religious affiliations or religious presuppositions?"

A few hands went up. They went up slowly and with effort.

"Don't be shy," said Ted. "Are there more?"

No other hands went up apart from the few.

"Over there, in the gray jacket . . . what religion are you?"

The student, knowing the professor was speaking directly to him, said, "Catholic."

"How about you in the middle?" Ted pointed to a young woman in the middle row.

"Christian," replied the student.

"And you . . . let me guess, a Muslim?" Ted noticed the hijab she was wearing. It was evident to him what she was.

"Yes!" replied the student. "Okay, we have a Catholic, a Christian, and a Muslim. I will not put you three on the spot, but I will talk about your beliefs, of which I know you are ashamed. These three are responsible for some of the great atrocities of our time. Why do people espouse these worldviews? It is because they are holding on to something they believe will justify their atrocious behaviors. And when you test the ideas brought about by Catholics, Christians, and Muslims, you discover that they cannot be scientifically proven."

"Um, Professor?" Madison raised his hand again. Looking down at him from behind, Oden rolled his eyes upward.

"Go ahead," said Ted, pointing at Madison for the second time.

"You said that religious people are responsible. But is it only religious people? There have been many atrocities committed against innocent people by non-religious people."

"That is true," replied Ted. "What you need to understand is that commonly held ideas enforced among a people group, whether religious or not, are a hindrance to a student's intellectual growth. Religious people are the most notorious, is what I'm saying. They tell you to have faith and not question these beliefs."

"But what I understand," replied Madison, "is that faith is not what religious people would call blind faith."

"I understand that reasoning," replied Ted. "Much of what is advanced in the name of Christianity, Roman Catholicism, and Islam comes from a book that was written many centuries ago. They cannot be verified because, for one, they are not original writings. And it is on the lack of evidence that religious leaders tell their adherents to 'just believe.'"

"That's where I'd pause, Professor," said Madison.

By now, Oden had grown restless as he glared at Madison from behind. Hearing this extended exchange, Oden threw his arms over the back of his seat, stretched his legs out, and assumed a recumbent position.

"Though I do not share their beliefs, I feel empathy for their beliefs and what they call faith."

"What is your name?" asked Ted.

"Madison."

"Okay, Madison, what do you think they mean by the word faith?"

Madison paused for a moment. He knew that the way he answered this question might determine how the few who raised their hands appeared in the eyes of their peers. But he had no time to look at them.

"I think faith is what they would call trust in a source that is the foundation for all things that exist."

"All that exists?" asked Ted. "No one, until this day, has been able to account for this invisible man in the sky. Religious people claim that he is the foundation for all that exists. Well, anyone who has ever been serious enough to think about these things has come to understand how pointless these things are."

"Well, sir . . ."

Without allowing another word, Ted interrupted in an elevated tone. "Could everyone who does not understand the reason why they are here please stand up?"

The call was met with stone silence, even from Madison himself. Madison did not know how to respond to this sudden intrusion by the professor.

Ted continued in a shout to the entire group. "I would have you all reminded of the reason why you are here. This class is the Philosophy of Science Ontology, which comes from the Greek word 'Onto' which means 'existence' or 'being realistic.' In the study of all that is real, we must be realistic. If it is not testable, then it is not real. And if it is not real, then it is not to be tested. It does not belong in this class nor in this field of study. No matter how committed believers are, religious worldviews, are only intended to make people feel better or, in some cases, make them better. If telling stories makes you better, then tell stories. As far as my class is concerned, you will be studying all that is testable, and only that which is testable."

Madison raised his hand, in hopes of either asking another question or getting another point in. Still, Ted waved his hand dismissively at Madison. "That is enough! We will begin on our class requirements . . ."

Madison felt eyes all over him. This didn't bother him in the least. What did bother him were the questions that had been left unanswered, there and then. As the professor suggested, Madison would have to do most of his learning outside the classroom. *"But will this be learning without restrictions?"* he wondered. Professor Johnson had already marked out for the class what wasn't real, and he had laid the ground rules that these unreal things should not be tested. This scratched all religious suppositions from the list. This was day one of what would be Professor Johnson's Ontology.

Madison was never a believer in the supernatural. What qualified as supernatural are untested things, among those things that are realities outside this universe. Madison was not going to say that there were other universes or gods outside of this one, but neither was he going to say that they were not there. To deny that something or someone existed, for Madison, was no different from claiming that they did exist, without evidence. He was more inclined to not jump to conclusions. That was why he asked questions to no end.

Madison had had his share of church attendance. Born of a Jamaican mother and a Trinidadian father, Madison was raised in a home where there was a fear of God. Madison would ask about God only to get unsatisfactory answers, such as "He is always here," and "no one can hide from him." Madison was never satisfied with this kind of response. His grandmother took him to church each time he'd visited her. Madison had asked her questions, but he could not get a reliable, logical answer, for his grandmother only spoke the language of faith—whatever that is. Madison had only been in a Sunday school classroom twice in his life. In the two encounters he had with Sunday school teachers, he was told to ask his parents, because they were the best teachers in the life of the student. But Madison was never satisfied with his parents' answers. In the end, Madison resigned himself to not believing as some did. He understood that others had faith and that they had their reasons for that. Madison also had his reasons for not having faith in the unseen. He simply hadn't been able to fully grasp what faith is.

Madison walked into the café after the first day of Johnson's class. To his disappointment, every table was taken. Madison thought of joining any new foreign student with little knowledge of English. At least he would not have to say much because of the language barrier. He only wanted to be alone with his thoughts. Madison scanned the busied café for that foreign student. No one appeared to be speaking Russian, Farsi, or Cantonese. No one seemed foreign by the way they dressed. This was disappointing to him. Then as he scanned the back of the café, near the window, his eyes caught Oden's. Oden was at a table of five. They were conversing. Madison saw the vacant sixth seat, and Oden motioned for him to join them.

Madison joined the group of five students—Oden, Paula, Kenny, Darla, Seth.

"Nice to see you at this time, Madison," said Paula.

"By the way, Maddi . . ."—Maddi is an abbreviation Kenny loves to use when referring to Madison, and he adds a Jamaican accent to it—"How are you making out with that professor?"

"It's too early to give an answer," replied Madison.

"I don't think they're off to a good start," said Oden. "If it were up to Madison, they would have spent the entire morning talking about the Bible and the Qur'an."

"I know what that class is for," replied Madison. "It's the way the professor put the three students on the spot, just because of their religion."

"He did not put them on the spot," retorted Oden. "The professor was only exposing their beliefs."

"And what exactly are their beliefs?" asked Paula.

Before Oden could go any further with his version of the story, Madison jumped in. "One is a Muslim, one's a Catholic, while the other is a Christian."

"What did he say about these beliefs?" asked Paula.

"That they cannot be proven as true. Thus, these beliefs do not belong in our class research," said Oden, who had to jump in before Madison could twist the story in defense of the three students.

"Do you agree with the professor, Oden?" asked Paula.

"I agree with him," said Oden. "These things only belong at home, the church, or the mosque, but not in the university or the real world."

Paula turned her attention to Madison. "Do you agree with him?"

Madison knew that no one at the table professed to be a follower of any religion. "I believe that if some people see the truth-value in these systems, then they should be free to talk about them. I'm only saying—"

"The professor made it clear to the class," said Oden, "that there isn't any truth in these belief systems."

"How does he know that?" asked Madison.

"He's the professor. And professors know a lot because they study a lot."

"I know of professors who wouldn't agree with Professor Johnson. They've done their homework as well," replied Madison.

"What are they saying?" asked Paula.

"Some scholars make sense of this world by talking about artists and engineers. The reason why things came to be is because someone willed that things should come to be. I have nothing against that." Madison briefly looked in Oden's direction. Oden looked irritated by Madison, though he wasn't looking at Madison. Oden's disdain-filled eyes were locked into dead space. Madison continued, "You don't have to see it the way I do."

Seth chimed in, "I'm with the professor on this. There's a place for these things. Sorry!"

"Well, I . . ." Kenny believed he should vouch for Madison, in case Madison felt outnumbered. "I'm going to side with Maddi on this. Oden, I'm not going to let your boy look silly, so I'm going to take it on myself to look silly with him."

The group chuckled.

"I think God belongs in that class every bit as much as Oden's smelly feet belong in that class." The group, except for Oden, burst out in laughter.

Oden reached out for Kenny, while Kenny shielded himself from Oden's grip. "Why should the entire class wonder where that smell is coming from, and not ask where everything else came from?"

The group continued their laughter.

Paula responded, "So, you're saying, Kenny, that everything else came from God?"

"That's what it looks like," replied Kenny.

"But that's a non-sequitur," barked Oden.

"What's a 'non-sequitur?" asked Kenny.

"It's one of the new words Oden learned in class today," said Madison. "He means that what you said about God doesn't mix with everything else that came into being."

"Or," added Paula, "everything else that was created couldn't possibly point to God."

"I already knew what that word meant," said Oden.

"Then why do you think this is a non-sequitur?" asked Madison.

"Because that is lazy reasoning. We don't even know where God came from if he even exists," replied Oden.

"I'm not saying that I know what God looks like," said Madison. "I couldn't say what he's like, what his real name is, or if god is really a machine."

"That would have to be an invisible machine," added Kenny. "If everything came from an invisible machine, I'm sure everything one day will be sucked back into this invisible machine. I hope both Oden's feet will get sucked in as well because he got the baddest smelling feet on this side of the Province."

The group, except for Oden, broke out into a guffaw. Oden got up from his seat to clubber Kenny, but Kenny got up in time. He made a mad dash to the exit, with Oden close behind. The others dispersed, as the clock signaled the start of the next class time.

How everything came to be. . .

The first day of classes came and went. Day two, and the halls were not as frenzied as the previous day, simply because, by now, the entire student body knew where they were going. Ted stepped out of the teacher's lounge to make his infamous stride to the lecture hall. This time he took his coffee thermos. For one, this thermos had a handle and was small enough to carry effortlessly, and the bonus was that it had a lid to prevent spills. He didn't want yesterday's mishap to repeat itself.

Ted walked by students as he went. A few greeted him, and he didn't answer them. He went, turning neither left nor right as if he were on a mission. Professor Johnson was on a mission—a mission to instruct and shape the minds of the next generation.

Ted walked into the already full class. The same group of sixty to eighty-five students looked expectantly at him. He placed his thermos down by a ledge then spoke.

"Good Morning. There will be a quiz."

Ted thought he could hear the reactions of more than eighty unprepared students.

"Before we go into the quiz, I will be showing you a thirty-three-minute documentary on the universe's origins."

Ted could hear sighs of relief throughout the room.

"Pay close attention and take notes, for right after it ends, I will be quizzing you on the details of the film."

An hour later, the students turned in their quizzes. After the last student turned his paper in, the professor rose from his seat and stood by the lectern.

"Now that we're done, we can now discuss the film . . ."

Professor Johnson started to ramble off over technical details that would put the average person to sleep. Most of the students nodded off. It comes to show how average they are. The eyes that did not grow heavy widen in amazement at the extent of knowledge. Out of the few that stayed awake, one person wasn't satisfied with the answers.

The first hand went up, and it was Madison's. Ted pointed to Madison. "Now, Professor, we know that the scientific community agrees on the stuff of the universe and how they came to be. But even scientists disagree over what came before the stuff of the universe. Could you also talk about the disagreements among scientists on this one thing?"

Ted knew that at some point this semester, he would have to answer this question. He had done it so many times in the past. And no matter how many times he addressed this question, he was still irritated by one proposal. *One would have to be dense to believe someone spoke this universe into being and fine-tuned it, without the use of instruments, so that billions of people could live on one tiny planet in the darkened region of one tiny galaxy. People would have to be real simpleminded to believe this. It cannot be supported within any stretch of the human imagination. Even if the entire universe and its properties came by the will and intent of such a powerful being, one would need to ask if he is even aware of the billions of people on this planet. The dangerous conditions on every planet known to man should tell scientists that life, especially intelligent life, is unintended."* Ted stepped out of his thoughts to answer the student.

"Yes, there are disagreements among scientists. It's an age-old question—"

Professor Johnson didn't finish his sentence when the lights blew out. The eighty-plus students reacted with whispers. Other students were more audible. The large room was light-dependent because of the windows lined along the back of the lecture hall. Because of this, the students couldn't see the professor any more than they could see one another.

Professor Johnson hollered. "Everyone, calm down. It's just a power failure. I'll go talk to the school janitor. Maybe he'll get the power started again."

Ted shuffled towards the entrance. He was thrilled only to see the lit exit placard that hung over that entrance. Ted turned the nob and exited.

Ted returned eleven minutes later and saw that no one left their positions. Maybe it was too dark to maneuver through the classroom without stumbling over fellow classmates. Ted smiled as he walked into the room. No one could see his smile.

"Good news, everyone. We'll have light soon . . ."

Thirty-five minutes later, the lights came on. Professor Johnson was perturbed. He began.

"What were we talking about before all this happened?"

A student hollered. "We were talking about creation . . . or how things began."

"That's it," Ted replied. "How things began. Let there be light."

The students laughed at the professor's attempt to make light of a quote from the Bible.

Ted was relieved the moment he saw a hand that was not Madison's. He pointed to the student.

She spoke. "Doctor Johnson—"

Ted interrupted her, "Professor Johnson."

"Sorry," she said. "I was thinking about the film. People in the film were saying that the universe was very hot in the beginning. And they said that it was then that something exploded. If something came from nothing in only seconds, what is the best answer for all these things just appearing from out of nowhere?"

"Good question!" replied Ted. "What happened, and how it all happened, within the first ten seconds of the Big Bang is mindboggling, as you saw in the film. The best possible answer is what careful thinking will lead you to."

Madison raised his hand again. It was the only hand that was up at that moment. It appears that the students were too timid to raise their hands, fearing that their questions might make them look stupid. They could be too prideful to raise their hands because they had too many answers to condescend to ask questions. Ted pointed to the one student with a question.

"Professor Johnson—"

Ted interrupted as he pointed, "You call me 'Doctor Johnson.'"

Madison continued sheepishly, "Dr. Johnson, the universe is beyond our mental abilities to fully grasp. Light is hot. It's powerful. But, as you see, see need it. Something this great might never be understood in our lifetime."

Ted said, "You are absolutely right about that. It may never be fully understood, but we are heading in that direction. Don't you think that this is enough?"

Before Madison was able to reply, Ted continued, "This question is not only for you but for all students. We need to wrestle with these questions. What we can't afford to do is stop at the religious, the-book-says-it-and-that-settles-it approach. That is not the approach you should be using. For when you do, you run the risk of total failure in life, and this class."

"You mean a failed grade?" asked Madison.

"I would be doing you a favor by failing you," replied Ted.

"Then, you are ruling out any answer coming from students who happen to be religious?"

"I rule these answers out simply because all personal study and reason are retarded by 'Only God has this knowledge.' This is not good enough. That answer hampers your research and is why it is deserving of a failed grade."

Madison did not answer. He could not answer, so he sat in silence for the rest of the session.

After the class was over, Madison found his way to the library. He noticed that it wasn't crowded; compared to the other facilities, this one wasn't busy. There were two floors for students in this library, yet only a few were present. Madison began his walk through the aisles and bookshelves. He found a few reading materials, then he found a corner for himself.

A moment later, Oden walked into the library. Somehow, Oden could pick up Madison's scent. He found the corner where Madison sat, relaxed, and undisturbed by his surroundings. That would soon change.

Oden stood by Madison's table. "Hey, I was looking for you. What are you reading?"

Madison lifted the book and turned the front cover up for Oden to see. "*The Kalam Cosmological Argument.* William Lane Craig. Isn't he that Christian apologist?"

"Yup," replied Madison.

Oden had on him the look of disdain. "How did that get in here? And why are you reading it?"

"I want to understand the Christian worldview," replied Madison. "And if I must look at some of their best scholars, I'll do it."

"Brother, you are wasting your time," said Oden. "That isn't even on the list of assigned readings."

"Neither does it have to. I read it because I want to go further in my search for truth."

"You're not going to find the truth there."

"The truth is that this book does talk about the universe's origins from the Christian's perspective," said Madison.

"It looks scholarly in the way it's written," said Oden.

"Craig is a scholar, and I am a truth-seeker," said Madison.

"How about you tell me what you've read so far? Tell me one thing in that book appealing enough to get my attention and that of other readers."

"Okay, I don't know what would get your attention or that of others, but in this book, Craig talks about Geoffrey Leibniz's answer. If I can use layman's language, to Leibniz, the universe is a big, jumbled-up system, with a lot of tiny parts and details. But all this came from a system that was very small and simple. I think Leibniz was saying that something basic can only be understood using basic language. Meanwhile, something that is very advance or very jumbled up needs more explanation."

"How I see it," explained Oden, "is that it's not the tiny parts of the Big Bang that need lots of explaining, but it's the actual event that needs much explaining. Something big happened at the beginning of the universe that I don't think anyone can explain."

"It was a big event. I know that, Oden. No one has the answer. I'm trying to understand what the issue is with someone greater than us already having the answer. It may not be the God of the Bible. Yet I take no issue with a supreme being creating the universe."

"I'm not ready to concede that," said Oden, "because, as the professor said, people gave up all reason just for the sake of the religious elders and some rite."

"Well," said Madison, "despite that, I'm every bit as spellbound by the Big Bang event as you are. But I still think the option of a person with lots of power is a good answer. In this page referring to Swinburne, Swinburne calls God the simplest answer."

"His answer is too simple," cried Oden.

"Shush! Please!"

Oden turned to see where the voice came from. It was the librarian who demanded that he keep the noise down. Oden looked around to see all eyes on him and realized just how loudly he must've been speaking. The librarian turned her gaze back to her computer, and Oden sat on the chair across from Madison and spoke in a more hushed tone.

"If we were in public, I know she couldn't talk to me like that."

"You were talking loud," replied Madison.

"Listen," said Oden, "that is way too simple an answer for intelligent people like yourself to buy."

"I don't think so. I see it this way: God doesn't get in the way of the system. The system is the way it is, whether you believe in God or not. I see myself looking over his shoulder to find out how he did it."

"You'd have to explain to him and where he came from," replied Oden.

"Oden," said Madison, "that is out of our reach right now. All we have is the system he created."

"The idea of someone creating something this vast is unthinkable," replied Oden.

"We couldn't explain this being. I thought about the machine. If the creator were no more than a mindless machine, or a robot, then there would be no answer for this universe. But I think there is an answer."

Oden raised both hands in a show of surrender, as he rose from his seat. He turned and started walking. "See you in class!"

When everything came to be. . .

At 7:45 AM, on the following Monday, students were entering their second week of classes. Madison and Oden sat behind the steering of Oden's Nissan Sentra. Usually, it would have taken them thirty minutes from Madison's house to the campus, but this morning was different. Looking over Oden's dashboard, Madison could see taillights as far as his eyes could take him. A traffic jam stretching as far as twenty-five to forty kilometers was causing trouble for the morning commuters. They sat on the main road. They felt like the car was parked. Oden was going to take the freeway, but there was a backup. Oden was left with no other choice but to ride this through to his destination.

The roads were clear from snow, sleet, and ice. If there was black ice, it would have been too late for the persons involved in an accident to find out.

Madison had on him the apparent look of regret. "Had I checked the traffic reports this morning."

"I don't think there was a thing you could have done," replied Oden. "You couldn't have expected this. This probably happened not long before you left."

"You're right. But I got to appreciate you coming this way for me."

"Come on, Mad, you know I would come this way for you. I'm sure you would have done the same for me."

"Of course," confirmed Madison, "I would have done the same."

"There's another thing," added Oden.

"What's that?"

"You got to stop holding up the class."

"I'm holding up the class?"

"That's what you've been doing for the past week."

"I'm not sorry! I make no apologies for asking questions," said Madison.

"Problem is that you've been asking these while he is teaching."

Madison sat with his eyes flushed on the license plate in front of them. His mind was really on events of the past week, and this old accusation Oden was pinning on him, again.

"You always do this. For as long as I've known you, you've been holding up classes. Mr. Roberts didn't like it, and Mrs. Jones didn't like it. Ms. Slowly didn't like it. Mr. Graham was annoyed by it. And now, Professor Johnson."

"Oden, you just never know who could benefit from this. Classes are full of students that are too shy to ask questions. In the end, their questions are never answered."

"In the end, the lesson is never taught because you're holding up the class. You do know that two hours' worth of lesson time had to be carried into this week because of you?"

"I never thought I was that important that I could spoil it for everyone."

Just then, the traffic started to free up. Oden was able to move. Now he was driving at fifty kilometers an hour.

Madison looked down at his phone. "8:25?"

Fifteen minutes later, Oden pulled into the campus parking lot. "Ah man, there's no parking. I have to drive to the other lot. And that's a far walk."

"Yeah, and we're late," agreed Madison.

A loud horn from behind startled the two. Oden looked behind him and saw a black Audi. The person getting their attention decided to sit on his horn.

"Who's doing that?" asked Madison with a look of shock.

"It's the professor," Oden replied, casting a knowing look behind him.

It happened that Oden and Madison were not the only ones in traffic. Professor Johnson was also caught in the gridlock, for he was coming from the same direction as the two students. Oden yielded the right of way for the angry motorist, who then ripped past him to get to the reserved parking.

"This is going to save us from having to explain to the professor what happened," said Oden.

Madison and Oden arrived at the classroom twenty minutes late. They went to their seats. Not long after, the professor walked in, carrying his briefcase. No coffee for him. No coffee, so there was no telling how irritable he'd be this morning.

Ted laid his briefcase on top of his desk then walked over to the lectern. He looked up and around and saw vacant seats. It appeared to him that several students were not in class because of a setback he knew all too well and had fought through.

"I apologize for my tardiness," Ted started. "We have now entered week two. I am sure that by now you have all finished your required reading. I would like to believe the same for those who are not present at this time. I would like to bring up this important point that, I believe, will segue into the lesson topic. By now, you all should know why you are here and the role this class, the Philosophy of Science Ontology, will play in your career ventures. Some of you will become computer engineers; some will become astronauts; some will become owners of corporations; some will become published authors, while a few will become philosophy professors, like me."

This fifth option stirred laughter throughout the room.

Ted continued, "And wherever your life tends, you will understand the importance of time. Time affects us all in many ways.

Forty-five minutes later, the students got up and started to leave. They walked by Ted, who stood over his desk with his eyes fixed on his notes. Madison lingered by his seat as the students left. Approaching from behind him was Oden, who was also heading for the exit. Oden shot Madison a derisive look the moment they locked eyes.

"The prof shut you down," whispered Oden, quietly enough to stay out of the professor's earshot.

"Get on with your ignorant self, OD." No one really understood why Madison called Oden "OD." It could be short for Oden's given name, or it could really mean "Old Devil."

The last student was on her way out the exit when Madison approached Professor Johnson's desk. Ted sat and kept himself immersed despite the unexpected visit. Madison stood over the desk, opposite Ted.

"May I help you?" Ted asked in a tone, meaning, "This had better be important."

"Dr. Johnson, this has something to do with the textbook I asked about days ago. Normally, I would have all my books before the beginning of the semester. I tried a third time to get one of the assigned books on Amazon after they ran out of copies in the bookstore. After they canceled the shipment on me the second time, I thought my book was on its way."

"Did you check the tracking reports?" asked Ted.

"I did. And just recently, I found out that Amazon was sending the wrong edition."

"You need the eighth edition," replied Ted. "You will be needing it throughout the semester. Most tests and assignments will come from this book."

"They sent me the seventh edition."

"And why is that?" Ted asked, now looking Madison in the eye for the first time.

"I don't know why the seventh edition came."

"You sure it wasn't a typo? A slip of the finger on the screen?" Ted asked with a hint of irony.

"Couldn't be, sir!"

"Then, what are you going to do?"

"Maybe ask one of my classmates to photocopy a chapter for me."

"And how often and for how long will you be doing this?"

"Hopefully, until I can get my copy."

"Okay, now that you have your temporary answer, what may I do for you?" asked Ted, hoping for some alone time.

"I'll have to fix that problem. But regarding our topic, I've been thinking about the so-called reality outside of this universe. Whatever it is, it cannot be subject to time as we are subject to time in this universe."

"I must tell you that I do not debate my students," Ted said, now butting in. "You must have mistaken me for some atheist professor on some show or some movie. Unless they are my peers or equals, I'll only allow students to ask me questions. Now, do you have a question?"

"I do, sir. Are the different time slices equally real? At what point are these time slices no more? I'm saying this because I can only wish last month was as real as this month. At least I could travel back in time to get my textbook from the bookstore, and not go through Amazon."

Ted smiled gleefully at the comment. "Time is, indeed, a mystery. It doesn't have physical properties like hands or feet. It doesn't have a body of any sort. But this reality controls the universe, and it controls life on this planet. We do not control it right now, so we must conform to it. I have no final answer to the thing we are trying to understand more. Will there be wormholes one day by which we may transport ourselves to another time? What motivates me on this quest is the time slice that we are in. A moment ago, I did not know what you wanted. Now I do. What amazes me is the fact that that moment was every bit as real to me as this one."

"What amazes me about time," added Madison, "is that as time goes by, you get older, and as you get older, you become wiser."

"Good thought!" remarked Ted. "You, like myself, are learning more. You are on your way. Go get that book and learn more."

Ted lowered his head once again to return to his work. Madison, with no more questions left on his chest, nodded slightly before stepping out of the lecture hall.

Why everything came to be. . .

A month later, after several tests and quizzes and a paper that was due in the first week of February, Madison was winded. He had other classes with other assignments. Madison had never worked as hard as he did the past month, courtesy of Professor Johnson's course. Not only did he have that first major paper to complete and turn in, but he also had a smaller one to complete.

It was Monday of the first week of February. Without Oden's car, Madison had to wake up an extra hour early to make it to class. He thought to himself, *"Had my old man paid to keep me on campus . . ."* The cost of living might have been different, but at least Madison would be on campus. Study time and preparation would have been much more manageable. Even time in the library would beat time on the bus since he had to bounce from one bus to the next. Only twice had Madison missed his stop. It took a considerable amount of time from him, especially that second miss, where he had to stay on the same bus until it returned him to his destination. Another peeve was that while on the bus, Madison had to put up with the distractions around him. He had to put up with silly teens and their aimless chatter; he had to put up with the passenger with poor hygiene; he had to put up with the young mother with a bawling child; he had to put up with the person with the headset playing the kind of music Madison didn't care to listen to. And it was usually so loud that Madison wondered how this person hadn't blown his hearing long ago.

Madison hopped off his first bus. Normally, he would walk across the street to take the second bus. Time was limited, so Madison decided to take the faster bus. But to make it to this bus, he would need to cross the park to get to that terminal. This walk was long, but if time could be saved by doing this, it would pay off.

Madison crossed the park with his backpack over his shoulder. He had his work with him, including the paper that was due that day. He walked past the soccer field in the crisp winter morning air. Thankfully, the ground was not covered with snow, for this would have made it more challenging to cross. He continued his walk with the terminal now in view. But something caught his attention, which was an unusual sighting. Two dark scarves twirled violently in midair. They landed on the ground, once or twice, before retaking midair. Madison heard the high-pitched sounds from a distance and knew the squeaking was coming from forest creatures. The dark, ribbon-like animals were squirrels. And they appeared to be fighting over something. Madison continued walking, almost tripping along the way, as his attention was still fixed on the squirrels. The squirrels fought violently, swirling into midair, biting and clawing at each other. Then they both landed on the frozen grass. This time one remained still. Madison saw the other squirrel still moving, but violently. It scrambled back and forth with abandon. This was not a dance of victory; it was a dance caused by madness. The squirrel had rabies.

The creature saw Madison and started racing towards him. Madison saw this and ran with all his might. His heart was in his throat as he ran and did look back. Madison saw what looked like the terminal, but his mind was lost in what was behind him that he couldn't see what was in front of him. Then he felt the scurrying of claws on his back; the thing he dreaded was happening. Madison heard the squeak that almost pierced his eardrums and screamed. He fought violently to avoid getting bitten by the squirrel as he ran. Madison didn't know where the critter was. He knew that it was on his back, on his head, and on his shoulder. Madison fought and bellowed as he ran. He didn't see the curb until it was too late, because he tumbled over onto the concrete, backpack and all. He rose from the embarrassing fall and still felt the scurrying of claws. Madison saw the squirrel on his left shoulder and bawled. He fought and ran as the critter scurried all over him. Madison ran until the creature was finally shaken off. He got to the terminal, saw a crowd at the bus stop, and pushed past the easily angered bunch to get onto the bus.

Madison found his seat. He huffed and puffed after having spent most of his energy. Madison searched his jacket, and himself, for claw marks, especially bite marks. He was relieved when he found none.

Madison knew that he was on schedule. He wondered what would have happened had he decided to stay at his regular stop. Madison would have lost twenty minutes. Instead, he had gained twenty minutes. Then Madison wondered if coming all this way to get to the terminal was worth the hassle. He was saving himself time and lessening the chance of late arrival because Professor Johnson seemed to be marking students for lateness. *But nothing was worth having to coming face to face with a ravenous squirrel.*

Despite that horrific experience, Madison was relieved to know that he was on the bus and en route to the university campus. He knew that he was bound to arrive at the college and in the class minutes before the start time. Just then, he felt a strange feeling, as though something was missing—his backpack. As Madison tumbled over onto the concrete, his bag had gone down with him. And in the confusion of the moment, Madison had gotten up without grabbing his backpack.

He cursed himself for leaving his backpack on the curb. All that was important to him was inside that backpack—his smartphone, his tablet, his textbooks, his folder, his paper that was due today. Now all that was inside his bag was still lying on that curb. The bus was almost at his destination. How could he possibly get to his backpack? And if he were to go back and ask about its whereabouts, there was no guarantee that he would find it. Technically, everything of importance was gone, all gone.

Madison cursed himself again. This time all the other passengers could hear him.

Madison arrived in class on time, but empty-handed, as students filed into the room and found their seats. Madison looked behind him and towards the end of the aisle and saw Oden. Oden had never been one to carry a bunch of items with him. He would never bog himself down with a carry-on. A booklet or small binder was all he needed. Oden had a binder with his paper. At least he had his report. Madison, on the other hand, had to come up with an explanation for why he didn't have his.

Professor Johnson stepped into the lecture hall with his coffee thermos and briefcase. He placed the briefcase on his chair while leaving the desk bare.

"Good Morning! As you all should notice, my desk is bare. By the end of class time, I expect this desk to be crowded with reports. You had well over two weeks to complete it. Thus, you are without excuse. Putting that aside, I'd like to read a quote for you by Terry Eagleton . . ."

After the quote, Ted paused to scan the room for faces.

"I can see you are thinking about this quote by one who, I will say, is a literary genius. With this quote in mind, I'm assuming you all have this in common: you're all in need of improvement. You all want to grow. That is why you're all here—to earn your degree. And this is a big leap for anyone who enrolled in this university. You heard the quote, 'Knowledge is our greatest pursuit in life.' But what does this knowledge involve? In other words, what kind of knowledge are we after? Anyone?"

A hand went up, and it was not Madison's. Ted pointed to the young woman in the middle of the fourth row. Madison looked on and recognized it to be the Christian.

"Thanks, Professor. I'm not one-hundred percent sure what the writer meant by knowledge, but I believe we're after meaning."

"And what do you mean by meaning?"

"I mean that there's always something more that we need to know about our lives and about ourselves. When something's not right, we learn that we need to change that thing."

"What you're saying is that the meaning we are in search for has already been established before we were born, and cannot be otherwise?"

"I believe there's truth to what the writer wrote. But I also believe that there is an absolute truth that things should be."

"You said, 'should be,' or 'ought to be,'" Ted said. "If such is the case, then is the knowledge we should be after supposed to be obtained by all persons living?"

"I would guess so," replied the student.

"When you learn that the 'ought to' isn't happening for some, what would you say to those individuals? What would you say to those who are content the way they are, and sense no need for improvement or change?"

"Well, sir, that would depend on the kind of need."

"How about this as an example? You are a physically trim size six, and you have a friend who is oval-shaped and obese. What would you say to that friend who loves her body and is still healthy despite her shape and size? What would you say to her? Is there an 'ought to'?"

"I wouldn't say anything. I have friends of different shapes and sizes."

"But is there an 'ought to'?"

"Personally, I believe that we were created by God. I believe that our bodies are designed. And if we are good for our bodies, there's a chance that we might live longer."

On hearing this, the professor paused in silence, hung his head, and exhaled in his disappointment. After what had to be a minute of shaking his head in disapproval, Ted finally looked up.

"Young lady, what you just did was throw God into the picture, as though he were responsible for our being here."

"I think he *is* responsible."

"That's what you've been taught to believe. Most of the students don't believe that he put us here. And they are leading lives no different than you are. Some seek improvement, and some don't care for improvement. Why should there be an 'ought to'?"

"I think we're all designed the same," replied the Christian.

"But it does not make us all alike, does it?" countered Ted.

Another hand went up. It was a student in the second-to-last row at the opposite end of where Oden was sitting. Ted pointed to him.

"I think we can learn the truth about ourselves—the way we are wired. At the same time, I think we can make our lives meaningful without being told that we are here for a reason."

Like a light that had been switched on inside this lecture hall, Ted smiled with approval. "That is a beautifully well-said answer. I believe in absolutes. I believe in that which is true as it pertains to the way things are at this moment in time. To posit the idea that there's a reason why we are here is to say that we are here because of someone's choosing. There is no way on planet Earth that we are going to know that."

Madison would have raised his hand and volunteered his answer, but he was too depressed and upset after having lost his backpack on his way to the station.

Another hand went up. Ted pointed to the person in the back row. "Thanks, Professor. Going back to what the author was saying and what you're saying . . ."

"Sir, I can barely hear you," Ted jumped in. "You're going to need to speak up."

"Sorry, as the author and you were saying . . ."

"I still can't hear you."

Ted faced someone at the corner of the room. He then pointed to a soundboard at the front of the hall and at the far right. Knowing what was expected of him, he walked to the soundboard, turned it on, then tuned the dials and keys. It took him under two minutes to do this. He took the mic that was sitting on the soundboard, tested it, then walked it over to the student in the back row.

"Go ahead," Ted said while staring at a clock above the entrance.

"Thanks, Professor. Going back to what the author was saying and what you're saying, I think we can see our roles in . . ."

Ted saw his lips moving but heard nothing. Ted looked over to the soundboard and gestured to the one controlling the sound. The young man played with dials and levers, but still, there was no sound. He searched in a cabinet for batteries, figuring that might be the problem with the mic. After finding out that they were good, the young man touched one of the connections. Then a loud screeching sound startled the entire room. A few students fell off their chairs while most writhed in pain with their hands covering their ears. Ted was the only person in the room who was not startled. He was perturbed. The student holding the mic spoke again. There was no sound.

Ted grew impatient. "I don't think I can wait any longer. From what I just heard, the student said that we can see our roles and where we fit in our society. If your reason for being alive involves others, then that's something you have a good reason to pursue. Seeing we are struggling with the sound, I will move on to our next segment."

Ted continued the lecture until the time of the quiz. Then the time came for the students to turn their papers in. Ted sat at his desk as students walked by and turned their reports in. Ted stared at the exit. Therefore, no one could slip by without first turning in their paper.

Oden walked to the professor's desk and laid his paper on the desk before exiting the room. Madison saw this and waited until the last student exited. Madison walked over to the professor's desk. By then, there was a big pile of completed papers on his desk. Ted looked up at him.

"Why, Madison, it's strange that I haven't heard from you today. Are you well?"

"I am well, sir," Madison said with a sigh. "I was meaning to tell you that I lost my backpack with my phone, tablet, and paper."

"Oh! That's not good! And how did you lose your backpack? I'm taking that you lost it on your way here?"

"I did."

"And what could be so worthy of your attention that it caused you to lose your bag over it?" asked Ted in a tone of sarcasm.

"I was chased this morning by a ravenous squirrel."

"Excuse me?" Ted turned his left ear in Madison's direction to be sure that he had heard right. "Did you say a ravenous squirrel?"

"Well, in fact, it was a rabid squirrel."

"Oh, a squirrel with rabies," said Ted, returning to his tone of sarcasm. "The classic excuse would be, 'My dog ate my homework.'"

"It's true! I was chased by a squirrel," said Madison, trying to be persuasive but to no avail.

"Doesn't make a difference," replied Ted, changing to a more serious tone. "You don't have your report with you. And this means that you'll lose a mark."

Madison was stunned and even shell-shocked at hearing that he would lose a mark. His heart sank.

"Don't worry. It's not the end of the world or even this class. You'll still get your marks, but you'll just lose this one. Call it absence from class. It was as if you were absent today."

"There's no way that I could get it back at the end?"

"No. You cannot get it back at the end of the semester. Just be sure to get things together, or it'll be the end of this class for you."

Madison left the desk and was about to leave the room when he stopped and turned to Ted. "I remember what Nancy, the Christian, said. I think we can learn something about ourselves and about life that's universal, a standard of some sort."

"Be careful when you say there's a standard that we are all supposed to follow. There are no standards that apply to every person, or else you're going to say that someone has set the bar for all of us to reach. And that is preposterous."

"I'll be honest that we shouldn't have to be religious to believe there are meaning and purpose that applies to everyone."

"You cannot believe in purpose without believing in a god who has created you with purpose and meaning."

"Even though I don't know who or what this god is, I can still live to understand that there is an 'ought to.' I don't think I need a god to believe that."

"You still don't understand where an 'ought to' could lead. You and I know that you don't need a god to understand your life. You can make much of life, or your grades, without feeling that you owe all this to a god. This is what people like Nancy feel indebted to."

"Problem I have with that worldview is that they feel as though they have it all figured out. My folks introduced me to people who believed they had it figured out. My grandmother, bless her soul, believed she had it figured out. I'm the sort to ask questions about these things."

"That's good," interrupted Ted. "It is good to ask questions and to raise doubts about religion."

"But I'm also asking questions and raising doubts about naturalism because I'm wondering if it's even enough to say that we should make the most of our lives now."

Ted raised his finger to stop Madison. "We make most of it simply because of the brevity of life as we know it. We do not have to inherit longevity. There's no promise you'll live past eighty. With that in mind, you should make the most of life."

"My problem with naturalism is that we have nothing in our worldview to motivate us to make the most of life. Christianity has the Bible, and it has motivated many to make the most of their lives."

"You're right about the Bible. Only that the Bible has also motivated people to do destructive things, all in the name of eternal life. I take no issue with the good as motivation in the Bible, but with the fact that the Bible can also motivate people to do evil."

"Isn't it the other way around? That people who are motivated by evil are using the Bible?"

"In any event," replied Ted, "the good is organic and has been a natural response of good people. Good people wrote a book to motivate people to do good. That's all it is."

"If the good is induced by good people, what happens when that good is downplayed by the call to make tough decisions, like kill someone? How can that good be a natural response of humans?"

"Hope you're not in the mood to kill someone. If that is the case, I would ask that you allow me some time to exit the school campus."

"No, no," giggled Madison.

"I was only jesting," said Ted. "By the way, we are always placed in situations where we must act. There are times when we must lie. There are times when we must kill to defend ourselves. You should be able to kill a mad rodent and not feel guilty about it. At times, what people would call 'the right decision' may go against any written code of ethics, like the Bible. This tells me that good is and has been, induced by good people who mean well. Our decisions are inherited or past down to us by our fore-parents. Memes are passed on like genes through generations."

"I'm wondering, sir," replied Madison, "whether these codes of ethics are really coming from memes. If the right decisions keep getting downplayed or overridden, then something tells me there's something that runs deeper than what we know. Isn't there a reality that runs deeper than what we know? One that tells us how to study hard to pass, and how to handle a failing mark?"

"Life is short, and it ends at the grave," replied Ted. "As I said, we must make the most of it while we are here."

"Meanwhile, something in a book tells me that there is more to our lives than being good or experiencing success and failure."

"Something more to life is your assumption. Go see about your lost backpack. Now, if you'll excuse me, I have work to do. Also, I must prepare for the next class."

Madison nodded, his eyes still locked with Ted's. He then turned and exited the room.

What or who is behind everything. . .

Months later, through May, and as the semester was coming to an end, Madison and company were working through different class assignments. Madison, Oden, Paula, and Kenny found an outdoor seating area, away from the traffic of student bodies that would often be found in the cafeterias, the hallways, and the libraries. Madison would regularly meet with Oden and the others between classes to review notes, have discussions, and prepare. By studying together, the students would feed off each others' strengths.

Madison had since retrieved his backpack, and all that was in it, with the help of his Christian classmate, Nancy. Nancy had noticed something unusual about Madison that morning—that he had come to school empty-handed. She contacted a friend whose cousin's neighbor's father's co-worker's husband's brother worked for the city. He conducted a search party, which led to someone finding Madison's bag. But Madison's fortune would have never happened had Nancy not noticed him. Madison thanked Nancy and invited her to join him and his friends anytime between classes.

Madison and Oden arrived a little later than Paula and Kenny. Their class was recently dismissed by Professor Johnson. Another pop quiz, another lecture, and another Q&A and another exchange between Ted and Madison went over class time. Oden was relieved at the thought that this semester was coming to an end. He had a few scares midway through the semester, and towards the end, because he had bitten off more than he could handle with the beauties, he couldn't keep his eyes off. He eventually had a fallback in his timing, which led to his pleading with Madison for help, in hopes that he could get caught up. Madison did help him while making sure that everything Oden turned in was Oden's work. Oden thanked him and stopped criticizing him for asking too many questions. In fact, Madison asked the professor the right questions, questions that Oden needed answers to, but was too proud to raise his hand.

The foursome sat at their preferred meeting spot that mid-morning. The sun was beginning to make its presence known to all who'd chosen the outdoors. Every now and then, a few friends would walk by only to say hello, chat a little, then go their way. Out of the group of four, Madison appreciated the visitors the least. He did not want the socials to get in the way of the much-needed thinking time. But the one student he had come to appreciate was walking towards their table—Nancy George.

"Hi, Madison! Hi, Oden! Is this empty seat taken?"

Madison spoke before anyone else could answer. "No! Please join us."

"Thank you."

"No, thank you for joining us. Nancy, you haven't met Paula and Kenny?"

"It's really nice to finally meet you, Nancy. Madison told me so much about you and what you did for him a few months ago."

"Hi, Paula. Well, I'm only thankful for the opportunity to be of help. It was a one-time incident many months ago."

"Well, Nancy, I am eternally grateful, and I will never stop thanking you."

"You're sweet. I can say that I'm glad to be of service."

"Madison told me that you were among the few who raised their hands to indicate to the professor that you were a theist."

"I had to tell the professor where I stood as a believer in God, despite the pressure to keep silent."

Madison jumped in. "I must tell you, Paula, that I admire Nancy's boldness. I admire this and the Christianity that emanates from her kindness."

"You're sweet, Madison."

The women didn't see this, but the moment Madison glanced in Oden and Kenny's direction, he saw the watermelon-sized smiles on both their faces. They both knew where this flattery was going. Already, Kenny and Oden were beginning to picture themselves as Madison's groomsmen.

"Madison told me that the pressure from Professor Johnson was overpowering," Paula said. "The professor said that you and the others were ashamed of your religions because of the lack of proof."

"I need to say this," replied Nancy, "I was scared at a certain point. I was wondering how he was going to react if I told him that I was a Christian. I admit that I was fearful at first, but I was never ashamed. Neither do I have reason to be ashamed."

"Nothing against religion, but why aren't you ashamed?"

"Thank you, Paula. I'm so happy you asked. I don't know what Madison told you about what the professor said. Still, he says that creation, or creation in the Book of Genesis, is not a statement of science."

"I'm sorry, Nancy, but I have to agree with him that it isn't a statement of science."

"Well, I agree that it is not a statement of science . . ."

Madison's ears perked up like a pair of extended antennas. Though he was already listening, what she just said piqued his interest even more. *"Is it true that Nancy, the Christian, is now conceding her worldview by telling the group that she has been wrong the whole time?"* Madison thought.

"but what happened in Genesis," Nancy continued, "has value in the study of science."

"How could this be?" asked Paula.

"We may know how things came to be; still, knowing how things came to be doesn't rule God out," replied Nancy.

"But as we move forward in our understanding, we will discover more about how things came to be without the need for an agent."

"It's easy to believe that," replied Nancy, "when you're committed to the idea that there is no god behind the physics or the biology. But we know the cause and effect structures of our world. Though some are saying that things can assemble by themselves over time, many still wonder if they could possibly function together without the need of an agent."

Oden felt the need to weigh in. "I'm sorry to burst your bubble, sweetheart—"

"Sweetheart!?" Paula grimaced, reacting to Oden's show of male-macho-bigotry.

"Okay, okay, okay," said Oden, backing down from his poor choice of words. "I remember our professor saying that Christianity has a bad track record, and their book is not a reliable source. If that's the case, then how can you argue that it has value in the study of science?"

"Bad track record has always been a problem for people who follow a religion. But you don't judge the book by its followers; rather, you should judge the followers by the book."

"Well, even if you say it's a good book, you cannot trust it with all its errors."

"But, Oden, that book with errors is like none other. It is a series of books that stretch over a millennium. And they speak for one another. Errors? Are you talking about copyist's errors? I am not a follower, but that book has made many believers," Madison weighed in.

"By whose lenses were they reading?" asked Oden.

"Through the lenses of skeptics turned believers," replied Madison.

"And, are you saying that you are convinced?"

"I am convinced that this book should not be taken so lightly," replied Madison.

"I know you, Madison," Paula said. "You're the type to show openness to different points of view. Is there any reason why you are not a believer?"

"You can compare me to Socrates. I am not a stakeholder of any one religion. I have yet to take that step of faith. Just call me a truth-seeker."

"In the end," said Nancy, "you may never come to know the one truth. Something will still be out of your reach. At some point, you must determine the best answer by what is most reasonable. I chose Christianity because it is the most reasonable."

"For you," replied Oden, "for you, sister."

Paula turned to Nancy. "Is Christianity the most reasonable? Other religiously devout people would say otherwise."

"You are right, Paula. My Muslim classmate and others would say otherwise. But I have taken the time to look at them and think them through. And the Bible is the clearest and most readable source of them all. And it talks about the beginning in both Genesis 1 and John 1."

"And our professor said that a plan or a blueprint goes against the laws of physics and could not have happened moments before the Big Bang," Oden added.

"I challenged the professor on that one, Oden. He makes it appear as if he's in no position to answer this."

"I don't think he should be forced to answer this," quipped Oden.

Madison faced Oden. "Here is where I see the value in Nancy's Bible: it talks about God and his Son's involvement at the beginning of creation. I asked the professor if there is anything technical that the Creator knows that we also must have known.

There were things I didn't know until the moment I asked the professor."

While Madison was still speaking, Paula and Oden noticed, from their angle, a figure that looked like Professor Johnson. Madison and Nancy's backs were facing that angle. Madison and Nancy noticed the two fixing their gazes on something, then turned. They saw Professor Johnson walking some twenty meters away from their table, who hadn't noticed their stares.

Ted made his usual relaxed, unconcerned, and casual stroll from one building to the next. It wouldn't matter if he knew that he was being watched, simply because he didn't care. Ted walked with a leather binder in one hand and a lit cig in the other. He walked by students and faculty without looking any in the eye. He stopped outside a set of doors and took several more puffs of his cig. A moment later, Ted threw the lit stub into a small trash bin before finally walking through those doors.

The group looked at each other.

"Why did we stop our conversation to look at the professor?" Madison wondered aloud.

"I don't know," replied Paula.

"Maybe the fact that he became the topic of our discussion?" suggested Nancy.

"Maybe the fact that he got swag," Kenny added. "Did you see the way he threw that lit cig into the recycle bin?"

"You mean the trash bin?" said Oden.

"Nooo. The recycle bin," said Kenny. "The trash bin is to the right of the recycle bin. The man just threw the lit cig into the bin to his left."

"As I was saying," Madison continued, "just because a blueprint with intentions isn't a statement of science, it doesn't mean that there was no blueprint or intentions."

"Maddi has a fear of a God whom he doesn't believe in," Kenny said.

Nancy turned to Madison. "It sounds like Kenny is sharing something deep and personal about you. Is this true, Madison?"

"Well, Nancy, though I'm not a stakeholder in any religion, I live my life as though the God of the Bible exists."

"And do you give credence to the Bible?"

"I have to. If any religious book were to tell me about me and the world around me, then it has gotten my attention."

Just as Madison was speaking, a loud commotion was heard from behind him. The group looked on. Madison turned to see. The bin lit up as though engulfed in a flame of fire. The inferno lit only one side of the container, the recycling section. That alone caused a few students to scurry. One student attempted to douse the fire by emptying a half-liter bottle of water on it. Another student tried to out the blaze by throwing a handkerchief on it. One with more sense removed the t-shirt he had on and used it to fan the flames. And, of course, none of these were of any avail. Finally, after one side of the bin was charred and partiality melted, the custodian ran with a fire extinguisher and hosed down the inferno.

Madison left the table, walked towards the bin, observed it, and then returned. "Kenny, you were right. That was the recycling bin."

"I could never imagine your philosophy professor having this much effect on the student body," Kenny said in a jovial tone. "Look, he affects them without knowing what he just did."

The group responded with a mixture of smiles and chuckles.

Madison replied, "Professor Johnson is long gone. He's still an arsonist, even though he may never know what he just did."

"I think you're right," Nancy replied. "Speaking of arsonists, people would call the creator the great arsonist who lit the torch, caused the fire, then walked away."

"What gets my attention about the Bible is the idea that the one who started it all did so without walking away," Madison said.

"And it's because he didn't walk away from that we have all this beauty and order."

"Very stimulating!" said Paula.

"Chaos is the norm, as the professor would say," replied Oden.

"I don't think we'd have the right to call anything chaotic if that were the norm," replied Madison.

"As far as I see it," countered Oden, "our existence is all a part of an unguided chain of events. A fire breaks out, and somewhere out of the burnt refuse, new life emerges."

"Let's say that you are right, Oden. Then the sanctity of life could be devalued at any time. I should be able to light a torch, burn the school campus down and mean it, take hundreds of lives, and not have to answer for it. I don't think we would ever have the right to call an event a travesty, because chaos is the norm. OD, my brother, you must take these things more seriously."

"What do you mean I don't take these things seriously?"

Nancy began her meager attempt to separate the two. "I can see you have been raising many questions on these things, Madison."

"As long as I've known myself, I don't speak flippantly, because I take these things seriously."

"And you say I'm flippant?"

"Maybe you need to raise your hand in class more, instead of just quoting our professor."

"I quote the professor because what he said makes sense."

"And you leave students like me to wrestle with what the professor said?"

Nancy got between the two again. "I'm glad you guys are speaking about these things. Maybe this will lead to more truth-seeking."

"Truth-seeking?" replied Oden. "It depends on where you choose to look."

"All the reason not to cherry-pick at sources," retorted

Madison. "Why some atheists are very selective is because they have already made up their minds on what they're going to reject."

"And, you are the open-minded one?" asked Nancy.

"Just call me the truth-seeker."

"I've known Madison for some time, and he asks a lot of questions," added Paula.

"Truth-seek your tailbone, Madison," said Oden. "I can read a Bible, explain it, then prove to you that I'm not the selective one."

The four stopped to notice Kenny sitting silently, watching them, all smiles. They wondered what was on his mind.

He then spoke with pizzazz. "We have it. It is set. Tomorrow, same time, same place, on this university campus. An event, Nancy, you won't want to miss. A group of atheists is going to wrestle over a tough topic. We're going to have a Bible study."

The group erupted in laughter.

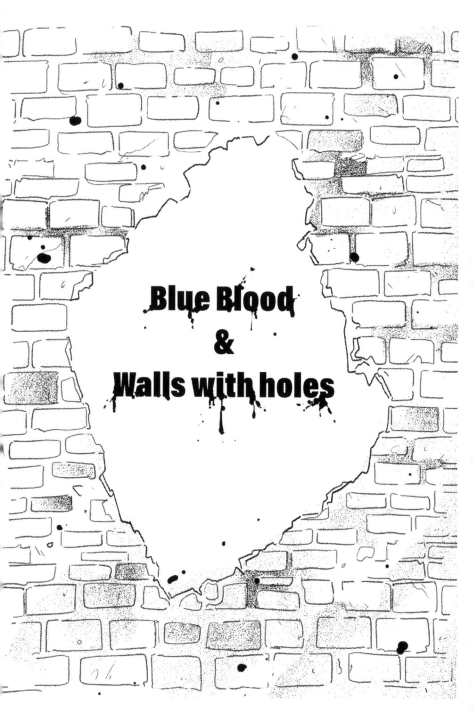

Blue Blood
&
Walls with holes

On Monday, June 10th, Jay Stropolis ended a call with his half-sister. It was either a personal call made professional, or a professional call made personal. Jay felt it was the former. He loves his sister, so he did not expect her tone to change to a more professional one. Gale Stropolis was asking a favor of her older brother—that he mentor her daughter, Alyssa.

Alyssa and her brother, Andi, were both adopted by Gale and her wife, Lolita, when they were still toddlers. Alyssa was into her fourth year of high school, while Andi was into his second year. As a part of her school report, Alyssa was told to find a mentor who was a professional. Alyssa first wanted to shadow her mother, but as a secret service agent, Gale felt that her career was much too dangerous for her daughter. Gale advised her daughter to see what Jay did for a living; at least what he did as an attorney was safe. Alyssa followed her advice. Hence, Gale told Jay to expect her.

Jay enjoys his niece's company, but he was hoping he wouldn't have to deal with distractions during work hours. Oddly, Jay's work hours also extends into the non-work hours. It is almost impossible to set up a time with Jay unless you're one of his clients. Some of his clients are demanding, almost dangerously demanding. Working with ex-cons with a checkered past and a reputation for violence is not a position that is envied. Also, there are days when Jay's job doesn't pay well.

It was 11:00 AM. Jay's eyes and mind were lost in his work when he heard the gentle knock on his door. If it were Gladys, his secretary, she would have knocked harder and called out from the other side of the door. Whomever Gladys let through was now standing outside his office door.

"Who is it?"

"Uncle Jay?"

"Oh, Alyssa, come in."

The door opened to a young, comely brunette. Though seventeen, Alyssa appears older by three years. Alyssa has a business-like aura about her that makes her seem more mature than she really is. She is a brazen beauty who is not afraid to step out of the mundane for the sake of a new experience, and who would go off into a tizzy before she allows herself to be boxed in by common stereotypes.

"Thanks for coming, Alyssa. Please, have a seat."

"Thanks, Uncle!"

"By the way, where's Andi? I know that he was also doing a report. I was hoping that your mother would send him as well."

"He doesn't want to come."

Jay looked quizzically at her. "And why not?"

"He wanted to go with Mom."

Jay's confused look morphed into an understanding one. "He wants to go with her on one of her assignments . . ."

"Um . . . assignments, Uncle? Andi is at the parlor with Mom."

Jay knew that while Gale worked as a part of the secret service and military intelligence, Lolita owned a hair parlor and nail salon in the inner-city.

"Oh, Andi didn't tell you? He wants to become a hairstylist."

The room entered a moment of silence.

"Well, at least he knows where he's going. As for you, young lady, you have yet to come to a decision. But don't worry. For some students, this decision will come with time. Others have made their decision during adulthood. Don't feel pressured. For you, your decision may come after being exposed to different careers."

"Mom told me that your career isn't dangerous at all."

Jay raised his eyebrows. "Oh, did she?"

Jay thought about what he was going to tell her. He knew that his job did not require putting himself in a position where someone could use him for target practice. But having clients that could be dangerous was no day on the beach.

"I want to know what it's like to be a lawyer."

He thought about warning Alyssa about the dangers that can

go with the work he does. Still, he shook his head and decided to tell her about the technicalities of his work instead.

"Let's go for lunch."

Jay sat across from his niece at a busy restaurant, downtown Sacramento. After wolfing down two double cheeseburgers, two large fries, a batch of chicken fingers, a bunch of onion rings, guzzling four liters of chocolate milk, and gorging two pieces of double chocolate cheesecake, the two were ready to talk. Jay only had a Caesar salad, a grilled chicken sandwich, and an iced tea. He knew Alyssa had an appetite large enough for two. Still, he wondered where all that food went and how Alyssa has managed to maintain such a sinewy frame.

"I have a fast metabolism," Alyssa said.

"I see!" replied Jay. "I understand you'd like to know about the work that I do?"

"I'd like to know. Mom only told me that you stand before the judge and the jury and the witnesses. She said that you will tell me the rest."

"Okay, well, that's a good starting point. Yes, I do stand before those people. But that's not where my job begins."

Alyssa was wide-eyed at hearing this. "It isn't?"

"No, it isn't. What your muscle-bound, army-boot-wearing mother hasn't told you is that before I see all these people, I first see an important someone."

"I wonder who that important someone is," Alyssa wondered out loud.

"That important someone is my client."

"Oh yes," said Alyssa, with a burst of realization.

"My clients . . ."

Alyssa jumped in to answer this question for herself. "Let me guess. These are people who sue other people for money."

"No," Jay quickly set the record straight. "No, I am not that kind of lawyer. Yes, some lawyers prosecute or go on the offensive against troublemakers. But my job is different. I go on the defensive for people—my clients—who are in trouble."

"And let me guess," Alyssa said with a smile. "These are people who are fighting parking tickets or traffic tickets. So, they come to you to get themselves out of trouble."

"Well, there are defense attorneys who do that. But the people whom I often call my clients are usually in more trouble than that."

"More trouble, as in they might be going to prison?"

"Exactly."

"My role is to either influence the judge and the jury to lower the sentence—"

"Or to drop the charges," said Alyssa, in another attempt to finish his sentence.

"You are absolutely right. Okay, I see you're familiar with some court slang."

"I've watched some of those reality shows."

"Okay. These shows give you some idea of what goes on inside the courtroom. But my role involves understanding what happened with my client and why he or she is in trouble. Learning what happened takes a lot of my time and energy. Often, I will meet with people in hopes that I will learn what happened. But, Alyssa, this search has brought me before some of the most interesting people."

"Interesting people?" asked Alyssa. "What kind of interesting people?"

"I've met some brilliant and educated people. I've met very creative people, people who were inventors, and people who were novelists. I've met people who were of great character, and I've met people who were the opposite. The latter were people who did an excellent job of hiding the fact that they only intended to hurt people."

"Wow," replied Alyssa, "your job has a lot of mystery."

"It does, no doubt. So, as I am learning more about what happened with my client, I am learning more about my client."

The window behind Jay was knocked by a few bodies. With the bang came a blending of angry voices.

Alyssa shifted her attention over her uncle's shoulder. On the other side of that window was a crowd. They were huddling around something. Jay heard the commotion outside the restaurant. He furrowed his brows as he turned to the cause of the uproar and saw the crowd outside the large glass window. Another spectator, in a burst of excitement, bounced against the window. This startled Jay. He figured they had to be a group of rabble-rousers.

He rose from his seat to meet the bodies causing the clamor outside and motioned his niece to stay seated as he walked towards the doorway. Some of the staff and customers made the doorway into a makeshift row of seats. Jay pushed past the crowd at the door to meet the group outside the restaurant. The first thing that caught his attention was the lit beacons of two police cruisers. He wondered who was in trouble now. As Jay found his way through the warm bodies, he saw what was causing the commotion. There were two uniformed officers with a teenage boy on the ground, whom they managed to subdue. Two other officers stood as backup and for crowd control. Jay looked down at the teen and noticed that he was gasping for air. Meanwhile, an officer had him in a chokehold. Many from the crowd shouted at the officer on the ground with the young man.

Jay quickly turned to one of the officers and asked, "What happened?"

"This kid held the convenience store owner next door at gunpoint. We caught him as he was stepping out with the bags of cash."

"What of the store owner?"

"Thankfully, no one was harmed."

Jay pointed at the teen in the police's grip. "Well, someone is about to be harmed, and I'm looking down at him."

The officer turned to Jay and looked at him for the first time. "We tried to get him into cuffs. He was playing tough with us, so Thomas had to play tough, too."

"And his gun?"

"We have it," the officer said.

"Well, just get him into handcuffs. What he's doing is unnecessary. Look at him! He's suffocating him! I'll be sure you get in trouble for this."

"Sir, who are you? And why are you barking orders?"

"My name is Jay Stropolis, and I am an attorney . . ."

"A defense attorney."

Jay quickly turned to see where the voice came from. And, sure enough, it was Alyssa's.

"I thought I told you to stay inside the restaurant."

"Actually, you didn't, Uncle. You only waved your hand at me to stay seated. You didn't tell me to stay inside the restaurant."

"But stay seated means stay inside the restaurant."

"You didn't tell me how long I should stay inside the restaurant."

"I'm sorry to get in between a family discussion," the officer interrupted, "but I'm going to ask you both to step back."

The two standing officers motioned the crowd to give them more space. Some stood their ground before more police arrived on the scene.

Jay again stepped forward to speak to the officer. "Where will you hold this kid?"

"We're taking him to the nearby station. You can talk to him about defense there. Now, step back, please."

The officer waved at Jay and the entire crowd to step back. Meanwhile, two others managed to get the teen into handcuffs. Then they walked him to one of the police cruisers.

Bad people and bad things. . .

Jay drove to the station. Alyssa went along for the ride. Jay walked, with Alyssa in tow, through the entrance and into the station, which had a mixture of uniformed persons and locals. He had to look around to find police he recognized from the scene and the teen who was about to be held in custody. Jay looked around and saw the teen from a distance. He then turned to Alyssa. "Now, Alyssa, I'm going to speak to the police over there. I'm now asking you to go to the waiting area and stay seated. And do not come unless I tell you to."

Alyssa obeyed and strode towards the waiting area.

Jay continued his walk towards the desk and the police who were on the other side. He pulled out his business card and presented it to the first officer he approached.

"I'm a defense attorney. I would like to have a moment with the teenager who was taken in a moment ago."

The officer smiled with irony. "Which one?"

"The armed robbery just off 12th Street. I was inside a restaurant when he was tackled."

"I know that one. The kid's name is Jayden Isaac. They got his fingerprint. They're taking his photo for records."

"When can I see him?"

"Hold for a moment."

The officer walked to a group of uniformed staff who were with those who were in custody. This was a long wait for Jay. After what had to be less than five minutes, the officer returned. He opened a four-foot swing door to allow Jay to walk through. "Follow me."

Jay followed the officer through the office area and to the soundproof room where they had Jayden Isaac. Jayden sat at the table, an empty chair across from him. One of the uniformed staff stood by Jayden, as Jay walked into the room.

Jay couldn't recall what the suspect looked like because his face was down while he was being choked by the officer. He was a young African American boy in his early to mid-teens. One of the officers told Jay that he was fourteen years of age. This number matched what Jay saw in his youthful features. He wore a premature goatee. He had a haircut with a fade, and the top of his head was neatly braided. Jay knew what to expect on the first introduction—a coldness of demeanor that would take some time for him to break out of. Jay looked down at him, and he looked up at Jay with anger and a sullen dislike for what he saw.

"Jayden Isaac, my name is Jay Stropolis. Feel free to call me Jay. I'm a defense attorney, and I deal with situations like yours."

"I don't know who you are, neither do I care to know who you are," the youth said defiantly.

"That's understandable. Given where you are at this moment, you might need to know who I am."

"I don't need no one to represent me. I'm not gonna allow myself to be cold-macked by some sleazy attorney. People like yourself want more cash than what you're worth."

Jay held his composure. "I understand that you have your suspicions of me. That's why I ask for nothing . . . nothing but your side of what happened. They said you ran out of the convenience store with a backpack with bundles of cash. They also told me that you were armed. By how this sounds to me, you threatened the owner to give you cash from the register."

Jay left that question in the air, hoping it would be answered. After a while, it was beginning to feel awkward. Jay glanced up at the officer who stood over Jayden. And on his face, Jay read the look of expectation. It was a look that said, *Do you have any more questions for Jayden before I lock him up?*

Jay continued. "Jayden, do you know that theft is a federal offense? You can be locked away for a long time."

Jayden finally spoke. "I know it's an offense."

Jay was dumbfounded. "But why?"

The officer standing over Jayden took the liberty to answer. "Maybe he's in search of attention?"

Jay remained straight-faced. "I know you're not in search of attention."

"Nah, man, I did it 'cause I got no money. And I got no money 'cause life is hard."

"And you chose to rob a store owner of his hard-earned money?"

"I can't believe what I'm hearin'. That money is not hard-earned. That fool robbed me thrice. Three times I came to buy a pack of chips, a candy bar, and a soda. And each time I come through his store, he bumps the price on me. And this man charges more than any other store does. I only buy from him 'cause the others are too far."

"And the fact that this man charges a lot justifies you robbing him at gunpoint?"

"I'm jus givin' him his dues."

"There is the option of seeking employment there."

"I did. And he tol' me they're not hirin'. What else can I do?"

"So you decided to give him his due? Now you do realize that your attempted robbery did not go as planned because the man is unharmed, and you are right here. And I don't know how long they'll keep you here."

Just then, the officer standing over Jayden leaned over and whispered to Jayden. "We might keep you here for a looong time." The officer extended the adjective "long" to heighten its effect on Jayden. "A looong time," he repeated.

Jay tried not to smile as he continued. "The truth is that they could send you to juvey. But I want to keep that from happening."

"That's not gonna happen," Jayden retorted. "I won't allow that. I don't need you. Go find some other pocket to pick, White Colla'."

Jay maintained his calm. "I tell you what, I won't ask anything of you, only that you allow me to understand your situation some more."

"You got nothin' on me, White Colla'. I got nothin' to say to you. Another thing, there's nothin' fo' free in this country.

Everything you do has a price. Don't give me that. Lawyers lie, and you a two-faced sleaze like the rest of them."

Jay paused for a moment. He thought about what he would say to win Jayden over. He briefly looked up at the officer who stood behind Jayden. The officer gestured to Jay with both hands that the floor was still his, for soon Jayden would be taken to juvenile detention.

"I get it. I understand that I have yet to gain your trust. I will have to earn it. I'll leave you for now. But I will return soon."

Jayden did not respond. He only looked away. Jay looked up and nodded at the officer before he stepped out of the room.

Jay walked over to the seating area where Alyssa was. He was ready to leave, so he beckoned for her to come, but to his surprise, she didn't budge. She only sat still and looked at him. He gestured to her again and got no response. He was wearied and annoyed by her unresponsiveness, so he marched over to her.

"Alyssa, didn't you see me calling to you?"

"I saw you were beckoning to me, but you said not to come unless you tell me to. You beckoned, but I heard nothing."

Jay gave a smirk because of the irony in his niece's humor and her ability to catch him in his speech. He knew she hadn't gotten this from Gale nor his sister-in-law, Lolita. He knew Alyssa had gotten this streak of sarcasm from him.

"Let's go," he said firmly.

Instead of driving Alyssa back to his office, Jay chose to drive her to that convenience store that was robbed. He parked the car and looked over at her.

"Now, Alyssa, I am about to speak to the store owner. Please do not tell him what I do for a living. I think he might hate me for my profession and not want to speak with me."

Alyssa smiled. "Okey-doke!"

Jay walked into the store with Alyssa behind him. He looked ahead and saw what seemed to be the store owner. This was an older, balding man with a pointed, greyish beard. He appeared to be of Middle Eastern descent and of average height. By his facial expression, this owner seemed to border between harsh and unyielding.

Jay walked up to the counter where the owner stood.

"May I help you?" the owner asked sternly.

"Yes, you may. My name is Jay. Don't mind my niece," he said, glancing back at Alyssa. "We're returning from the station."

At that moment, the owner raised both eyebrows with sudden interest. "He's in prison?"

"They have him in custody."

"Well, good," the owner said with enthusiasm. "That's one less hoodlum to deal with."

"You said, 'One less hoodlum.' Are you telling me this happens often?"

"These crazy teenagers come here every week. They don't come at night as much, because I set up a strong security system. They cannot break-in at night, so they come and cause trouble during day hours."

"They come during day hours. What do these kids look like? For example, their ethnicity. Are they white, black, Hispanic?"

"Most of these troublemakers are black."

"Okay, and when they come, what do they do?"

"There are two kinds of troublemakers: One is the thief that takes what he didn't pay for and pockets them in hopes that I don't see him. But I have cameras. And there's the troublemaker that wears a mask and points a gun at me because he wants money from this register."

"I can tell that what happened earlier was not the first time."

"Of course not. This is about the fourth time this has happened. That is why I have an emergency button behind this counter. I pressed it the moment I saw the mask."

"And when did you see the mask?"

About then, a woman stood behind Jay with a growing expression of impatience. The owner pointed at her, which directed Jay's attention to her.

"I'm sorry," Jay said to her with a faint smile.

The woman stepped ahead, paid for her items, and quickly exited the store. Jay turned back to the owner, who was becoming more annoyed by Jay's line of questioning.

"Tell me something, sir, are you an investigator that you would spray me with these questions?"

"Actually, I am not. I'm an attorney."

"I hope you are the type that tries felons and puts them behind bars."

"Well, I fall in those lines. But you need to tell me if you saw the youth before he put the mask on."

"I saw his face when he first walked in. And that was before he put the mask on."

"Have you ever seen this kid before?"

"I've seen him before. I've seen some of his friends. They are those hoodlums who wear blue colors all the time."

"Oh, you're talking about one of the Crip sets? There is the Son of Samoa SOS Gang, the El Camino Gang, the Nogales Street Gangsters—"

"I don't really care which," the owner interrupted. "They are all the same. They are all bad."

"Well, the word 'bad' has taken on different meanings. Bad or evil is only behavior or a condition of a thing. People can call something or someone bad, depending on what the person understands to be bad or evil . . ."

"And I call those who he calls friends bad, especially the evil twins."

"But it's only a word that people use to describe other people or things."

"Well, I can tell you that something or someone is bad or evil because they are bad according to the law of my God."

Jay looked briefly at Alyssa, who looked back at him. Jay wondered how he was going to answer this. "Your God? You sound very religious."

"I am a Muslim," the owner announced.

"That's fine," Jay replied. "But you know nothing of this kid's background or of his situation. He told me that he came one day in search of a job, but you denied him. What he did was bad. I'll grant you that, but I'm wondering if that makes him bad."

Now the owner became very suspicious of Jay. He locked eyes with him over the counter. They appeared to be in a staredown. He broke his eyes from Jay's and looked at his niece's. Jay saw the owner locking eyes with his niece, making her very uncomfortable. Jay attempted to redirect the owner's attention back to him.

"Sir, I—"

"You are lying! You are a defense attorney."

"Sir, I don't know what you're talking about—"

"It's written all over your niece," the owner interrupted.

"Sir, just because—"

"You want to represent that bad boy!"

"Do you want to see my—"

"I see your niece," the owner continued. "You have no dealings in my place of business!"

"I'm only trying—"

"And I gave you enough," the owner interrupted. "Now, leave this place." The owner pointed at the front entrance.

Jay backed away in silence while moving Alyssa towards the front door with his outstretched arm. They stepped out of the convenience store and walked toward Jay's car. Before pulling away, they just sat inside the car for a moment.

"Uncle Jay, were you going to lie to that man?"

"I was not going to lie to him. I was only attempting to get some information from him. Well, that failed, because he read my niece's facial expression."

Alyssa stomped her right foot. "Uncle, I didn't know that there was a kind of look that I was supposed to give that man."

"No, don't worry about it," Jay said with a sigh. "I was trying to have him play over in his mind what happened."

"Shouldn't it be simple? Like, I mean, he was held at gunpoint or something like that?"

"Putting what he knows about me aside, I could surely use tips such as the thug's choice of words and his movements. These snippets of information will either work in favor of the teen that robbed the store or against him. Do you understand where I'm going with this?"

"I understand, I guess. But isn't this something that investigators should do?"

"Yes. But call me the concerned citizen whose profession also involves asking questions. Sometimes you will come across persons who give you a hard time, like that owner in the store. If you do end up with short answers, piece them together with other answers from other sources."

"I think I understand," said Alyssa, "but what do you mean by piecing answers together?"

"Jayden told me that he came looking for a job but was turned away. He told me that this owner has been very unfair with his pricing on candy bars and other things. The owner told me that he has seen Jayden's friends, and they look like they belong to a Crip gang set. I don't have all the answers that I need. What I do is try to make sense of all these short answers. They are all a part of one big answer. Make sense?"

"I guess so."

"I guess that is a good enough answer."

Jay and Alyssa looked to their left and saw a group of adolescent men walking into the convenience store. There were ten of them, and they all entered through the front door. They were not wandering into the store; they were walking with purpose. Jay thought there was a kind of uniformity about the group—could be in their clothing. The second-to-last customer had a dog on a leash. It was not just any breed; it was a pit-bull terrier. On all fours, this dog stood at three-and-a-half feet in height, and it was monstrously built. The person holding the leash could have easily read the "No pets allowed" sign, but he wilfully overlooked the posting as he walked the dog into the store. To Jay, these delinquents were looking for something or someone. He tapped Alyssa on the leg.

"Excuse me for a moment. I need to go grab something. I'll be back."

Without another word, Jay followed the group into the store. He held back at a distance to not make himself noticeable to the group. As he walked on, he saw the men surrounding the cash register. One of the young men went into a face-off with the store owner. He pointed at the owner's hand. "You betta back away from that button, son. I see where you goin'. You send for five-o's, you're gonna have another problem."

"I want you out of my store," barked the store owner. "You and your hoods."

"Listen, ol' man, we don't have time for this. You tell us where they took our boy, Tio."

"I don't know who Tio is, and why you come to me," the owner replied.

"You very well know why we come to you. Don't give us that. Last Tio was seen here, five-o's took him. Napa and Scarp are lookin' for Tio. And we not leavin' without an answer, yah feel me?"

Just then, one of the other thugs deliberately knocked over a magazine rack. The rack crashed to the floor, causing the magazines to spill over onto the floor. Another thug began to trample on the magazines and kick some across the floor.

"Don't do that!" cried the store owner. "Look at what you're doing!"

"I am waiting for an answer," the lead thug said forcefully.

"I don't know where they took him!" shouted the owner. He looked over at two thugs whose faces were blurred from the vapors protruding from their marijuana sticks. The owner pointed to the two smokers. "You, put that out."

Neither of the two obeyed. One took another puff of cannabis before blowing the smoke in the owner's direction while swaying his head like a cobra.

The lead thug knocked all the items off the counter to recapture the owner's attention.

"That costs money," the owner barked.

"Shut up!" the thug shouted back.

With caution, Jay walked by the group of thugs to the counter, where the two stood. What he did not realize was how close he was to the pit bull. It growled. It sounded like something huge with massive jaws. Startled, Jay looked down at the large head with rows of teeth ready to snap, and then up at the thug holding the leash. He didn't appear any less unfriendly to Jay. He only looped the leash around his arm twice more to shorten the dog's reach. Jay walked to the counter. The lead thug and owner stared at him as he approached. Both wondered what the first words would be to come out of the mouth of this well-dressed stranger.

"Fellas, please. I know where Jayden is."

"Who are you?" snapped the thug.

"My name is Jay Stropolis, and I am an attorney."

An unexpected voice came from behind Jay.

"I hope you're the type that defends felons in court and keep 'em outta prison."

Jay turned to see another thug who appeared to be the lead spokesperson. He had a muscular build and a handsome facial structure. He had a medium complexion, a well-trimmed beard, and a neatly shaven head with short dreadlocks that spiked from the top. This thug wore a fitted, white long-sleeve shirt with blue designs that striped down one side of the chest. And in that fitted shirt, his muscled v-shaped torso was hard to overlook. He walked ahead. And from behind him came his identical twin. He was equal in height, built, and attractive appearance. The only difference was in his hairstyle and wear. He had full dreadlocks to his shoulders, plaited down from one side. He had a well-trimmed beard and wore round-framed glasses. Added to his more cultured and classed appearance was his fitted white dress shirt hanging over a pair of fitted dark dress pants and dress shoes. It was known that while his twin brother was the hands-on, industrial type, this one was the more business-oriented intellectual.

"By his intro, I can tell that he is," said the second twin.

"Excuse our intrusion," said the first twin, "but I hope my brother is right about you."

"Allow us to introduce ourselves," said the second twin. "My name is Elmo Carter, aka 'Scarp.' This is my twin, Ethan, aka, 'Napa.' That brother you just spoke to, we call 'Flint.'"

Napa spoke. "And now that we've introduced ourselves, tell us your real purpose for stepping in. We were just in the middle of an interrogation."

"Well, interrogate no further," Jay said, "because I know where Jayden is being held."

"That was easy," said Scarp.

"Too easy," agreed Napa.

"I know the deal," said Scarp. "Any man decked in a tie, and nice suit puts a price tag on everything, including his time."

The group of blue-wearing bandits nodded and muttered in agreement. Napa spoke.

"So, tell us, White Colla,'" Napa said, "what's your price?"

"You can call me Jay. Otherwise, you're not the ones asking for my time. Right now, it's the other way around."

"You offer your time knowing that there may be a lawsuit?" Scarp asked.

"There could be one," answered Jay. "There could be charges pressed against Jayden. He may receive extended jail time."

Napa slowly turned from Jay to the store owner. "Is there going to be a lawsuit?"

The store owner stood speechless now that all eyes were turned on him.

"I cannot tell you whether there is going to be one." He turned to Jay. "|And you, I knew it. You are a defense attorney. I don't want you to ever set foot in my store again."

"You did not answer the question," Scarp insisted. "Are there going to be charges pressed against Jayden?"

"Listen, you have nothing here—"

"You will not answer the question?" Napa interrupted. "You put our boy, Tio, through this. So you're going to pay for his release."

"No, I will not." the store owner retorted.

Napa turned and nodded to the thugs around him. They turned and began knocking items off shelves and even turning over standing ones onto the floor.

"Guys, you don't have to do this," Jay called to the group.

"Stop!" the owner shouted.

Flint turned to the owner and punched him, causing him to land on the floor. The owner attempted to reach for the emergency alert button. Still, before he could do so, Flint walked over to him and kicked him in the head, knocking him unconscious. Flint then bent down to the downed owner and began pummeling him. Jay ran over in attempts to stop this when he was tackled to the ground. He attempted to wrestle his way out of the thug's grip, but the thug was much too powerful. He had Jay pinned. A loud scream came from around the corner, piercing the ears of all, including Jay. Alyssa was horrified as she looked down at the thug who had Jay pinned.

"That's my uncle!" she shouted.

Another thug grabbed her. It only took one to subdue her.

"Please, don't hurt her," Jay called out.

Scarp stepped forward. He spoke to Jay while keeping his eyes on Alyssa.

"And who is this?"

"She's my niece," replied Jay.

Scarp turned to the ones who held them. "Let them go."

They released both Jay and Alyssa. Alyssa ran to her uncle and squeezed him for all she was worth.

"Now that you've had your reunion," Napa interjected, "we want ours with our lil' gangsta, Tio, our fam."

"I'll take you," said Jay. "But you should never have done this. Look at what you've done to his place."

"That is not for you to worry about," Napa replied.

"Your business is to take us to where the five-o's have Jayden," Scarp added.

Jay paused for a moment before answering. "Only on one condition."

"Name it," replied Scarp.

"You can't take the entire band with you. This will surely draw attention."

"Done," replied Scarp. "Anything else?"

"Only you, and maybe one of your friends, can come. I'm hoping that the one you choose also knows decorum."

"Done," Scarp replied.

Napa drew closer to Jay until they stood eye to eye. Jay held his ground, trying not to tremble.

"What you sayin', White Colla', that I lack décor?" Scarp held his arm out to hold Napa back.

"I can tell you, Jay, that Napa has decorum. But I can see where the counsel is going with this. Both of us will draw too much attention. Let me go, and we will fix this."

Napa was hesitant. Then he said, "Wait."

Napa walked over to the cash register, grabbed it, lifted it over his head, and slammed it onto the floor. He then grabbed a baseball bat from one of his companies and used it to smash the register until it finally popped open. Napa reached down to the destroyed register, pulled the hundreds, the fifties, and twenties from its shattered remains, walked over, and handed the money to Scarp. He then turned to Jay.

"Now you'll know, White Colla', that I got decorum. You can't free him without cash."

Goodness and good behavior

Inside the holding cell of a police station in Sacramento, Jayden sat waiting for the next worse thing that the law had in store for him. He was one among several other inmates who sat waiting. He could recall the play by play of the armed robbery.

He had walked into the convenience store. He had meandered aimlessly into that convenience store. The store owner was there at the time, and his clerk wasn't. And from the moment Jayden walked into the store, the owner eyed him. Before that day, this store owner had accused him and two friends of his shoplifting. They had made themselves look suspicious to the owner, so the owner walked over to the three and pressed them. It soon came to the owner's, and even Jayden's attention that one of his friends had pocketed a pack of chewing gum. That first meeting ended with Jayden and his friends being chased out of the store. The next time Jayden stepped into that local convenience store was when he needed school supplies—lined paper, note pads, and pens. The items he took from the shelves were priced. And when he went to cash out, the store owner overcharged him. Jayden later learned that he paid more for the supplies than he should have. He went back to that store later that year when he needed milk and eggs. He pulled them out of the colder section and walked them to the cash register. Jayden paid for the items. He didn't look at his receipt until he arrived home. The owner had overcharged him again.

Jayden went back and confronted the owner. That's when the owner gave him his reasons. The milk and eggs were on sale, but the special was over by the time Jayden had gotten there. Jayden did not set foot back in that store until he was bold enough to ask for a job. The clerk was alone. He told Jayden to come back another day. When Jayden went back, the owner said to him that he wasn't hiring. Jayden fast-forwarded to that final visit to the convenience store. As he looked over his shoulder, Jayden had noticed the owner eyeing him. There was a look of mistrust on the owner's face. Jayden could not hide between shelves without drawing suspicion. He felt the Hi-Point 9mm pistol that Napa had loaned to him in his right pocket. He felt the winter hat, with holes to see, in his left pocket. Then he lifted the headgear, ducked and slipped it over his head, slid the pistol from out of his right pocket, and ran to the register, with the weapon pointed at the owner.

"Get your hands up! Get 'em up! Do it now."

The owner obeyed, though he stalled for a moment.

"Open the box."

"You mean the register?" the owner asked sarcastically.

"I don't care what you call that thing. It's outdated, like your pants. Now, open it!"

Slowly, the owner opened the register.

"Get a bag and fill it with what you have in there."

"You cannot hide, because I know which one you are," the owner said while filling a plastic bag with hundreds, the fifties, and twenties.

"Drop the chitchat. I didn't come for backtalk. Just fill the bag," Jayden looked desperately behind him, splitting his attention between the owner and the door. The owner filled the bag to the last dollar bill. Jayden grabbed the plastic bag and made for the door.

"Freeze! Police!"

A few armed, uniformed men rushed Jayden and tackled him to the ground.

Jayden thought about that failed attempt to get away and

wondered what he could have done differently. He thought about the short history between himself and the store owner and reasoned within his mind that he had good reason to point a gun at that man. The owner had robbed him twice. Not only that, but the owner had also turned him down when he needed a job. He had accused him of theft, when, in fact, it was his friend who had stolen the chewing gum. *He had made him out to be something he was not—a thief. The truth is that the owner was the thief. He had stolen from Jayden twice, using his smart tactics against a poor customer. So if anyone was the victim here, it was Jayden, not that store owner. When Jayden pointed that gun at the store owner, he was really just giving him his dues.*

"*Shout out to my homie, cuz, mah original gangsta, Napa, Luz the nine, cuz. Good looks.*" Jayden looked down at his empty hands and was reminded that he no longer had that nine-millimeter pistol because the police took it. What trouble could Jayden be in if he were to be freed and return to Ethan without his handgun?

"Isaac!"

Jayden snapped out of deep thought. He recognized the voice as belonging to one of the officers. He followed the sound and saw the officer who had called out.

"Jayden Isaac, someone's here to see you. Come with me."

The officer opened the cell and led Jayden to the small room where he'd met that lawyer almost a day ago. The officer sat Jayden on a chair at a table. There was another chair on the opposite side of the table. The officer did not remove Jayden's cuffs; instead, he opened the door and in walked Elmo Carter. Jayden's face showed elation. Scarp's face wasn't as animated. With the officer behind him, Elmo stepped forward to greet Jayden with a simple handshake. Because of where they were, and the situation, Elmo and Jayden couldn't greet each other with the same kind of energy they usually would. They both sat on either side of the table. Jayden leaned forward so that only Elmo could hear what he had to say.

"Good looking, BG. Fuzz got me on watch. Now I'm ready to bounce."

"Not that easy, Tio," replied Scarp, also lowering his voice out of the police's earshot. "They're going to try you in court before they decide what to do with you. You can get six years for robbery. You may not get out before your twentieth birthday."

"I'll do days in dis pen. But I refuse to spend a year."

"You can get twenty simply for armed robbery."

"Nah, Nah, cuz. That can't happen."

"It will happen unless you have an attorney to represent you. A lawyer who goes by Jay Stropolis came the other day. Let him handle this."

On hearing this, Jayden's reaction made it clear that he didn't agree. "I don't trust dat low life."

"Don't have much of a choice, son. You don't know the man. Another thing, he told me that he saw everything. Hiring Stropolis can be your ticket out."

"Still don't trust him. He looks like money, and I got none. And I'm not down for getting chooched."

"If you think you're going out on bail, then you're perpin'. Napa thought it would work that way. The lawyer had to correct him and remind him that they don't do cash bails no more because of a recent Senate bill that was passed. You're staying till they decide what to do with you."

"Nah, cuz. You're not gonna leave me hangin'?"

"No, we're not. That's why you gotta let Mr. Stropolis handle that. He can go into your records. And, Tio, this is your first time in the pen. Let him prove that you're not a danger to the public and that you did what you did out of a grudge."

"Yeah, in the end, he'll cost an arm, a leg, and mah rear end."

"Listen, your only concern right now is getting out. We'll worry about the other stuff later."

Scarp waited for Jayden's response. After stalling for a moment, Jayden nodded before turning his face back to the bare wall in front of him. Scarp rose and stepped out of the room. Five minutes later, Jay Stropolis stepped in. Jay stared straight at the empty chair as he walked towards it. He sat and then turned to Jayden.

"Jayden, you know why I'm here."

Jayden stared at the wall behind Jay, and without regard for the questioner, responded, "Yup."

"Any parents or guardians you know in the area?"

"My mom."

"Has she been to the station?"

"Yes."

"And what did she say?"

"Nothing much. My mom told me that it's my decision that put me in here, and I'm to stay until I decide what to do."

"By now, you should know that you could spend years behind bars because of what you did. Because of what Elmo told me about you—"

"What did he tell you about me?" snapped Jayden.

Jay kept his calm. "It's important that he tells me about you. I can use what I know in your defense. Elmo told me that you're straight. What I want to do is go around and talk to people who know you: school teachers, neighbors, coaches, if you're into sports, and so on."

"I' ma tell you, White Colla,' that I don't gang bang, I don't sell crack, heroin, meth, keta, or any drug, I don't nap hookers or sell 'em. I ain't wit none of that."

"Well, that's good. We can start there. What I'll need are people that you know. They'll tell me what they think about you. While the prosecution will be in search for every ounce of dirt, I'll be searching for people who can explain how that little dirt first turned up. Makes sense?"

Jayden didn't reply. He only nodded.

"Good. Then give me some names of people and tell me where I can find them."

Jayden thought for a moment. He then gave Jay a list of names, including teachers, neighbors, active members in the community, and local business owners.

Jay took the names and made a brief list. He shared them with Alyssa, knowing that she had come as a part of her school report. She would be eager to do something, and this was her chance. He would give her a list of names, coach her, and then send her to the individuals while shadowing her.

Their first stop was at his apartment building. Jayden had given Jay two names. One is a disc jockey that lived on the first floor, while the other is a family that lived a few doors from him. The truth is that they were new to the community, and they'd only known Jayden for a short time. Jay decided to throw a curveball in this investigation and not visit the named persons. Instead, he would have Alyssa stop random persons at the apartment building as they walked by and ask them if they knew Jayden. Those that did would be fielded with questions by Alyssa herself. Jay thought it fit that Alyssa did the questioning. If a grown-up stranger, like Jay, were to stop residents and ask them about Jayden, the people who knew him would know that he's in trouble with the law, or possibly the FBI. At least the questions coming from an adolescent would be perceived as innocent, especially a female adolescent.

Jay and Alyssa were heading from the car to the building's main entrance when they saw, on their twelve, someone exiting the building from a side entrance. Jay nudged her. Alyssa walked ahead to meet this person. He was a middle-aged man, with his head shaved bald and a clean goatee. He stood five-feet-four-inches tall, had a stocky build, and looked neighborly. With Jay standing six feet away, Alyssa approached.

"Excuse me, sir."

"You are excused," the man smiled.

"I'm asking about Jayden Isaac. Do you know him?"

"Young hood, handsome, medium built. Are you his girlfriend?" the man asked, now looking like the questioner. He looked her up and down with growing interest. He could be thinking that Jayden had to be popular for a nameless woman to track him down.

"No, I'm not his girlfriend. I would like to know him."

"I'm sure you would," the man smiled, then became more solemn. "How may I help you?"

"That man in the suit is my uncle. He's Jayden's defense attorney."

He looked at her with a side glance. "He's in trouble?"

"That's why I'm doing an investigation on Jayden's life. I'm interviewing people who know him, in hopes that they can tell me what they think of Jayden, based on their own experiences with him."

"I haven't seen Jayden as of late. Why . . . the five-o's have him?"

"Yes, he's in jail right now, and your answer is critical. That's why I'm here."

The man looked at Alyssa as though impressed by her spunk and the quickness and depth of her perception. "I'll tell you what I know. I've seen, and I've known troublemakers. I've never known Jayden to be one. The only way he would do something wrong, I guess, is if he had been pushed to his limit. And, by the way, who do I know that isn't like that?"

"Do you know, or have you seen, his friends? You can know people by their company."

"That's true. If loitering was a crime, then Jayden and his hoods would be found guilty. That's all I've seen so far. Maybe I'm too blissful to not be ignorant. It's all I know."

"Thank you so kindly for your openness and sincerity. I'm Alyssa Stropolis. And what is your name?"

"Anthony Bryant. Folk from around here call me AB."

Alyssa thanked him again as they parted ways. Jay drew closer to Alyssa. They then turned their attention to the three-story building. The yellow-brick building stood as a duplicate of a collection of other yellow-brick buildings on that street. Jay and Alyssa walked up a set of steps and into the lobby. Jay tried the glass door and, amazingly, it opened for him. They walked past a set of elevators, towards a door marked 'Superintendent.' Jay would have stopped at the disc jockey's unit since he also lived on the first floor, but he chose to interview those whom Jayden Isaac would not expect. It's unlikely that this superintendent was a friend of Jayden.

Jay and Alyssa walked the hallway, and as they passed doors, they smelled the aroma of a medley of dishes coming from different cultural backgrounds. It was as if they were picking up the scent of delectable dishes of Mexican, Chinese, Indian, and Mediterranean cuisines. But combined, they formed an amalgam that made Jay want to gag. They came upon the superintendent's door, and Alyssa could swear that she smelled the stench of urine stains on the walls beside the door.

Jay knocked, and the door opened to a dark-complexioned man with a head of short, nappy hair. His round face was clean-shaven, and he wore silver-framed glasses. This man wore a white sleeveless vest with two small holes where his potbelly was, plaid shorts that blended the colors blue and red, and no shoes. He gave a questioning look to his unusual visitors.

"Yes?"

"We are sorry to bother you," Jay spoke, "but we are here to do an investigation. I'm Jay Stropolis, and I am Jayden Isaac's attorney. This is my niece, Alyssa."

The man said nothing.

"She's assisting me today. Something happened to Jayden a couple of days back. They have him in jail, and they have yet to try him in court—"

"And we're going around the neighborhood in hopes of finding and speaking with persons who know Jayden," Alyssa butted in. "Could you help us?"

The man looked at Alyssa, and his face seemed to say, *"This has to be one bold and bright girl. I'm going to listen on to see what else she has to say."*

"Yeah, I can help you. Come in." The man cracked his door open so that both Jay and his niece could enter. They walked into a shabby unit. The man took a dry wash rag to beat the dust off one of the two-seaters before motioning Jay and Alyssa to sit. They sat.

"I didn't get your name."

"Quincy."

"Thanks for your time, Quincy. Do you know Jayden well? And how long have you known him?"

"I don't know the boy that well. I've seen him many times. I don't know for how long."

"What were your experiences with Jayden, from past leading to present?" Alyssa asked.

Jay smiled approvingly at Alyssa's take-charge approach.

"Aside from the regular meetings when his mother's rent was due—she usually sends him with the cheque—I only see him on random occasions. There were times she was behind or short on her rent. Then again, that's not his problem. Off and on, I would see him and a few of his boys. They would loiter in the halls or the stairwell until someone reports them to me—"

"Then, you would ask them to leave?" Jay said, finishing Quincy's sentence.

"Yes," Quincy replied.

"Have they ever offered resistance when you confronted them?" Alyssa asked.

Quincy gave a vacant stare before saying, "No. Never. But I had to do this more than once. The thing about these kids is that they're creatures of habit. And they make a habit of loitering. This boy plays loud music on earbuds. I don't know how they get that sound cranked so high that they can still cause a disturbance. Neighbors complained about him just because he passed their doors."

"He loiters, and he causes disturbances," Alyssa noted, "but have you ever seen him lash out? In other words, have you ever come across any violent behaviors in Jayden?"

"Jayden, deep down, is a decent kid. He gets lost in that device of his, a lot. It's in those moments that he becomes motionless and shows no emotion. I have never come across a violent attitude in him. Now you tell me," said Quincy, "what kind of trouble did that boy get himself into?"

Jay and Alyssa looked at each other. Jay gave her a slight nod before she turned to Quincy. "He robbed a store at gunpoint."

Quincy turned and heaved his chest before exhaling deeply. "Which grocery store did he rob?"

"The Sholes Convenience Store," Alyssa replied. "It's right by this nice local restaurant. You need to try their apple pie and their cheesecake—they're to die for."

"I just might," Quincy answered. "I think I know that one. Middle Eastern man? Ornery fellow?"

"I think you got the man," replied Jay.

"I don't think this justifies what Jayden did, but I don't think Jayden is the only person who has had run-ins with this store owner. I went to buy two bags of ice one day, and I saw him get into a heated argument with this Spanish lady. She sounded like someone who doesn't take foolishness from anyone. They went back and forth for a while. I asked to be excused, so I could pay for my things and get out. And the man motioned with his hand for me to wait until he was done telling off this woman. By the time he was ready for me, the ice was half-melted. I told him to wait while I went to the back and got two different bags. Then we got into an argument over those bags. I wanted to drop the bags on the counter and walk out. But I couldn't stand in there those twenty minutes for nothing."

"I can't thank you enough, sir. I'm listening to your story, and I'm comparing it to Jayden's story. You, Jayden, and the Spanish lady have had not-so-pleasant experiences with that owner. You all decided how you were going to react. Jayden also decided what his reaction would be. From what I've received from my uncle, Jayden has been to that convenience store on several different occasions. I guess Jayden was at his breaking point."

"That don't justify what he did," corrected Quincy.

"I couldn't agree with you more. What I see with Jayden is what I've seen with many in his age bracket. Ask me, I'm also a teen. A young person will let out or give off the anger and frustrations that have built up over time. Before that, young people are like sponges. I could be wrong. I read this report by the American Psychological Association that among the risk factors causing aggression in teens are dwindling or lost economic opportunities. Then there are the disadvantaged communities, thus are socially disorganized and plagued with crime. And I cannot leave out the influence coming from peers with a track record for aggressive and violent behavior. There are others. But you will understand Jayden's position when you consider the likely causes for his behavior, which then led to his course of action."

Jay smiled and lifted his chin as he listened to his niece.

Quincy arched his eyebrows. "I could go with that theory. I think I'm looking at the product of an upbringing. In the end, I see Jayden making his own choices, however misguided."

"As my uncle often tells me, decisions are affected by brain states and by one's surroundings. I think brains can be defective."

Quincy was puzzled by that. "To know why a person is making bad choices, we have to examine his brain?"

Jay stepped in. "We're not saying we should examine his brain for defects, but that we could better understand the possible causes for Jayden's decisions."

Quincy paused by what he'd just heard. "I'll give you my

contact. Let me know how the case goes with the boy. I still think he's a decent kid."

"Thank you, Quincy. And we will."

Teaching and counseling

Jay and Alyssa left the apartment building, and the next stop was the school campus. Jayden gave him the name Gerald Pinn, who was the gym teacher. Jay went instead to a list at the head office. One of the names that came up was Marisha Applegate, the English teacher and guidance counselor. At this time, Ms. Applegate would be moving between classes. In a figurative sense, she would remove one hat to put on another. With one hat, Ms. Applegate instructed her students in speech grammar, writing skills, reading, and thoughtfully critiquing works of literature. With her second hat, she assessed the student's abilities, interests, and personality types to help them discover their career paths. With this hat, Ms. Applegate also gave special attention to emotional problems and gave sound advice depending on the need.

Jay and Alyssa found the room that Ms. Applegate would be in. Alyssa knocked. Opening the door from the other side was an attractive brunette who was good-looking in a wholesome way. Marisha's brown attire spelled modesty, as her skirt flowed down past her knees, and she wore loafers on her feet for comfort. Her shapely body was borderline heavyset, and her hair was long and in a clean ponytail. As she opened the door, her eyes rested on Alyssa.

"Hi there, I wasn't expecting visitors."

"Oh, hello. My name is Alyssa. Are you Marisha?"

"The one."

"This is my uncle, Jay. I hope we're not intruding on your timetable."

"Well, I was expecting a student at any moment."

"I am so sorry to intrude," Alyssa said, stepping back slightly. "We'll come back—"

"Oh, nonsense," interrupted Marisha. "I'll spare you a moment. Knowing my student, he has a way of not arriving until twenty minutes later, and that's after he remembers that he was supposed to meet with me."

"Oh, we so greatly appreciate this. We hope we won't hold up your time."

"And when my student arrives, I'll have him wait until we're finished."

"Thank you, Marisha," Jay said. "This shouldn't take much of your time."

"Come in."

Marisha directed Jay and Alyssa to a two-seater that sat across from a comfortable armchair. The room was small enough to be considered cozy and was suitable for a few persons. They all sat.

"What may I do for you?"

"You have a student who goes by the name Jayden Isaac," Alyssa said.

"Jayden Isaac. Yes, he is a student that I normally meet with. He is also one of my English students."

"Then you would know plenty about him," said Jay in a matter-of-fact tone.

"Strange, I haven't seen Jayden in days."

"That's why we came to ask you about him," said Alyssa. "Days ago, there was an incident involving Jayden."

Marisha froze as though she dreaded what might be reported to her.

"Jayden is in prison because he robbed a convenience store," Alyssa continued.

Marisha's jaw dropped, and she covered her mouth with her right hand.

Jay took over to give her an important note. "Jayden is in custody with the local police. He will be tried in court in a matter of days, maybe months. This will determine whether he will be going to juvenile detention or not."

"And we're hoping that you could tell us what we need to know about Jayden, from your experience," Alyssa added.

"I'm sorry, this is all coming as a surprise to me," Marisha's voice matched her stare of disbelief. "I've known Jayden for a short time. I wouldn't have expected this course of action from him. Maybe I was too naïve. Jayden has been battling his demons. He is the elder of two siblings in a single-parent household. His mom works at the postal office, doing all that she can for her children. Because of what Jayden has seen in his community—disadvantages and poverty rates—he has been carrying the loser complex."

"The loser complex?" asked Alyssa.

"The loser complex. Jayden feels that in a community where there's no hope, he is hopeless. Because many blacks are jobless, he feels that he, too, will become jobless."

"Wow, I didn't know that someone his age could think this way."

"And this has affected his schooling. For one, he lacks motivation, believing that there's no hope."

"And these are the demons you were talking about?"

"Yes. Fear of the unknown. That is the reason why I've been trying to get him to think more about his education. It becomes a challenge when your peers are not thinking about their education."

"Wow, and when Jayden needed others to help push him forward, most were only holding him back."

"I can understand why some have committed armed robberies. I was hoping that it wouldn't come to this for Jayden. I can see it in him that, deep down, he wants to do well and to make most of his life."

"And now he's not where he should be. We are hoping that Jayden doesn't end up with a fifteen-year prison sentence."

"That is why I am motivated to help in any way. One of

the areas I've been trying to help him with is his grammar. Good communication is an aid in a job search. With Jayden, he uses improper English both on the street and in English class. Young people often use slang to express themselves, especially when speaking with peers. Problem with Jayden is that he has yet to master the art of checking his use of slang at the door. This becomes a problem, especially for older teachers who don't understand emojis or text language."

"Oh, I'm like that as well. I use slang with my girlfriends. And I do have my moments when I find myself using slang in the wrong places, like really."

Marisha smiled. "And slangs do change with trends. Putting that aside, I'm hoping Jayden can find a community with the right people. I know his mom. She's honest and hard working. Jayden will need others to inspire him, a community, such as a church."

"That's a good suggestion," Jay remarked. "But he'll need to take the meat of good moral teachings, chew on the marrow, then spit the bones out—I'm talking about the dogma."

"They can do that, council. And I think youth could benefit without the dogma. But what you need to understand is that the dogma is the skeleton of the good moral teachings. You admitted this. You can remove the meat from the skeleton, but the skeleton is what causes the moral teachings to stand. It is the foundation."

Jay's face twisted into a grimace on hearing this. "With all due respect, Ms. Applegate, I don't think the dogma is the foundation."

"And why do you think the dogma isn't the skeleton?"

"Because Jayden doesn't need religion to be good."

"He does not need religion; you are right," replied Marisha. "He needs to know that religion was supposed to have meaning in the life of the church."

Alyssa stepped in. "And that meaning is to serve the communities and to not allow oneself to become corrupt. That's what their Creator would want them to do to thrive."

"Alyssa, I believe you've hit the proverbial nail on the head," said Marisha.

Jay turned and gave Alyssa a quick side-glance in annoyance, thinking, *What has Gale been teaching you? Or is this coming from Lolita?"*

"I was watching YouTube one day," Alyssa continued, "and I saw this evangelical preacher. That's where I got the idea."

A knock on the door alerted the three.

"I think my student is finally here."

The three stood, and Alyssa extended her hand to Marisha. "Ms. Applegate, we can't thank you enough."

"You can thank me by taking my contact information with you."

Jay extended his hand next. "We certainly will. Thank you."

Law and order

Jay and Alyssa walked through the near-empty halls of the high school and towards the set of doors that led to the pickup and drop-off circle. Just as they passed the first set of doors to the second set, they noticed two young African American females who stood at the far right. The girls were both facing the driveway. They appeared to be Alyssa's age. Jay had his hand on the door handle when Alyssa pivoted towards them instead.

"Excuse me, does anyone know Jayden Isaac?"

"We both do," one said. Alyssa pulled away from Jay and walked towards them.

"What do you know about him?"

As Alyssa drew close, she saw two good-looking teens— one was fair complexion, while the other was dark complexion. Neither appeared to be thrilled to see Alyssa. The darker one looked at Alyssa with scorn. She could be thinking, *"Who is this white chick, and what does she want with Jayden?"*

"I'm sorry to be abrupt, but Jayden is in trouble with the law. My uncle, a lawyer, and I are looking for people who know Jayden. We're hoping to get as much from the community that when my uncle stands before the judge, he'll make a good defense for Jayden. It will help to keep Jayden out of prison."

Both teen's facial expressions suddenly changed towards Alyssa. The one with the fairer complexion spoke first. "Okay, what do you need to know?"

"Thanks, How often do you see Jayden?"

The teens looked at each other.

"As often as I would see the others," said the darker girl.

"When you say the others, are you talking about his friends?"

"Yes."

"And what do you see Jayden and his friends doing, whenever you see them?"

"I would see them in the hall."

"What would they be doing?"

"Doing nothing."

"Do you ever see Jayden go to class?"

"Everyone goes to class, or they'll have to see the principal."

"Does either of you know whether Jayden is involved in any activities, like sports or a debate team?"

The two looked at each other.

"I know he don't do basketball," said the fairer girl. "But I know he spits rhymes."

"I always hear him spittin' rhymes in the halls," the other added.

"And, has either of you ever seen Jayden in fights?"

The two looked at each other. The girls gestured that they were both clueless.

"I never seen him in a fight," the fairer one said. "He and his friends play around. That's about it."

"That's all I've seen," the darker one confirmed.

"You both have been a big help to us. My name is Alyssa. And your names are?"

The darker one responded, "We both like Jayden, but we don't want to have to stand in court."

"Oh, I understand," replied Alyssa. "Being called to the stand can be nervy."

Alyssa looked over to her uncle. Jay nodded.

"Okay, we have other witnesses, so you'll be off the record."

"My name is Bree," said the darker one.

"And my name is Eisha."

After thanking them again, both Jay and Alyssa continued through the second set of doors to his vehicle.

Days later, Alyssa trod up the steps of the Stropolis office building. Outside the building and inside, she passed other professionals in business wear. What struck her was that there was a realtor office in the building. Most cannot tell the difference between a lawyer and a real estate agent. They carry the same aura. Realtors are salespersons, and so are lawyers. For Uncle Jay, it was a little more complicated. He sold his services, not homes. Jay once told Alyssa that sometimes he wished he was selling homes and not his services to would-be criminals, who would come looking for him if all were to fail through a court decision. The real estate agent would simply lose potential referrals from their clients.

Alyssa walked up to the door that read "Stropos Firm." She walked in and saw Gladys at her desk, tapping away at the desktop keyboard. Gladys was so plugged in that she barely noticed Alyssa walk in. Alyssa also noticed voices coming from her uncle's office. She heard Uncle Jay's voice. She also heard another. It sounded much like a heated argument. She decided not to bother Gladys, who was more likely to hear Jay and his visitor than Alyssa sneak in. Alyssa walked towards Jay's door. She knocked and then walked in. Jay and his visitor stopped speaking the moment they heard the gentle knock.

"I'm sorry to intrude. Uncle Jay, is everything alright?"

The visitor, a tall Eastern-European-looking man with blond hair, slicked back into a ponytail, a goatee, and a suit turned to Jay.

"I will give you three days to think about this. Three days. Do not allow this to drag on any longer. Goodbye." Then he walked out.

Seeing and hearing all of this, Alyssa turned to Jay.

"Uncle?"

"It's okay, Alyssa. That man who just stepped out is the state lawyer."

Her features were sullen. "Oh, the prosecution's attorney."

"He's offering me a plea bargain stating that Jayden will not have to go to trial, providing he admits his guilt."

"What did you say to him?"

"That I'm not ready to accept this plea bargain, because I haven't received a yes from my client. I haven't yet spoken to his friend, Elmo, about this deal."

"I can tell he's forceful, just by listening to him a little."

"He insists that I take the offer of a lesser charge and not let this go to trial."

"What happens if Jayden were to accept this? Wouldn't he be getting jail time?"

"He would. And lesser jail time. And if he does plead guilty, and later the store owner decides to press charges, then this former case would hurt Jayden."

"Despite what we've heard from Quincy, Marisha, Bree, and Eisha, Jayden is still guilty. Many conditions affected Jayden, but he still made a bad choice."

Jay paused, and with a deep sigh, said, "Yes, you are right. He made a bad choice. If this case goes to trial, it'll be in the hands of the judge or jury to decide what to do with him."

"The jury could vote that he is guilty. And then Jayden could get twenty years in prison. If you do accept this plea bargain, Jayden could get about two years. I'm only wild guessing."

"It's around there. Now, I could advise Jayden to accept. And, by the way, it's unlikely that I will be paid for my services. Elmo, who goes by the name Scarp, will say that I'm bailing out too soon."

"Jayden is fourteen. If he were to go to juvey for two years, he'd be out after his sixteenth birthday."

"Then again, from what we heard from the building superintendent, the school counselor, and the two teens, Jayden is a low-risk offender. He could be eligible for house arrest."

"Is that where he has to live with an electronic device?"

"They call it SEC, which is short for Supervised Electronic Confinement. He will not be free to travel. At least he won't have to face jail time."

"That sounds like a good alternative."

"But, Alyssa, to get house arrest, the case would have to go to trial. The prosecutor and the store owner would have Jayden face jail time." Jay paused as though he heard something.

"What is it?"

"I don't know. Let me see."

Jay rose from his seat and walked to the door. The moment he did, the door opened, and two figures stood outside the office. Jay wouldn't have been able to withstand them, for both were hugely built. They dwarfed him in size. Scarp and Napa walked in, and they passed Jay on either side as they both took seats. Napa took the chair beside Alyssa and turned it around before sitting on it. Alyssa was about to get up when Napa motioned her to stay seated. Scarp sat on the corner of Jay's desk.

"Elmo, I was just about to contact you."

"It's been days," replied Scarp.

Gladys stood at the door. "I am sorry, Jay, I tried to stop them, but they insisted that I let them in."

Just then, a thug appeared from outside the office, and then another one. The second thug was monstrously large. He stood at six-feet-nine-inches and weighed over three-hundred pounds, with massive arms and hands. The first thug, Flint, stood over Gladys and barked.

"Lady, sit down! Go back to your seat!"

"I will not be pushed—"

Just then, the big monster pushed Gladys to the floor. He did this with minimal effort. Still, Gladys landed hard. Alyssa did not see how she fell because they were outside the office.

Jay protested, "Hey! She's seventy-three years old."

"She will heal," replied Napa with cold resolve.

Flint closed the door, leaving Napa and Scarp alone with Jay and Alyssa.

"Back to what I was saying," Scarp continued. "It's been days since I've last heard from you. Do you have enough evidence to free Tio?"

"Not to free Jayden, but to prove to the courts that he's not a risk to the public."

Napa spoke up. "What's that supposed to mean, White Colla'?"

"That he will not have to go to prison or juvey. Instead, he'll be on house arrest."

"House arrest would mean that Tio is guilty," replied Scarp.

"Then why did we hire you?" asked Napa.

"Gentlemen—"

"We are not gentlemen," interrupted Napa.

"Okay, boys, I wanted to understand Jayden's situation. Now I do. Because of the people myself and Alyssa spoke to, I know that Jayden is not a risk to the public. The prosecution's office is offering me a plea deal—"

"And what if Jayden were to reject it?" Scarp asked.

"Then he would have to take this case to trial on a losing cause."

"You say this is a losin' cause?" barked Napa.

Alyssa jumped in. "People say that Jayden is a decent kid. It doesn't make him not guilty. Because of the offense, the judge and jury may not hear the case. No matter how this case ends, Jayden would still be guilty. They know what he did. It's the State against Isaac. I'm not telling you to . . . but I'm thinking that you should talk to Jayden and tell him that this is the best thing to do. He can take this to trial. But we hope they put him on house arrest and not let him do time."

Alyssa stopped the moment she saw Scarp and Napa look at each other. Alyssa knew they weren't taking to the proposal. Napa broke into menacing laughter. It unnerved her. Scarp didn't laugh; he just held his humorless stare at Alyssa. She wondered what he was thinking.

"You're serious!" said Napa. He turned to Jay. "Now, I'm convinced that this is truly your niece. She got sass, like any firm with attitude. She is destined to become one."

Scarp spoke with his eyes still pinned on Alyssa. "Then you and I will be seeing your client. And you will tell our lil' G what you can and can't do."

A heavy thud was heard at the front office. It was coming from Gladys's desk. Then there was another booming sound, then another. Alyssa saw Napa rise from his seat to see to the cause of these sounds. And just as he opened the door, Napa stood before a five-feet-nine, lean brunette, who appeared to be in her late forties. This one was not one to be trifled with.

Jay said, "Gale?"

Alyssa's eyes widened. "Mom!"

Napa stepped back as Gale walked in. He walked to the door and peered around to the front desk.

Napa turned to Gale. "They're all lying unconscious! What did you do to them?"

"I put them to sleep. Your friends will be out for a while."

"Okay, little sis," said Jay, "I wasn't expecting you so soon."

Scarp kept his cool. "Are we going to get more family involved in this? You are not making this easy, Jay."

Gale turned to Scarp. "And you are not making it easy, Mr. Carter."

"Even Wonder Woman got tabs on us," said Napa. "I knew she was a fed."

"Yes, Carter number two. I've got enough on you to make hell very real in your world. You are worried about your friend when a litany of lawsuits can be filed with your name on them. Your friend has a chance to live a normal existence outside the darkened walls of a state prison, or juvey."

"Not while tethered to some tracking device," replied Scarp. "That's not freedom."

"It's much better than what your twin could get for his offenses. With what we have on file for him, I don't think the courts will so much as trust Ethan Carter in public. You can make this easy for us all—tell Jayden Isaac about the conditions and rally your friends to clean up the Sholes Convenience Store. Or you can make this difficult for us all. And I'll assure you that when you do time, you'll have your friends as your company. So what will it be, Carter?"

The twins turned their heads in annoyance as they wrestled with this choice. Scarp turned to face Jay as he spoke to Napa.

"What do you say, Napa?"

Napa wrenched as he said, "Yeah, go talk to our boy about the conditions. Get him on house arrest." He then turned to Gale. "And what of the store owner?"

"I had a talk with him. Immigration has enough on him to have him deported. All I'd have to do is lead them to him. He won't be filing any suits against your friends. If you send your friends to undo the mess they made, we will not have to talk about charges."

Napa turned and started walking towards the door. Gale called to him. As he turned, she took a small white sack from her jacket pocket and tossed it to him. He caught it.

"Wake your friends on your way out. They have a lot of work ahead of them."

He took the sack, turned, and walked out.

Scarp followed and stopped at the door. He turned to Alyssa, then to Jay. "Meet me at the station. We both will talk to Tio."

A day had passed. Jay and Alyssa met with Elmo Carter, who then spoke to Jayden Isaac at the station. After a little persuasion from Scarp, Jayden was ready to accept the conditions. Jay talked to the prosecution's office. He told them that both he and his client would take the deal only on terms that Jayden's sentencing would involve the halfway house and the SEC program. The prosecution's office granted this request.

Jayden Isaac pleaded guilty for charges of armed robbery. He stood before the judge and jury. Marisha Applegate, Quincy Abioye, and Anthony Bryant gave their written statements in support of Jayden's request. Although they were not eyewitnesses of the armed robbery, they knew Jayden, thus making them character witnesses. Those who didn't know Jayden well could testify, from their experience, that he wasn't a danger to the public.

The judge's final verdict included a three-year house-detention sentence for Jayden. Under the California Penal Code Section 1203.016, Jayden would be free to hold a job. He would need one since he would be paying twelve dollars a day for the electronic monitoring device. Marisha Applegate would assist Jayden in his search for employment. Under that penal code, Jayden would be free to attend family gatherings, religious gatherings, classes at a school, college, or university. He would be free to see the dentist, visit the doctor's office, and go to the gym. That is freedom and a far better alternative to imprisonment.

A day following the decision, Alyssa went up the steps and through the doors of the office building. She walked by lawyers, realtors, and other tie-wearing business bodies to get to Stropo's Firm. She opened the door and was greeted by Gladys, who was where she would usually be. She went to Uncle Jay's door and knocked.

"Come in."

"Uncle Jay?"

"Your knock was louder than normal. Wouldn't have thought it was you."

"Maybe it's the excitement I'm feeling right now."

"Oh? Before you tell me about your reasons for barging in, tell me what you think about the recent days you had with me, in this office, on the field, and in court."

"I have to say, Uncle, that your job is not as boring as Mom made it out to be. And this is the reason why I came and am excited. I've decided on my career path."

Jay pushed himself forward and almost off his seat. His heart pounded. He had to hear this. "Yes, Alyssa, so you've decided to become a—"

"Police detective or a private investigator."

Jay's face froze.

"I want to become an investigator. After our experiences in the field talking to different people and making friends with some of the most interesting people I've ever met, I can't see myself doing anything different."

Jay was almost speechless as he said, "Oh, I was beginning to think that you liked my job."

"No offense, Uncle, but I want to carry a gun and be trained to use one. I want to practice martial arts like Mom. I think lawyers are too defenseless."

Again, Jay's face froze.

"Then again," added Alyssa, "I have come to understand what has been missing in my life. I appreciate my moms. They have been an encouragement to me. I have a good friend in mom."

"What are you saying?" asked Jay.

"Being around you, I feel . . . I don't know . . . accepted by a gender that I respect and see as a role model. For some reason, I feel I need to be accepted by a man in my family. I want to be sure that what I'm doing is right . . . that's it."

"Your mothers can help you in that area just as much."

"It's not the same, Uncle. My moms are strong women."

You can say that again," added Jay.

"I need a strong male presence in my life. I'm not talking about the one that would later want sex from me. I'm talking about someone I can look up to, like a father. You are that father. I want to know that I have your approval."

Jay looked at her for a while before smiling. "Alyssa, whatever you want in life, I'll stand by you in full support. You are my niece, and I'll always be there for you."

"Thank you, Uncle Jay."

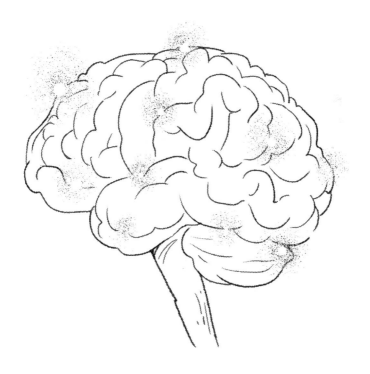

THE BRAIN FACTORY

On Friday at 4:15 PM, at Cromwell University, Jeff stood in the lecture hall as a guest speaker. He spoke to the more than six hundred students as a part of a weekend conference that would extend into Sunday.

Jeff was neither a philosopher nor a theorist, but he had friends that were. For decades, he has operated on the human brain and was fascinated by what went beyond the grey matter. The concepts of consciousness and freewill drew Jeff's attention. This was where he deferred to his philosopher and theorist friends for their answers to this mystery. After decades of working with the physical stuff and learning about how it could tie into consciousness and free will, Jeff wanted to pass the knowledge on to students on college campuses. The topic itself was out of his field of expertise, but he was up to the challenge. After his talk and the Q&A session with more than six hundred students in the auditorium, Jeff experienced push back from several bold students.

Jeff's eyes moved from the questioner holding the mic to the line behind him. The students standing along the aisle were a minority compared to those that stayed seated. Since the beginning of the Q&A, Jeff had been fielded with questions from believers in the supernatural. He wondered how much longer it would be until all the questioners got their turn at the mic. He might not be able to get to every question. In fact, it was likely that many would be forced to return to their seats with their questions unanswered. Then, there was the hall and then the lobby with the book signing. *"This is going to be a long afternoon,"* Jeff thought.

Jeff's eyes darted back to the student with the mic, the student who was speaking directly to him. Jeff listened more intently to the last line of his long, technical question. Jeff had missed some of the details. He wondered if any of the other students understood what this questioner had said.

"Could you rephrase your question? Most of that went over my head."

The students throughout the auditorium broke out in laughter.

The crowd guffawed for the space of a minute. That bought Jeff time to briefly scan the room. He wondered how many people shared his views and how many didn't. He hoped there would be more people on his side. Jeff then turned his eyes back to the student. At least now, Jeff could catch what the student said. It was apparent that the student was deeply embarrassed by the doctor's response.

"I meant, do you believe that the many neurons that work in the brain as a unit are aware of what they are doing?" the student rephrased.

Jeff's eyes lit up in a that-is-more-like-it kind of way.

"Thank you for the question. Dumbing down does have a way of shortening our speeches."

The students broke into more laughter. Jeff gestured for them to stop it.

"In response to your question: No. The neurons don't know what they're doing, though they are animate objects that are very tiny. They work together as they fire through channels and communicate through synapses. These cells function in a certain way, just like the cells in the human heart function. It's amazing how billions of these cells function automatically or mechanically—however you'd like to describe it. But we should never suppose that these neurons know what they're doing."

Jeff pointed to another student holding a mic, a youthful-looking, sandy-blond-haired twenty-something-year-old of average height and weight. The student didn't look intimidating. He held the mic in one hand while keeping his other hand behind his back. "That's *a clear sign of confidence. But confidence in what?*" wondered Jeff. He hoped this student's confidence was in that which was rational, and not what was beyond the physical.

"Dr. Measly, thank you for the work that you do. To be in the same room with the patients and their families must be quite an experience. To have patients with a form of dementia or Alzheimer's is a sobering reality. They've arrived at a point in which some of their brain cells no longer function. What happens to some of their memories of past events? Even though they're able to recall some details of their past, what happens to the other details?"

"Thanks for your question. Thoughts of past events, from distant to recent, are images that are etched in our retinas. Those living cells in the cerebral cortex of our brain will then send signals to other cells throughout other regions of the brain. When some neurons die and cease to function, some thoughts will no longer register in the mind of the host—the patient."

"That makes sense! But what I'm trying to understand are the thoughts belonging to a conscious adult who is one-hundred-percent healthy and in the right state of mind. While he's aware of his surroundings, he entertains thoughts of what happened and what could have happened."

Jeff twitched. "As I'm looking at you right now, I'm thinking that I should have worn my belt. I feel like my pants are about to fall off my waist."

The auditorium erupted into laughter.

After the chuckles died down, Jeff continued. "I didn't mean to be so vulgar. With all the busied cells, we all would be surprised at how much goes on in our brains. It should not surprise us whenever we think of what would have, what could have, what should have happened. Neurons are functioning as they should. But what if some of these cells were to die? Then there would not be a lot of thinking. This is where families and friends with working brains can step in and care for the person who has become helpless."

"What I'm trying to hint at is that someone made a conscious decision, even to leave important things behind before coming to this conference . . ."

The crowd reacted in a cacophony of laughter, giggles, crows, cackles, and whispers.

The student continued. "My apologies if I sound personal and direct. I understand there's much activity in the brain. How do we explain conscious, sane, and thoughtful persons making decisions regarding their families? What is happening with the neurons?"

Jeff gave a gleeful smile before answering. "What is your name?"

"Jared."

"Okay, Jared, I thank you for your question. And no offense taken. You and I both have something in common—we are conscious, sane, and thoughtful. Consciousness, thoughts, and life-altering choices are something remarkable. How brain cells work into this is a mystery. And I have friends who could explain the art of consciousness in ways that will blow your minds. We can compare the functioning of a human brain to that of a computer . . ."

Just then, the moderator quietly walked to the podium. He took a mic with him and spoke to the people in attendance.

"Thank you for your questions. Here ends the Q&A."

The crowd, disappointed, released sighs of disapproval. Jeff's eyes widened. They wanted more. He looked at the moderator and thought, *"I love this man! He came right when I was ready to retire for the day."*

The people continued in hopes that the moderator would extend the Q&A. The moderator, who would not be persuaded by their reaction, continued. "For those with questions, you can still see Jeff Measly in the lobby. He'll be happy to answer your questions there."

"No, I will not," thought Jeff, as he walked over to his briefcase. He gathered all his notes, folded his laptop before loading it into his briefcase slot, and walked off the stage in search of an exit point through which he could sneak out of the building unnoticed.

Jeff did not find that exit point and so was deluged by students with many questions. He found himself in the lobby signing many books. He wondered why he wrote to begin with. Then he was reminded that he wanted to teach students what he had learned about the brain. And to write books of this sort did have a price— many buyers would come in search for a signature.

The following week at the clinic, Jeff sat at his office desk. The image before him on the screen was Neville Brown's brain, as was seen through the MRI scan. The side of the cranium was on a split-screen view with the top of the head. Even the loud banging of the MRI scanner was drowned out by his intense focus. Jeff had to see whether something new had turned up since the operation. The glioblastoma cancers, such as what Neville Brown had, were unpredictable. And just when it seemed they were all gone, new seeds of the disease could reappear. Jeff had success in removing every trace of the disease. However, due to some reports he had read of patients dying post-surgery, he decided not to take the chance with his patient.

In the adjoining room, Neville Brown was laid on the table before he was sent through the scan. They had to sedate him because of his fear of closed spaces. He had a traumatic experience as a child, but he never told Jeff what led to his claustrophobia. He was too embarrassed by the details to share it. The radiographer stood by the MRI scanner as Neville lay still.

Jeff stared at the split images on the screen for unusual patterns or slight changes within the brain. He was able to capture the crystal-clear resolution of contrasts between grey and white matter. If a new sign of brain cancer were to appear, Jeff would detect it.

Robby, who was one of the technicians, walked over to Dr. Measly's desk. "Maybe it's me, but I thought I saw Mr. Brown's foot twitch."

"It's you, alright. It's the coffee," Jeff said with comical air to his voice.

"I doubt that it's the coffee, sir. I know that I saw his foot twitch."

"Well, if it does, he will not be able to escape, seeing that we strapped him to the table."

"Simone told me that he is dreadfully afraid of closed spaces. I hope the belts are strong enough to hold him. Look!"

Robby pointed to the MRI scanner. Jeff quickly turned and saw Neville's feet kicking wildly, with abandon.

"They didn't strap him down? Oh, no!"

The next thing he saw was the radiographer's attempts to hold the patient's legs down. That turned out to be a foolish move, for Neville lifted his right foot so wildly that it connected with the radiographer's jaw, knocking him out cold. Robby ran in with hopes that he could calm Neville down. By now, Neville had pulled himself out of the machine and was already on his feet. Robby tried to calm him. What Robby must have forgotten was that Neville was six-feet-two, and two-hundred-and-fifty-four pounds. As a Jamaican immigrant, Neville never played American football. Still, to Jeff, Neville looked like a retired left tackle for the BC Lions. Neville charged forward, knocking Robby off his feet and causing his back to slam hard against a wall. Just then, two large men in lab uniforms tackled Neville to the ground. As big and as powerful as these men were, they had a difficult time wrestling Neville to the floor. He was much too strong to handle. Neville was like a mad bull that had just been spooked.

Jeff shouted to the men. "Let him go!"

The men let Neville go. As quickly as these men were able to spring to their feet, Neville also got to his feet.

Jeff raised both hands as he spoke directly to Neville. "Neville, are you alright?"

Neville replied with clarity, though he sounded as if he was coming to himself. "Oh my, I'm alright, doctor. I'm sorry! But you know how I feel about these closed spaces."

"I'm sorry that I didn't check the drug dosage they gave you. You were not supposed to come to so soon."

Robby struggled to his feet, for he had just had the wind knocked out of him. A nurse tended to the radiographer who had his lights put out.

Robby stumbled over to Jeff. "Sir, are you now going to consider open imaging MRI systems?"

Gary A James

Life in the system

Jared Kensington lived an ordinary life off-campus. He's the only child of a single mom, who had far too many aspirations to bother with him. Ever since she left for New York City to further her career as an artesian and architect, the responsibility to raise little Jared was given to her mother. From the moment he learned to crawl, his grandmother was the only guardian Jared ever knew. She taught him how to walk, to potty, to say 'thank you,' to complete a sentence, and to say grace. Jared's different stages of growth had been under her watch. Before he was sent off to private school, his grandmother home-schooled him. Jared owed his life to his grandmother. She taught him the important lessons of life—most importantly, a relationship with God. Apart from his grandma, Jared had no recollection of the woman who abandoned him. Now, at the age of twenty-two and working towards his major in neurobiology, Jared hoped to become a neurosurgeon. His fascination with the human brain was not the only thing that drove him in this direction. The woman whom Jared had been depending on has now become dependent on him.

Wilma Kensington now had a severe case of dementia. It was a degenerative brain disorder called Creutzfeldt-Jakob disease. This was not the off-campus kind of routine that Jared hoped for. Now at seventy-three, Wilma was into her second year since being diagnosed. She lost much of her memory, outside of the distant ones, and had also lost control of her speech. The most apparent symptom was in her walking and in her balance. The loss of coordination, in addition to her frequent muscle spasms, made her more dependent on her grandson for mobility. Jared was the only relative she had in the Province, so whenever Jared was at the campus, a hired caregiver would come in to assist Wilma.

Jared pulled up to the driveway of that single car garage. He would have pulled in had the caregiver's vehicle not been parked and blocking him. That was always a good sign, for it tells him that somebody cares enough to stick around. Jared has had the experience of the one caring for Wilma leaving the house without notifying him. He had to get a hired caregiver.

Jared walked up the steps, slid the key in the door, and opened it. He walked in to find his grandma where she would usually be. She was on her favorite recliner. The caregiver walked from the kitchen to the recliner with a teacup on a saucer. The content was semi-hot earl grey tea.

"You're here," said the caregiver. "Good. Now I can leave. Today's mail is on the kitchen table. Also, there's chicken soup on the stovetop. I fed her about a half-hour ago. Feel free to help yourself."

"Thank you, Janice. I believe she would have praised you had she still been able to speak."

The caregiver smiled as she walked to the front door.

After she closed the door behind her, Jared walked to the mail that was on the table. He checked the names along with the addresses. Some of the institutions he recognized. One of the letters addressed to Jared A. Kensington caught his attention. It was an institution he did not know: Brain Developer Solutions.

"Brain Developer Solutions? This has to be new," thought Jared.

He opened the letter addressed to him.

"Scientists have now come forward with a breakthrough cure for Alzheimer's, Creutzfeldt-Jakob, Huntington's, brain tumors, and other degenerative brain diseases. These computer-generated molecules . . ." Jared lowered the letter. "This has to be some type of scam," he said to himself.

He thought about crumpling the letter and throwing it in the trash, and then a thought came to him: he should put it aside and read it later. So that is what he did.

Wilma called to Jared. "Is everything alright, son?"

Jared called back. "Everything's alright, Grandma."

"I heard you say scam. What is it?"

"Nothing important, Grandma," he replied. He took the letter, rolled it up, and stashed it in his pocket.

Weeks went by, and Wilma showed more signs that she was worsening. Her movements were made with more effort, and it took more out of Jared and the caregiver to help her eat and go to the bathroom. Wilma cried during the day and often into the night because of the intense pain she was feeling. She had also since lost most of her sight. Everything in view was a complete blur. She had a difficult time telling her grandson and the TV stand apart. She was getting worse. Jared could no longer fully understand his grandma. Her speaking sounded like a line of a slur. Wilma knew her grandson by his speech and by his touch. Because her memory was going, it came to a point where Wilma could not remember Janelle leaving her son behind. Wilma couldn't recall Janelle ever giving birth out of wedlock. Jared went home to his grandmother one day, and she couldn't remember him. He told her that he was her grandson, but even that did not ring a bell for her. One day, with the caregiver still there, Jared asked to be excused. He walked to his car, drove to a nearby parking lot, set it into park, and held his head as he sobbed uncontrollably.

It was on a Saturday at 10:00 AM. Jared had just finished breakfast with his grandmother. After cleaning up and before going to his study, he took his dirty clothes and was preparing to throw them in the laundry. Rather than blindly throwing items into the washing machine, Jared would search the pockets to be sure that nothing important was being thrown in. This he did with all pants and shirt pockets until he came across a rolled-up letter. Jared wondered what it was. Then it dawned on him that weeks earlier he had stashed it into his pocket. He had forgotten about this envelope and why it was addressed to him. It was BDS—Brain Developer Solutions. Jared pulled the letter out and began to read.

"Scientists have now come forward with a breakthrough cure for Alzheimer's, Creutzfeldt-Jakob, Huntington's, brain tumors, and other degenerative brain diseases. These computer-generated molecules, scientists call N1H, are engineered to counter the effects of prions, by preventing the misfolding of the remaining proteins. They prevent further build-up of amyloid plaques while repairing damaged cells. This medical breakthrough will help restore chemical signals and reception within the neurotransmitters, allowing the brain to function as intended."

Jared held the letter in his hand as he thought to himself, "Could this be true? Can computer-generated molecules be injected into the human brain and then do all of that? This cure sounds much like human engineering. It sounds unnatural, almost like science-fiction."

He thought about the far-fetched possibilities while being struck by his own reality—his grandmother no longer remembered him. Jared took the address and hastily went for his grandmother.

Jared pulled up with his grandmother to the center where this medical breakthrough was being administered to patients. He helped Wilma into her wheelchair and then pushed her into the building. It was 11:15 AM, and the line-ups were long. Jared knew that it would be a long wait for himself and his grandmother. Given that he didn't have much to lose, Jared thought the trial would be worth it.

While sitting with his grandmother, Jared looked up at the screen. He noticed a commercial that played over and over like a broken record. It was repeated to grab the attention of those with eyes to see and ears to hear. Jared noticed a man with a full head of wavy blond hair. He appeared to be the founder of Brain Developer Solutions. This man stood with the strength and stamina of a thirty-five-year-old, though his face and speech told his audience that he was decades older. Words appeared on the screen: John Burgess, MD, Founder of Brain Developer Solutions.

He spoke into the camera. "Friends, as you are watching, you may be thinking about that loved one who has Alzheimer's or Huntington's or a serious case of dementia of another sort. Maybe that member has Parkinson's. You can only imagine what life would have been like if things went back to normal. Maybe that family member has a grade three or four brain tumor for which there may never be a cure. Tumors can be removed, only to reappear later. Are you stressed even as you're thinking about your loved one's condition? Then have no fear, because our doctors and scientists have now come up with a medical breakthrough that will reverse the effects of these terrible diseases. Through our tests, many of our patients having incurable brain diseases, and even brain damage, are now living and functioning as normal. Are you skeptical? I understand. That's how I felt when I first came across this possibility. After becoming a witness, all my fears and concerns have dissipated. So why wait? Give BDS a try. You'll go home satisfied and thankful that you did."

Jared turned his attention from the screen the moment he saw that the video was playing over again. As soon as he lowered his eyes from the screen, they met with the eyes of one of the most beautiful faces he had ever laid eyes on. Jared was almost bashful, but he held his stare. This woman appeared to be of Aboriginal descent, and about Jared's age. He smiled. She smiled back as she averted her eyes from his. She had long, flowing, dark brown hair, which she moved over one shoulder. He had to say something, at least, "hi."

"Who are you here for?" Jared asked, hoping she heard him. She turned to him. "Excuse me?"

Jared felt a little queasy, unsure if this first meeting was going to be pleasant. "I was asking what you are here for."

"Oh, I'm here for my grandmother, who is still to my right."

Jared looked to her right and noticed, for the first time, an older woman that appeared to be in her seventies. "Oh, this is your grandma?"

"Yes, she is," she smiled.

Jared thought about the next thing to say, and quickly before things got awkward. "This is my grandma."

"Oh, that's nice." The young woman looked at Wilma and smiled.

"She has CJD," Jared continued.

"And what is that?" the young woman asked.

"It is Creutzfeldt-Jakob disease. We found out two years ago. And now she's only getting worse."

"I'm so sorry," the woman replied.

"And what is your grandma in for?"

"She has Parkinson's."

"I see," replied Jared. "How long has this been going on?"

"I haven't gotten a count on the number of years. But it has been for a long time."

"I'm sorry!"

"Thank you!" The woman smiled politely, waiting for Jared's next question.

Jared was sweating on the inside. He hoped he could continue the conversation, but he was out of things to say.

"I'm Jared. And you are?"

"Kaya."

"Nice name. My last name is Kensington."

"And mine is Deloria."

Jared thought about the direction of their conversation. This name exchange had better lead to good interaction, or it would have been for nothing. "I attend Cromwell University, and I'm majoring in neurobiology. I'm hoping to become a neurosurgeon."

"Wow, that's impressive," Kaya replied. "That's a fitting career."

"I'm hoping to get my hands busy in this field for my grandma, and for others."

"That's very noble of you."

"What are your plans, career-wise?"

"I'm working towards my major in economics. I'm working towards an MBA."

Jared smiled. "So, you're the business and money type?"

"I guess I am." Kaya smiled back.

Just then, Kaya looked up at the board. At the same time, the device the people at the desk gave her both lit-up and vibrated.

"I see our number. Well, it was nice talking to you."

Jared hurriedly lifted himself from his seat. "It was nice meeting you, Kaya. I was hoping that you and I could get together. Maybe I could tell you about some of the things I've learned."

Kaya smiled. "That would be nice."

Both Jared and Kaya exchanged phone numbers, with emails and social networking page monikers as a backup. Jared wanted to be sure that he did not lose contact with this one.

An hour had passed since Kaya and her grandma had gone into the lab. Jared jolted from his slumber as he felt the vibration of a device on his lap. He looked down and saw that it was the device they had given him. He looked up and saw their number on the screen. Jared stood and wheeled his grandmother to the desk, where they would direct them to the lab. They were given instructions before and after the procedure. One of the nurses dressed Wilma and prepared the back of her head for the injection. And the process was quick and easy. Jared would never have expected this kind of easy—but it was.

On their way home, Jared stopped at the library to drop a few books off. He would never have expected what happened next.

"Your mother used to stop at the library on Saturday

afternoons. She was a creative type. And here I have my wonderful grandson—the brainy type."

Stunned by what he heard, Jared turned to look at his grandmother.

"Is everything alright, Jared? You're looking at me like you've just seen a ghost."

Jared did feel like he had just seen a ghost. Sitting next to him was the grandmother he knew as a child. It'd been days since his grandmother last looked at him, weeks since she last spoke to him in ordinary English and more than a year since she called him by his first name. A tear streaked Jared's cheek.

"Grandma! You know that it's me?"

"Yes, son. And thank you for taking me to the clinic. I feel a whole lot better. Why don't we go in and find some more books on the brain?"

"I'd love . . . but Grandma, I feel uneasy having you out and about like this."

"Oh, nonsense," replied Wilma. "I know you want to go in and learn more about the brain. Just go in, and I'll tag along."

Jared felt very uneasy. After thinking about it, he finally gave in. He walked over to the passenger side to get her wheelchair, but Wilma was already on her feet.

"What do you need that for, Jared? Are you alright?"

Jared's eyes widened as he slapped the top of his head. "You can walk?"

"Of course, I can walk. I did say that I feel much better. Come on!"

Jared walked into the library, and to the section where he would find books on the human brain. Wilma tagged along, and she started reading almost every book that he browsed through. She did not stop. Jared thought he was the only one checking books out. To his surprise, he saw his grandmother about to check out a book also.

"What do you have there?"

"I was hoping you could check this one out for me. The book is entitled *The Big Questions in Science and Religion* by Keith Ward. I've read the first few pages; it is an interesting read. In this book, Keith gives answers to questions like 'Is evolution compatible with religion? Do the laws of nature exclude miracles? Is it still possible to speak of the soul?' and others."

Jared frowned. "I was hoping you would not put such a strain on your brain."

Wilma patted him on the shoulder. "Ah, don't worry about me, son. I'm fine. And I will be fine."

After considering for a moment, Jared took Ward's book and added it to the others he was checking out.

Weeks went by, and Jared watched his grandmother cautiously. Whenever he went to the campus, Wilma was alone. He couldn't convince her to accept assistance. She loved her independence. Without her knowing, Jared requested that the caregiver stay close by. He gave them a set of keys in case they had to check on her.

Jared and Kaya had started seeing each other. He felt a closeness to her, as though they were meant to be. They shared much in common. Both had grandmothers who needed to be attended to. Both of their grandmothers showed dramatic signs of recovery since the injection. They were both students living off-campus while working towards their advanced degrees. However, Kaya was a year or two ahead of him, since she was a year and a half his senior. Getting close to and dating an older woman thrilled him. But the one thing that excited Jared most was their faith. Both were believers in Jesus and were regular church attendees. They would often speak over the phone into the late-night after they had finished their studies.

One late Tuesday evening, both Jared and Kaya were on the phone. It was during the late hours that they'd set aside the head details and talk about their childhood and the funny things that happened. They would reminisce over their elementary, middle, and secondary school years, and all the silly things they did and what they saw others do. These were their more relaxing moments when they could once again be ordinary people. It was 2:00 AM, and Kaya was the first to bring their conversation to a close. They said, "Goodnight" before ending the call. Jared laid on the bed, but he thought he heard something. He got up and put his ear to the door. That's when he heard his grandma. It sounded like she was talking to someone. Jared opened the door, and using stealth, he crept along the floor until he got to her door. He heard her talking, but to whom? Jared was curious not because of whom she might be talking to but because of what she was talking about. He thought he heard her talking about the technical details a person could only get from a scholarly book on the brain. She was uttering mathematical equations and computer algorithms from off the top of her head. Jared knew that he did not have the intellectual depth or capacity for this. He knew some of the math, but not at this level.

"Something is wrong," he thought. He opened the door and noticed that grandma did not have a phone in her hand. She was talking to herself.

"Grandma?"

She turned. "Oh, hello! May I help you?"

"Grandma, I heard you talking to yourself, and I was wondering if everything was alright."

"Yes, I'm alright." She squinted at him. "Do I know you?"

Jared's eyes widened. "Grandma, it's me, your grandson, Jared."

"I am going to have to ask you to leave my house right now." Wilma started towards Jared in her attempt to push him out of the house. Suddenly, she twitched, and her movements became more unstable. Jared caught her just as she was about to fall. She struggled to get out of his grip. "Unhand me! Let me go!"

Jared picked her up and carried her to the wheelchair. She fought and resisted until he strapped her in. Wilma tried to break free but to no avail. Jared was in a state of total confusion. He did not know what to do. The only thing he could think of at that late hour was to call Kaya.

"Hello?" Her voice was still groggy from getting only forty minutes of shuteye.

"Kaya, it's me. You wouldn't believe it. It's my grandmother. She's not well."

Kaya was speechless, mainly because her hand was over her mouth in shock.

"After we hung up, I heard her talking to herself in some of the headiest jargon. When I went into her room, she didn't remember who I was. Something is wrong, and I can't call the people."

"Oh, no!" Kaya finally replied. "And you probably paid them ten-grand."

"So far, I got down six. I'm on a payment plan. Now I'm wondering if I'm getting my money's worth."

"I wonder if we did the right thing by BDS."

"And I know I can't call them at this hour."

"You're going to need to go in the morning."

Life in the brain

Hours later, Jared called the center. He made sure to call the school and tell them the reason for his absence. Jared took his grandmother to the center. The only advantage of going in early was that he didn't have the long lines to deal with. He wheeled Wilma to the information desk, where a woman with a friendly face greeted him.

"Good morning, and welcome!"

"Hi."

"Are you here for your mother?"

"My grandmother, actually."

"Are you ready to go in for the procedure? And how are you paying?"

"I've already paid. And I was here weeks ago."

"And did your grandmother get the procedure done?"

"Yes, she did get it."

The woman's smile suddenly disappeared. "Are you saying that she already had it done?" She observed the blankness behind Wilma's eyes.

"Yes," replied Jared.

"Could I get your first and last name and your grandmother's full name, please?"

"My name is Jared Kensington, and her name is Wilma Grace Kensington."

The woman scrolled through her database until she stopped somewhere on her screen. She rose from her seat. As she prepared to speak to another staff member, she turned and looked at Jared.

"Excuse me." She walked over to another woman who appeared to be the one in charge of that department. They spoke out of Jared's earshot. They whispered. And by their expression, he could tell that not all was well at Brain Developer Solutions.

After the lengthy exchange, the woman returned. "I apologize for the wait. And even more for the trouble. I was just told that the doctor is willing to see you soon."

Jared was surprised and a little skeptical.

The woman continued. "On behalf of Brain Developer Solutions, I want to humbly apologize for all the trouble this might have caused you. And as our pledge to repay, we will waive the outstanding debt that is on your account."

Jared knew this was coming. It didn't bring him an ounce of comfort, nonetheless. "And what am I going to do about my grandmother?"

"That's what I was getting to. Our doctor will see you right now, and he will fix this problem right away."

Approaching the woman from behind, while keeping his eyes locked with Jared's, was the doctor. He approached with humility.

"Hi, Mr. Kensington, we are ready to see you."

Jared wheeled Wilma as he followed the doctor to the lab. They walked through three sets of doors until they came across a line of chairs. Another set of doors stood between the group and where they were going. The doctor walked back to where Jared stood and placed his left hand on one of the handles of Wilma's wheelchair.

"You can stay out here and read some of the magazines. We will take it from here."

What was strange about this doctor was that he spoke with a firmness that Jared did not hear at the front desk. Even his eyes, he showed the kind of determination that would not take no for an answer.

"I came with my grandmother. I go where she goes."

The doctor pressed him, "You being present will be of great disservice to your grandmother. You need to allow us to do our jobs. If you will not, then we can do nothing for her."

Jared wanted to take her and walk out of the center, but he figured since they'd come that far, they shouldn't back out now. *"Why the closed curtain?"* he wondered to himself. *"What are they hiding? What nefarious plot are they up to?"*

"Go ahead," he consented.

One out of the two male nurses stood between Jared and his grandmother's wheelchair as the other took the handles and walked Wilma through the next set of doors. The doctor walked ahead of them. Forty-five minutes later, the doctor and nurses returned with Wilma. Jared rose to his feet.

"Thanks for your patience, Mr. Kensington," said the doctor. "Your grandmother is fine, and she will be better from here on."

Jared reluctantly thanked the doctor before taking hold of the handles and wheeling Wilma out to the front.

Wilma got better. As she did when the cure was at its peak, Wilma called her grandson by name, she spoke with clarity and moved about freely without the need for aid. One Thursday evening after Wilma made supper, Jared called Kaya's number. She answered in a heartbeat. The only problem was that there were sounds of frustration in her voice.

"Hello?"

"Kaya, is everything alright?"

"It's my grandma," Kaya exploded. "She's shaking like a leaf." Kaya dropped the phone and sobbed loudly. Jared called to her. For a while, she did not answer; he could only hear her sobbing.

"Kaya?"

"Yes?"

"Is there anyone with you?"

"Yes, my father and my younger brothers."

"I went through the same problem the other day. I'm thinking we should see a radiologist sp that he could examine her brain. I think by finding out about her, I can also figure out what they did to my grandma."

Jared waited for a reply but only got silence on the other line.

"Kaya?"

"Yes. I think we should do it."

That Friday, Kaya took the day off classes to take her grandmother in for examination. As Jared suggested, Kaya decided to take her grandmother to the St. Luke clinic. For something of this sort to happen to the only two patients they knew was no coincidence. The cure for the defective brain must have a defect. Jared thought about the numbers, sets, and figures that his grandmother spouted out without ever studying at that level. He thought about the change of facial expression the lady at the desk had the moment she heard about the defect. Jared also thought about the doctor's cloaking and daggering, and his insistence that he stayed outside. At the same time, the issue with Wilma's brain was being corrected. All these things added up. Jared had to go with Kaya and her grandma on this visit to the clinic. By doing so, he could find out what was going on inside his grandma's brain.

Jared took Kaya, her little brother, Turner, and their hunched over and trembling grandmother to the clinic. They walked her into the building and to the information desk. Kaya spoke to the lady at the counter. "We're here to do an examination on my grandmother."

The greying-haired lady handed Kaya a clipboard with a questionnaire. It didn't take her long to fill it out and give it back to the lady. Then Kaya, Turner, their grandmother, and Jared sat in the waiting area. Not long after, the lady at the desk called Kaya. She walked to the counter, and standing behind the lady was another woman who appeared to be the radiologist. She wore a white lab coat over light pink scrubs. She had red hair that was tied in a ponytail and donned attractive features. There was a professional aura about this woman that could not be overlooked.

"This is Dr. Katy Palmer," the lady at the desk said. "She'll be your neurologist for today."

Kaya greeted her and asked, "Could my brother and my friend come in?"

"I don't see why not," the doctor replied.

They followed her through a set of elevator doors. After they got in, the elevator opened on the second floor. They walked to a large room with a desk and screen. In the adjoining room, a technician was tinkering inside a box by the machine. Dr. Palmer broke away from the group to talk to Robby, the technician. The group was close enough to hear their exchange.

"Robby, what are you doing?"

"I'm sorry, Katy. This machine is under repairs."

Agitated by this, she asked, "Now? Is the machine being repaired now? What happened to yesterday and the day before?"

"I'm sorry! My hands have been tied the past several days with the other technical issues. I finally convinced Jeff to opt for open-imaging. And you know I've been busy with that."

Kay lifted her hands in frustration. "What are you suggesting that I do?"

"The open-imaging scanner is ready for use. You got to go check it out."

"I'm trying to check out a woman's brain. This is not the time to be testing machines."

Robby raised both hands as a show of surrender. "Hey, I can only do my job."

Katy broke away from him to rejoin the others.

"Unfortunately, we will not be using this machine today. Follow me. I'll take you to another scanner."

Katy led the group back to the elevators. They walked in. This time, the elevators opened on the third floor, as she led them to another large room. This room had all the same items that the first room did; the only difference was that the machine was not as big as the former. The former was tube-like with a narrow closing. This second machine was more open. It was more likely to accommodate obese patients and those with a fear of closed spaces. Katy asked for Kaya and Jared's assistance.

"Jared is the budding expert here," said Kaya. "He wants to be a neurosurgeon."

Katy raised her brows as she said, "Then I could certainly use your help."

"Sure," said Jared.

"What I'm going to ask you to do is tell me what you see in

Emma's brain while I put her through the scanner." Just then, Katy felt her jacket pocket. She pulled out an iPhone and answered. "Hello? I'm in room 300. I'm with a patient. You're coming? Okay, great."

Katy ended the call. As she turned her attention back to the group, she noticed that they were watching her with curiosity. "That's Dr. Measly. He'll be here in a moment."

"Dr. Measly?" asked Jared. "He was at my school months ago."

"Oh, then you can both get acquainted, seeing that you're hoping to become a neurosurgeon."

Jared felt a burst of excitement about getting the chance to meet and speak with Dr. Jeff Measly. He had heard and read of Jeff's many exploits. His feats were legendary. And now Jared would get the chance to speak with the person he hoped to learn from. Jeff walked into the room, his eyes and attention only on Katy. It was as though she were the only person in the room. She soon directed his attention to their visitors.

"Jeff, I would like you to meet Kaya and her grandmother, Emma. She's our patient. This young man is her brother, Turner. And this is her friend, Jared."

"Nice to meet you all," Jeff said.

Jared extended his hand to shake Jeff's. "It's a pleasure to meet you again, sir."

Jeff looked at Jared with a quizzical look. "Again? You speak as though we've met before."

"It was at my college, at Cromwell U. We even spoke after your talk."

Jeff looked directly at Jared. Then the quizzical look changed to one of recognition. "Oh yes, my conscious, sane, and thoughtful friend who never forgets his belt at home."

Katy and Kaya turned to each other, puzzled. It didn't matter to Jeff, for all that mattered to him was that Jared knew what he was talking about—and Jared did.

"Nice to see you again." He turned to Katy. "I see that you'll be the first to test this machine."

"Apparently so," replied Katy with a tinge of displeasure. "That's what I got from Robby. I don't know what is to become of this test, but we'll soon find out. Kaya told me about their visit to Brain Developer Solutions and what they did for her."

Jeff said nothing. He only raised his brows as though spellbound by what he had heard. They turned to the open MRI scanner. It was shaped like a donut. This allowed the patient's head to pass through the scanner without having the feeling of being closed in.

Jared joined Jeff in staring at the split imaging on the screen.

Jeff turned to Jared. "What do you see?"

"It looks like a broken-down structure of what a normal brain is. And the gaps are wide."

"What else do you see?"

"Wait a minute . . ." Jared peered more deeply at the images. "Is that supposed to happen? I see signaling where the dopaminergic activity has ceased."

"And if there were recent activities in the dopamine neurotransmitters, you would have to explain the state of her brain right now. The structure looks like it has been like this for some time."

"What are you saying, sir?"

"If she has been functioning as normal until yesterday, as your friend says, her brain should not look like—not this soon."

"So, you're saying that the computer-engineered chemicals responsible for the motor function in her body have now malfunctioned, causing her brain to collapse?"

"I'm not going to jump to conclusions, but this cure reeks of criminal activity."

Jared's chest sank. "This is beginning to make me worry. My grandma—"

"Was she treated?"

"For CJD."

"That's not good. For a patient with a case of Creutzfeldt-Jakob disease, this can be dangerous. Where is she right now?"

"She's home. I've been seeing a lot of red flags with BDS."

"If you can, Jared, go and get her."

Jared went for his grandmother, while Kaya agreed to stay at the clinic with her brother and grandmother. Jared convinced his grandmother to go for a ride with him. When they returned an hour later, they found Jeff, Katy, Kaya, Turner, Emma, and Robby in the office. The doctors were talking with Kaya about her grandmother.

"Dr. Measly," Jared said humbly, hoping not to barge in on their conversation. "This is my grandma."

Wilma turned to Jared, then to Jeff. "His grandma has a name, and it's Wilma. Pleased to meet you."

Jeff took her hand. "And you as well. Mrs. Kensington, I hope you know why your grandson brought you here."

"He told me that something was wrong with the cure. But how could that be? I feel like a million dollars."

"We heard that patients have been feeling this way ever since the treatment was introduced. But your grandson has something to say to you. Jared?"

Jared was not expecting that he would be placed in the hot seat. All eyes were turned to him as he thought about what to say to his grandmother.

"Grandma, do you know calculus?"

Wilma looked at her grandson, dumbfounded. "Jared? What is the meaning of this?"

He inhaled deeply, then exhaled. "Days ago, you were spouting out mathematical equations and computer algorithms. I was wondering what you were talking about because I don't know that stuff on that level."

Wilma was confused, and her eyes showed absence. "Computer equations and math—Son, I don't know that stuff either," she mumbled.

Jeff and Jared looked at each other. "Mrs. Kensington, will you allow me to do an MRI scan on your brain?" Jeff asked.

"I don't see why not," Wilma replied.

Katy guided Wilma to the open MRI scanner. Jeff, Jared, Kaya, and Robby watched as she got into position on the table. Once she was positioned, the four persons turned their attention to the screen. And Wilma's brain appeared as whole as one belonging to a healthy person.

"Something is fishy about her brain," said Jeff. "At first glance, you can see that the cerebellum looks normal."

"If Mrs. Kensington's brain is connected, the way it should be, then what is the problem?" Kaya wondered.

"Well," said Jeff, "We still don't know how she was able to spout out mathematical equations and computer algorithms." He turned to Robby. "This falls in your area of expertise. Can you explain what's happening?"

"I'm sorry, doctor." Robby shook his head. "That is where my knowledge comes to an end. There's only one person we know who can explain this enigma, and that's Zack Howard."

"Of course!" replied Jeff. "Call him and tell him to meet us here."

Robby called Zack. Zack arrived in less than five minutes. Jared turned and saw what looked like a real techie. He stood at six-feet-one. Zack was a lanky, dark-haired specimen with a scarce and scraggly mustache. He wore large rims he called glasses, and a lab coat, which hung from his thin frame.

"Jared and Kaya, I'd like you to meet our lead techy, Zack."

"Salutations, and a most cordial welcome to you all," said Zack.

"Weeks ago, both Jared and Kaya took their grandmothers to the Brain Developer Solutions clinic. They've received treatments for Parkinson's for Kaya's grandmother and for Creutzfeldt-Jakob for Jared's grandmother. The treatment was simple, well, too simple. It's a new technology whereby they inject fluids into the brain. And these molecules would then perform some type of neuroregeneration. These molecules would bring dead neurons back to life while restoring circuitry between neurotransmitters and channels. This is where you have patients with dementia and other brain diseases functioning as normal. And when you look at the patient's brain structure," Jeff pointed Zack to the screen, "you will see the normal structure. In Kaya's grandmother's brain, we saw the signs of decay and shrinkage that is normal in untreated patients. From Kaya's report, her grandmother was fine until yesterday. The decay would normally be gradual for her grandmother. However, when the neurochemicals in her brain ceased to function, everything went south in a hurry."

Zack looked on as he rubbed his chin.

"I see. From what the images on the 3D and cross-sectional formatting suggest, the neurotransmission and receptors are controlled by a computer-enhanced neurochemical that assists in the normal motor and cerebral functions of the brain."

"That's what we've gathered so far," said Jeff.

Zack continued. "From my observation, the computer-enhanced neurochemicals could be doing more than merely assisting the brain in its normal functions. The neurochemicals could also be gathering information via the host, which, in this case, is Jared's grandmother."

"What would they want from our grandparents?" asked Kaya.

"There is a high probability that your matriarch is not a specific target," said Zack. "To get to a specific target, the people in question would need to go through an untold list of patients in order to arrive at one. Then there could also be the systemic attempts to globally track and keep tabs on a populous."

"How could we be sure about this?" asked Jared.

"The night your matriarch regressed to her degenerative state, you said that you heard her utter a string of mathematical equations and computer algorithms?"

"Yes."

"To restore her faculties, you took your matriarch back to the center where she was first treated?"

"Yes."

"And did you see the procedure as it was being done the second time?"

"No. The staff kept me away from the room. So, you're saying that while the doctors were using computer assimilation to make her better, they placed a global tracker inside of her?"

"It is unfortunate that I should arrive at this inference, but yes!"

"One would expect scientists to find some exotic plant in a distant island," Jeff said. "At least that would have been natural. But this?"

"I can envisage the brain structure bearing properties of a neuroregenerative nature. Even the prospect of a brain repairing itself would have been a befitting alternative."

Jared spoke in frustration. "But isn't this illegal? They've placed a tracker inside her without telling me."

"To do so without the written consent of a family member or caregiver is illegal," said Jeff. "The only case in which this is not illegal is when the moral character of the family or caregiver is held in question."

"You mean if they were criminals?" asked Jared.

"Precisely," said Zack.

Kaya sighed. "Is there any way that we could tap into this advanced technology?"

"Our purpose should not be to tap into this technology," said Jeff, "but rather to detect it. And to be quite ingenious about it, this is an unauthorized tracking system. And this should be detected. It runs counter to Canadian privacy laws and should be reported."

Jared shook his head. "How can we provide proof of this?"

"What we can do," said Zack, "is use this open MRI as a GPS detector. Though the tracker is in liquid form, we can pick up the pulsing of infrared signals on the camera. On another note, I acknowledge the apparent feelings of solicitude you might be feeling. For I, too, can identify with your feelings of concern, because my own father's life was cut short due to the degenerative disease we call Alzheimer's. Just maybe in my desperation, I, too, would have petitioned the agents at Brain Developer Solutions for their help."

"I'm sorry for your loss," Kaya said. "It must have been hard for you."

"Much obliged. It was. But I have found peace amidst the predicament in which I have found myself."

"That's comforting to hear. We need to know a depth that will outlast the misfortunes that life will throw at us."

"Indeed. And you are a person of faith, might I presume?"

"Both I and Jared and our families we've brought with us. We are followers of Jesus."

Katy joined in. "Zack, I and others in the building are Christian."

Jeff turned to Robby. "I guess that leaves you and me, buddy."

"Hey, Jeff, I'm not an ardent atheist."

Jeff threw his hands up as he looked upwards and sighed. "I'm surrounded by Jesus people."

Katy stood as a barrier between Zack and the group. "I would ask that you all step back and allow Zack to work."

"You're an atheist?" Kaya asked Jeff.

"I wouldn't necessarily call myself an atheist. I'm more of a humanist. I can tell you all that I've lived in a time when the people throughout this region were almost entirely non-theist. Times have changed," Jeff said with grim features.

"Jared and I would also call ourselves, 'humanists,'" said Kaya

Robby said, "But Jeff is a secular or non-religious humanist."

"You don't have to spell it for them, Robby. I think you'd be of more help to Zack."

Robby shrugged his shoulders as he walked towards the machine to join Zack.

Kaya spoke. "I think you can be a good humanist simply by caring. So far, Doctor, you have shown that you have a genuine interest in my grandmother's welfare."

"It's a part of who I am. It's only a shame that people are disingenuous in their reasons for coming up with a cure for her disease."

"Not surprising to me," said Kaya. "That's what human nature has always been."

"But it's not who you are," replied Jeff.

"What I understand Kaya to be saying is that the decision to put another's interests over your own goes against your selfish ambitions," Jared explained. "If the people at Brain Developer Solutions are using patients for a goal, then I wonder if their concern is curing brain diseases."

"Whatever their goals may be, this organization is already on to something that we have known the whole time—the human mind stores information like a computer. The computer-enhanced neurochemicals are what connected your grandmother to a network or a source somewhere in this city. To these people at Brain Developer Solutions, her brain is a computer. That is why they were able to accomplish this feat."

"I remember your last comment during that Q&A. If the human brain is no more than a computer, then who is controlling the cured patient? I'm really hoping that the people at Brain Developer Solutions are not the ones controlling my grandmother."

"Well, she did spout out a string of computer algorithms and mathematical equations."

"But she was rambling. And when we asked her, she told us that she didn't know what she was talking about."

"There's a part of me that believes they're controlling your grandmother. But I'm convinced that's not the case. It's the information that's inside her brain that's controlling her."

Jeff looked over to Kaya and noticed her squirm a little.

"You alright?"

"I'm fine."

"There is a ladies' room a few doors down."

"Thank you, Dr. Measly."

Jeff turned his attention back to Jared. "I have yet to wrap my mind around what happened to Wilma that night. If the people at BDS can control her from a remote location and cause her to speak a computer language unknown to her, then that reminds me of our potential to understand consciousness and free will. You did listen to my lecture?"

"I did while I was in the audience. I understand where you were going with the cells. They are billions of androids working in sync to create a mind."

"And I'll remind you, Jared, that there's no determining what their values are. There's no telling whether this doctor will exploit the sick for profit or live in complete denial of his own interests for the sake of the sick."

"I remember you making a comment much like that. I have yet to wrap my mind around what BDS was trying to do with my grandmother that night."

"Maybe their computer crashed, and they were trying to solve that problem in your grandmother, remotely."

"It sounds like they can turn a dead brain into a computer."

"A brain is a computer, Jared. They were able to make Wilma blurt out complex math problems and algorithms without knowing what she was saying."

"What I still don't understand is BDS and their part in this. If they really controlled my grandma's brain, did they do so on purpose? It doesn't seem like they had a reason for what they did."

"What do you mean by that?"

"If the people at BDS are not conscious that their brains are computers, then I wonder if there's any point in restoring my grandmother's brain. They're every bit as dead as she is."

"There is an illusion of awareness. One thing that cannot be denied is the fact that the hardware has been functioning as it should. What BDS was trying to do was restore your grandmother to health. Their reasons remain hidden from us. It could be that they have been functioning as doctors and scientists. And their moral could have been shaped by the greed and apathy around them. Maybe I would have been like them had I been working for BDS."

"I'm hoping to find out if the same is true about every person working for BDS. Are there any employees that see through the greed and apathy and want to leave BDS for that reason?"

"Well, we may soon find out."

Robby left Zack to join the group.

"We're ready."

"What did he do?" asked Katy.

"He turned the MRI scanner into a GPS detector. We are now able to track what's inside her brain through this computer and through my phone. Now check this out."

Robby slid his iPhone open. Already, the screen was on the detector. A pulsing red light glowed brighter each time Robby pointed his phone at Wilma.

"Follow me, guys."

Jeff, Jared, Kaya, and Katy followed Robby as he held his phone out. They followed him into the elevator. They each peered onto the screen of his phone and saw the red light. Only now, the straight image in the screen switched to a navigational plain revealing a pulsing blue for their location and a pulsing red for Wilma's current position.

"Zack was able to link the neurochemicals inside Wilma's brain with the radio waves that point the scanner to it. He then connected my personal phone to the scanner. It will not matter where I carry this device. I will be able to track Wilma's whereabouts."

"And you can do this because of the neurochemicals they injected in her brain?" Kaya asked.

"Exactly. You'll also notice that as we move further from Wilma's position, the navigational plain zooms out. This allowed us to see a wider view of our mapping." They looked at Robby's screen and saw what he described.

They were on the main floor. Kaya excused herself to find the ladies' room, as Jared turned to Robby.

"I wonder if Zack will be able to use my grandma to find the people with the controls?"

Jeff mused over the question. "Never thought of the possibility. Maybe we could."

Life in the controllers

Jeff had always thought Zack could do it. To Jeff, Zack had always experienced oneness with technology. It's almost as if they were one and were meant to be inseparable. Zack always wanted to remind Jeff that he was not born with a motherboard on his lap. Zack's ingenuity and rare mental capacity to recall a long string of numbers did not help him to fully understand the human brain. Zack stressed that the human brain is far more complicated than a computer, though they bore many similarities. To Zack, the intricate details of the human brain and how it ties in with a person's existence made the most advanced supercomputers look prehistoric. Even the most intelligent and creative minds would need to unravel the mysteries of the human brain. They have yet to create a likeness to it.

The team turned their attention back to Wilma and Emma. Two stimulation probes were implanted in Emma's brain. Kaya, and later her father, agreed to the procedure. Wilma, who was her energetic and feisty self, for now, would be taken back to the center. They would use her as a means for finding the people holding the controls, but not without resistance from the patient. Wilma considered it an insult that they would use her as a Guinea pig. Without her knowing, Wilma had been used as a Guinea pig by the people at Brain Developer Solutions. Jared was determined to get to the bottom of their organization. As a graduate student majoring in neurobiology, Jared had the impression that something was wrong. What the people at Brain Developer Solutions was doing had little to do with the wellbeing of their patients.

Jeff would have held it against BDS for their unnatural means to cure their patents. Yet this would have made him look like a hypocrite because he had been using technology in the same way. He used stimulation probes and batteries to aid a Parkinson's patient, which didn't make Jeff any different from the doctors at BDS. The difference was in Jeff's truthfulness about his use of devices in hopes of reducing patient's tremors, and BDS's deception about their use of computer-enhanced neurochemicals to cure their patients. Also, BDS used neurochemicals that had a tracking feature. Jeff believed that to track someone without written consent went against Canadian Privacy Policy. The differences between what he was doing and what BDS was doing were as apparent as night and day.

Jeff wanted Zack to hack into BDS's system to see what BDS had phished from their patients so far. But Zack told Jeff that a task like that would take days, knowing that their system would be encrypted.

Jared wanted to barge into the center, but Kaya reminded him that doing so would be an emotional, not-very-wise response. In the end, Jeff told Jared and Kaya that he would be accompanying them, but would be bringing company with him.

On Saturday, sometime mid-morning, Jared drove his grandmother to the BDS center. It was 8:33 AM by the time they walked through the doors and to the waiting area. The number of waiting patients did not surprise Jared. Other family members entertained the same idea of early arrival that Jared did. Some sons brought their fathers, daughters who brought their mothers, parents who brought their children, and so forth. And there were a variety of sicknesses that were represented in the waiting room. There were different types of neurological disorders, degenerative diseases, mental disorders, brain damages, brain cancers, and even headaches. Many of the patients had faces lit with expectancy. Some were skeptical, and Jared could read it on their faces. "*If they only knew what I went through with my grandma, many of them would not be here,*" He thought to himself.

Time went by as Jared sat and waited with his grandmother. She sat to his right, with her mind still intact. Wilma was plugged into her grandson's ASUS phone, playing her favorite pastime: a rigorous game of Lumosity.

"I'm kind of worried whenever I see you on that one."

"Aw, don't worry about me, son. You should see my score. Just on my speed and my memory, my LPIs have gone up dramatically."

"I'm only saying, Grandma, that you should give your brain a break."

Wilma exited the app and lowered the device. "Okay, but this means you'll need to talk with me. Talk is the only thing I enjoy more than Lumosity."

"Okay. So how are you feeling?"

"Not bad at all. This morning I did the laundry. I managed to get four loads in."

"I thought I heard the washing machine and dryer at 4:00 AM."

"That was me, alright."

"4:00 AM?"

"4:00 AM is a good time because it saves on energy. It lowers the electric bill since fewer things run during those hours."

"I never thought of that."

"Then what time have you been doing the laundry?"

"Around noon."

Wilma frowned. "It's about time you reconsidered the time you do laundry."

"I will," Jared replied with a grin. "I can say this, although we're in this building, I'm enjoy sitting here and talking with you."

"Yes, I remember the day you learned your first word."

Jared turned with a look of interest. "You remember that? I'd like to know what it was."

"It was 'foot.'"

"Foot?"

"It kinda sounded like 'foo.' I tried to make it out. You were only eleven months old."

"Sounds like I was trying to speak with my head down or with my eyes on someone's feet."

"You were adorable. You might remember this. There was a time when you came across an old VHS cassette that I had hidden. Apparently, you didn't know what it was. Even during those times, people didn't know what a VHS was. Blu-ray discs were becoming the in-thing, while the DVD era was ending. You picked up that VHS cassette took out the reel and put it inside another cassette. Well, that cassette was borrowed from the library. Imagine, VHS still being found in the library. I returned that cassette. I later picked up the cassette you found. It was then that I remembered that it was a recording of my wedding anniversary. Well, I slipped it into a VHS player, and to my surprise, I was watching *Ghost* with Patrick Swayze and Demi Moore."

The two shared a laugh.

"I did that?"

"That was the beginning of your mischief."

"Did you ever get the cassette back from the library?"

"I went to the library, praying that there weren't other old fogies like myself in the area who were big fans of Patrick Swayze."

The two shared another laugh.

"As a matter of fact, I did get it back. I did have to fake it as if I were too in love with that movie to not see it again. I had to find someone with the skill to disassemble and reassemble parts. You did this with ease."

"I remember, though vaguely."

"You were seven. Even then, you were taking things apart and putting things together. In my opinion, I think you were meant to be a brain surgeon."

Jared smiled. "That's encouraging."

The two continued to wait and converse as the clock rolled into the eleventh hour. Not long after, the device Jared held lit up. He looked up and saw their number. They both walked to the desk.

Moments later, they were in the room exchanging stares with Dr. Knolls, the doctor Jared had met at the center only days earlier. He looked Jared in the eyes with slight concern. To Dr. Knolls, Wilma appeared to be in the right state of mind, so their presence drew suspicion.

"Thank you both for coming here. How are you, Mrs. Kensington?"

"I am fine, thank you."

"And how have you been keeping? Have you been feeling any pain, any numbness, any dizziness, problems with your vision?"

"I feel as fit as a fiddle."

The doctor managed to conjure a smile. "And Jared, from what you've seen, were there any recent signs or symptoms—sudden outbursts, anxiety, depression? Has her speech been slurred, or has there been a lack in her balance or coordination?"

"Quite frankly, I haven't seen anything. But that's not why I'm here."

"Do tell," replied Dr. Knolls.

"To have my grandmother here and in her right mind is huge for me. What your people did and how they did it is beyond the field I'm training in."

"What field are you training in?"

"I'm training to become a neurosurgeon."

Dr. Knolls raised his brows with interest. "Well, isn't that interesting? The most helpful field, given your grandmother's former condition. Brain surgery is a critical process that takes flawless precision. The components are so intricate that the wrong move can be devastating."

"Well, you understand. But the approach you took in correcting the problem in my grandmother is something I've never come across, certainly not in my studies."

Dr. Knolls was skeptical of Jared until he saw the sincerity. "Our founder, Dr. John Burgess, and his team of scientists started this medical procedure a year and a half ago in Seattle, Washington. This is a ground-breaking medical procedure that has never been seen in all of neurobiology. You saw when the neurochemicals were injected into the back of the patient's skull. The chemicals we call N1H were scientifically tested."

Jared interrupted. "What is N1H supposed to do?"

"These neurochemicals travel throughout the different regions of the brain and charge already dead neurons, thus bringing them back to life. The circuitry is restored between the pre- and post-synaptic clefts in areas where there was no activity. The ratio for failure is slim. Your grandmother's case was among the few that needed rebooting."

"I find it interesting that you use a computer term like 'reboot.' I didn't get to see what you did the other day because you barred me from the room. Is my grandmother's brain a computer hardware to you?"

Dr. Knolls laughed while holding out his hands in deference. "No! Far be it that I should look at your grandmother the way I would a computer. But, in the end, you will have to admit that the brain circuitry does work a lot like computer circuitry. I'm convinced that your grandmother's consciousness is linked to her brain. When that's affected, her conscious state is also affected."

"Because my grandmother's brain is like a computer, you should be able to reboot the system remotely while you're here and she's home. Can you do that with N1H?"

"We may arrive at that level in our advancement someday."

"I have no doubt, Doctor, that her consciousness was affected. But are you saying that even her decisions are coming from her brain's circuitry?"

"I've considered the other possible answers. There's no better way to explain it right now. When the brain is deleteriously affected, consciousness is affected, and the ability to make decisions is also affected."

"So conscious decisions are lost as the brain's functions are lost?"

"That's what it has come to, even for many patients, until the day they came to our center."

"I admit that because the brain is the command center of the body when that goes, then everything shuts down. I believe in the brain's role. That is why I'm studying in this field. You know more than I. When you got my grandmother's brain working, did you add new information? You did say that the brain is a computer."

"Well, of course not. We only used what we knew to make your grandmother better."

"And this information did not come from a computer?"

Dr. Knolls was a little irritated by the question. "It came from us. This new medical breakthrough is human-engineered."

"Good to know that while the human brain functions like a computer, the conscious decisions, which include adding new information, came from humans."

"I can say this, Jared, we have yet to fully discover the science of it all."

"And we have come so far to make computers that can beat us in a chess game."

"Well, a product of many human minds," added Dr. Knolls.

"A product of many human minds," repeated Jared.

The door opened, and in walked Jeff Measly wearing a black coat and tie. He was accompanied by a man and a woman who, by their aura, appeared to be agents. Two of Knoll's male nurses and the pleasant-looking woman from the front desk followed.

Dr. Knolls turned to this new train of visitors with a look of surprise. "What is this? Who are you? And why are you all walking in unannounced?"

Jeff proceeded to speak. "Hi, I am Dr. Jeff L. Measly, and these are two of my CSIS friends, Lacy Pearson and Paul Ryan. Since the others work here, I assume they need no introduction."

Dr. Knolls was visibly troubled by the comment. "And why the agents? Lauren, please explain."

Lacy stopped Lauren as she proceeded to speak. "I'll answer that. Dr. Terry Knolls, we're doing an investigation on the neurochemicals that are used as a treatment at this facility, and the security risk they pose to citizens."

"Security risk?" Dr. Knolls repeated gobsmacked. "I know of no such risk."

Jeff held out a binder. "My friends and I can inform you of what's been going on at this center. What I'm holding is a binder with charts showing the scans of both Wilma Kensington and Emma Deloria's brains." Jeff handed out the different charts to Dr. Knolls. "Observe. This is Emma Deloria's brain at 10:05 AM, Friday. This one is Wilma Kensington's brain at 12:25 PM, Friday. And this is Emma Deloria's brain at 1:08 PM, Friday." Jeff paused for a dramatic effect. "You'll notice that while Wilma's brain was intact, and Emma's was not, Emma's brain showed dramatic changes for the better as time went by. Emma's brain at 1:08 PM looks better than it did at 10:05 AM, which draws suspicion."

Lacy turned to Jared. "Do you have the recording of this conversation, Jared?"

"I do," said Jared. He reached over to his grandmother, pulled her shirt up, stripped away a small sticker holding a small device, and handed it to Lacy.

Dr. Knolls rolled his eyes. "You bugged your own grandmother? And for what?"

"My grandmother's brain is a computer that blurts out computer algorithms and math equations. This medical breakthrough is what I call your advanced technology," Jared replied.

Lacy continued, "And you chose to keep this from the patients and their families. Neither was there any written consent from the families. Both the Kensingtons and the Delorias showed me their signed documents from BDS."

Dr. Knolls was flustered. "And for what reason do they need written consent?"

Paul, the male agent, spoke as he held out his tablet for Dr. Knolls to see. The doctor looked at the screen and saw what looked like a navigation plain with pulsing blue and red light.

"What is this?" asked Dr. Knolls.

"That's what we would like to know," replied Paul.

"These neurochemicals are much like computer chips implanted in the brain. And these chips can be tracked from here," explained Jeff.

"Dr. Knolls," said Lacy. "I hope you understand that your business is under scrutiny because what you do poses as a security risk. In the next week or so, we will be sending our people. And you will be expected to give us tabs on what your organization is doing."

"And why should we be forced to?"

"Because of what this technology can do to citizens. Someone from your organization could invade the privacy of citizens. Because of the neurochemical tracking feature, the government needs to know what your organization will do. We will be leaving you, but some of our people will be staying for a while. Every day this center opens, some of our data gatherers will be here. Do not refuse them. Do not get tough. Some of them are trained in combat. Either you're going to have our people to deal with, or this business will go under like a sinking ship. So what will it be, Doctor?"

Dr. Knolls looked up at Jeff, Paul, Lacy, and Jared. He sighed as though he were ready to give in.

"Sure. By all means, send your people in."

For the next number of days and weeks, the Canadian Security Intelligence Service Agency worked closely with Brain Developer Solutions to keep a close watch on their online activity. What the CSIS found were attempts to steal data from citizens and from governing officials, with the help of families that were supposedly cured of brain diseases. Dr. Knolls had much explaining to do.

Thursday, May 23rd. Jared and Kaya met together outside the St. Luke's Clinic. Dr. Karen Valkyrie, a neurologist, would give them both reports on their family member's condition. The brain-imaging tests showed no abnormalities in neither Wilma nor Emma's brain. Both Wilma and Emma were ready to return to a normal life. This was a surreal experience of delight for both Jared and Kaya. Even for a medical procedure that has found success, its duration was uncertain. Even a technology as advanced as N1H could fail in a world that is subject to decay. Jared stayed hopeful for his grandmother, whom he was more than happy to have back.

Jeff accompanied Jared and Kaya to the main floor. They exited the elevator and headed towards the exit. "Don't hesitate to stop by whenever you're in the area."

Kaya said, "Yes, we will. I look forward to learning more from your staff," Kaya said.

"I really meant the staff learning from you," said Jeff. "Our financial department can learn from your acumen when it comes to money management."

Kaya smiled.

"I will be stopping by," said Jared. "Not very far in the future, I will be joining your team."

"We can use another valuable player." Jeff smiled.

THE U

Tuesday, September 24th. The former lieutenant, Dave Travis, and Eugene Ellis stepped out of an elevator. They were on the first floor, heading to the cafeteria. Dave looked down at his phone and saw 12:15 PM. Eugene looked down at his Apple watch and saw 1:00 PM. Dave looked over at Eugene's watch.

"1:00 PM? Is my time right?" he asked.

"Your time is right," Eugene said. "I set my time forty-five minutes ahead. This way, I'm never late for an appointment. I'm never late for anything."

"That's awfully frugal of you," said Dave. "That could take away some of the stress from you."

"I need to correct you, Dave. It does not stress; it's what you call passion."

"If that's what you call passion, I would hate to see what you look like when you're upset."

"Well, you might get to see me upset once you see Jerry Paulo and me in the same room."

"Yeah," Dave replied dismissively. "Well, it's good to know now that you're in the clear with the two bogus reports about the two lifeless planets."

"And you know me better than that, Dave. I take my work too seriously to make up a story about life on two Earth-like planets where there are no conditions for life. When I see Paulo—"

"Let it go," interrupted Dave. "And another thing, there's no way you can trace that one to him."

"That forged letter has his name all over it. I know others are out to get me, but I don't know anyone more capricious than Paulo. That looks like something that he would do."

"Well, we'll need to look more into that one. There's something unrelated I'd like to ask of you—" Dave looked down at Eugene's tray. "You're going to eat that?"

"Yes. And why not?"

"A slice of pepperoni pizza, with a side of onion rings and a can of soda to wash it all down. A tube of Pringles to snack on, and a pack of Skittles for the road. Eugene, this is unhealthy eating."

"It's my diet of choice, and I'll eat whatever I want. And another thing, for the work that I do, I can use all the sugar, fat, and cholesterol that I can get."

Dave raised both hands in deference. "It's your diet."

"You were about to ask something of me?"

Dave snapped his fingers. "Oh yes, a bunch of foreign students will be visiting the center for the next few months. It's for one of the programs."

"Tell me that these are hopefuls and not the undecided who may later branch off elsewhere."

"From what the director told me, our center is training grounds for these students. I was told that these are bright students. This program will encourage future innovators in STEM. And no, they're not tourists."

Eugene released a sigh of relief. "Good. And you would like me to get involved because these students could be our next scientists, technologists, engineers, and mathematicians?"

"I would love for you to get involved. And yes, there's great potential in this group."

"No can do." Eugene sat. And as soon as he did, he yanked a large piece of his pizza with his teeth.

"Why not? This would be a great opportunity to not only become acquainted with students from different backgrounds. You could also find yourself teaching and mentoring future scientists."

Eugene looked down at Dave's tray. "What is a man the size of an ox going to do with one little burrito made almost entirely of lettuce?"

"If you eat healthily, you'll live longer. It does well with my daily workout regimen."

Eugene pointed at the items on Dave's tray. "I think that's a tangerine. And what is that green liquid?"

"I'll assure you it's not a shamrock shake. It's a smoothie, a blend of green apples, bananas, kiwi, green grapes, kale, and spinach."

Eugene guzzled some of his soda. "Well, that's all fine. But that's all you're going to eat? You could starve in the next hour."

"I assure you that I will not pass out while on the job."

"Look at you, you're more than twice my size. Your biceps are larger than my thighs. And I'm not speaking hyperbole."

"What I'm eating will suffice until supper time, which is around 4:00 PM. By what I see on your tray, it doesn't look like you'll be eating your next meal anytime soon."

"Supper, if that's what you call it, it will not be until 11:00 PM, if I'm lucky." Eugene took several small packets of vinegar, opened them, then doused the onion rings with their contents. He began to gorge himself with the onion rings.

Dave continued. "Back to my question. Why not address this group or spend a little time with one student?"

Eugene held up his index finger until he was done chomping on what was in his mouth. "I've been busy. I have a large to-do list, what you don't understand."

"I'll tell you what, why don't you look at the group that is expected to visit tomorrow, which is Wednesday? There are about twenty-six students—kids from Eastern Europe, East Asia, Africa, the Middle East, and South America."

"And please tell me they speak English."

"They do speak some English, though not fluently."

Eugene took a layer of chips from the Pringles tube and wolfed them down. Dave looked at what Eugene was doing and remained quiet.

"Okay, I'll do it. I feel like I'm doing you a favor. I'll stop and look at the group. But I'd rather remain hidden."

"I don't know how you can successfully accomplish that. You do tend to draw a lot of attention to yourself with that Einstein hairdo."

Eugene was about to chug the bag of Skittles down his throat when he stopped. "Hey!" he said, taken aback by the comment. "What's wrong with my hair?"

Wednesday, September 25th, 1:20 PM. At the visitor center, a guide led a train of students through the different exhibits. Their ages ranged from eleven to eighteen. They listened intently and with awe as the guide led them through the Space Operations Learning Center, the Ozone Garden, the Goddard Moon Tree, the Solarium, GLOBE Hall, Neighborhood Earth, and the other spaces. These foreign students, who were entering a higher stage of education, were not very fluent in English, according to the average American's standards. Nonetheless, what they knew was enough to get them by. The visible items at the exhibits that responded to touch needed no previous training in English.

Eugene and Dave stood behind the group, unnoticed when they visited the James Webb telescope. This wasn't the real telescope. It was a replica of the craft that had yet to be launched. This exhibit was important, even to Eugene. As one of the latest additions to the Goddard Space flight Center, this telescope would take space observers unimaginably farther than the Hubble space telescope did. That was crucial to Eugene. But while the guide took the group through the telescope's different components and unique features, Eugene noticed that the guide was overlooking some of the critical elements. This frustrated Eugene. And as the guide continued, Eugene eventually reached his tipping point.

Eugene broke away from Dave, walked to the front, and stood by the guide. Seeing Eugene, the guide immediately gave the group an introduction and shared with the group his credentials, accomplishments, and ongoing work.

"That was long. You sure you don't want to share my biography?" Eugene thought to himself as he looked at the guide. The floor was given to him.

"Thank you, Steve. And thank you all for taking the time to visit the Goddard Space Flight Center. I trust that you are learning as you go. As Steve said earlier, this newest telescope will change the way we see distant galaxies. Who has ever looked through a telescope?"

The question was left in the air as Eugene waved his finger over the group. Seven hands went up.

"Out of you seven, who can share what he or she has seen and what he or she has learned?"

All seven gave their answers. All answers came in the form of experiences they'd had in their respective countries. They all gave their responses based on what they understood about the cosmos. Eugene was impressed.

"Good answers!"

Eugene spent the next half-hour with the group, sharing details that caused eyes to widen. The students took it all in, even while the floor was open for questions and answers. Eugene then turned the reigns of tour guidance back to Steve.

The guide took the group through the 3D tour. Eugene returned to where he was standing by Dave.

"Doesn't sound like the Eugene who was too busy to speak to the students, much less to see them."

"It's the least I can do. Steve did a good job, but not good enough."

"I can always count on you to fill their heads."

"I already know that the lesson is not gluten-free," Eugene responded in an almost singsong voice. "They're a smart bunch. They can handle that."

"Then again," said Dave, "they sound like a knowledgeable bunch. I was listening in on the exchange, especially between you and that student from Iran, and the one from Zambia. How about that one from Russia?"

Eugene's eyebrows arched. "That student from Zambia, I'd like to pick his brain some more."

Dave turned to Eugene with a scolding look. "Pick his brain? The only way you can do that is if you were a brain surgeon."

Eugene rolled his eyes. "Okay, I'd like to pick his mind. I'm going back to my work. What are your plans for the next few hours?"

"Projects, and more projects. What more can I add to my list?"

"I think that when you were an astronaut, your job was easier."

"You can say that again. Those were the days—"

Before Dave could finish, he was distracted by one of the students. Eugene also saw the student frantically searching his pockets, then turn and start walking towards them.

"What's the problem, son?" asked Dave.

The student contorted his face, not entirely understanding what Dave said.

"What are you looking for?" Eugene asked.

"My phone," the student said in an Asian accent.

Dave turned to Eugene. "I'll take him, though I'm not sure where he could possibly find his phone. Steve could tell me where they were, and we could retrace their steps in hopes of finding his device."

Dave took the student's phone number. After five call attempts, he walked by the students to get the tour guide's attention. The student relayed to Steve what he'd told Dave. Steve turned to the other Asian students in hopes of finding a fellow countryman who could help to translate but found none. None of the other students had seen this student's phone. Steve had a job to do and would have to put what he was doing on hold to find a missing phone. Dave knew this wasn't going anywhere, so he decided to take the student to the exhibits that Steve said they'd visited.

As Dave and the student were about to part from the company of other students, one of the African students tapped Dave from behind. He looked to be around thirteen years of age. Dave turned to him. "What is it, son?"

The boy smiled, turned to the Asian student, and spoke in an Asian language that Dave did not know. They continued their short exchange. Dave tapped the African student.

"What did he say?"

"He said he is looking for his Google Pixel 5. It is a clear white with a glass back and Alpine case. It has a megapixel camera."

"Okay, now that we know what the phone looks like, does he remember where he last saw it?"

The African student turned back to the Asian student and continued their conversation in that student's native language.

Dave interrupted. "You can speak his language. But I thought I heard you say that you're from Zambia?"

"I *am* from Zambia," replied the student. "He is from South Korea. We are speaking his native dialect called Gyeongsang."

"How did you come to learn his language?"

"Before I came to this country, I went to UST—the University of Science and Technology in Daejeon City in South Korea. I knew English before I left Zambia. I was in Daejeon for two years, where I got my engineering degree."

Dave arched his brows. "You spent two years in South Korea? No more than that?"

"There, I learned the Chungcheong and Gyeongsang dialects. I know the Seoul dialect, though not as well as the other two."

"And you studied in Korea for only two years? And how were you funded?"

"Yes. That is where I earned my bachelor's. And I was funded by the Korean Government Scholarship Program."

"And how old are you?"

"I am thirteen."

"Impressive!"

"I wanted to go to Beijing or to Massachusetts. My family could not afford to send me to either. Now with the different scholarships coming to me, it will be possible."

"Despite that, I can see you have a thing for linguistics."

"My first language was Nyanja. From there, I learned Tonga, Barotse, Mambwe, Tumbuka, and well-known Bemba. I learned these through the many friends I had. And, of course, I learned English while in school."

"You're pretty fluent."

"I can improve. And I also learned French from one of my teachers."

"N'est-ce pas vrai?"

"Effectivement! Vous parlez francais bien?"

"Well, I only speak a little for show. You speak it fluently."

"In conversation and in writing."

"I'm Dave. My scientist friend over there is Eugene. And you are?"

"Geri Kubota. You can call me Geri."

"I certainly will. We need to take our friend to retrieve his smartphone."

"That will not be a problem."

Geri pulled out a smartphone from his pocket and took it out of airplane mode. With it, he also pulled out a smaller device, which was small enough to enclose in the palm of his hand. He attached it to his smartphone. Geri tapped that little device. It reacted with a pulsing blue light, which lit intermittingly.

"I see that you are going to track it?"

"Yes," replied Geri. "How will you be able to detect his device?"

"By any information that he has on that device—his name, email, and other personal information. These will appear on my smartphone. This device is compatible with any smartphone."

"What if the lost device were turned off or set to airplane mode? Any pocket thief can do that."

"This device will track the phone to where it was last turned off and track the owner's fingerprints by matching that data with full name and email address."

Dave did a double-take. "I know of the tracking technology that tracks devices to the point where they were last turned off. I've never heard of any that tracks fingerprints."

"This device does more. It matches images of the owner in the file section and reflections on the blank screen."

"It does all that? Who's the manufacturer of this new technology?"

Geri paused for a moment, then grinned. "Me."

Dave was ecstatic. "This is amazing, Geri! What would this technology do about the smart thief that hacks into the encrypted device and pilfers all the important data from it?"

"This technology memorizes not only recent fingerprints but also facial prints of persons who look into the phone screen."

"Well, lead on."

Dave, Geri, and the Asian student, Ji hun, were exiting the exhibit when they were intercepted by Eugene.

"How about I take these students?"

"Are you okay with that?"

"Yes, I'll spare a little time."

"They're all yours! Meet Geri and Ji."

"I'll work on that as I go." Eugene turned to Geri and Ji hun. "Come on."

Eugene, Geri, and Ji hun followed Geri's tracking device through the corridors and out of the visitor's center. The tracking device pulsed as they continued their walk through the GSFC grounds. Both Geri and Ji hun knew where they were earlier and were able to backtrack. It was now a question of where Ji hun last had his smartphone and what had happened to it since. One of the unique features that Geri did not tell Dave about was this technology's ability to work as a compass. The arrow on Geri's phone would either point towards or away from an exhibit. The device pointed them north-west. Eugene knew the operation center for the Hubble Space Telescope was in that direction. He followed the students to the unknown point of destination.

"So . . . Geri . . . Did I get it right?"

"Yes, you did."

"How and where can I get my hands on one of those? Does it work with iOS?"

"It does. Only that this is the first of its kind."

"You invented this?"

"Yes!"

"And you can use it to find other items, like USBs?"

"Yes," replied Geri.

"We could use more young blood at the center."

Geri ruminated over the thought of being called 'young blood.' "I'm getting used to your American way of speaking. When you say 'young blood,' did you mean 'young person?"

"Yes," replied Eugene. "But young blood is more advantageous to the rest of my colleagues."

They were on the sidewalk when Eugene's eyes caught a glimpse of an approaching figure. It was strange that of all the people employed by NASA that he could bump into, the one he despised most was approaching. Eugene recognized Jerry Paulo from a distance. This time he was alone. There was no one to restrain Eugene. He had the mind to run ahead of the students and take a swing at Paulo. But this wouldn't do well for his credibility in the eyes of the young visiting students. Eugene chose to restrain himself, but not without biting his lips. He walked behind Geri, in a way using him as a shield to protect Paulo from himself. Jerry saw Eugene and the students approaching but chose not to detour. There was a head-on collision coming. What would be the result of this meeting? Time would tell. In a moment, the two were face to face.

"Ellis," Jerry said in a formal tone of voice.

"Paulo," Eugene returned in his mock decorum.

"I can see that you have a pair of young foreign students. Hope you're learning something," Jerry said, moving his eyes from the students to Eugene.

"They are learning something," Eugene said impatiently. "Let's go." He pressed his hands against Geri and Ji hun's back to push them forward. Jerry stopped them.

"What are your names, and where are you from?"

Both students answered; first, Ji hun, then Geri.

"You're from Zambia, and your name is also Jerry?"

"No," corrected Eugene. "His name is spelled with a G, one R, and an I at the end. This is the more accurate spelling. The American version is the twisted way of spelling the name."

"Okay, Eugenie," replied Jerry in a sarcastic tone. "Like you have the corner on the world's correct spellings and pronunciations of names."

Eugene grew more impatient. "Are we done here? We are trying to find this student's phone. Can we go now?"

"Not yet," replied Jerry. "You've been bringing up my name these past few months."

"Oh, have I?" Eugene replied with irony.

"About the reports on the two Kepler missions, I did not forge your signature. I did not attempt to spoil your credibility with the board. I didn't even tell the administrator that you were that dumb."

"You expect me to believe that, Paulo?"

"Listen, Ellis, I am not the only person at GSFC who doesn't like you. There are others. I suggest you widen your search for culprits."

"And the next person is going to deny that they did it."

Jerry shrugged. "Not my problem. All I know is that I did not do it."

Eugene pressed his hands against Geri and Ji hun's back. Before Eugene could say, "Let's go," Geri paused. Not because he had found the missing phone, but because he had lost the signal. Jerry saw this and commented.

"Unless Ji hun's phone crossed the event horizon of a black hole, Geri's tracking device has now ceased to work."

"I hope you would one day cease to work and that you get sucked into a black hole." Eugene forcibly pushed the students forward to get away from Jerry Paulo.

The empty space

They were three blocks down from where they stood. They looked intently at the device, hoping it would light up again, but it did not. After a few technical procedures to correct the problem, it still couldn't pick up anything belonging to Ji hun. Eugene had Geri test it on his smartphone, and it worked. They now knew that Geri's invention did not malfunction. The only problem was that it could not lead them to Ji hun's smartphone.

"I wouldn't be surprised if it were that Paulo," Eugene said grudgingly. "Another way to find the lost mobile is by his IMEI number. Have you taken that route?"

"I did," replied Geri. "Though I was able to pull up his IMEI number, there were no responders on my engine search. I can only suggest that we continue in the direction that my device last pointed."

"Good idea," said Eugene. "Let's go."

Eugene and the students continued their walk towards the Space Telescope's Operation Control Center, where Geri and the others had visited earlier.

Ji hun turned to Eugene. "That man, what did he mean?" he asked in his slow, broken, simple English.

"Him? He's being what he's wired to be, and that's a fool and a stupid, bumbling idiot."

"Scientists have yet to discover the mass of a black hole," Geri said.

"What is further from their understanding is what happens at the event horizon. In the center of galaxies, stars are getting pulled into black holes. That is where all light is trapped in pitch blackness. Black holes are still a mystery because no one has sent anything near a black hole," Eugene replied. "We can tell that these were once stars that collapsed in on themselves, but no one knows the size of this compressed matter. By its force of gravity, it can pull many stars hundreds of times larger than our sun towards itself at a speed that is half the speed of light."

"Earlier, you said sucked in?"

Eugene threw his eyes upwards before turning them back on Geri. "Yes, I said, 'sucked in.' In truth, things are not being sucked in the way things are sucked into a vacuum. Because of the size of the mass, the gravity is powerful. Things fall into a black hole. The temperatures inside a black hole are billions of degrees Fahrenheit. It's not like we could send a craft with a camera past the event horizon in hopes that it will not melt."

Eugene paused.

"Even scientists wonder what's on the other side. Some wonder if these are spawning other universes."

Geri rubbed his chin. "And many scientists believe that hypertime travel will be possible?"

"This is their guesswork," replied Eugene. "Speaking of the mass of the black hole, a black hole is like a massive bowling ball that is dropped on a mattress. Because space-time is flat in the way a mattress is flat, the massive bowling ball, or the black hole, would cause a curvature in space."

"The holes in the mattress are the wormholes that scientists are talking about?"

"Correct! Some of my colleagues . . . okay, fewer of them believe we can do hypertime travel by using these wormholes as ports."

"But you don't believe it?"

"I'm not convinced by this," replied Eugene.

Geri jumped in. "Why are you not convinced?"

"There's no guarantee that wormholes would take a person to another point in space-time any more than they could cause that person to land in a parallel universe."

"Suppose we could travel hyperspace through these holes and go to another galaxy, would this be time travel?"

"Though there are still unknown possibilities, we humans are now constrained by our four dimensions of length, width, height, and time. Will we be able to control matter in such a way that we can overcome all the hurdles in space? Time will tell."

"Do you believe that could happen?"

"I don't rule out the power quantum computers could later have. Time travel would be more far-reaching than space travel. I choose the latter. Understanding the warping of space and time can point us scientists to other worlds."

"Do you mean other Big bangs or other beginnings?"

"That may or may not be what's on the other side."

"I can say that our God created a universe that is full of mystery. He has left it for us to explore."

"Woah, hold on, young man," said Eugene, waving both hands back and forth before Geri.

"Not so! We have yet to fully understand our universe. To throw a supreme being into the mix will compel scientists to try to understand this being. If he transcends space, like some of my colleagues believe, studying him would be an impossible task. I have advised many to abandon that task. And I will say so now."

Geri said, "To study God through science methods would be an impossible task."

"I don't mean to interrupt, but I know where you're going with this. To understand God would mean that you would need to understand his self-revelation?"

"Yes," replied Geri. "I believe that this is the only way you could know God. You said that we are constrained by our four dimensions, which includes time. But God does not have to be constrained by length, width, or height. He can dwell in the other six smaller dimensions, and beyond. That is what makes Him the Supreme Creator of all things. If we were to try to understand Him, we never would. He would have to come into our four dimensions and reveal Himself to us. And I believe that is what He did through His Son, Jesus."

Eugene stared at Geri with a frowned look. "You don't surprise me, Geri. I have African colleagues who are also people of faith. I see that Africa is a cultural milieu of faith."

Just then, the three were at the outer doors of the Space Telescope Operations Control Center.

Eugene turned to Ji hun as they were walking in. "Ji hon . . ."

"It's Ji hun," corrected Geri.

"Yes, Ji hun." Eugene nodded apologetically. "What did you last do with your Pixel 5 smartphone?" Eugene hoped Ji hun understood his slowed, broken, and simplified attempt to communicate with him. This worked to little avail.

Geri turned and spoke to Ji hun in the Gyeongsang dialect. Ji hun replied. Geri then turned to Eugene. "He was taking video footage of the operations center. He did so while walking through the different rooms. He said that he could have left it beside one of the computer screens."

Just then, Geri looked down and noticed his device had lit up as it did the first time. The light pulsed more rapidly, showing that the three were close. They were inside the lobby. But the map on Geri's screen did not point them to the control room. It led them towards a small desk in the lobby. A buff woman stood by the counter.

"Mary," Eugene said in a not-so-thrilled-to-see-you tone.

"Eugene," the woman countered.

"This is Ji hun. He is looking for his phone."

"What does this phone look like?"

Eugene turned to Geri as though he were giving the floor over to him for the answer.

"It is a Google Pixel 5," Geri replied. "It is a clear white with a glass back, and it has an Alpine case."

She reached behind the desk and pulled out a phone that fit the description to a tee. "Then, this has to be it."

Ji hun's face lit up as he thankfully took the smartphone.

Eugene turned to Mary. "How did you come across this phone?"

"One of our operators found it, and he turned it over to me."

"Could you tell me who that operator is?"

"That is confidential. This worker handed it to me. And now the rightful owner has it."

"Mary," Eugene replied with a tinge of annoyance in his tone. "It is important that I know this. I want to be sure that it did not fall into the hands of someone who may have hacked it."

Compared to Eugene, Mary was physically imposing enough to hurt him if he wasn't careful how he spoke to her.

"Eugene, you are bothering me. Unlike you, I have enough faith in my colleagues to believe that they would never do such a thing. A person who lacks moral integrity doesn't deserve a place in this space center. I know these people better than you do."

"What I'm hearing now is the kind of naivety that allows mischief and danger to run amuck." Eugene shook his head disapprovingly.

Mary began taking steps towards Eugene. And he started taking steps backward, as he allowed the young students to shield him.

"Eugene, I am about ready to open you up and feed you to the seagulls."

"No, you are not," countered Eugene as he continued walking backward. "Such violence is unbecoming of you. What of your morals?"

"Yes," spat Mary. "My morals will stay intact as long as you get out of my sight." She turned to Geri and Ji hun with a forced smile. "Thank you, both for coming. Please come again, and I will be more than happy to show you around." The moment she turned her eyes back to Eugene, her features reverted to anger.

Eugene took the students with him as he walked over to another section of the building. He turned to Ji hun. "Can I see your phone?" He took it out and handed it to Eugene. Eugene examined the Pixel 5 from screen to back cover. "Looks normal. And he locked and encoded the device. Good."

Ji hun turned to Eugene. "Why she was angry at you?"

Eugene grumbled to himself, "The hippopotamus." He then said more audibly, "I do not trust people the way that woman does. She was angry at me because of that."

Ji hun gave Eugene a quizzical look. Geri clarified in Ji hun's dialect what Eugene had just said. Ji hun then smiled approvingly.

"I would like time with the Hubble," said Geri.

"The main attraction for visitors. Everyone who visits this flight center wants to see through the Hubble," Eugene replied.

"Can we?" Geri asked with enthusiasm.

"Yes, you can. Unfortunately, to get this, you would need to bump a lot of scientists and educators that are also vying for time with the telescope. You would need to fill out a director's discretionary time form with a proposal, and so on, and so forth."

Geri slumped, showing his disappointment. Eugene saw this. "Then, there is the option of joining me in my slot a week from now."

Geri's face lit up again with hope.

"But, you would need to be here then."

Geri nodded with glee.

"You would have to be here in Maryland, not somewhere in Massachusetts."

The three noticed they were standing before a display guarded by a glass. The exhibit showcased the earlier equipment used for Hubble that was now obsolete because of more up-to-date equipment.

"Looking at all of this, it now looks ancient to me. It's strange, that is not what I was thinking back in the nineties."

"I wasn't yet born then," Geri observed. "I am fascinated by the effort they took back then, with the limited technology, to go deeper into the universe's past."

"Yes," agreed Eugene. "We are still limited. Yet we're at the doorstep of a deeper look into the universe's past."

"I would like to see through James Webb."

"I hope I'll be the first." Eugene smiled.

Eugene turned and saw, at a distance, one of the senior astronomers, one of the few persons on planet Earth that Eugene highly respected, Greg Cobalt. Eugene noticed that he was coaching a youth who didn't look much older than Geri and Ji hun. Eugene walked towards the two. Geri and Ji hun followed.

"Dr. Cobalt."

The man turned to Eugene. "Come on, Eugene. You've known me for so long, and you still address me by my title?"

"I'm sorry, Greg. When you are in the presence of a god, the human impulse is to call them 'doctor.'"

Greg chuckled. "That's fine. Hey, I would like to introduce you to my young protégé and future astronomer, Nikita. And who do you have with you?"

"Yes, I have with me two exchange students, Geri and Ji hun."

"Oh, that's nice. And what would you both like to be when you grow up?"

"An engineer," said Geri.

"Astronomer," said Ji hun.

"Oh, that's nice," replied Greg with a big smile. "Maybe you both can come and be mentored by yours truly."

Eugene turned to Geri, "You don't know this, but when I was a young kid like Nikita, Greg took me under his wings and mentored me in the same manner."

Geri was in awe by this.

"Yes, that was a good while back," Greg added. "More than thirty years ago."

"Greg is one of our surviving dinosaurs. You will learn a lot under his tutelage."

"Thank you, Eugene for the kind words . . . and for calling me a dinosaur." They shared a laugh. "Now, if you'll excuse us both," Greg continued, "we have some work to do. I hope to see you again, Geri and Ji hun."

Greg and Nikita started in one direction as Eugene and the young students went in the opposite. The three left the control center and began to backtrack to the visitor center where they had left the others.

Eugene turned back to Geri. "About your electronic device tracker, maybe it lost its connection to Ji hun's device because it was outside a specific radius?"

"That was not supposed to happen," replied Geri, "because the connection was first gained by satellite. The device was found on this tracker, then it was lost—"

"As though someone interfered deliberately," Eugene finished his sentence. "Who would be so interested in his smartphone, unless they wanted to hack into this device? It is a nice phone. Don't get me wrong. Most hackers are complete strangers, but they can also be people you know and are acquainted with."

Geri spoke. "Then, there is the possibility that someone found the device, put it away safely, and then gave it to the owner."

"My problem is that you were tracking it one moment, then the next, you lost it on your screen. That would never have happened unless someone interfered with it."

Geri changed the subject. "There is a technology building. Can I go to that?"

"Listen, you really should be getting back to the others. I'm sure you're missing out on lots."

Geri and Ji hun bowed their heads. Ji hun also knew the

language of technology and wanted to go. Eugene looked at the two and was sorry he did, for all he saw were the pouting lips and puppy dog eyes that could soften the most hardened person of them all.

"Okay, we'll go. For a half-an-hour max. No more."

The faces of the two lit up. Eugene detoured to Building 29, and the students followed. They walked around the building to find the entrance. They came across landers and rovers, each weighing more than Geri, Ji hun, and Eugene. As they moved farther, they saw other robots, and these had remotes by them. Geri and Ji hun did not waste any time as they picked up remotes and started playing with their knobs. Fortunately for them, the rovers responded to the controls. The robots moved as Geri, and Ji hun handled the controls. No one could have expected what happened next.

The robot that Ji hun controlled ceased. Geri's robot also stopped. Other robots stopped, even those that were being controlled by other means stopped. Soon, the computers shut down without warning.

"What's going on?" Eugene asked as he turned to staff that were present. No one had an answer, but the engineers sprung into action and attempted to fix the problem. The center with the kind of toys that would make Geri and Ji hun smile became off-limits to visitors until the issue was fixed. Eugene turned to Geri and Ji hun. "Let's get out of here while they fix the problem."

The two followed Eugene and made their way to the visitor center. They arrived and stood in the lobby by the entrance. The other foreign students were about to leave. Steve walked up to Eugene with an almost worried look.

"Did he find his phone?"

"We found it," replied Eugene in his attempts to calm Steve down.

"Because they are about ready to leave."

Eugene turned to Geri and Ji hun. "I'm sorry, kids. Your class is about to leave. But please, come again."

"I will be here next week for the Hubble," Geri reminded him.

"Yes, we see the Hubble shots together."

Geri looked around. The other students looked around. Steve and Eugene looked around and noticed the screen images switching to screensavers before turning off. The lady at the welcome desk looked down at her screen with a confused look. She was having computer issues. Other digitally controlled items began to malfunction as well.

"I don't remember this ever happening," said Steve. "Is this happening for the first time?"

"This is what happened back at Building 29."

Steve gathered the students as they exited the visitor center. Eugene followed.

Geri returned to his home away from home. Since his arrival in the United States, a family living in North Bethesda had graciously taken him in. After living with the Evanses for a short time, Geri learned that this family had a tight relational bond. What he also learned was that this family was made up of people of faith. They prayed and read the Bible together. The Evanses talked about things that were important to each member. And God was at the center of every discussion. To Geri, this reminded him of home in Zambia. His family prayed together and read the Bible. They posted Bible verses throughout their home, and God was at the center of every talk he had with his mother and father. This is what Geri remembered growing up. And he was happy to know that he could live with this while in the west.

The Evanses were kind. This family received Geri into their home, and Ji hun also, seeing that they both hit it off from the start. Geri would often communicate with Ji hun in his language as the translator between Ji hun and the Evanses. In contrast, Ji hun was getting more fluent in his English. The Evanses also benefitted, because Lisa and her daughter, Jasmine, were learning French. And who better to help them in their lessons than Geri? Charles Evans, the man of the house, and his youngest daughter, Julia, both hoped to travel to South Korea in the future to teach English as a second language. Both Ji hun and Geri helped them learn the Korean language.

That Wednesday evening, as Geri and Ji hun returned to the house, the unexpected happened: every electronic device crashed, from desktops to handheld devices. The Evans family also noticed that their flatscreen TVs went blank. Charles checked the internet modem to see if it was receiving signals. There were none. He picked up the house phone to call one of their neighbors that lived three houses away. They were using the same service, but they were not having the same problem.

"We have a problem," said Charles.

"A moment ago, my computer crashed," said Lisa. "I'm wondering what's really happening."

"Mr. and Mrs. Evans, when did this happen?" Geri asked.

Charles answered, "The moment you and Ji hun walked in. Everything was fine until then."

The controls in the sky

Dr. Geri Kubota is a leading spacecraft engineer for NASA. He leads in aerospace research and technology. His goal is to send humans to the far reaches of space so that they might go where no human has gone before.

It had been more than eighty years since President Kennedy's address to the nation, along with his prediction that NASA would one day send a man to the moon. Many years later, Geri was at the center of man's first mission to Mars. Along with the tireless efforts of other leading engineers, Geri had helped to make it possible for people to stay on Mars for periods. Engineers had designed protective space suits to shield them from the lethal doses of solar ultraviolet radiation and the superoxide effect coming from the Martian soil. They had also created protective habitats for the human explorers, which could withstand the dust storms and other harmful elements. And the Reconnaissance Orbiter had tapped into the abundant water resources that were able to sustain human life on Mars.

While GSFC was on their mission to send the first man to Mars, Geri had his sights on the mission to Jupiter's moon, Europa. This project was headed by the Jet Propulsion Laboratory in Pasadena, California. Geri wanted to be there to witness history. The team at JPL made history as they sent the first lander on Europa. A decade later, they'd sent the first man to Europa. The precautions they had to take on this icy planet were different from those they had to take on Mars. For Europa, there was no question whether there was water or not. They had been able to understand the chemicals on that moon's surface and in that moon's water. The design for space suits was different, and the kind of habitat to be built was also different. Geri's skill and creativity became the inspiration for the technology that was on board for the first mission to Europa. As an astronaut, Geri hoped to later visit Saturn's moon, Titan.

There was no question whether Geri was qualified. With a bachelor's degree in computer engineering from the University of Science and Technology in South Korea, Geri had moved on to get his master's degree in mathematics at the University of Massachusetts. He then earned a second master's in aerospace engineering at MIT. He then went on to get his doctorate in geology at Georgetown University. The right training was always crucial to Geri. To send any Joe to Mars, Europa, or even earth's moon without a degree in engineering would be catastrophic.

On the first Monday in March 2043, Geri kissed his wife, Bora, a woman born to a South Korean mother and a Zimbabwean father. He kissed her, but she didn't want to let him go. What made this extra challenging for Geri was that Bora was also an engineer at Goddard Space Flight Center. This was how they first met. Now that Geri was preparing for his mission to Europa, Bora also wanted to go.

"My Bora, you have to let me go."

"You are not leaving without me this time. I let you go on that first and second trip to Mars. Now that you're going to a more dangerous planet, I cannot bear to stay home or at the flight center while you are risking life and limb to show the world you hit a plateau in your life."

"Honey, please understand that it's not about me, it's about the mission."

"Well, if it's not about you, then I'm coming."

"No. I cannot have this. There's no guarantee that I will be back."

"Then I'm coming. And I'll make sure that you do come back. You have a daughter here, remember?"

"Yes," Geri said with sadness in his voice.

"Then it's final. I'm coming."

Bora insisted that she go on this trip to Europa. She would not be told otherwise. When the candidates were named for the next mission to Europa, Bora made sure that her name was listed. Bora wanted to go on this mission, also to return and to receive a medal from the first black female US President ever. Geri would be joined by a team of astronauts and his wife for this next exploration to Europa.

On Saturday, and before their mission, Geri and Bora visited a senior astronomer by the name of Eugene Ellis. Eugene was not the one to give them marriage advice, for this was never his forte. Instead, he told them about his understanding of Jupiter and its moons.

"Good luck on your six-hundred-and-thirty-five-day trip."

"It's been said that the trip will last that long," said Geri.

"Six-hundred-and-thirty-five days with perfect alignment

between Earth and Jupiter's moon. When you get there, providing you get there safely, your worries will only begin. The radiation blasts from Jupiter are deadly and constant. The last team was lucky enough to dodge that bullet. There's no telling what it might do to you or your surroundings. To this day, my colleagues haven't found any biosignatures coming from life on the planet."

"Thanks, Eugene," replied Bora. "We already know about the risks."

"I don't want to be the doomsday preacher on your path to discovery, but I've grown fond of you both."

Geri turned to his wife with an I-told-you-so look. "You see, Bora, the risks are great. And Goburra can't afford to lose both of us."

Bora narrowed her eyes at Geri.

Eugene continued, "I say that if you should go, then you should go out with a blast."

Geri turned to Eugene with a look of disbelief. "What?"

"I mean that if you both should go, you should go out in style. Your sister will take care of Goburra while you're both gone. With the chances for survival being slim, you both could be gone for a very long time."

"Thank you for those going-away last words," Geri said with irony.

"What now? You want me to encourage you both? You want to be encouraged, so I'll give you the encouragement you need. Unlike me, you are both young and attractive. And I have to say that you would make two beautiful corpses . . ."

Their jaws dropped.

"Well, you heard it from me. As you religious folks say, God's speed!"

"Well, Eugene," replied Bora. "I don't know what else to do with this type of bidding, but to say thank you."

The next day, which was Sunday, Geri, Bora, and the other astronauts were strapped into the cockpit of the spaceship that was about to launch. They joined the other members of the crew in a time of prayer to ask for the Lord's protection throughout this voyage. Sunday was a day to be in church, so they had church in the cockpit, and they felt as close to God as they'd ever felt. They wanted to launch into chartered territory with a mission that would benefit human civilization. That is what God would have them do. He would not have allowed them on this mission if it were to be a failed one. Thoughts like this flooded Geri's mind as he sat with eyes closed, ready for the next space mission.

"It's a liftoff." Geri knew this as he felt the turbulence during liftoff. If the team could break through the earth's gravity pull, they would be on their way to Europa. This would be a more than three-hundred-and-sixty-five-day trip. And they might not arrive at their destination until more than two years later.

For the crew, life on the spaceship was never a problem. There was enough fuel to take them to Europa. Geri and one of the members on board had already been to Mars. No one on board had been to Europa. This is an experience to tell grandchildren if they survived to see their grandchildren.

Geri had designed the spacecraft to withstand the harsh radiation coming from the gas giant. The electronics aboard Europa Astrobiology Tracker, or EAT, was also built for that purpose.

By the time the crew was close enough, the trip felt like it took them a lifetime to get there. The spaceship flew by Callisto, then Ganymede. Geri, Bora, and the crew could see Lo and the massive Jupiter at a distance. Then there was Europa.

They prepared for landing as they flew within Europa's orbit. Where they would land was critical. To descend closer to the pole, and close to the dark brown stripes, was their goal. They made it. To land human exploration on Europa was challenging for the crew as they landed near the equator. They survived, but not without a big scare. The team on board ship EAT landed where they needed to. The team went into a time of thanksgiving to the Creator of the universe for that successful landing.

Before stepping onto the planet's surface, the team prayed again, asking for the safekeeping and wellbeing of the entire crew. The team climbed into spacesuits that were designed for landing on Europa. The suits were also equipped with heaters for their walk on this frigid planet. They were not bulky like those used on Mars, but lightweight and fitted to the body for maneuverability. The gloves were also close-fitted and had friction pads on the fingertips, allowing the crew to work more efficiently. Geri exited the lander, then Bora, then the other crew members. The team looked around at what looked like Antarctica. The only difference was the appearance of the sky.

Bora said, "Jupiter is so massive! It takes up almost half the sky."

"Yes," agreed Geri. "And look at the sun. It looks much smaller than how it would look from home."

Another astronaut, named Bob, joined them as he said, "It's almost insignificant from this planet."

"No wonder it's so cold out here," said Bora.

"It is," said Geri. "By the way, we've got lots of work to do."

Just then, the surface rumbled from below. It frightened the entire crew. Geri wondered if this was it. Before another word could be said by anyone, over the horizon, a massive explosion of what looked like water. With force unlike anything Geri had ever seen on earth, the water shot upward into the sky. Like a gigantic fire hydrant, it shot thousands of feet into the air. This rocked the surface on which the team stood, knocking them off their feet. Everyone looked up with awe at this display of power, until droplets of water landed on them.

"Eugene told me about the plumes on this planet," said Geri.

Bora said. "I wonder how frequently this happens. If this happens often, I wonder how much we can get done sitting down."

"We'll get a lot done before we return to earth. We need to work while avoiding high radiation zones."

"Oh, that won't be easy," remarked Bob, the other space traveler.

The team explored the surface while trying not to stray too far from the lander, where they would be staying for the next three days. They used land equipment with wheels to get from one point to another. Geri and Bora traveled in an RV. He drove along the brown surface while maintaining communication with the team back at the lander. The lander was built to withstand the deadly radiation, but not the RV in which Geri and Bora were driving. They drove for a reasonable distance. Geri and Bora stopped where they could see along the sky, the beauty of creation. They stared at Callisto and Ganymede, which were larger than Europa. They stared at Jupiter and the smaller moons.

Bora turned to Geri. "Shouldn't we be working?"

"Yes," replied Geri. "But it's hard to not be distracted."

"Tell me about it," agreed Bora.

Geri looked up, and what he saw shocked him. "Bora, I think we better go."

Bora reacted with a quizzical look. "Go?"

Geri grabbed her and turned her to see what he was looking at. "Oh, no!"

"Let's get out of here!" Geri shot, as he grabbed her arm and pulled her into the RV.

They climbed in. Geri started, turned the vehicle, and drove it at full speed. Behind them was a piercing glow coming from the high energy radiation belt that Eugene warned them about. It was like lighting – only that it was like a straight sheet made of light. And it was coming their way. The glow was getting closer by the second. Soon they would be fried by the radiation. They were getting closer to the lander. The light was much too fast. Soon it would be too late for Geri and Bora Kubota. Coming from the lander at full speed was Bob, the other traveler. The moment he got close enough to Geri and Bora, he jumped out of his RV with a black tarp that could withstand radiation and threw it over Geri and Bora's RV. The glowing light hit Geri and Bora's RV, but they were under the tarp. Unfortunately for Bob, he was not covered by the tarp when the radiation hit him. Geri and Bora watched in horror as they learned what Jupiter's radiation could do to a man's body.

Geri and Bora looked at Bob's remains and lamented over it.

"He risked his life to save ours," cried Bora.

"I know," replied Geri, with eyelids tightened with grief. After a while, he said, "We know that his death was not in vain."

Geri looked over to the team as they approached. They looked down at Bob's remains with great fear. Then they looked up and noticed that the radiation did more than fry Bob, the astronaut, it also caused significant interference on everything electronic.

Geri pulled out his electronic device and tested it. "Oh, this is not good."

The others tested everything electronic that they could get their hands on, and nothing worked. Even their RVs did not work. "This is not good," repeated Geri.

Then, another astronaut, said, "Let's go back to the lander to see whether things are working. And we need to get back quickly because of the after-effects of this blast and what it could do to our bodies."

The team walked briskly to the lander. Fortunately, the lander wasn't a far walking distance. The crew stepped into the lander. All electronic things were working. The giant plant's radiation could not penetrate the lander because it was built to withstand the heavy doses. Geri laid down his device, which was no longer working, then picked up another instrument. Then a strange thing happened the moment he stepped out of the lander. That new device shut down.

"Oh no," Geri winced. "I need this device for this mission, or else we are here for nothing."

He looked around at the others. They all knew that if they were to expose their electronics to the dense radiation effect in the air, their devices would not work. Geri knew that he needed his handheld device to explore the planet and to continue his work. The massive doses of ultraviolet and ionized particle radiation would explain why this had happened.

Geri was about to go into his quarters to sleep and think of a solution when he came across a computer monitor. It was on. He stepped closer to see what was running on this device. That's when he saw the data files being opened remotely by the team back on earth. They were able to access this computer through the orbiting satellite. Geri ran to another computer and contacted the team at NASA's JPL. "Geri Kubota here. What time is it? And how is the weather?"

A voice from earth replied, "Good to hear from you, Geri! It is Friday at 11:45 AM, Rocky Mountain time. It's a beautiful ninety-two-degrees Fahrenheit weather with scattered clouds."

"That's good. We have a problem. Our hardware died. And the team told you about Bob?"

"Yes," replied the staff member at JPL in a somber tone. "We have the data from his hardware."

"Oh, do you?" Geri asked with interest.

"If you look at one of the screens, we have your data. I believe that's your device."

"One moment, please." Geri excused himself to go to the running monitor. He opened data files and saw videos and images of the open landscape that both he and his wife drove through. He opened another and saw footages that he could not remember. These were coming from another device. They were footages of the landscape. Geri walked back to the other screen. "Files are coming from another device."

"That was Bobby's hardware," the member from JPL replied.

"His device is dead."

"We can pull up data from it."

Geri stepped out of the lander.

"Where are you going?" asked Bora.

"I need to see the device that was left on Bob's RV."

Geri drove an RV to the other RVs that were left behind. He walked over to the RV with the device that was left behind. Geri picked it up, held it, and knew that this device was dead. He looked it over and felt around. Geri smashed it against the surface of the RV, opened the back, and pulled out a computer chip. He held it up and knew that this device was also connected to the satellite.

Geri lifted himself from his position, looked around, and saw pure darkness. He peered to his left and saw Ji hun, who was fast asleep. Geri soon came to himself. *"I was dreaming the whole time?"* he thought. He then turned his eyes to the Pixel 5 that Ji hun had on a nightstand by the bed.

There is time

On Tuesday, October 1st, Geri arrived at the Goddard Flight Space Center by 11:00 AM. Charles Evans dropped Geri, and Ji hun there and promised he would return at 3:00 PM. They would join Eugene during his time slot and cycle that was scheduled for 12:30 PM. Both Geri and Ji hun arrived at the spot where they were to meet with Eugene. He had promised to capture the Hubble images with them. But Eugene was not there.

"Maybe he is busy," Geri thought.

Geri and Ji hun browsed the lobby, making as though Eugene would be there as promised. They would not wander too far, lest Eugene would arrive and not see them. They looked along the walls and saw some of the spectacular images taken by Hubble over the years. Pictures of quasars, comets, and nebulae caught their eyes as they scanned through the different photos on display.

"What beauty . . . like all of this was made for our eyes."

Geri turned to the male voice to see who it was. It wasn't Eugene. A tall, dark-haired man with handsome features stood by Geri. He turned their attention back to the images.

"And that one, which exploded some ten billion years ago, looks much like a crucifix." The man turned again to the two. "Oh, where are my manners? I'm Warren. I'm one of the astrophysicists for NASA. And you are?"

The students replied with their names. "Well, nice to meet you, Geri and Ji hun. I hope you're enjoying your time here at Goddard Space Flight Center?"

"Yes," replied Geri. "We are supposed to meet Eugene, the astronomer, here before 12:15 PM."

"Hmm," looking down at his watch. "It's 12:00 PM now, and you have not seen him?"

"So far, no."

"Okay, I have his number. Let me see if I can reach him."

Warren pulled out his smartphone and tapped away at his touchscreen, then listened. He tried the number again and no response. Warren lowered his phone.

"Hey, fellas, I really don't know what to tell you. So far, he's not picking up."

"What will happen with his 12:30 time slot?" Geri asked.

"That's a good question. Excuse me."

Warren broke away from the two to join one of the staff whom Geri recognized from the other day. Warren spoke with Mary in a whisper that neither Geri nor Ji hun could hear. Another man joined them. He appeared to be more mature than Warren. They continued their three-way conversation, and neither Geri nor Ji hun could listen to them.

"What are these adults talking about?" Geri wondered, noticing Mary taking glances at him. He usually didn't feel uncomfortable around adults in these positions, but it was how she looked at him. Geri tried not to make too much of this. He turned his head in the opposite direction, and the moment he did, he saw a blond-haired

teenager at a distance. Geri did not get a good look at him. In the split second that he turned the youth slipped behind a wall. Geri didn't think much of it until it dawned on him. This looked like the Russian kid he had seen a week earlier. Warren returned. Mary followed.

"Good news, kids. We've solved the problem. That fine gentleman we spoke to over there is a professor at Penn State University. He's on the same cycle and was scheduled to look through the Hubble at 1:00 PM. He has graciously offered to take Eugene's slot in place for his."

Geri smiled. "Thank you, Warren. Do you think Eugene will be here soon?"

"I don't know," replied Warren. "Eugene tends to be unpredictable. By the way, I would like you both to meet Mary. She is one of our staff at this center."

Mary spoke with a forced smile. "Yes, we met a week ago. It is nice to see you both again."

Ji hun looked at her but did not return the smile, and Geri smiled faintly. They shook hands with her, but reluctantly.

Mary held her forced smile. "Well, I hope you both will have a good time looking up at the stars."

The two only looked at her while slowly nodding. Mary and Warren spoke before Mary bid them goodbye. She then walked away to another part of the building.

Warren turned to the students. "There's a seating area." He pointed to a seating area with comfortable-looking, beige-colored sofas that were interlocked in a semi-circle. "Let's sit over there until Eugene arrives."

The three walked to the seating area. Geri shared with Warren where he was from, what he had done, and hoped to do in the US, and the career path he had chosen. Ji hun did the same. Warren then shared with the youths some of the work he had done and what he hoped to do in the days to come.

"Guys, this is all fascinating. Very impressive! I wish I had given myself the kind of head start that you did. You are both on your way."

Geri looked down at his phone. "It is 12:45 PM."

"I wonder where Eugene could be," Warren said.

In a moment, the man they'd been waiting for walked in. Eugene appeared as though he were coming from a marathon. He was sweating, and he looked peeved over something.

"And here's our guy," Warren announced.

"I'm sorry for my delay. You should have seen the beltway. It was bumper-to-bumper, and for what? The stupid construction crew decided to block four lanes. Four lanes! And leave us with no more than one lane. Ugh, this is ridiculous. Don't they know that people have jobs to get to?"

"I even called you."

"Yeah, yeah, yeah. I saw your number, but I couldn't answer, because my hands-free wasn't working. I lost my earpiece to the washing machine, and a cop cruiser was on my tail the whole time, daring me to pick up my device and answer."

"Well, Eugene, despite all of that, you will get your time with the Hubble."

Eugene gave Warren a look of shock. "What? What happened?"

"A professor from Penn State has volunteered his time in place for yours. He's with the Hubble now. You have 1:00 PM instead. So, you can relax until then."

Eugene sat. It appeared to the others that this was the first time he really exhaled in hours. "Thanks, Warren, I appreciate that. And for entertaining these kids."

"Hey, don't sweat it, Eugene. They are a lot of fun to be around. They have a lot of fascinating things to share about their lives. I'm going to leave you for now. It was nice speaking with you both."

The three bade Warren goodbye as he walked off.

Eugene turned to the young students. "What fascinating thing would you like to share with me?"

Geri told Eugene about the vivid dream he had had a few nights earlier. He told him every detail from start to finish.

"Wow," replied Eugene. "Now, that is what you call a vivid dream. Often when I dream, what I see is fragmented and rarely makes any sense. For example, one night, I dreamt that I saw Doctor Greg Colbert looking through a telescope. It was one of the old ones, like what Galileo would look through in his day. After turning my head for one second, Doctor Colbert transformed into this blonde babe . . ."

Geri and Ji hun laughed.

"Now, if you're looking for a vivid dreamer, I am not one of them. But that's interesting, Geri. In 2043, you will head a mission to Jupiter's moon, Europa. And by then, humans would have already made footsteps on Mars. I believe this will happen. Let it be. I'm glad that I will live to see it. My hair white, and my back arched, but I will see it!"

"I wish it could happen sooner," Ji hun added.

"Yes, I'm with you on that one, Ji hun. Right now, we are limited by our technology, because we don't know everything that is yet to be known. Future engineers like Geri will one day do what engineers today cannot."

Geri looked down at his smartphone. "It is 1:15 PM."

Eugene cursed as he jumped from his seat. "What is that professor doing in there? Ugh, look at the time, and he's still in there."

People throughout the lobby heard him. The staff at NASA were not surprised, because they knew Eugene to be that way. Eugene looked back at the students who were looking up at him with stunned faces. "Pardon my French."

Geri, who knew the language, said, "That is French?"

Just then, the Penn State professor returned from the Hubble telescope. And he was walking hurriedly. He approached Eugene.

"I am so sorry about the amount of time I took. I got carried away. I don't get this opportunity every day."

Eugene wanted to punch him in the gut. But he was reminded that he had two young students with him. It would not be good mentorship if Eugene were to resort to violence. So, he retrained himself.

"I hope you found what you were looking for out there," Eugene said with the most cheerful smile he could conjure.

"I think I did. The universe is a wonder. If only all my students back at Penn State could see what I saw."

"Yes," Eugene thought. *"If only all your students could see your googly eyes, you fat . . ."*

"And the resolution is amazing," said the Penn State professor. "I cannot wait until the James Webb is ready. My students and I will have to make a bus trip out of this."

"Yes, do that," Eugene thought, *"on a day that I choose to leave the state."* Eugene turned to Geri and Ji hun. "Let's go." They followed him to the Hubble. Geri turned back to the seating area. He thought he had seen a familiar face among the staff walking by.

At the GFSC, Eugene, Geri, and Ji hun gathered around a computer. Eugene turned to Geri. "I am going to receive new images. They will turn up on this screen."

"What are you looking for?" asked Geri.

Eugene kept his eyes straight. "Yes, I am looking billions of years into the past where there were larger clusters of galaxies. What I'm looking for is the denseness and activity of dark matter. Normally, you will not see the dark matter out there until the interstellar light produced by rogue stars shines on them. I'm also looking at the busiest star- and galaxy-forming periods of our universe's evolutionary history, to see how these galaxies were first formed. And I'm also looking within this galactic region for an Afro-Asian girl named Bora."

Ji hun laughed. That answer got a smile from Geri.

"There is much to be seen in our universe's past," Geri said.

"And there's so much more to discover and learn about the cosmic past. When the JWST comes into use, we'll be able to look even further into our universe's past. Oh, the suspense."

"Some scientists believe that time is an illusion. It sounds like you believe that time is real?"

"Yeah, I believe that time is real. We are constrained or limited by time. It's like our three dimensions of height, depth, and width; we are limited by these."

"I, too, believe that time is real."

"Yes, time is real," agreed Eugene with weariness in his tone. "It'll be interesting to discover what's beyond Planck time, or the space-time beginning."

"What would you do if you were to see darkness?"

Eugene paused for a moment. "I don't know. What would I do if I were to see signs of another universe or another space-time? I'd throw a party, maybe."

"The JWST will answer many . . ."

Just then, the screen on Ji hun's Pixel 5 shone. Then the strangest thing happened. Geri looked around to see everything electronic begin to act strangely.

Eugene turned to those in his company. Speaking out of his frustration, he said, "Please tell me this is not happening." Eugene briefly looked around. "Not on my watch. Oh, come on!"

Eugene blew by Geri and Ji hun to where the others were waiting to use the Hubble. Geri did not go after him. In the lobby were other scientists, educators, researchers, and coordinators. Geri could hear them quarreling over this sudden failure. Out of those that went into a fit, Eugene was the loudest. Though reluctantly, both Geri and Ji hun joined them. Geri looked around and tapped one of the coordinators on the arm. The coordinator turned to Geri.

"Excuse me, Miss. The cause is not in the spacecraft. The cause is down here." The researchers and scientists began to turn in Geri's direction.

The coordinator asked, "You know the problem?"

"I think I do."

Geri turned to Ji hun. "Can I hold your Pixel 5?"

Ji hun handed it to Geri with a look of curiosity.

Geri handed it back. "Could you open it?"

Ji hun did this using the pattern unlock.

Geri held out the device to the coordinator. Eugene drew close to see what he was showing her. "I am looking through his browser, and I see the landing sites . . ." The coordinator held on to the device Geri was holding.

"Can I see this?"

Geri let go, as she looked more intently at the screen.

Eugene drew in.

"This device is supposed to hold no more than 128 gigabytes worth of data," she said. "What I'm seeing is info that has not been made available to the public." She turned to Geri and Ji hun. "How did you end up with this?"

Ji hun shrugged.

"I don't know," Geri replied.

"This is serious," the coordinator said. "How could you not know?"

"I was with them," Eugene jumped to their defense. "These kids are not the sort to do this."

"We still have a problem. We need to know how this kid ended up with this on his phone."

In a mode of frustration, Eugene ran both hands through his hair. "Okay, we'll take him to the board of directors."

Right then, Warren returned, walking side-by-side with a man both Geri and Ji hun knew.

Charles Evans raised both hands. "There you are. It's a quarter to four. I've been looking for both of you. Are you ready to go?"

"Far from it," answered Eugene.

That answer triggered a puzzled look on Charles's face.

"What he meant," the coordinator interjected, "was that we have a lot of questions for them."

"What type of questions?" asked Charles.

"Questions that are having to do with this young man's smartphone. We saw a wealth of information on his phone that hasn't been made public. And we would like to know how all this information ended up on his phone."

Warren turned to Charles. "You don't mind waiting around?"

He shrugged. "It's not like I have a choice."

The controllers from Earth

Later that evening, Geri and Ji hun sat in a small room, in the company of some of NASA's heads in the technology and information departments. Dave Travis, Warren Reed, and Eugene Ellis were also in attendance. Charles Evans, though reluctantly, waited outside. Orville, the chief man in the technology department, grilled the two students with questions about Ji hun's Pixel 5 and what had been found on it. His query came back as void. Neither Ji hun nor Geri had an answer for the latest finds by scientists, and inventions by engineers that turned up on that one device. Neither of the two was there to steal data. For all this data to have turned up on Ji hun's phone had even him wondering. "Who has been using the IMEI number for my Pixel 5?"

"Where did you find this phone?" asked Dave.

"A lady," replied Ji hun.

"And that lady is Mary Wind," Eugene added.

"My guess is that she found this missing phone," Orville said.

"That's what it looks like so far," replied Eugene.

"What you have is a phone that went missing," said Orville. "Mary, from our engineering department, finds it, and now we're wondering how on Earth all this data ended up on this phone." He paused, then continued. "I sense Charles's restlessness. Let him in."

One of the technology department leaders walked to the door, opened it, and motioned for Charles to come in. Charles walked in. It did not take him long to sit on the vacant seat.

"Thank you," he said. "As you would guess, I'm filled with questions."

"So are we," replied Orville. He then looked around at the faces before continuing. "Then, there's the other question: How did this device cause other electronic devices to malfunction?"

"The sixty-four-million-dollar question," said a member from the information department.

"If that were really a sixty-four-million-dollar question, I would be cashing in my millions," Eugene stated as a matter of fact. "This Pixel 5 could not be the cause for the malfunction, no matter how advanced the troublemakers are. If that amount of radiation could be emitted from a handheld device, it would have been felt. Just imagine. That amount of ionization is enough to make our friend sick. He's still standing. No, there's another source affecting the computers around us."

Dave turned to Ji hun. "How are you feeling?"

"I'm fine," Ji hun replied.

"That answers one question," Dave said.

Warren turned to Eugene. "You also have the corruption of computer circuitry caused by positively charged electrons, caused by a stray neutron from a secondary cosmic ray shower. Though this single event could tear at the nucleus of the silicon atom of a RAM, these rays do not harm human cells."

Charles spoke up. "Hello, layperson here."

Warren chuckled. "My apologies, Charles. What I said is that cosmic rays from supernovas happen every now and then. They happen so quickly they could cause our computers to crash. At the same time, they are harmless to our health."

"Does this permanently damage computers?" Charles asked.

"No, it does not," replied Warren. "These are soft errors, as is the case for Ji hun's phone and other devices. So no, it's not permanent."

Eugene turned to Warren. "You are talking about a rear event. We are talking about an event that has happened more than once. There is no coincidence. This led to data popping up on Ji hun's smartphone on more than one occasion. Someone has the use of a nuclear reactor that is being controlled at will."

Warren paused as his eyes widened. "Last night, my father was at Building 29. As the lead custodian for the center, he often walks throughout the center, to be sure that the different exhibits have been cleaned. While walking, he stumbled across a handheld fission reactor."

"A fission reactor?" asked Orville, now wide-eyed.

"A fission reactor. Dad did not touch it. He told me where he found it, but by the time I got there this morning, the reactor was gone."

Orville held his stare. "Who and why?" He turned to Eugene and Geri. "From what you've just told me, this has happened more than once?"

"Yes," confirmed Geri. "This also happened at the house where we stayed." He turned to Ji hun. "Ji hun, did you see anything on your phone that looks like it belongs to a member of the Evans family?"

Ji hun struggled to process the question. Geri repeated in the Gyeongsang dialect. Ji hun replied to Geri, using the same manner of communication. Geri then turned to Orville.

"He says that he saw things on his phone—"

"What did they look like?" interrupted Orville.

"He says, 'like Lisa's personal documents, and pictures from Jasmine's phone'. . . that is one of their daughters."

"Thank you both for being clear, and for being honest." Dave turned to Orville. "It sounds like new technology. We need to call it a day."

Orville looked at Dave before turning to the others. "You're right. We should call it a day. We should be able to sort this out in the morning."

Charles turned to the young students. "Let's go, boys."

"Uh, Charles," Orville raised his index finger. "Could you have Ji hun leave his device behind? for security reasons."

"Security reasons?" shot Charles.

Orville continued, "We'll keep the device locked."

"I could hold it for you if that will give you comfort," offered Warren.

"Or I," said Dave.

"I'm holding the device for these kids. At least they've been around me the most. They've been around me long enough to trust me," said Eugene.

That option received smiles of approval from both Geri and Ji hun.

On Wednesday, October 2nd, Eugene stood in front of a flip chart easel with black marker in hand, doing what he enjoyed most—crunching numbers. Eugene thought, talked, ate, slept, and breathed numbers. Numbers were his life. Those numbers could affect space flight, or even measure distances between space bodies. Space bodies are those light-years away from the Milky Way galaxy and those on a collision course with earth and could arrive in less than fifty years.

In his mind, the numbers sailed in a harmonious and unbroken symphony. Eugene was lost in his craft, while Ji hun's Pixel 5 sat along a ledge untouched by another pair of hands. A sharp knocking on the door alarmed him, throwing off his flow.

"Yes!" shouted Eugene in his annoyance. The door opened, and a head peeped through. Eugene knew this face to be Greg Cobalt's.

"Hiya, Eugene. Did I come at a bad time?"

Eugene's anger abated. "No, for you, it's never a bad time. Please." He beckoned for him to enter.

Greg walked in and walked up to the flip chart that Eugene had in front of him. Greg's eyebrows and mouth arched as he looked over Eugene's math.

"Okay. Well put! But what do you think about this?" Greg picked up a marker from the ledge and began marking on the paper, using his own math skills. Eugene made the same face that Greg had made earlier.

"Okay. Hadn't considered that one, yet."

"Well," said Greg, "I was once your mentor. I was teaching future scientists then, and I am still teaching today."

"You will always hold that pedestal in my mind."

Greg chuckled. "You and I know that our understanding is constantly expanding, just as the universe is constantly expanding. I find myself learning as an old man. There's no telling the limits to which we will go as a civilization. I predict that in another thirty years, we will have traveled past Pluto, past Eris, and into deep space."

"By that time, you will be dead."

"It doesn't matter. Just the thrill of knowing that I am right keeps me up late at night and wakes me hours before dawn. It is my thrill."

Greg was interrupted by a gentle knock.

"Come in!" hollered Eugene.

The door opened, and two young faces appeared. They were Geri and Ji hun.

"Ah, it is good to see you both again," said Greg.

The two smiled and waved at him.

"I was not expecting you both so soon," said Eugene.

"Were you expecting them?" asked Greg.

"You see, the phone that I have on this ledge belongs to him."

"Did he forget it?" asked Greg.

"No. It's a long story."

"Do tell."

"You see, Ji hun lost his Pixel 5 phone on his first visit to the center. We searched. One of the staff from the engineering department found it. Ever since he found it, strange things have happened."

"Like what?" queried Greg.

"Ji hun's smartphone contained data from NASA's central database, important data that has not been made public."

Greg rubbed his chin as he mulled this over. "Interesting."

Geri and Ji hun walked over to the flip chart to look at the math. Ji hun picked up the marker that Greg had put down and started to draw figures on the same paper.

"This is what I'm talking about," said Greg. "As the universe continues to expand, knowledge is increasing. There's no telling the great lengths to which our increased knowledge will take us."

"Now, that increased knowledge could cost us. And there's no telling who has all this data."

Greg's eyes widened. "You are right about what's at stake. Whoever has it, there's no telling what they'll do. But you do have to hand it to this group—whoever they are—for being shrewd. Still, we must find out who they are before something critical happens."

Greg and Eugene turned to the flip chart. They hadn't noticed the makeover the math had undergone. Ji hun, while they were speaking, had added some changes to their math. Both Greg and Eugene arched their eyebrows and mouths.

"Okay," said Greg. "We have another Einstein here."

Eugene turned to Ji hun. "Thanks for this. But the people in the technology department haven't yet sorted through this. It's around 9:00 AM. It's early."

"We will walk around the center for a while," said Geri.

"Good. Do that," Greg agreed.

Geri and Ji hun walked to another building. They found electronics and began to explore that exhibit. Visitors and staff strolled by, some doing what Geri and Ji hun were doing. forty minutes had passed. Geri picked up a remote and pointed it at a screen from ten feet away. Under that screen was a sign, and beside it was a younger man walking by.

"Wait," Geri thought. "I know that face. That's the boy from Russia."

The youth walked on, not knowing that he was being watched. Geri followed. This young man, who Geri believed to be Nikita, walked purposefully to another section. Geri stayed on his tail, but at a distance. Nikita walked on until he came upon a door. He opened it and walked through as though he were given access. When the door closed behind him, Geri stopped and waited for a moment. He then slowly opened the door and peeped around. His eyes were locked with Nikita's. Nikita looked over his shoulder as though he had heard the door when it clicked open. His back was almost completely turned to Geri, so Geri stepped forward. The moment he did, Nikita had on him the look of recognition. He turned and walked on.

Geri called out, "Wait!"

He followed Nikita. As he did, Nikita picked up his pace. Geri picked up his speed. Nikita stopped at the door, opened it, then walked through. The door closed behind him. Geri arrived at the door the moment it closed. He tried it. The door was locked. He attempted to force the door open by rocking the handle, but to no avail.

Geri turned. And the moment he did, he came face to face with a woman's chest. Geri almost bumped into it. He looked up into Mary's face.

"Hi," Mary said with her counterfeit smile. Geri stood frozen, not knowing what to do, nor what would happen next. Then he did what was in his impulse to do.

"Hi," Geri replied.

"How did you get in here?" asked Mary.

"I was following this other kid named Nikita."

"And why were you following this other kid into this restricted area?"

"I was walking to him. Then he ran. Then I ran after him."

"You shouldn't be here."

Mary took hold of Geri's right arm. He felt the tight vice grip of her hand as she walked him down the hall. He felt like the blood circulation in his arm had ceased. As they approached a set of doors, they opened, and in burst Eugene. He looked as if he were searching frantically for someone.

"There you are! You can't split— What are you doing to his arm?"

Mary pushed Geri towards Eugene. "You need to tell these boys that there are places that are off-limits."

Without replying, Eugene turned to Geri. "What were you doing? I saw Ji hun, but you were gone."

"I told her that I saw this other kid, Nikita."

Eugene gave Geri a look. "Russian kid?"

"The one we met the other day."

Mary jumped in, "You both can carry on your conversation in the atrium."

Eugene turned to Mary. "Do you know the kid he's talking about?"

"Of course, I know the kid he's talking about," Mary said in a mocking tone. "He's one of our future scientists."

"Why did he run?" asked Geri.

"I don't know," shot Mary with a tinge of annoyance. Eugene turned Geri's face forward towards the door. "Let's go."

The two walked on, leaving Mary behind.

They walked to the atrium where other staff and visitors were. Ji hun stood solitarily, with his eyes glued to his phone. Eugene saw this and briskly walked towards him.

"If I knew that you were going to do that . . ." Eugene snatched the phone away. "I would have held this phone from you."

Geri reached for the phone. "I want to see this for a minute." Eugene handed him the phone. Geri looked into the files. "I don't see anything from NASA."

"Let me see it." Eugene grabbed the smartphone. He removed his glasses and squinted at the screen. He scrolled the phone's storage. "I don't see anything. Where did everything go?"

"It all makes sense to me," said Geri. "This smartphone was not used to store data permanently, but for a short time until the people controlling this phone could import everything to another device."

Eugene was deadpan as he handed the phone back to Geri. Geri searched the phone's back cover.

"What are you doing now?" asked Eugene.

"I need to open this."

Eugene looked around. "I think I know where to find small tools. Follow me. I'm going into Greg's tool pan."

They followed Eugene to a computer room. Eugene walked directly to a small tool pan under a table, put it on the table, opened it, and shuffled through it for a tool to open the Pixel 5. He found one. Eugene also found a compartment with memory chips and handed Geri the tool. Geri took it and opened the back of the phone. And what he saw shocked him.

"What is it?" asked Eugene.

"The memory card." He slipped it out to show it to Eugene and Ji hun. "I have never seen anything like this before."

"What is it?" asked Eugene.

"The average phone memory card holds up to 64 gigabytes of memory. This memory chip holds 100 terabytes of memory, equal to the most powerful computer in the world."

"What was this doing in Ji hun's phone?"

"I guess someone put it in there. I'm wondering if Lady Windbag is behind this."

Eugene looked into the tool pan compartment with memory chips. He took out one of the chips and held it up. This chip was identical to the one in Ji hun's smartphone.

The door opened and in rushed Nikita. The moment he saw the three, he froze. Time stood still as the three stared back at him. Another person came through the same door behind him. Eugene, Geri, and Ji hun stood ten feet away from Greg and Nikita.

Greg closed the door behind him. "Ah, Eugene, it's strange that I should see you now."

Eugene was visibly stunned. "You have 100 TB chips in your tool pan?"

"Yes, strange that I have them with me."

Eugene said, "Someone secretly slipped one in Ji hun's phone."

The door opened behind Greg and Nikita, and in walked the large-boned brunette.

"I'm that someone."

"I knew it," shouted Eugene. He stared at Greg. "Please, Greg, tell me what's going on."

"I'll tell you what's going on. And, thank you, Mary! What we have could change the world. There are times when we need to get out of our box and join forces with people who could help us move forward."

Eugene held his questioning look. "Who are these people?"

"People with enough resources to move us forward. We are only adding the brains. As people that are driven, there's no limit to what we can accomplish. Eugene, we could use you and your young friends on our team."

"How many people are on this team?" queried Eugene.

"On this side of the world, you're looking at the team. We are collaborating with others in Russia."

"It pains me to learn this of you, Greg, but I must pass."

Greg faked a heavy sigh. "It's too bad. I had a feeling you'd decline."

"You had a feeling that I'd decline?"

"Oh, you are really that honest type. It's one of the reasons why I had to soil your character a little. The Kepler missions . . . your name . . ."

"You did that?"

"Guilty," Greg said with a devious smile.

"Here, I was thinking that Jerry Paulo did it."

"Nope. Yours truly."

"Why?"

"I believe I've already answered your question, Eugene. Just as I've taught you from the beginning, we are nothing more than space dust. We came without purpose. And we will all merge with the space dust and gas from which we came. There's no purpose in this life. Thus, in the little time window that we have in this cosmos, we must find our purpose through our advancement. In this world, there's no time for morals. I've always known you to be a by-the-book kind of guy. I knew that I had to taint your record before the admin a little. If they trusted you less, it'd be more unlikely that they would ever suspect espionage of you or any crooked activity."

"What happens now that the three of us know what you're doing?"

"Oh, that's simple. We're going to erase this from your memory."

"And how are you going to do that?"

In response to Eugene's question, Mary let down a bag from her shoulder and pulled out three gas masks. She gave one to Greg, the other to Nikita, and held the third for herself.

"It's simple," Greg continued. "We are going to release a gas into the air that will help erase all bad memories . . . bad memories like this one."

Eugene rushed towards the door. As he did, he was met by Mary's crossing forearm, which knocked him to the floor. Eugene rolled to his hands and knees to prepare to strike back. As he jumped to take a swing at Mary, she dodged the force of his swing, caught his fist after it passed her, and returned with a crushing elbow to his jaw. She flipped him over, and Eugene was on the floor. Mary then lowered herself to his level and hit him in the face, breaking his glasses. Eugene was dazed from the blow. Greg, Nikita, and Mary slipped their masks on as Geri, and Ji hun stood by helplessly. Mary stood over Eugene. Greg had an unusually small gas tank with him, which was small and light enough to fit into a backpack.

The door behind Greg and Nikita burst open, and a voice shouted.

"Freeze! FBI!"

Six agents dashed in with firearms trained on the three assailants. Soon Greg, Mary, and Nikita were on their faces. Warren Reed and Dave Travis walked in behind the agents. Two other staff members stepped in to aid Eugene.

"Dr. Greg Cobalt," Dave said, "who would have thought that you would go this far and this low?"

"My father tipped me when he saw the fission reactor," Warren said. "He traced it to you. Also, your calls to that research organization in Russia have been traced."

Dave said, "We've always known you to be smarter than this."

Warren said, "But you've been leaving too many breadcrumbs. You've made it too easy for them to find you."

Greg stayed silent, while the FBI took them away.

On Friday, October 5th, Dave and Eugene stepped out of an elevator. They were on the first floor and were heading to the cafeteria. They went to the line and took their foods of choice, before finding an empty table—somewhere visible enough to be spotted by comers.

Dave paused as he sat across from Eugene. Eugene wore a different pair of glasses on a partially bruised face. The glasses he wore two days ago was damaged by a former engineer at NASA. That former engineer would join a former astronomer at NASA in a federal court. Both Cobalt and Wind would now have a big problem on their hands. The student from Russia, Nikita, would be deported back to his country. And the unknown research organization back in Russia had been exposed. They would soon have their share of problems with their government.

Back at the table, inside the cafeteria, Dave observed Eugene's tray. He saw a grilled turkey sandwich on whole wheat, a small bowl of vegetable soup, and a V8 drink. Dave searched Eugene's side of the table for other items and found nothing else.

"Eugene, have you changed your diet? I'm not seeing any of that stuff I'm so used to seeing you eat."

Eugene also looked down at his tray. "I don't have the stomach for that stuff anymore."

"Is this a permanent change to your diet?"

Eugene picked up his turkey sandwich to take a bite. "I don't know. Maybe."

"I gotta say that this is a change worth witnessing. And how's your jaw?"

"I still feel it. I think that woman broke it."

"Sorry," replied Dave.

"What dulls the pain is the fact that Mary is now gone with the wind."

"I'm also sorry about that thing with Cobalt. I would never have seen it coming."

"I'm sorry as well. You think the world of someone until he

shows his true colors. If it is to end this way, so be it. I just don't have the stomach for a lot of the stuff he has taught me anymore."

"Eugene, our world is broken. In our world, people are doing harm to others for the sake of gain. And if you are not at all affected by this, then we are no more than space dust without purpose or reason for living."

Eugene sat in silence as he took this lesson in.

Just then, Geri and Ji hun appeared and stood before them—both with their trays. Dave raised both hands in a welcoming fashion.

"I thought you guys would never come."

After joining them at the table, Geri spoke. "Me and Ji hun were preparing for the winter semester."

"I can't believe you will both be leaving for Massachusetts."

"We will be here until late December."

"And while they're still here, I'll put them both to use," Eugene said with the best smile his jaw would allow. "When I'm done with them, they'll know more than the entire university combined."

"That'll be a training session that I'd love to see."

Dave turned to the approaching figure on his right. He was a young dark-haired man who bore a resemblance to Dave. This newcomer wore a white long-sleeve shirt with a NASA logo and appeared to be not much older than Geri and Ji hun.

Directing the others' attention to this young staff member, Dave said, "Geri, Ji hun, I would like you to meet my nephew. He hopes to become an astronaut."

"Just following in my uncle's footsteps," the young man said.

Dave turned to the group. "Following in my footsteps, he is also enlisted in the army."

"That one I didn't know," said Eugene.

Geri paused to look intently at Dave's nephew. "I didn't get your name,"

"I'm sorry. My name is Bobby Travis."

Hearts of Steel
&
Concrete

O n Tuesday, April 2nd, somewhere east of Savannah, Georgia, a beautiful 20,000 plus square-foot estate sat in the open, surrounded by a semi-circle of trees. This estate overlooked a large body of water. The contemporary structure was a mixture of steel, stone, cedar, and stucco, and few travelers would come across this mansion. Anyone pulling a mile and a quarter from the nearest state route would marvel at its beauty. As lavish and as breathtaking as this estate was, it was also made from the type of material that was durable enough to withstand some of the most destructive forces of nature.

A king-sized bed sat at the center of one of the massive rooms, its occupant still asleep. A hand stretched out from under the white satin sheets, and then a foot. The blinders at the windows automatically slid open, the light of day providing clear signs that it was time to get up. But this occupant paid attention to neither.

A voice on the intercom broke the silence, and this occupant's eyes snapped open.

"Sapphire, it is time to wake up," demanded the voice on the intercom. "Your tutor will be here soon."

Sapphire shot up to a seated position. The fourteen-year-old sat upright with her right arm folded over her eyes, for the daylight was almost blinding. Her disheveled hair was lopped over to the left. It was the dark, kinky, shoulder-length hair that took a considerable amount of time to prep. She sat there in her underwear and vest, waiting for her eyes to adjust to the light.

The intercom spoke again. "Sapphire, are you awake?"

She spoke back to it. "Yes, Dotty, I'm up."

"You should have been up already. And you're still snoozing?"

"I set my snooze for fifteen minutes."

"Fifteen minutes was two hours and fifteen minutes ago."

Sapphire looked around, now concerned about the time. "What time is it?"

"It's 9:30 AM," barked the intercom. "It's almost 9:45. Christopher will be here soon."

Sapphire's eyes widened as she jumped out of bed. She shuffled into her bathrobe as she walked hastily towards her bathroom. She walked onto the beautifully tiled floors of her bath and into the walkthrough shower, which stretched for some fifteen feet. The moment she dropped her bathrobe and stepped onto the base, the warm water gently sprayed her from every direction. As she continued walking, it sprayed more vigorously. The water was now mixed with soap as the spray brushed in a massaging motion. As she continued walking, she was rinsed with pure water. And towards the end, it stopped. Then pressurized air blew from every direction at room temperature. She was thoroughly dried by the time she got to the end. The duration of this shower was one minute and fifteen seconds.

Sapphire stepped out of the shower, took another bathrobe, and covered herself with it. She stepped into her walk-in closet. This was where time stood still. Everything fashionable and ready-to-wear was staring at her. She had to decide and fast.

Sapphire thought of the zodiac sign of Aries, the day and month, and chose the color red. This narrowed her margin of choices for matched the color of her nails. Two was the second day of the month and the second day of the school week. She chose the second red thing that she laid her eyes on, from the second shelf from the entrance. She pulled out a J.Crew spring outfit consisting of a red skirt that fell above her knees, a long-sleeve fashionable shirt with a cross-color of red and neon green. On her feet, she wore neon Nikes. With no time left to do her hair, Sapphire tied a neon green headscarf around her head. She stopped to look down at her hands. They were as perfectly shaped, aligned, and painted as nails could be. Sapphire loves hands almost as much as she does nails. She is drawn to hands, which is why she would often look at people's hands. Hands revealed things about a person—their lifestyle, their situation in life, their character.

A woman dashed into the walk-in closet. This startled Sapphire.

"Dotty!"

"Girl, time is waning. Christopher is at the gate. You need to hurry up."

"I know," Sapphire replied in a singsong voice. "It's not like he's going to turn away from my house and find someone else to tutor."

Dotty sighed before speaking in a calmer tone. "Please, Sapphire, try to understand that Christopher works on a schedule."

Dotty was interrupted by the barking coming from a toy dog. And rushing into the closet and into Sapphire's arms was a black fluffy toy dog.

"Asha! How are you, girl?"

Dotty watched as the little girl and the little dog smothered each other with kisses. Sapphire embraced Asha tightly and rocked her.

Dotty coughed to get Sapphire's attention. "And your father has agreed to a time within Christopher's schedule. Be happy that he comes at 9:45 AM and not 7:00 AM."

Sapphire made a mock sigh. "I know. I know. It's because I like Chris that he has the job."

"Christopher is one of the best speech-and-writing tutors out there."

Sapphire rocked Asha again as she spoke baby talk to her.

Dotty coughed again. "And your parents would have you call him 'Christopher,' for he only answers to this."

Sapphire gave the look of realization. "Yes, because he's British. And, by the way, I love his English accent. Don't you?"

"Yes, I do," replied Dotty.

"I wonder how old he is."

"He once told me that he's twenty-one. In all seriousness, we need to deal with him as the professional that he is. And—"

Another voice came over the intercom. "Hello, Dotty," said a female voice. "Mr. Adams is in the waiting area."

"Thanks, Adrienne." Dotty turned sharply to Sapphire. "He's here. Let's go!"

Sapphire is the youngest daughter of Sheldon and Rachel Lehrer. Sheldon Lehrer is the founder and chief executive officer of LeXo. This multifaceted company provides the clearest resolution in visual technology, imaging, and sound technology. He was listed in Forbes as one of the top ten wealthiest businesspersons in America. Forbes had also listed Lehrer as the wealthiest African American in the country, with a net worth of 9.6 billion. His wife, Rachel, is a fashion design guru with a clothing line that has become a household name: RL. Her clothing line has appeared in every fashion magazine. And Rachel's net worth currently stands at 998.7 million dollars. She is soon to be added to the black billionaire's elite.

Sapphire was born and raised in wealth and privilege. She had never experienced a reality in which she had to be told, "No, you can't have it; it is too expensive," or "You can't go there; it is too costly." Sapphire was provided everything in advance by parents who were too engrossed in their businesses to oversee her. Sapphire's two older brothers, Shemar and Rahim, were off to college and a life absent of their little sister. Sapphire was simply without immediate family, which is why Dotty, the steward, has become the closest thing to family in her life.

Sapphire respects Dotty, who could be as old as her mother. She is a woman who always knew how to comport herself as a professional. As a black woman who came from hard-working parents and blue-collar work history, Dotty demonstrates the maturity and firmness that is fitting for her position as a steward.

Dotty led Sapphire by holding her hand firmly. They were walking to the classroom, where Sapphire would meet with Christopher. The room has the façade of a small library but is large enough to hold over a hundred students. The shelves accommodate books of many different genres. Throughout the room were lounging areas for booklovers, quiet rooms encased with plexiglass for study without interruption, and computer desks that were lined across for online research. In the center of this small library were roundtables, square tables, and smaller versions of these for one-on-one meetings. Christopher sat at one end of one of these little tables. Dotty and Sapphire joined him. Christopher, a handsome-looking figure, smiled as they approached.

"Thanks for waiting. I had to get Sapphire ready."

"Greetings to you, Dotty. That is not a problem. Hello, Sapphire. And how are you this fine day?"

"Hi, and fine." Sapphire smiled.

"Superb. And I understand that you are ready for our next phase in the study of reason and persuasive writing?"

"I believe I am."

"Excellent! I truly believe that our time together will be both illuminating and rejuvenating. And with the hopes that our time will not intersect with or overlap Orvis's math class, we will do all that we can in the interest of time."

Dotty waved her hand. "Thank you, Christopher. Now, if you'll both excuse me. I'll go tend to other things."

"You are most welcome," said Christopher.

An hour later, Christopher and Sapphire sat along a bench that was padded with soft carpet. Sapphire had grown restless and had chosen this spot to continue their lesson. Christopher willingly went along with her choice. At this point, they talked about a speech by the former U.S. president Barack Obama. They were reading his second inauguration speech, as it was transcribed. Sapphire felt engaged with the address and with the writing and felt a part of it. She did not pay much attention to politics, not nearly as much as she did to the things that affect young black Americans.

"I can see that you have taken a liking to his speech."

"Oh yes," replied Sapphire. "He is a very good speaker. I like it when he talks." She stopped to give a deep sigh.

"Is everything alright?"

Sapphire lay on the bench. She rolled over to position herself on her stomach so that she could face Christopher. She stared at him without saying a word.

"Sapphire? Is everything alright?"

She gave another deep sigh as she looked up at him. She kicked her legs upward.

"I love the way you say my name. Could you say it again?"

"Um . . . Sapphire?"

She giggled as she stared at him.

"This is getting a little awkward," he said. "Are you ready to continue?"

"I love your eyes."

Christopher blushed a bright red. "Thank you."

"And I like your hands."

"Why, thank you, Sapphire."

"They look gentle and well kept. There isn't a vein on them."

"Thank you again."

"They're like a woman's hands."

Christopher coughed. "I really don't find that very comforting—"

"Do you have a girlfriend?" she interrupted.

"As a matter of fact, I do," he replied.

"She must be nice."

"Indeed, she is."

"I was saying that . . ."

"Saying what?" he said.

"That we should get together and . . ."

Christopher turned and looked at her with one eye. "I say, aren't you too underage to be discussing these things?"

"No. I'm fourteen. So I'm not underage," Sapphire countered, as she sat up.

"And tell me, why are you not underage?"

"I can tell you that age is only a number. And readiness is only for the first person to decide."

"And why is the first person the only one to determine this?"

"Because too many people are deciding for the few that don't have a voice."

With a look of interest, Christopher asked, "And you have a voice to speak on behalf of all other young teens?"

"No. I'm just saying that society or government . . . whoever they are . . . has decided for everyone what the age is to be married, to drink, to smoke. Look at India and those far countries that marry twelve-year-olds to really old men. Over here, that would never happen, because America has already decided that the age to marry must be twenty."

Christopher stopped and stared at Sapphire for a moment.

"Suppose you were living in . . . say, India or the Middle East, would you have considered marrying a really old man?"

Sapphire contorted her face as though the thought was enough to make her puke. "No!"

"Do you think these children would have chosen them?"

"I don't know!"

He continued. "One thing is certain: it matters little to those adults what those children want. What matters is what those adults want. I do not believe that I need to ask you, but would you marry against your will? In the western world, marriage is for people who the government knows are mature enough and wise enough to make these decisions, and who are not at great risk of getting hurt."

Sapphire stared thoughtfully at Christopher for a moment.

Christopher continued, "In response to your question, yes, I would love to get together with you for ice cream. And if you wish, I will invite my lady to come along."

Sapphire's face lit up. "That'll be great! When do we go?"

"We do want to set a date, for this is what Americans call 'dating.'"

"What do you English people call it?"

"In your case, I call it getting together for ice-cream."

"Can I bring my pet Affenpinscher?"

"Christopher raised his eyebrows. "I don't see why not."

Hard hat

On Wednesday, April 3rd, a building project in Columbia, South Carolina, drew local onlookers. This project would take months to build. Surrounding the construction site were beautiful images of the future building. This business building would then bear the logo LeXo. It would become another landmark for Lehrer and his team, also the first LeXo skyscraper in this city. Blocks away, and in an industrialized area, LeXo recently opened another manufacturing building, where their products would be made.

At the site for the business building, the ground was being cleared and excavated for what would later be a fifty-five-story skyscraper—the tallest building owned by LeXo. Next to this excavation site was the center. At this stage, the gravel had already been laid. The base and foundation walls were established, and the framing erected for the main center. This base was five stories high. Men in orange neon vests, white hard hats, and steel-toe boots plugged through the different types of work. Some poured concrete. Others did the foaming, while others strung lines through the different levels of the building.

It was a busy work-day like the others before it and many others to come. The construction company that had been entrusted with this project was PnC, short for Phillips and Company. The company was named after its founder, Brian Phillips. Because this contractor didn't cover all areas of project building, other responsibilities, such as water and electrical, were entrusted to other contractors. As a general contractor, PnC had yet to provide these additional services. Despite their limitations, they were given significant projects in major cities across the United States. After two decades of service, the teams have been dispatched across the country to take on different projects. To date, PnC has over two thousand construction employees, over five hundred engineering workers, more than two hundred financial specialists, more than fifty IT professionals, and more than thirty architects. Out of this group came their executive team and board of directors. The workers were spread out according to the amount of work, as they tended to run different projects simultaneously.

Brian Phillips first went into the construction business when he lived in Calgary, Alberta. Since 1981, he has taken on many different roles, from a construction worker to management positions. Back then, Brian was working with EllisDon. In 1993, he moved to live with his wife in the state of Montana. In 1994, he launched his company, PnC, which is short for Phillips and Company. Brian started working various trades, such as carpentry, drywall, plumbing, pipefitting, and masonry. He hired others that were gifted in different occupations. They began with small projects. And over time, they took on larger projects. His company had since ballooned from a small contractor to a large corporation. Today, Brian is often seen on-site, not as a man passing by in a suit, but as one of the men walking about in a hard hat and vest, carrying a clipboard. Another distinct quality of Brian is that he is not afraid to get his hands dirty.

The skeletal framework for the free-standing structure was scaled by a tower crane controlled by a certified operator for PnC. He was guided by a construction supervisor.

Colin is an average-looking man with a potbelly, blond mustache, and a mouth that spoke louder and went further than his current status in the management hierarchy would allow. As a man in his mid-thirties, he acted like one with much to prove. He was so performance-based that a relational chasm was created between him and the workers. Colin did and said what was in the interest of his status before his higher-ups. Meanwhile, he cared little about the status of other workers. The worker with little to show for was the one to be pitied most when placed under Colin's supervision. Colin was often the subject of lunch break conversations.

From the fifth floor, Colin held radio as he guided Geoffrey, who then operated the crane. "Steady. Steady. Right there! Hold on! Back up a little. Right there. Hold!" Colin looked around. "Where is he? Tim!"

Patrick, a worker with bulging muscles, stood before Colin and pointed past him. "You don't see him behind you?"

Colin turned to see Tim, a tall, thin, dark-haired, youthful-looking novice with smooth skin. "Okay, daydreamer, I need you to set those boards to the corner, pronto. There's much to be done."

Without a word, Tim took a pallet jack, hoisted the crate with the boards, and did as he was instructed.

Colin spoke into his radio again. "Okay, Geoffrey, you can lower the generator there."

As Colin instructed, the generator was lowered, then settled on a flat surface so the workers could reach it. Colin motioned to Tim gruffly. "Come and help me un-strap this generator."

Tim rushed over to assist him.

When finished, Tim looked around at the rails and drywalls that were being put on the walls and ceilings. He then stared at the workers. His eyes fell on Patrick and on the other workers on that floor. He then turned back to Colin.

"Say, Colin, I've been working here for weeks. I would like to do the boards and drywall."

"You'll get to do the boards and drywalls when I feel that

you're ready. Until you can prove this, I'll have you do the odd stuff."

"I think I've been doing the odd stuff for far too long to not be entrusted with something more."

Colin gave him the look of a skeptic. "You think you're ready?"

"Yes," Tim replied without batting an eyelash.

"You want to be entrusted with more?"

"Yes," Tim replied impulsively. "I feel that I'm trained and competent enough to drywall; if not drywall, then plaster."

Colin stared at Tim for a moment before giving in. "Okay. Here's what I'll have you do." He handed Tim a drywall gun. "Here's what I'll have you do," Colin spoke condescendingly. "You're going to take this gun, position the drywall against the railings, then secure the drywalls while using this gun. Do you need me to show you?"

"I'll be fine," Tim said.

Colin looked on as Tim stepped forward with a drywall board and a handgun. Tim held the drywall gun in his right hand and the drywall in the other. The way Tim held up the drywall awkwardly was enough reason for Colin to put an x in the checkbox for his ability to hold up drywall. Tim leaned the drywall board against the railing wall. He raised it while pressing his left shoulder against it to hold it up. Meanwhile, the board slid against the railings. There was no way it would stay in place if Tim was going to press his shoulder against it.

As Tim leaned against the board with his left shoulder, he held the drywall gun in his right hand. He had a poor visual of the board and the wall where it would be staying. He pressed the nozzle blindly against the board, hoping that the nail would catch the railing on the other side of that board, but it missed. The nail barely grazed the railing, as it appeared on the opposite side of the board. The other men on the floor stopped to observe Tim's failed attempts to work as an expert. Two men struggled to stifle a laugh as they looked on.

Colin spoke, making it known to Tim that he had seen enough. "Please stop."

Tim stopped. The board swung from its position and looked easily removable.

"It's become clear to all that you don't even know what you're doing," said Colin.

Tim attempted to speak, but Colin stopped him with a raised index. "While Patrick was working, did you not even stop to see what he was doing and how the job should be done? Where were you the whole time?"

"Standing by and learning," replied Tim.

"It doesn't look like you have been learning from the pros. If you could just pull your head out from the hole in the ground, you might just learn something."

Tim raised both hands in defense. "Okay, I'm not as polished for a skilled worker."

"You don't even fit the skilled worker category. I don't know where your head is. You need to get your head out of Kalamazoo and come back to Columbus, where the other workers are."

Colin walked over to Tim and grabbed the drywall gun. Just then, the siren sounded. It was their lunch break. The workers shuffled over to their belongings, trying to save every minute and second they could. One group lumbered to the elevator, while others to the stairwell that led to their belongings.

As time rolled into ten minutes past the top of the hour, men were already at their spot of choice. The more reserved and introverted chose their personal vehicles. At the same time, the socialites gathered in their groups and on the floors where they worked. Then there were the few daring workers that sat from the second floor with their feet dangling over the edge. This was a far cry from the famous image from the Great Depression. In it, eleven workers sat on a girder with their feet dangling eight-hundred-and-forty feet from the New York City streets. Times have changed, and safety policies had cracked down on all types of comfort that appeared unsafe.

Tim Douglas sat with a group of four workers on the twenty-eighth floor. They sat on the almost dusted floors, each with his back against the wall. Donnie, a stocky worker with a thick beard, leaned over to Tim.

"Don't worry about it, you'll catch on. As for Colin, no one likes him. It's not the first time he's put someone on the spot."

Patrick, who heard Donnie, also leaned in Tim's direction. "That dude's got inferiority complex issues. Everybody knows this about the supe."

"Yeah," said Donnie. "And that's why he talks to people the way does."

Jordan, a worker with a ponytail tied in a bonnet, chipped in. "Back there, he had to make you look small so that he could look big. It's a shame this man would use you as his punching bag."

"Don't sweat it," Tim replied. "Maybe I haven't been putting my all into this line of work. I'll get it, eventually."

"And soon," said Donnie. "By the way, you've only been here for less than a month. What were you doing before this?"

Tim inhaled, then exhaled. "I was working at an office job. Unlike my work here, in the office, I wore dress shirts, dress shoes, and ties. I worked at an accounting office for five years."

"Why did you leave that job?" asked Jordan.

"Maybe it was me outgrowing my workspace. I had to get out and do something outside the cubicle. So here I am."

"Here you are," Patrick mocked.

"Here we are," echoed Donnie.

Patrick continued, "I've thought about shedding my dusty gear, this loud orange vest, and these big bulky boots to go hide in some cubicle."

Jordan looked as though he were studying Patrick. "Right now, I'm trying to picture that, bro—you in a cubicle."

The foursome broke out into laughter.

Donnie spoke first. "I think we're all wired differently. Unlike Tim, who has only been here for two weeks, you guys and I have been doing this for ages. This is all I know. And I'm fine with things as they are."

"I'm not budging either," added Patrick.

Jordan said, "I don't know how long you plan to be here, but we'll help you get as much as you can from here," Jordan offered.

Tim did not get the chance to reply with a "thank you" before the siren sounded for the second time. Back to work. The men got up from where they were seated, stashed their belongings, and each went back to his work position.

Tim was standing by, watching Jordan position then secure the drywall with his gun. Tim watched as Jordan did this with the fluidity of a seasoned pro with decades of history and the U.S. equivalent to the Great Wall of China under his belt. He worked with ease and rapidity. Tim watched in awe, and he grew more anxious to give the job another try.

Just then, Colin stepped from the elevator and onto the fifth floor. He spoke up so that the men in orange vests could hear. "I need a couple of guys on the ground level. Ronaldo and Tiny!"

The men looked around, wondering who the second person was that Colin was referring to. They knew Ronaldo . . . but Tiny?

Colin shot Tim a look. "I am talking to you."

Tim looked around at the men, then at Colin. "You just called me Tiny."

"Yes, I called you Tiny," Colin said in a condescending tone. "And when I say Tiny, know that I'm referring to you."

Tim and Jordan's eyes met. Jordan gave Tim that I-told-you-so look. With a little hesitance, Tim handed the drywall gun back to Jordan and walked to where Colin and Ronaldo were.

Tim had never had to answer to the name Tiny before. For one, he was not tiny. Tim stood slightly above the average height at six feet. And if there was anyone in the room who did not have the right to call Tim Tiny, it was Colin, who only stood at five-feet-six when he was at his cockiest. Why would Colin have the audacity to call Tim Tiny? Maybe Colin thought about the Dickens character and thought he could label or pin that one on Tim.

Without a word, Tim followed Colin and Ronaldo, who spoke and understood little English, into the elevator.

Tim turned to Colin. "Colin?"

"Yes," Colin said with ready attentiveness.

"I'm going to kindly ask you not to call me Tiny again. I am not Tiny, so I don't—"

"I know your name is not Tiny." Colin interrupted.

"Please don't," Tim said with firmness.

Colin raised both hands. "Okay, I'll stop calling you 'Tiny,' if that makes you happy."

"Thank you."

The sliding doors opened to the ground level. Colin led Tim and Ronaldo away from the building and to the unleveled grounds. He walked to a stop where he saw black plastic bags. He returned with two—one for each.

"The cement trucks will be here in an hour. What I need you to do is simple. Clean up the area until it arrives." Colin walked away without another word.

Twenty minutes later, Tim and Ronaldo were still searching the area, picking up trash from the ground. This was a daunting task for someone who would rather spend hours doing something else. Both Tim and Ronaldo used sticks with pointed ends to pick up the trash, and so avoided having to bend over much.

Tim had his eyes down before he looked up at three persons. It became clear to him that these people had just arrived, and they didn't come to get their hands dirty. One was a big bald African American man in a suit, with broad shoulders and arms that made Tim wonder how he managed to fit them into that suit. He dwarfed his company. The man was accompanied by a black woman with a small frame. The woman was accompanied by a younger version of herself, though they did not appear to be related. To Tim, this one seemed to be about fourteen years old, with attractive features. She was dressed casually in what looked like designer clothes. She also wore a bushy ponytail that went slightly past her shoulders. She held in her arms what looked like a little black fluffy dog. They were all given hard hats, which they put on. Meeting them was the project manager, a man named Kim Thomas.

Tim stole glances at them. They looked influential and important. Tim looked more intently to see the project manager speaking more directly to the woman and the girl, while the big man stood by. If the two are speaking to the project manager, they must have connections to the project itself. Whatever the people involved may have been talking about had nothing to do with him, so Tim turned and continued to pick up trash. He decided to mind his own business. It'd be hours before the day was over, at which time Tim would return home, crash, then prepare to start all over again come dawn.

A shout sounding more like a screech shook Tim out of his focus. The noise came from where the girl stood. Tim turned and saw that she was no longer carrying a little dog. She shouted in a direction. Tim looked and saw fluffy dashing towards the excavator. This machine was known to dig deep into the ground. It could be searching for bones. Fluffy was following her canine instincts when she dashed towards it, hoping to lay claims on one of the dinosaur bones. Just as this toy dog reached the steep incline, she tumbled down the landslide and towards the machine. Tim knew this puppy could get easily lost in that landslide. Being covered in dust and earth, it could easily blend in with the dirt. The operator would not see the toy dog, and as the machine moved, the dog would get caught under the tracks of that massive machine.

Thousands of pounds would quickly turn that toy dog into a slice of pita bread. The girl cried as the dog went down the landslide. Tim could not stand by and watch. He had to do something.

Tim dropped the stick and bag he was holding and dashed towards the landslide. His helmet flew off. He was not going to stop to go back for it. He had a dog to save. Tim came across the steep incline, and the earth gave way as he tumbled down the landslide. He never knew how steep this landslide was until now. This time, he heard other voices, and not just the girl's voice. Tim both felt and heard the thud of arriving at the bottom. He ignored the pain of the fall and jumped to his feet. Tim shuffled around in search of the toy. The excavator was quickly approaching, and as far as his eyes could take him, he only saw dirt. Dirt was moving; it was the earth that came down the landslide. Wherever that dog could be, by now, it would have been buried under piles of sand. Tim jumped in front of the excavator and waved his arms as he shouted. "Stop! Stop!"

The machine stopped. A stunned and curious operator opened his door and stepped onto the platform. "What's going on? Why did you stop me?"

Tim held his hand up. "Just hold . . . I'm looking for a dog."

"A dog?" shot the stunned operator. "Where is that dog?"

"I don't know. It's buried somewhere."

The operator shot his hands up as he turned, resigning to leave Tim alone.

Tim looked around and listened for a whimper but heard none. He dug through the earth frantically. The problem was that he did not know where to search. This dig might take hours, even if other workers were to assist. By the time they got to the toy, it would have already suffocated.

Tim had to act quickly. He did not have his work gloves on him, so he used his bare hands and continued to dig. He got up and ran to where he had landed and dug. He was almost a foot into the earth when he heard the small whimper. Tim stopped, listened, and discovered that the sound was coming from his right. He turned right and dug. And as he searched, something small began to move. Tim dug deeper. Then something small and furry moved under him—the girl's pet. The animal climbed out. A wave of relief washed over Tim's heart. The animal shook itself, almost causing itself to lose balance. The dog lifted its paws at Tim. Tim offered his hand. The pooch sniffed it, then licked it. Tim tussled its head. The dog twirled around several times and shook itself again. Tim lifted it off the ground and proceeded to carry it.

Tim looked up and saw that the climb was too steep. And just as he was about to climb, he saw a two-seater utility vehicle approach. Tim was surprised to see the person behind the wheel. It was the big boss, Brian Phillips.

"Get in, Tim."

"Thanks."

Brian, a man with a raspy voice, looked at the animal Tim was holding. "I can see you got her mutt. Good, you went down to save it."

"Who is that girl?"

"That's Sheldon Lehrer's daughter, Sapphire."

"That explains me putting my neck out to save the dog."

"At least that wasn't a failed attempt. At least the boss's daughter gets to keep her animal."

The utility vehicle climbed the dusty dirt hill with ease. It pulled to where the project manager and the visitors were. The girl stood with hands, overlapping her mouth. Her eyes were bubbling with tears until one broke free and streaked down her right cheek. Tim stepped out of the utility and handed the girl the dog. He then watched the unbreakable reunion between girl and dog.

"Thank you so much." She gave the toy to the woman, then grabbed Tim in a tight embrace.

Tim did not know how to react. He passively patted her back. "You're welcome."

"What is your name?" she asked.

"Timberland. You can call me Tim."

"Okay, Tim."

"What breed is that?"

"She's an Affenpinscher. Her name is Asha. She's only one-year-old."

"That was a gutsy thing you did back there," The woman joined in.

"It was nothing for me." He turned to the girl. "You're Sapphire?"

"Yes. And this is my friend, Dotty."

Tim thought, "This young girl has to be very mature to have friends this mature."

"How old are you?" he asked.

"I will be celebrating my fifteenth birthday next month."

"That will be quite a party."

"I'll have more than two hundred of my friends at my house."

Tim smiled as he now looked at the six-feet-two, muscle-bound shadow in the suit. The man quickly shook his head the moment they met eyes, telling Tim, *"You don't want to meet me."*

He turned his eyes back to Sapphire and Dotty, who offered her hand to Tim. He took it.

"Thank you," she said.

"It's my pleasure. And again . . . it's nothing for me."

Dotty turned to Brian and Kim. "This is Sapphire's first field trip to the site. We never expected her to take her pet."

"She's my pet," defended Sapphire. "People take their pets wherever they go."

"They do not take their pets everywhere," countered Dotty.

"No worries," said Brian. "I used to take my pet Spinone, Freddy, with me on the different sites."

Sapphire turned to Dotty with an I-told-you-so look.

Brian continued, "Had him with me for many years."

Kim jumped in. "That dog is a legend. Wherever people saw

Brian, they would see Freddy. Brian, you had him for more than two decades?"

"Yeah, he's pushing eighteen years now. He's an old boy."

"You mean Freddy's still alive?"

Now excited, Kim followed with a crack.

"He's still alive, alright. Still on all fours till this day."

"No kiddin'?" replied Kim.

"Strong as a bull elephant for his age and as stubborn as one. I tried to keep him indoors 'cause, with age, he's as blind as an ol' bat. He still insists on coming, though."

Kim laughed. "Just like his master. I got to go see that boy."

"Why don't you let him come?" Sapphire asked.

"Keeps bumping into things. Took him out this morning. We came across some steps. Boy tumbled down the steps."

Sapphire reacted. "Oh, no!"

"No worries. There were only three steps. All the reasons why I don't take Freddy on the site anymore. Couldn't stand to see him tumble down ten steps or more at a time."

Dotty raised her forefinger. "Is it one of those shaggy breeds?" Kim decided to answer.

"Oh yes, Freddy is a shaggy type. Now he has that scruffy grey beard. He's the spitting image of his master." Hearing this, Brian smoothed his hand over his scruffy beard.

During this time, Sapphire could not help but notice Brian's hands. There was dirt underneath his short fingernails. His hands were large, strong, and they had small nicks and calluses that were caused by the ravages of hard work. And he had what looked like a splinter in one of his palms. These were the masculine hands that belonged to the natural tough guy, who cared little about much, who would do all he could, no matter how tedious the job was. This group was declining in their numbers, as they are slowly dying out.

Sapphire looked down at Tim's hands—not as big or as rugged as Brian's hands. Before Asha ran off to make friends with the monster in that big hole, whatever Tim was doing, had to be unrelated to his previous job. His hands did not look anything like this line of work. The few cuts and scrapes look more recent. However, he did climb down the hole without gloves to save Asha. Despite this, his hands did look more like office hands.

Sapphire turned to Kim, then to Brian Phillips. She said to Brian, "Could Tim come with us to the next building?"

Brian, almost stumped by the question, said, "Don't see why not."

Just then, Colin returned to the ground level and saw Tim talking to Brian Phillips, Kim Thomas, and the guests. He joined the group, giving Tim a stern look, telling him that he had no business here. Brian turned to Kim, who then turned to Colin.

"Colin, radio Dennis or Norman to come and take Tim's place. Go."

Without a word, Colin walked off as he fumbled with his radio. Brian turned to Tim.

"You can join Kim and the owner's daughter on this walk to building one."

Brian excused himself from the group, turned to Tim, then motioned with his head for him to follow. Tim followed Brian a reasonable distance until they were out of everyone else's earshot. "Take my clipboard with you. As Kim takes the group through the manufacturing building, I want you to make notes on everything that needs to be done."

"Thanks again for hiring me and for entrusting this to me."

"Not a problem. Just don't mess this up." Brian grinned as he slapped the clipboard against Tim's chest.

Tim held on to the clipboard. "It's been two weeks, and some are already saying that I'm incompetent."

Brian turned as he prepared to meet the others. "Don't worry about it, kid. You'll catch on. Who doesn't have a pair of left-hands at something?"

"My pop would thank you for this."

Before taking a step, Brian stood still and sullen over that last sentence. "Yeah, I know he would."

Brian walked off, leaving Tim alone with the clipboard.

Tim was deep in thought as Brian joined the others. He was reminded of his father—an electrician with forty-plus years of service under his belt. He ran his own company—PowerSix— and had worked on different projects with Brian. Tim's father, Tom Douglas, was approaching retirement. At the time, he had only a few days to go before he hung his belt and turned the reigns of the company to one of his lead men. Then the unthinkable happened. Tom was resetting a few fuses at a building's power source when something triggered an explosion. He caught on fire before dying at the scene. This month would be one year since that tragic accident.

Tim opened his tear blurred eyes and saw that Kim and the others were ready to go. He walked on to join them.

Neon vest

Several blocks away, a beige Nissan Rogue pulled up to the driveway of the LeXo manufacturer building, followed by a silver Escalade stretch limo. The limo stopped. Sapphire and Dotty's big shadow got out, walked to the side door, and let them out. They stepped onto the fresh pavement of a new driveway. The employees of LeXo would park in this lot when complete. Inside this newly built manufacturing building, PnC workers walked about in their yellow helmets, and yellow neon vests. Employees of PowerSix, Tom's former company, wore their blue neon vests, as they took care of the electrical components. A painter company, with men wearing white painter hats and clothes, came in to do paint jobs at the office. Inside the factory was where the heavy work was.

The painters had already finished painting this factory. The white finish of the walls, ceiling, and floors gave this factory that clean look. This was where the machines were being created. They were designed accordingly. There would be a total of one-hundred-fifteen machines, made for different purposes. These would be used to create the most advanced and up-to-date equipment in sound and visual. This was where mechanical engineers and IT professionals went to work.

Kim Thomas led the three, and Tim followed with a clipboard in hand. They were greeted by black turf carpet somewhere between the outside entrance, and the inside access to the factory. The floors throughout were spotlessly clean, so much that a loose piece of paper thrown on the floor would be frowned upon. On the floor, the clicking of shoes was heard. These were not footwear that either Sapphire or Dotty was wearing. The clicking on the solid floors came from Kim's steel-toed shoes and two other agents walking towards them.

"Mr. Kim."

"Mr. Jack and Mr. Ben. How are things?"

"Not bad," Ben said. "You got company?"

Ben Rogers is the chief strategy officer, and Jack Tipperton is the chief information officer for PnC. While Ben was heavily involved in the planning, Jack had been the intelligence to the public, even via web media.

"Jack and Ben, I would like you to meet Mr. Lehrer's daughter, Sapphire, and one of his aids, Dotty." The four greeted each other formally.

Jack spoke as though he were talking to a five-year-old. "And, Sapphire, what are you hoping to get from this field trip?"

"Information, I guess," Sapphire said, wondering if there could possibly be a better answer than this.

"Information," repeated Jack. "That is my area. If there is anything that I could do to help you out, you just name it. We are here for you."

Sapphire smiled, not knowing how to answer this.

Kim turned to Sapphire and Dotty. "Could you excuse us for a moment?"

"Sure," they said simultaneously. Sapphire, Dotty, and their chauffeur turned to leave the group. Sapphire tugged on Tim's shirt as she invited him to follow her. He did. She continued to stroke Asha's head. The dog looked like Sapphire had taken the time to groom her on their drive to the factory. Tim reached down and stroked her head.

"I see you've cleaned her up."

"I did on our way here."

"Her coat is black once more. Doesn't look like the one I dug up earlier."

Sapphire smiled. "Yes. Again, I want to thank you for saving her."

Tim smiled. "You're welcome."

"Tim . . ." Sapphire paused, "you don't look like a construction worker."

"Am I that out of place?"

"I'm jus' sayin'."

"What do I look like to you? I wouldn't be surprised if you guessed right."

Sapphire pressed her forefinger against her lower lip. "You look like a store clerk."

Tim's eyes popped in surprise. "A store clerk?"

"Yes, because you're a tall, lanky white kid. How old are you?"

"I don't mean to answer a question with a question, but how old do I look?"

"Fifty-five."

"What?" shot Tim.

"Gotcha!" Sapphire said, pointing her index finger at him.

Tim chuckled.

"Okay, I'm serious. You're twenty-one."

"Not bad! I'm twenty-six."

"Wow, you're that ancient?"

"Come on, Saph, twenty-six is not that old."

"Just kiddin'. For you to be around that long, what were you doing before?"

"I was a finance accountant for a financial company."

"Wow, interesting. That explains your hands."

Tim looked down at his hands. "What of my hands?"

"They're softer than the average construction worker's hands. They're not dry, crusty, or chipped. The nails are aligned. They don't look like you've been here for long."

Tim raised his eyebrows. "Wow, my hands have given me away."

"How did you end up here?"

"Interesting story. And in a way not so interesting."

"I'll determine that," Sapphire said.

Tim laughed. "Okay, I did accounting for five years. I sat in front of a desk much of the day."

"Wow," Sapphire said without another word.

Tim continued. "As you would guess, I was bored after five years. I grew uninterested in my job. Then something happened: they fired me. I was without a job for a while."

"Oh, no!" Sapphire reacted.

"I went in search for different jobs. No one hired me. I was depressed. My father had me working with him, doing something that I was not good at. He then told me about Brian's company. I said that I would give it a try. He tried to convince Brian to hire me. During that time, Brian was cutting back on his workers. They weren't taking anyone but ITs and engineers at that time. I slumped back into depression. Then the worst thing that could ever happen . . ."

Tim paused and inhaled deeply, then exhaled.

"My father died in an accident."

Sapphire overlapped her hands on her mouth.

"I don't know how it happened. The fire marshal told us that it was caused by an explosion."

Sapphire spoke with sorrow. "I'm so sorry!"

"Thanks."

"You were unemployed, and now without a father."

"After he died, I continued to fall down a financial hole."

"When did your father die?"

"A year ago. As you can guess, this dragged me deeper into depression."

"How did you get over that?"

"Prayer was helpful."

Sapphire obviously wasn't expecting this answer. "Prayer?"

"Experiencing the peace that Jesus promised helped. Then came the open door for employment, which came through PnC."

"When did this company hire you?"

"Two weeks ago."

"It sounds like Brian knew your father. How did he take it?"

"Very hard. He was my dad's brother-in-law. Brian is my uncle."

Sapphire gave Tim the look of realization.

"You don't look related."

"I don't know how related we are supposed to look."

"I don't know. Same eyes, same hair . . . You certainly don't have the same hands."

Tim looked at his hands again. "He's my mother's older brother. I would guess that I have my mother's hands . . . in a way."

"What do you do in construction?"

"I'm trying to learn everything—to see where I fit most."

"Do you know where you fit?"

"Nope."

"No?"

"No. I like the idea of building things. But I feel myself leaning in another direction."

"Where?"

"I've been thinking about my father's death. Lately, I've been taking courses to join the fire department."

Sapphire's eyebrows arched. "Ooh, Mr. Fireman," Sapphire playfully poked Tim's chest. "Mr. Fireman, put out the fire, man."

Tim laughed. "Brian has friends in the fire department. I'm hoping to speak to them."

At that moment, Kim, Jack, and Ben returned.

Sapphire looked down at Kim's hands. For masculine hands, the skin was well proportioned with medium-length fingernails. These nails were almost perfectly trimmed, without an ounce of dirt under them. They looked like hands that hadn't seen hard work in decades. They didn't look like hands that had seen a pen or keyboard in months. She looked at Jack's hands. Like Kim's, there weren't any dry spots on them. The fingernails were low-trimmed except for the pinky fingers, which were so long they had begun to curve downward. What stood out most on Jack's hands were the tattooed Jewish star on the back of both hands. Sapphire looked at Ben's hands and what she saw mortified her. They were dry to the point where they had begun to chip in seven thousand different places. The fingernails were chewed off, even past the fingertips. And the fingers looked like Ben had started chewing on them after the nails were gone. These looked like hands with work history, even though they didn't appear dirty. Almost blurred at the back of his hands were tattooed writings that were too illegible to read.

Sapphire drew her own interpretation while looking at these three pairs of hands. Kim was a clean-cut individual who cared about not only his appearance but also his status. He seemed to claw at every opportunity he could get to boost his standing. Jack was not like that. He cared about his appearance. He obviously came from a proud Jewish heritage by the tattoo markings on the back of his hands. Sapphire tried to understand what was up with his pinkies. Jack appeared to be the type to not reveal his intentions until the last minute. Either that or Jack would grab at everything that others would leave behind. He would take the thing that appeared to be small and insignificant and transform it into a giant. Ben looked like one with much on his mind, most of which was not work-related. He was burdened with many worries and many regrets. He seemed to have given up. Sapphire wondered if Ben had seen his hands as of late.

"Thanks for your patience," said Kim. "Jack just told me about the public responses to this project. Most are good responses on Twitter, in the comment section and at the bottom of our webpage on LeXo . . ."

Sapphire interrupted. "Good responses on what?"

"Good question. The good responses are for LeXo and their advanced equipment, and the prospect of having a LeXo in town."

Sapphire looked dissatisfied. "I'm interested in bad responses."

Jack laughed, attempting to minimize this response.

"They're not that bad. You only have a few that are still on the old prehistoric hardware and are miffed over the 'consumerism.' There's nothing to be worried about. Yes, new things cost money. Meanwhile, there's always the need to advance. Simply, there's a supply; subsequently, there's a demand. Your father's company supplies." Jack then squinted one of his eyes at Sapphire. "Is any of this making any sense to you?"

"Yes."

Sapphire could not put her finger on it. There was something about this Jack Tipperton that she did not like. There was an aura of phony about him that she did not want to be around for long.

What part of the public responses had gotten her attention? The answers that said that the public wanted what LeXo had to offer were fair. Those comments outweighed the bad comments. That's what mattered, right?

"Sapphire," Dotty waved in her face to get her attention.

"Yes?"

"Are you okay? You were lost for a moment."

"Oh, okay."

"Kim just asked if you are ready."

Sapphire looked around and saw all eyes on her. She smiled faintly. "Yes, I'm ready."

Kim and the company parted ways with Ben and Jack. He led Sapphire and the others to the different machines, where engineers and IT specialists were still working. They were working on the machines. Employees of LeXo came to test the engines. Sapphire and Dotty approached and asked questions. This was important for Sapphire. In a decade, she would be co-owner of LeXo. She would make critical decisions. On this field trip, she was seeing through the eyes of a consumer who was no different from the thousands of other consumers. These may never get the chance to meet Sheldon Lehrer in their lifetime. She was the daughter of the renowned billionaire, and yet no different from the average consumer.

Sapphire thought about Tim, who was Brian Phillips's nephew. If Tim wanted, he could push to become the heir apparent to his uncle and make PnC his own. Tim was thinking about his contribution to society rather than a goal to claw his way to the top. A firefighter? What did that have to do with PnC? Could Brian hire firemen as insurance in case something terrible happened? Tim's aspirations had nothing to do with PnC. It was a career path with other people in mind. Tim's father had died. What Tim hoped to do could never bring him back, but others may find themselves in a situation like his father was in. Tim hoped to save them—complete strangers. What profit would this bring to Tim, other than knowing that he had saved someone from a burning building? Certainly not money.

"Sapphire."

Sapphire turned.

Dotty touched her shoulder gently. "Are you okay?" Dotty asked, now with a concerned look.

"I'm alright," Sapphire said apace, with hopes that Dotty would not ask again.

"Okay," said Dotty. "I hope you got all of what Andre, the IT, said."

"I got it all," lied Sapphire. "Can we stop for today? I want to go where my dad is."

Everyone stopped with puzzled looks.

"Are you sure you don't want to see the other machines?" Dotty asked.

"I got all that." Sapphire didn't have to lie then. "I know what I'm going to see. I want to go now."

Dotty turned to their driver. "We'll be outside in a minute."

The big man in the suit turned and headed to the exit.

Just then, Tim returned after scouting the new facility, with a clipboard, paper, and pen. Sapphire walked over to him with her eyes on the paper.

"That's a lot of writing."

"Nothing that can't be corrected," said Tim. "There were a few things that our people brought to my attention. A few other things I found. Nothing to be alarmed about."

"I believe you," Sapphire said as she turned.

After only knowing Tim a little, Sapphire felt that she could trust him. He was the person that stuck his neck out to save her dog. Tim had shared with her his hopes to become a firefighter, which involved rescuing people. If Tim was so eager to protect people, what he said to her could be trusted.

Tim had searched the new manufacturing building for small problems, just as he had said. But what Tim did not tell Sapphire was that he had also found another problem in the building, and this problem was too big to be called human error.

Steel-toed boots

On Thursday, April 4th, the construction crew for PnC cleared the way at the main building for the window company to install windows. The workers for PnC knew that the window company would be around for a while, especially since the fifty-five-story skeleton for the skyscraper was finally up. The glass would be the beatifying feature of this skyscraper. The PnC workers knew that the window crew roles would now be front and center. So, while PnC had workers on the different floors of the five-story building, others were outside with the cement trucks.

At 10:35 AM, Brian stood by the cement truck as its cement mixer stirred the mortar for the concrete. The front of the main building was already paved, from the driveway to the visitor's parking. The hardened concrete stopped at the back where the men stood. The drum turned on the cement truck as the driver prepared to pour its contents onto the empty space where Brian and the others stood.

Patrick pushed a wheelbarrow towards where Brian stood, with his hands held firmly against its handles. His tight grip caused his veins to pop and muscle definition to show on his massive biceps. The wheelbarrow, which had a three to four hundred kilogram capacity, bore a weight that surpassed its limit. Patrick believed that this tool could hold a mountain of gravel, while others doubted. As he pushed the mountain towards Brian, Colin and the others watched, speechless. Brian stood with a shovel in hand and watched as Patrick approached.

"Making one trip out of two?"

"Yeah!" Patrick stopped.

"You just pushed close to eight-hundred pounds up the slope."

"Missed my workout this morning."

"Good. Go ahead and dump it into the hole, Patrick."

Immediately, Patrick heaved and turned the contents of the wheelbarrow into the two-foot groove where Brian stood. Brian then used his shovel to even out the gravel inside the slot.

"Need more gravel."

Patrick turned as he said, "I got it."

Brian then turned to Colin. "Call a few others. There are other wheelbarrows. We need to get this done."

Colin walked off in search of others. Fifteen minutes later,

Patrick returned with his third mountain of gravel. Behind him were three other workers holding onto wheelbarrow handles, while pushing their own piles. None of the other workers dared try to create a mountain. One worker leveled the gravel at its brim. The other two workers took less. One of these workers was Tim Douglas. He lagged while the others were ahead. On two occasions, Tim's barrow with gravel tipped over, because he couldn't hold it up. The second time, he had tumbled over with it. He got up quickly, hoping that the others had not seen. This would become the subject of a parody. Tim struggled up the hill as he attempted to catch up with the others.

The three arrived at the stop and dumped their contents into the groove where Brian stood. After one more trip, he motioned to the four to stop for a while. Brian then turned to Colin.

"Grab a shovel and help me out." Though reluctant, Colin did as he was told.

The others watched as the two bosses pushed through the gravel. As they watched, they noticed that for Brian, this work was second nature. He had to be almost twice Colin's age. Brian did the task effortlessly. For Colin, it was a different story. His forehead broke out in a sweat. Soon, his shirt was soaked, and streaks of liquid poured down to the seat of his pants. Colin huffed and puffed, as he struggled through his potbelly and the three hamburgers he had the previous day, to get through to the gravel. He frequently stopped to take breathers, and to arch his back, maybe because he felt it. For the workers that watched, this scene was almost comical, a subject for a parody. Few muffled their laughs, hoping that the bosses did not hear them.

The two finally stopped, and Brian motioned to the truck driver to pour the cement.

At that moment, two figures approached. One was Kim Thomas, and the other was Jack Tipperton. They wore white hard hats as the workers did. They only stood out by their usual gear of suit and tie.

Unlike Brian, the workers would only see these men on the occasion of a worker's meeting and on the day of a project's completion. Thomas and Tipperton approached Brian with the knowledge of a visit from someone important. Brian pulled a dry rag from his back pocket and dried his forehead. The moment Jack saw Colin, he smiled fiendishly.

"I see you've gotten some much-needed exercise out of this, Colin. Just a few more crunches, and you'll be looking like Patrick."

Those that heard it laughed. Colin only smiled sheepishly.

Kim turned to Brian. "You don't think that the window company came a little early?"

"I think they should come."

Jack squeezed through. "You sure about this, Bry? Even Ben claims that with the rocks flying, it isn't good timing for the window company."

"In case you forgot, Lehrer is putting the squeeze on our operation. They want to hasten the project."

Kim spoke more directly to Brian. "Brian, you and I know that this is a recipe for disaster. We need to cover a lot before they call on the window company to come in."

"Not my call," said Brian. "Mr. Lehrer insisted on it."

"Speaking of Mr. Lehrer, the man will be here soon."

Brian shot his arms up in disbelief. "Ah, come on! Couldn't he even tell me ahead of time? This man suddenly decides to pop in!"

"I'm not liking this either. But it sounds like Mr. Lehrer wants us to follow his timeline to the tee."

Out of anger and frustration, Brian dashed his shovel on the dusted ground, causing the tip of the shovel to bend. It bounced and landed at Tim's feet.

They all turned to see an entourage of men approaching in suits. Two out of the six approaching figures were the size of NFL centers. These two would have successfully guarded Matt Ryan against a barrage of linebackers. The other four men were average-sized but built. And, by the creased looks on their faces, they looked as if they could hold their own in any street fight. As an act of courtesy, and a response to the protocol, the six wore white hard hats, just as the workers on site did. Only the seventh man did not wear a hard hat. This man led the pack, and Brian knew this man to be Sheldon Lehrer.

Brian stepped ahead of the others to meet with Sheldon. He grabbed his clipboard as Sheldon drew closer. By the time they were a foot from each other, neither offered a hand.

"By the look on your face, I can tell you weren't expecting me."

"Good perception," replied Brian.

"I decided to pop by and see your progress."

"I've already told you where we are."

"I need to see it for myself."

"Got no issue with that."

"I also came to see another party that will be working around the same time as you."

"You had Kim send for them. And, as you've requested, they're inside the building."

"I also have to tell you that you and Kim will need to expedite this project with a new finish date. By December of next year, my skyscraper should be up."

"No can do."

Sheldon raised an eyebrow. "Why not?"

"We've already set a date for April, three years from today."

"And I am asking for a new projected date."

"Listen, three years is my crew on steroids. You're now asking for the impossible. Why the urgency?"

"I don't think that's any of your business."

Brian stopped and dropped his head for a moment. "Right, it's none of my business. The problem is that you made this project my business. I'm telling you what's my business, and that's what happens on this site." Brian shouted as he pointed at Tim. "Every worker you see on this site is my business! Every piece of equipment that we've paid for is my business! When something breaks down, or one of my crew gets injured, it's my business!"

Sheldon calmly took a white handkerchief from his pocket and wiped the string of saliva from his tie. He looked down at Brian's right forearm. On his arm was a tattoo depicting an open book with fine writing and laid on top of that book was an automatic pistol. To Sheldon, the image looked much like a Bible.

"I can tell by the look of your tattoo that you are Bible-belt religious?"

"'Bible-belt religious' is not how I describe myself. If I could speak for myself, I am a follower of Christ."

"A follower of Christ," Sheldon said mockingly. "I couldn't tell the difference between followers of Christ and Bible-belt religious folk if you paid me. Maybe because I don't think much of either."

"You don't surprise me, Mr. Lehrer."

"I told you before, call me Sheldon."

"Sure . . . Sheldon. You don't think much of either, yet you brought it up. It sounds like you don't think too highly of Bible-belt religious folk."

"You guessed right."

"And why is that?"

"Bible-belt religious folk are some of the most stubborn of land animals. You ask a simple thing of them, and there's no compromise."

Brian turned and looked at Kim before turning back to Sheldon. "That's it?"

"Even you know that's never it. There is a dozen."

Brian took one step towards Sheldon. "Like what?"

"I never came here to talk about religion. It's time-consuming, and it destroys communities."

"I'll tell you what destroys communities," shot Brian. "Arrogant people destroy communities. Men, whose heads are too large to fit inside a hard hat, destroy communities. Religious or not, they destroy communities. Do you have another thing that miffs you about religious people?"

Sheldon took two steps back. "I'm done here. You've heard my request. You have until December of next year to complete this project. If it is not completed by then, know that this will be your last project with LeXo or any company. I'll see to that."

As Sheldon said this, he turned and headed back the same way he came. His six shadows followed. Brian and his crew stared at them as they headed to their vehicles. These visitors had come with a mission to see Brian Phillips and his company. The window company, Brian noticed, had been forgotten. The truth was that the window company did not have the central role in this project. That explained why Sheldon only came to see Brian. Brian's team would determine the pace of this project. The pressure was now on Brian to build a fifty-five-story building in one year and eight months. This was a project that would typically take three to four years to complete.

As the vehicles disappeared, Kim said, "This is crazy! There is no way that we can do this in only one year and eight months. This is insane."

Brian did not turn in Kim's direction but held his stare at the spots where Sheldon's cars were parked. "It's insane, but we're going to get as many bodies as we can to do this."

Both Kim and Jack gave Brian looks of disbelief. "You are serious?" asked Kim.

"I am," Brian replied.

"This is madness," Jack said. "How can we possibly build a fifty-five-story skyscraper in less than two years?"

Kim took one step in Brian's direction. "I'm telling you, if you were to speak to Ben, he would call this madness. We will be ruined as a company."

"It is madness. And that is why we are going to attempt it." Brian turned and walked away. The team, the crew, and Tim stared at Brian as he headed in the direction of his utility vehicle. He stepped in, started it, and drove into the dusty distance.

Tim now knew what would be expected of PnC. His uncle would need all the help he could get to finish this project at an earlier date. Tim had his sights set on embarking on a new career as a firefighter, but now he was considering putting his plan to leave on hold. Brian required all the manpower. He needed his nephew now more than ever. And with what Tim knew about the manufacturing building, Brian would need his nephew in more ways than he could imagine.

On Friday, April 5th, east of Savannah, Georgia, a beautiful twenty-thousand-feet estate sat looking over a large body of water. At 12:30 PM, and after Sapphire's break time, she would return to Orvis for round two of their math lesson. Orvis was as humble as he was knowledgeable. He was knowledgeable to the point where he put Sapphire to sleep with his knowledge. Orvis was young—only twenty-five—and a good-looking African American behind a crooked pair of glasses that needed fixing or replacing. Orvis would have been an interesting person to Sapphire had he not been so geeky.

Sapphire was about to join Orvis in her library when her phone chimed. She pulled it out and looked at the screen. The name was Tim Douglas.

"Orvis, I need to answer this. Thank you!" She stole away without allowing Orvis to respond. She slid the screen to the green icon. "Hello?"

"Hi, Sapphire?"

"Oh, hi," Sapphire's face lit up. "You're calling me now? I thought you're at work."

"It's my lunch break. I hope that's not a problem on your end?"

"No, it's not."

"That's good. I was meaning to ask how you're doing. Since breaking away to see your father, I haven't seen you."

"I'm fine," Sapphire said, ill at ease.

"I hope you caught up with your dad that evening."

For a moment, there was silence on the phone. "Not really."

Tim's heart sank. "I'm really sorry, Sapphire. Did you see him at all yesterday?"

"Last night." She said nothing more.

Tim felt that he shouldn't probe any further. "I understand that this meeting had to be short."

She gave no reply.

Tim knew the silence and what it meant. Already, he was able to envision Sapphire's meeting with her father the night before. Anxious to see him, she had rushed in his direction. As enthused as she was about their engagement, Sheldon did not share the same emotion. While she embraced him tightly, he squeezed her a little, reached for her head, and pecked it before pulling away to something more pressing on his mind.

The meeting in question had to have been a real disappointment to her, which explained her silence.

"I don't know what he was doing or where he was going. I only know that he didn't look happy."

"I think I know why he wasn't happy." Tim left his answer in the air, hoping that Sapphire would reach for it.

"What happened?"

"I checked our website last night. They're talking about the false report on the forty-story residential PnC built in Atlanta, Georgia."

What does that have to do with my father?"

"I think he read it."

"Um, you lost me."

"Your father read a false report about the forty-story building on our website. It wasn't built in one year. That took two years and five months to build. And that building did not have some of the special things your father's fifty-five-story building will have."

"You think my father saw that?"

"Why would he ask my uncle to build his skyscraper in one year and eight months? Someone saw the story on the forty-story building and pointed it out to my uncle. Well, Brian was not happy. Yesterday, he had someone correct it on our website. Now it says, 'two years and five months.' Brian fired Jack and gave someone else his job."

Tim did not get a response from Sapphire then. He could almost hear her cup her hand over her mouth.

"Are you still there?"

"Yes. My father wanted your uncle to build his building in less time?"

"Yes. Sheldon demanded this from Brian. Brian told Sheldon that it can't be done. Sheldon then threatened Brian. When Sheldon went home, someone must have told him that what PnC did on that forty-story building was false."

"You mean that it was a hoax?"

"If you want to call it that, then that's what it is. I'm now wondering if the pressure is still on."

"I don't know." Sapphire shrugged. "You're asking the wrong person."

Tim smiled faintly. "Yes, I understand. I thought I should pass that on to you."

"Thanks."

"Take care, Saff."

"Bye."

Safety glasses

Time went by. April eventually gave way to May, then to the summer months, which led into fall, then to the colder months. The time clock rolled into the New Year. It wasn't long before the crew for PnC saw another April. Then the intervening moments went by. The team was into the late of November before they knew it.

On Wednesday, November 25th, at 11:00 AM, Brian stared upwards. Kim joined him as they looked from the paved sidewalk to the top of the almost fifty-five-story building. The sturdy structure stood firm and free as the glass reflected the sun's light. The reflections of other buildings were seen from the ground up to the eighth floor. Not only was the window company not finished, but there was also much left to be done on the upper floors. Brian and Kim looked up at the incomplete building and wondered what Sheldon's reaction would be.

Since the reports on the forty-story residential came out to be false, Brian had not seen or heard from Sheldon. He did not share what he had learned with Brian. To Brian, it was apparent. He couldn't see Sheldon conceding to anything, so the pressure to complete this project by December of this year might still be on. But from what Brian and Kim were seeing, the project would not be finished by then.

It had been more than a year since Jack Tipperton was terminated. Since then, another problem emerged, in that several mishaps delayed PnC's operation. Two tower cranes malfunctioned while working on the skyscraper; an incident happened on the site that almost caused a fatality. An electric blowout occurred at the center; on two occasions, there was a flood at the factory and near the electronic equipment. And then there were the fire and explosion hazards that Tim pointed out to Brian. The last-minute decision to fix these problems helped prevent those dangers from happening, but also set the project back and slowed their progress. Even with the increased number of workers, Brian and Kim had seen this project fall back.

Brian and Kim looked up at the floors the glass company had yet to finish. "I wouldn't worry about it."

For a moment, Brian turned to Kim. "Who said anything about worry?"

"I'm only saying," replied Kim, "that I think they'll be finished by next April."

"Everything should be done by April," corrected Brian.

"What I find interesting," said Kim, "is that the false report put out by Jack on our website is becoming more believable."

Brian smirked. "While firing him is becoming less noble."

Kim reached into his jacket pocket and pulled out an electronic device shaped like a pen. He held that silver pen against his mouth and pressed a mounted green button. The grey fumes that this electronic device projected gave off a minty scent. Brian thought about the peppermint tea leaves that suddenly sprouted throughout his backyard.

"I wonder about the government and why e-cigarettes are not yet illegal. These sticks are more toxic than traditional cigarettes."

"I wouldn't know," replied Brian. "I quit smoking six years ago."

"Good for you," replied Kim. "That saves you the burden of a new and more dreadful addiction."

The two stood blissfully, not noticing the two men that stood beside them. One of them coughed, and Brian and Kim turned to the men standing by them. They were Hispanic. Both had an olive complexion and wore jackets. The slightly darker complexioned man was larger than the other and looked much like Dwayne Johnson. The smaller one with a fairer skin spoke first.

"Mr. Phillips?"

"Who's asking?" Brian asked.

"Hi, I'm Ulysses Antúnez. And I am here on behalf of Sheldon Lehrer."

Ulysses extended his hand to Brian, who did not take it. Ulysses looked down at his own hand with a look of wonder at being snubbed. He looked up at Brian. "Sheldon cautioned me that you would not be happy to see me. And I under—"

"What are you here to tell me?" Brian interrupted.

Ulysses cleared his throat. "On behalf of Mr. Lehrer, I am here to inform you that there has been a change to the deadline—"

"Change to the deadline?" interrupted Kim. "What do you mean a change to the deadline?"

"It means what it says," countered Ulysses.

Brian spoke. "The truth is that this should be coming from our end, not from the owner. A new deadline hasn't been agreed on."

"Yes," answered Ulysses. "But I'm here to inform you that the deadline has been pushed to February of next year."

"February of next year?" asked Kim, now flummoxed over the audacity of Sheldon Lehrer. "Well, now that's quite generous of him," Kim said sardonically.

Brian stepped forward and pointed his fore and middle fingers at Ulysses' chest. The Dwayne Johnson look-a-like stepped forward to intervene. Soon, a bunch of figures in hard hats and neon vests emerged, and Ulysses and his companion were surrounded.

"You go and tell that boss of yours that there are no boys in this business," Brian demanded. "If he wants to do business with me, he needs to get out of hiding and talk to me like a man. No dates are set without the project manager or me knowing about it."

Ulysses straightened his jacket. "Then it sounds like you have a later date in mind? What do you want me to—"

"I want you to tell him to talk to me!"

"Would you like him to call you?"

"I don't care! Then tell him to call me."

Ulysses stepped back. "As you wish. I will have him call you ASAP. Sorry to bother you."

Brian and Kim turned from their visitors as they walked away. The workers on the site dispersed, then Kim faced Brian.

"He's asking us to cut it close. Things tend to slow down during the colder months. I would guess that what the project manager has to say doesn't matter anymore."

"You're running the operation here." Kim rubbed the back of his neck. "I think there's more to my job than what happens on the different projects. I think I'm losing touch, especially with

Mr. Lehrer opening his mouth. Who'd ever think the wealthiest African American would be so arrogant?"

"The truth, Kim, is that's human nature for you. It can happen to the best of us. Somewhere in the Bible, it tells us to guard our hearts. Out of it flow the issues of life."

Kim smiled with a thumb up. "True to the Bible, as always."

"With my words, I think I've made it clear that I haven't always been true to the Bible. That's why I'm thankful for grace. And that is why I'm a follower of Christ. And as a follower of Christ, I don't want to take His grace for granted. I want to guard my heart always because the same cares that have taken hold of Sheldon's heart could also take hold of mine."

"Well said," Kim replied. "Speaking of cares, I've been making a lot of preparations for that hospital that we're going to build in Richmond, Virginia."

"I can see you've been busy. That's why I've been pitching in every way I can, even with the physical work," said Brian.

"How old are you again? Sixty-two? And you're as tough as flint. This may take a toll on you later. I'm fifty-one. It's been countless years since I've last touched an iron bar, pushed a wheelbarrow, or dug with a shovel."

"What do you do at home?"

"I pay others to do it." Kim grinned.

"I see you're living the dream."

"You think Sheldon will call you? It's unlikely he'll be making an appearance anytime soon."

"I think he will call me."

Late that evening, Brian received a phone call from an aide to Sheldon Lehrer. The person on the phone asked if the timing of the call was okay. Brian accepted the incoming as the right timing. That was when Brian was put on hold for five minutes.

The next voice he heard was Sheldon's. They spoke for a while, and Sheldon told Brian of his conditions. Brian told Sheldon about his conditions. In the end, Brian's conditions won over Sheldon's. Sheldon had to give in to Brian's terms, knowing that the weight of responsibility had been placed on Brian and his company. Sheldon would never have done this in the hearing of his employees, his bodyguards, or his aides. It wouldn't have looked good on his image. As for Brian and his team, they knew how much weight they could handle, and so they should be the ones to determine the deadline. The deadline was changed to August. The question now was, how well could PnC perform?

After the call ended, Brian laid his phone down and was about to open his fridge when his phone chimed. He thought to let it ring until it stopped, but the ringing sounded like a clanging cymbal in his eardrum. Brian couldn't ignore it. He picked it up to see that the call was from Tim. He answered.

"Yeah."

"Uncle Brian, Tim here. I was hoping to talk with you before you left, but you were already gone."

Tim listened for a response. No response came, so he continued.

"I told Kim about it. I took the test for the state fire department and passed."

"That's great! I knew you would."

"I think you know what this means?"

"Of course, I do. You take a job, then you move on."

"Yeah."

There was silence on the line for what felt like two whole minutes.

"Well, first I need to thank you for hiring me . . . for giving me a chance."

"Don't mention it, kid. But don't get ahead of yourself. First, you need to get a job before you do the farewells."

"Yes, you're right. I thought that I should thank you in advance."

"Well, you're welcome. Not sorry that I did. You did help us with what you knew about fire prevention."

"Yeah."

There was a pregnant pause on both ends.

"Until they start calling, don't leave yet. We still need you."

"I know you still want me around. There's another reason why I called. About the hazard, I saw at the manufacturing building . . . I saw the same thing in the two business buildings."

"Are you talking about exposed batteries for the alarm system?"

"It's almost a trend. Someone left a piece of steel wool lodged somewhere, and just above the exposed batteries. I saw exposed batteries at the other buildings as well. You would think they would discard the steel wool after they're finished. But they left the steel wool there. I don't think it was unintentional."

Brian stayed silent for a moment.

"Are you still there?" Tim asked.

"I am. Just wondering to myself who this could be. Either a disgruntled employee, former employee, or one of Lehrer's cronies."

"Didn't you ban Tipperton from all premises?"

"I did."

"You think he might be behind this?"

"You saw the open terminals before and after I fired him. Unlikely."

"What do you think about Lehrer and his company?"

"He would have me done by December. A fire breaking out or an explosion would delay that. I don't think he would do that to himself."

"Maybe one of the guys is dissatisfied with his pay, and before he quits, he wants to do damage to his employers."

"I don't think there's an employer who will pay him enough. Tim, I got some stuff to mull over."

"This is not food, is it?" Tim said in his attempt to lighten up the tone of the discussion.

"No, it isn't," Brian said, keeping his austerity.

"In any event, Happy Thanksgiving!"

They ended the call. Brian placed his device on mute before turning the face down, for he would not be accepting any more incomings. He would not be seeing his workers on Saturday, but he would be seeing his board on that day. For Brian, it was a time to reflect, reconsider, and preplan his next move.

Tim lowered his device. He left it on in case there were unexpected late callers—family, maybe friends, or coworkers, or perhaps a potential employer who'd consider him. Though it was late into the evening, a job opening for firefighters might be forthcoming. *"It can happen,"* Tim thought to himself. But to become a recruit would mean to drop PnC on a dime. He hadn't forgotten what Brian and PnC had done for him while he was on his face unemployed. To Tim, it seemed like an act of betrayal, but Brian reminded him that he was just responding to their need for workers. More than that, he had gone above and beyond their expectations. His recent interactions with a real fire marshal had given him an eye for fire hazards. Because of this, Tim had detected things that others might have overlooked.

Just as Tim was about to go into his living room and prop onto the sofa, his phone chimed. He turned to his phone and peered into the screen. It was a number that Tim didn't recognize. He pondered a little while it rang.

He answered it. "Hello?"

"Hi, is this Tim Douglas?"

"Yes, who's speaking?"

"Oh yes, my name is Dan from LeXo. The manufacturing building. I'm one of the operations managers. While you were doing an inspection, we exchanged numbers in case anything came up."

"Now, I remember. That was a while back. Is everything okay over there?"

"I know I shouldn't be calling you, now that PnC is no longer responsible for the building's condition. I don't know how to say this . . ." Dan, the caller, stopped for a moment before continuing. "I remember telling you before PnC cleared out that there was an unusual amount of dust in the ducts. I know your guys had work to do and that it was dusty. I later told you that these had to be cleaned before your team left. I remember you jotting this down before you left. I had a duct person over earlier today, and he saw enough dust to cause a fire—"

Tim interrupted. "Before the last day, I brought this to our project manager's attention. And it wasn't cleaned?"

"No. Now I don't want to start pointing fingers. I really want to say to my higher-ups that this oversight was unintended. It's one thing to leave while not knowing there is dust. But it's another to neglect this, knowing that this could cause a fire. I would like to believe that your company would not do this on purpose. I'm just pointing this out to you, hoping that you would be more cautious when you see these things. That's it."

Tim was silent.

"I hope the line did not go dead."

"No. I'm just thinking about what happened, what might have happened, what didn't happen, and so on."

"I see," Dan replied. "I hope this one incident doesn't spoil the trust between our company and PnC?"

"I hope it doesn't. You gotta excuse me, I'm still processing this."

"I understand," Dan replied sympathetically.

"I will have to share this with Kim, our manager."

"Thank you, Tim."

"Thank you for calling me this late and for bringing this up. And, for what it's worth, I'm sorry about the oversight."

Tim ended the call. Now he had time to think about what happened, what might have happened, and so on. Tim played back in his mind a course of events that by now would be in distant memory. Tim remembered bringing this matter to Kim's attention. He had also told some of the workers that were there at the time. They knew about the mess that needed to be cleared. Even then, there was a group of PnC workers in the factory that removed their equipment and trash in the open. If they knew about the dust in the ducts, how would they all leave this problem unanswered? This had to be deliberate.

Tim thought about the group of workers that were in the manufacturing building at that time. His coworker Donnie was in the building, and so was Colin. Colin had since been too busy with the future business building to be concerned about what happened at the factory, which raised Tim's suspicions about him. Colin may have been soured over Kim's decision to remove Tim from his clutches. He wanted to make Tim look untrustworthy to his superiors. Lately, Colin had not been very popular with his managers. He had not been at the manufacturing building until the team left the LeXo manufacturing building. Tim had a solid reason to believe Colin ordered the workers to leave the ducts alone. Then there was the possibility that Colin had made a brief visit to the factory with no knowledge of the affairs in that building. He could have both entered and left with no knowledge about the ducts.

Tim decided to sleep on that thought.

Clipboard

Days, weeks, and months went by. The project continued through the colder months, but at a slower pace. After the phone conversation between Phillips and Lehrer, the project deadline had changed from February to a later date. That later date finally came in April of the following year.

On Saturday, April 9th, Brian, his nephew Tim, and Kim looked up at the completed LeXo building. The solid glass reflected the attractive view of the city, thereby adding to the beauty of this skyscraper. The crowning aesthetic was the signature 'LX' label that was mounted at the forefront of this structure. It was complete. And the beauty of the exterior reflected the beauty of the interior.

Life had changed for Tim, in that he had finally been recruited by the fire department in Atlanta. The night before, he was wearing firefighter gear with flat-hat and pick-head ax. As a new firefighter in the city of Atlanta, Tim had been busy at his new job. And Brian had since added a new responsibility on Tim's shoulders: Tim Douglas was named the Chief Safety Officer for PnC. Apart from his role as a firefighter, Tim would be visiting construction sites to help create a safe construction site for workers and visitors.

The PnC work crew had already moved on to a newer project in Richmond, Virginia. All had left Columbia, except Brian, Kim, and Tim. They were not wearing hard hats, neon vests, steel-toes, or any type of safety equipment. They wore their regular street clothes. Tim wore his long-sleeve dress shirt over his jeans. Brian was just as semi-casual, only that he wore a brown blazer. Kim wore a dark, navy-blue suit with an open-collar white shirt.

Kim looked down at the clipboard that Brian was carrying and wondered why he was holding onto that clipboard. "Brian, what is with that clipboard?"

Brian answered with calm resolve. "I've made a checklist of things that have been done, and things that need to be done."

Kim gave a mischievous grin. "There's no end to the project, is there?"

Brian did not know how to answer this, so he only nodded.

Kim continued, "Now that this saga with Lehrer is finally over, we can move on to new things with other owners."

"We'll be moving on from here, alright. I have since spoken to Lehrer."

"What about?" Kim asked with a probing look.

"About a future project somewhere on the west coast."

"I thought he had written you off since you haven't met his expectations."

"So I thought," answered Brian. "That was until he told me about a recent promise made by a certain someone who works for PnC, a promise that another member of PnC told me was true."

"A promise?" Kim raised his eyebrows.

"A promise that if this building was not completed by April of last year, PnC would refund up to twenty percent of its total earnings from this project. This, I did not know about until it was brought to my attention by Lehrer himself. Two PnC employees, I will not name, confirmed this."

Kim stood dumbfounded. "I—"

Brian continued. "Someone had to make this promise."

Kim said, "Wait a—"

"Years ago, I fired Tipperton for a false report on our website for a residential in Atlanta, Georgia—"

Before Brian could say another word, he lifted two layers of paper from the clipboard and shoved the clipboard into Kim's hand. "Read this."

Kim took the clipboard and read, while Brian spoke.

"You've been confiding in some on our team, but not all, certainly not me. You didn't think I'd get my hands on this. Still, a residential magazine tells of Tipperton's boasting about the false story. The team that updated our website received your approval for this false story."

"My approval?" Kim reacted with disbelief.

"Look at the signature. Isn't that your signature?"

"That's my signature."

"That is a promise that you made recently, to complete the hospital in less than two years. I did not know this. You've acted without my knowing this—"

"How is it that you did not know this?"

"Don't act like I was supposed to know! Truth is that I was not supposed to know."

"You were supposed to know," Kim said in his own defense.

"About something that was intended to ruin our company? Are you planning to take over? How long did you think I could be hoodwinked and bamboozled?"

Kim did not answer.

Brian continued. "Turn the page."

Kim turned the page. "I did something behind your back, something that you were not supposed to know until now."

"And what is that?" asked Kim.

"I've just promoted Rene to Project Manager."

"What!" Kim turned to Brian.

Brian grabbed the clipboard from Kim and barked. "You're fired. Now get out of my face."

Kim stood speechless and shocked. He did not answer. He looked both Brian and Tim in the face and saw that Brian was unmoving in what he had just said. Kim took two steps back, turned, and walked away.

Tim turned to Brian, who kept watch on Kim's form as Kim walked on. "I wonder if he admitted to the fire hazards?"

"He did not," answered Brian. "And it doesn't matter, because I've known Kim to be a liar for some time."

Just then, a dark forest-green Escalade stretch-limo pulled up to the curb where Brian and Tim stood. As soon as it parked, the driver, a stockily built man stepped out of the driver seat, walked back to the passenger door, and opened it. Out stepped a familiar figure that Brian and Tim knew. It was Sheldon Lehrer.

Sheldon stepped from the limo towards Brian. Tim was under the impression that Sheldon was expecting Brian to be there. Sheldon did not speak but looked up at the structure, then Brian followed his eyes. Both looked up, neither saying anything to the other. Sheldon then turned to Brian.

"This is a prelude to another that I expect to build in Seattle. You will be hearing from me."

Brian turned to Sheldon. "You know how to reach me."

Sheldon held his hand out to Brian for the first time. Brian took it with a firm grip. The two held that firm grip until they were able to crack a smile.

Tim turned and saw the driver open the limo door a second time. This time, two women stepped out. The first woman, Tim, recognized to be Dotty. The second woman, he did not recognize, but she looked familiar. *"Could this be Sapphire?"* Tim wondered.

Tim had spoken to Sapphire over the phone since the day they first met. The last time he saw her, she was almost fifteen years old. Three years had since passed. And the young woman – now eighteen – that stood before him was virtually unrecognizable. Sapphire now embodied beauty beyond her years.

"Hi, Are you . . ."

She smiled. "Hi, Tim!"

Tim hid his melodrama as he said, "Wow!"

Brian turned to Tim and nudged him. "Close your jaw, kid. Her father is standing here."

Sheldon heard it and chuckled as he spoke. "I take it you met my daughter a few years back?"

"I'm sorry, Mr. Lehrer. I did."

Sheldon raised his forefinger. "You can call me Sheldon."

"I will, Sheldon." Tim then turned to Sapphire. "It's really good to see you, Sapphire."

"And you as well. And congratulations on your promotion. A Chief Safety Officer and a firefighter. You'll be really busy."

"Yes," Tim replied. "I will be. And thank you! By the way, I see that you'll be busy too, not only as a university student but also as a spokesperson and a worker, meeting needs in different communities."

"Yes, I'll be busy as a student and as a philanthropist."

"Very good. What led you to this decision?"

"You did."

"I did?"

"Well, you did, as you inspired me by your selfless act. You saved my dog. Instead of hoping to take over your uncle's company, you told me that you want to become a firefighter. That is selfless."

Tim was only able to say, "Wow."

Sapphire continued. "I told my father that this is what I wanted to do. We have been doing this together since."

Sheldon butted in. "As father and daughter, and with Dotty's help." Dotty only smiled.

"That's great," Tim said. "I hope to stay in touch with you."

"We surely will." Dotty nodded.

Brian and Tim bade Sheldon, Dotty, and Sapphire goodbye as the three continued with their escort into the building through its main entrance. Brian turned to Tim. "When are you headin' back to Atlanta?"

"I believe Monday morning."

"You just got here."

"I know. That means I'm at your disposal until I have to leave."

"At my disposal," Brian repeated with irony. "I've got something for you to do."

"And what is that, Uncle Bry?"

"Let's get outta here." Tim smiled as they stepped into Brian's pickup.

"That is something I can do."

Reporter's Island

On Tuesday, March 10th, at 1:30 PM, a mall in the heart of Moncton was bustling with customers. People walked by, heading in different directions. Some carried shopping bags, while others meandered about empty-handed. Some traversed in groups, while others went solo. Some walked with purpose to their steps, while others sat and watched the passersby.

Two women strolled through the shopping mall, holding shopping bags in their right and their left. One appeared to be in her late forties, while the other appeared to be fifteen years old. Lacy and Sage strode through the mall with arms linked. They sang along with Ariana Grande as they danced and stepped to the music. This drew the attention of the sitting observers. All the better for Lacy and Sage, because they both loved the attention; it was one of the many things they had in common.

"I am going to remember this day for a long time," Sage said. "I really don't want this to end."

Lacy spoke between catching her breath and laughing. "I know you don't. At some point, this day will end, and March break will have to end. You will return to class, and I will return to work."

"It's not fair," Sage replied with a pout. "I don't know why it has to end. I wish this moment would last forever. I didn't know you were going to be off this week. Thanks for taking it off."

Lacy spoke jovially. "Hold on there, sweetie. I did not take this week because it is March break. March break happens to fall on my vacation days."

Sage smiled. "Yes, Auntie!"

Lacy's face lit up. "Aww . . . you called me, 'auntie!'"

"You *are* my auntie—my auntie and my new best friend."

Lacy jerked her head back. "I thought your mom was your best friend."

"I thought so too," Sage replied. "This wasn't an easy decision—but you won."

"Oh." Lacy grinned. "It's my honor. I just won't tell Staci that I won."

The two continued their stroll through the mall. Before they could make a last and final exit to the parking lot, Lacy and Sage had to stop at every department store. They had to walk through the newest stores, see the most recent arrivals on the stock shelves, and stumble across the best deals and sales. Due to the size of the mall, it would be a while before the two were ready to leave. They were testing their bags to see how much they could hold, when Sage said overconfidently, "Mine is not full."

An hour later, their bags hit their limit. Lacy knew it was time to load them into the trunk of her SUV. They were in Sally Maye, and Sage was at the checkout counter. Lacy looked around to see what she had missed. That's when a hand took hold of her elbow. This startled her.

"What the—"

"Lacy?"

Lacy turned to the figure. She was standing eye to eye with another woman. This woman's face was animated, as though she was thrilled to see Lacy.

"Hi, uh, do I know you?"

"Sorry to startle you. Actually, you don't," the woman replied. "But I'm one of your biggest fans," the woman said. She appeared to be a decade younger than Lacy, or more. "I'm always on the latest. When I don't catch *The Daily News* in New Brunswick, I'll get it on the website. And you are amazing!"

"Why, thank you," Lacy replied with a blush. "But I didn't get your name."

"My name is Jennifer. And it's okay if you forget my name in the first few tries. I can only imagine how many others you need to memorize."

"Thank you, and yes, Jennifer is easy to remember. Are you from around here?"

"Quite honestly, I'm from Hampton. It's a small town, which explains why I travel a lot."

"What do you do, Jennifer?"

"I'm a travel writer. I'm a contributor to travel magazines in different cities, and I give travelers heads up on the places to visit and the places to avoid."

"Now, that is interesting. I've been doing plenty of traveling. What is your last name? I may have come across some of your articles."

"Hampton."

"Hampton?"

"Hampton. You know, they named a small town after me."

"Oh, wow. Before traveling to Winnipeg, I came across several articles written by Jennifer Hampton on sights and entertainment. Are you *the* Jennifer Hampton?"

"Guilty!"

"Oh, my goodness," Lacy smiled. "You, too, are a celebrity in your own right."

Jennifer blushed.

Lacy continued. "When I read your article on the Enoteca restaurant in Winnipeg, I said, 'I have to stop there.'"

Jennifer touched Lacy's forearm. "Did you try the caramel and chocolate tartlet? It is to die for."

Lacy touched Jennifer's forearm. "Yes, I did."

The two women went into an outburst of giddiness. For a moment, they were two female adolescents reminiscing on where they'd been and what they'd done. The real adolescent, who had already finished at the checkout, stood beside Lacy, unnoticed.

"Oh, Sage, you're finished?" Lacy asked, surprised.

"I'm finished," Sage replied, stealing glances at Jennifer.

Lacy turned to Jennifer. "Oh, Jennifer, I would like to introduce you to a friend of mine, who is visiting from Saint John. She is the daughter of one of my colleagues."

Jennifer walked close to Sage and grabbed her hands. Sage was a little uncomfortable. "Let me guess, Staci Palmer?"

Sage jolted her head forward. Lacy jerked her head back. "How did you know?" Sage asked with a look of shock.

"Well, that's easy," Jennifer replied, letting go of Sage's hands. "You are the spitting image of Staci."

Lacy gave Jennifer a knowing look. She turned to Sage and said, in a matter-of-fact tone, "She is right, Sage. You do look like your mom."

"I know. I get that all the time," Sage said.

"Are you hoping to work in the same field?" Jennifer asked.

"Not only will I be in the same field, but I am also going to become a reporter just like Lacy."

"Oh, wow," Jennifer replied. "Then, you'll have a big pair of high-heels to fill."

Lacy chimed in, "Not only will Sage get to wear my high-heels, but she'll also outgrow them and become a better reporter than I."

Sage turned to Lacy with a look of disbelief. "There is better than you?"

"Oh, I believe there is."

"I don't think there is," replied Sage. "I think I can only become as good as you."

Lacy smiled and turned to Jennifer. "So, Jennifer, where is your next point of arrival?"

"Don't know yet. I'm going to play low key. Maybe write a few articles on places to be in Moncton, Saint John, Fredericton, and other places. Have you read about that coming thunderstorm? I read that it should be coming tomorrow evening. It's a big one, I heard."

"No," Lacy replied. "My table has been full. It's coming tomorrow, you said?"

Jennifer looked at Lacy with her jaw dropped. "You're the reporter, and you don't know this?"

"There are a lot of things a reporter doesn't know. So much is happening in the province, especially in the realm of political issues. Other reporters do the weather reports."

Jennifer snapped her fingers. "I get it. As a writer who focuses on an area, in particular, I should know this about reporters."

"No harm is done."

"Let's stay in touch. I could surely use an update on what's going on at different points of arrival." Lacy smiled.

"Let's." Jennifer smiled in agreement.

The two exchanged personal contact numbers before parting ways.

Lacy and Sage stood at the back of Lacy's SUV, loading the bags that were filled to their capacity. It was 5:30 PM, and Lacy was ready to call it a day. Sage turned to Lacy with a tinge of excitement.

"Let's do something."

Lacy jerked her head back. "You are full of energy."

Sage's shoulders dropped. "Are you tired already? Let's call your new friend. Maybe she'll know the best places to go to."

"I was ready to turn in for—"

Sage jump in. "Let's see a movie. You won't need lots of energy for a movie, just your attention."

Two hours later, Lacy and Sage walked out of the cinema with the new movie, *The Lovebirds*, on their minds. They both had their own thoughts on the film, which neither shared. Lacy thought about an episode in her life, in another city. Sage could swear she had come across a similar story in a romance novel. *"These are stories that are taken as fiction,"* she thought. *"But life in New Brunswick can become fiction at any moment. All that is needed are a few excited people in the same room. There is certainly going to be conflict. And this is how people come up with fiction."*

Sage turned to Lacy. "What do you think?"

"It was okay," Lacy replied.

"I was talking about weather reports. The weather reports that what's her name . . . Jennifer mentioned."

"Oh," Lacy said, now snapping back into reality. "Terrible, isn't it?"

Sage waved her hand at Lacy's face to get her attention. "Auntie Lacy?"

"Yes," Lacy was slightly annoyed.

"You're doing it again."

"Doing what, Sage?"

"What you're doing right now, and that's answering my question without giving my question any thought."

Lacy calmed. "I'm sorry, sweetie, my mind strayed a moment ago."

"What's on your mind?"

"My mind ran on my former life back in Saint John. Now that I'm in Moncton, I feel like life has changed."

"For better? Or for worse?" asked Sage.

"I don't know. I really don't know."

"How is that?" asked Sage.

"Maybe I find myself starting over, as though I've freed myself from the thoughts of a former mayor. In a way, life is bitter and sweet."

"Well, if Jennifer is right," said Sage, "life may become more bitter in less than two days."

"I'm no meteorologist, but my understanding is that these floods caused by storm surge normally happen in the fall or during winter. This is unusual."

"If it does happen, do you think it's going to be washing into this area?"

"These tides are big, and when they hit, they go far. Don't be surprised when this parking lot is flooded within forty-eight hours."

Sage gave Lacy a disgusted look and said, "I would not want to be around to walk through that."

Where did the water go?

On Thursday, March 12th, Lacy gazed through the living room window and onto her front porch. She had an open view of her front yard and street. The streets in the city were dark that afternoon. Hundreds of feet above the roads were menacing dark clouds. The cracking of thunder was heard, and it sent a booming echo across the sky and slight tremors on the earth. Lacy looked up to see flashes of lightning in the distant dark clouds. She looked down and saw raindrops fall. Soon, they assaulted the concrete, the lawn, and her truck. Lacy now wished she had parked in the garage. She could have; now it was too late. The shower became a downpour of rain, an assault that soon became a massacre. The gushing rainfall would typically stop with the passing of thunderclouds, but these thunderclouds did not go. They stayed. They stayed and angrily hovered over the entire city and region with a vengeance. There was going to be rising tides, with water levels at six meters, or even eight meters high. Either way, Lacy would need to get her rain boots ready for the early or late flood of the city.

Lacy had seen flooding back in Saint John in 2008, which was said to have surpassed the surge in 1973. Lacy was told about the severity of that flood. What made the flood of 1973 worse was that she'd seen it through the eyes of a toddler. Lacy had no clear recollection, other than the image of her mother pushing through waist-deep waters to get to her. Lacy could remember, though vaguely, her mother holding her in one arm while moving with great effort through the waist-deep waters. She could recall being laid in a canoe. Like other distant memories that fade, this one gave her an image gallery into her past. For Lacy, this wasn't enough, because these memories were fragmented.

Lacy could recall asking her mother, "Where did the water go?" There were no unscientific answers to this question. Lacy's mother dismissed it as one that she felt too unqualified to answer. Lacy had since asked a lot of questions of her mom, her Uncle Todd, Ms. Rothman, the teacher, Bobby the neighbor who knew a lot of things, and her father, who was an Anglican bishop. She had asked them questions, such as "What causes birds and planes to fly? What causes boats to float? Where does all the trash in the city go? Where do people get their last names? When people die, how do they get to heaven?" These questions, and many others, were given short answers, the kind that left her hungry for more answers because those answers were not enough. Lacy would then be dismissed by the annoyed adult.

The one person that should have given her a satisfying answer was her father, who had spent much of his waking hours in a church building. Lacy barely saw him. When she did, he would bless her ceremonially the way he would other patrons in the area. He would bless her, then go on his walk, leaving little room for answers to questions. When she was readying herself to go to college, Lacy's father encouraged her to go to Bible college. He felt that the professors would answer her questions. She went. And to her disappointment, none of the professors she encountered gave her reasonable answers to her probing questions. Lacy eventually dropped out of Bible college and began her quest for answers. This is what led her to journalism.

Her eyes began to regain focus on what she was gazing at. The street became a puddle. The rain had not abated in the last twenty minutes. Soon, the sidewalk would be covered in water, then her lawn, which was being drowned in the downpour of rain. There's no telling when this would stop. If it failed to stop, Lacy would have neither raft nor canoe to stay afloat. She suddenly wished she had followed through on the swimming lessons. The lack of time has always been the bane of this one goal. Now would have been an excellent time to be prepared.

The water had risen above the curbs. The lawn was covered in water. There was no question whether Lacy would need her rubber boots. If the water levels rose to her shoulders, she would climb to her roof and allow fate to decide.

Forty minutes had passed, and the fierce downpour abated and became a sprinkle, then sporadic rainfall. Lacy ran out onto her elevated porch and looked up. The dark clouds over the region had suddenly morphed to gray clouds. They sailed silently overhead and northwest.

Lacy was about to slip her rubber boots on when her phone chimed. She looked on the device and saw Sage's name and image. She picked it up and answered.

"Hey, Sage."

"Hey."

"What's up?"

"I'm just calling to find out if everything is okay over there."

Lacy looked out at the deluge, which was far less than expected. "Everything is okay."

"Did your streets get flooded?"

"If you call making a mess of your favorite pair of high heels a flood."

"Oh. You're saying that it wasn't bad?"

"Yes. The grey clouds are now heading northwest."

"Wow! From what Jennifer said, I was expecting worse."

"Well, many weather warnings are exaggerated. But it's good to stay cautious, I believe. What's the story in Saint John?"

"So far, it's all gray skies. A little sputter here and there. Nothing serious."

"Well, that's a good report if you ask me."

"So far. Mom told me that a big one is coming. This one is supposed to dump more water on our cities."

"A big one? When is that one supposed to hit?"

"I think she said next week."

"I know I'll be talking with Staci sometime next week."

"Are the waters high enough to stop everything . . . like you going to work?"

"No!" exclaimed Lacy. "I'm glad I'm driving an SUV. I could surely plow through this."

"That doesn't sound too bad," Sage said, sounding relieved. "Even if we were to get lots of rain, I now think it won't be as bad."

"I'll have my phone by me. Update me if it begins to grow intense."

"Okay. What are you doing now?"

"I'm about to step outdoors and say hi to a few surviving neighbors."

Lacy ended the call, and found her knee-length rubber boots, slipped them and her raincoat on. Lacy grabbed her car keys and stepped onto her porch, looked straight ahead, to her left, and then to her right, and saw ankle-deep water.

"Oh, this is nothing," Lacy said to herself.

She descended the steps to the water and noticed that the water was not ankle-deep; it was actually knee-deep. She also saw, at the corner of her eye, one of her neighbors. At the house to her right was Gina Preston. She, too, was descending her steps with the same purpose in mind. But unlike Lacy, who had an SUV with four-wheel drive strong enough to drive through the flooded streets, Gina had a 2000 Honda Civic that did not have the same features.

Lacy waved at Gina. Gina waved back.

Lacy said, "Are you okay to drive through that?"

"I don't know," Gina replied. "I guess I'll find out."

Lacy stopped to watch Gina as she climbed into her Civic. Fortunately for them, both of their driveways were inclined. Despite the water levels, pulling from their driveways would give them some momentum as they drove down into the water's depths. Opening her car door presented another problem for Gina. Some of the water rushed into her car, soaking her seat. She started her car, pulled out of her driveway, and set the transmission to drive. But this was only the beginning of her problems.

The moment she pulled ahead, her car tires spun. The easy drive to the nearby variety store, the library, and the post office became a blooper clip from an off-road motorsport event. The more Gina accelerated, the more her car spun. It swerved left; it swerved right. It then turned at one-hundred-and-eighty degrees. Lacy watched on and knew that Gina wasn't going to get far.

Lacy walked into the knee-deep water and waved Gina down. Gina saw Lacy and stopped. By then, the car was on her own lawn. Gina did not push her door open; instead, she climbed out of her window. Lacy went to assist her.

"Wow," Lacy said. "I didn't think it was going to be this bad."

"No, I didn't either," Gina replied.

"Just imagine what it would have been like if the water were shoulder deep."

"I don't even want to think about that," Gina replied.

"By the way, where were you going with your little Civic?"

"I was heading to work."

Gina Preston worked part-time at the local library. On the side, she is a freelancer who worked for several advertising firms. Gina is a bookish person who spends much time on her desktop, laptop, if not with her nose in a book. She is a gifted writer and drew from her ability to be creative. Gina's disposition to give herself entirely to her work had rendered her socially inept. Because of the extended amounts of time on her computer and reading materials, Gina had forgotten what it was like to relate to people. Lacy had gotten to know Gina over the past year-and-a-half since moving to Moncton. Often, she and Lacy would cross paths. Unfortunately, Gina's awkwardness would usually abbreviate those meetings.

"Okay. I'm heading out. I wouldn't mind taking you there."

"Oh, really? Lacy, you shouldn't."

"Nonsense. I'll take you there. Let's call this my deed for the day."

After struggling within, Gina finally gave in and said, "Okay, thank you."

Gina grabbed her handbag and other personal belongings and joined Lacy in her SUV.

Lacy turned to Gina. "You can leave your bag and personals in the back. They are safe back there."

"I'll be fine with them on my lap," Gina said forthwith.

Lacy started her truck, and it purred. She shifted to four-wheel drive and backed out. She drove effortlessly through the unusually high waters. The SUV sat on the road as it plowed its way to its destination. In less than thirty minutes, they were at the library. Their trip to the library was more comfortable than expected, in that not as many vehicles were on the road. What they saw on the streets were SUVs, Pick-up trucks, and large eighteen-wheelers. Even the police cruisers were SUVs. Gina knew that she didn't stand a chance driving in these conditions with her little Civic.

Gina turned to her chauffeur. "Lacy . . ."

"Yes, Gina?" Lacy replied.

"Thank you."

Without another word, Gina opened the passenger window and climbed out, with her belongings strapped over her shoulders. Lacy watched her as she trod through the high waters to the library's entrance. She did so without turning back.

Moments later, having shed water boots and changed into her usual flats, Gina walked through the library with a tray of books in front of her. She was placing the returned books back onto the shelves. It was a quiet Thursday afternoon with fewer local visitors than usual. Because of the weather conditions, some regular visitors chose to stay home. This gave Gina more elbow room to do her job. Some of her co-workers had decided to call-in.

There were only about twenty people at the library, all scattered through the aisles and lounging areas. Also, inside the building was another librarian who sat behind a desk with a computer monitor before her.

Gina's back was turned to her co-worker when she heard a woman approach the desk. The woman was making an inquiry that Gina did not pay any attention to—only that the voice sounded familiar.

Gina turned to the desk, her co-worker, and the woman that was speaking to her. It was Lacy. Gina's co-worker motioned to her. She left what she was doing to join them.

"Gina, could you help this fine lady find the national geographic section."

"Hi, Lacy."

"Do you know her?" Gina's librarian co-worker asked.

"Yes. And I thought you would, too. Lacy is on the Daily News channel."

Gina's co-worker looked at her, clueless. "Um, Gina, I don't watch the news. And I don't watch TV."

This response surprised neither Gina nor Lacy. She was ancient-looking enough to be both Lacy and Gina's grandma. She appeared to have been hidden from human civilization in recent decades.

"That's okay! I'll take her," Gina said.

Gina led Lacy to the section where the National Geographic magazines were. Lacy stared at Gina while her head was turned. She appeared to be very uncomfortable in Lacy's presence.

"Are you looking for history or nature?"

"No, cities. I'm looking for the more recent issues with Canadian cities."

"Okay. Is this work-related?"

"It could be," Lacy replied. "Really, this is for me. Oh, I did not tell you that I was off this week?"

"No, you didn't," Gina replied matter-of-factly.

"Well, I'm off this week until Monday."

"That's good."

With nothing else being said, the air was growing thicker with silence by the second.

"I was meaning to ask, how's life as of late?"

"Fine."

Silence. They both smiled awkwardly.

"I have known you for the last year-and-a-half. Until this day, we have never been acquainted. I didn't even know that you worked at a library."

"Well, this is where I am," smiled Gina awkwardly.

"Meanwhile, you knew who I was—that I'm a reporter for the Daily News."

"Yes, I did," smiled Gina awkwardly.

Without warning, Lacy locked arms with Gina and started walking.

"What are you doing?" Gina tried to pull away.

"You are coming with me, Missy. And if I must wrestle you to the ground, you are coming with me. We are going to chat a little."

Gina looked around nervously. "You know, I'm working."

"Five minutes is all I'm asking for, then I'll return to this NG section."

Twelve feet away, and at a small table, Lacy and Gina sat across from each other.

"Tell me a little about yourself."

"My name is Gina Preston. I'm thirty-seven years old. I'm unmarried. I'm a size six. And I wear size eight-and-a-half in women's footwear. My mother is from Italy, and my father is from Newfoundland. I lived in Newfoundland until I was nineteen. I moved away from my parents, earned a Bachelor of Arts in English. And I have been living in New Brunswick ever since."

Gina waited for a response. She looked around nervously, hoping that her co-worker would not catch her sitting. Lacy just sat and smiled.

"Wow. That's a good start. And why aren't you married? You are such a pretty woman."

"I don't know. I guess no one has asked me."

"Strange. I know men who would ask you to dinner, then to marry them, in a heartbeat. Maybe, you just need to get around more."

"Maybe. I've been really busy with work."

"Busy with work?" Lacy looked surprised.

"I did not tell you that I'm a writer."

"A writer? What kind of writer?"

"I'm a freelancer. I do everything from content writing to scriptwriting."

"Interesting. Now that definitely adds to your busy schedule. How long have you been doing this?"

"I've been freelancing on the side for twelve years. The library, six years."

"That's nice. I thought I saw a handsome-looking young man around the corner. Let me go."

"No!" Before Lacy was able to rise to her feet, Gina grabbed her arm. "No."

"Why not?"

Gina lowered her voice, hoping that only Lacy heard. "Not while I'm working." Gina looked sheepishly at the older man who listened to their exchange. "Not while I'm like this."

"Okay, I'll tell you what. You and I are going to hang out this weekend."

"Where?" Gina looked frightened.

"Trust me, you'll love it. You are going to meet some friends of mine who are also writers. You'll get the opportunity to talk about what you do. Maybe you can share ideas, some of which could be added to your memoir."

"I don't think I'm ready to write a memoir. I am hoping to write a novel."

"A novel?" Lacy shot her a look of interest. "You are full of surprises."

"I am hoping to get some inspiration as I go."

"Well, Gina, stick with me, and you'll get lots of inspiration."

Neither of them noticed, but Gina's co-worker strolled by and saw the two sitting comfortably.

"Gina?" her co-worker said with a questioning look.

Lacy continued her thought. "And you're suggesting that I use Turabian sixth edition when citing my document on famous Canadian cities?" Lacy stared into Gina's eye's waiting for her quick answer.

"Yes," she replied. "For this publication. I would suggest this over the Chicago seventeenth edition."

"Okay, if you suggest."

Gina's co-worker coughed. "Pardon me. Gina, could you watch the desk for me? I need to walk to the upper level to check on a few items."

Gina lifted herself from her seat. "Okay."

Lacy also lifted herself to walk to the National Geographic section. "Thanks, Gina."

"You're welcome," she replied.

Lacy had told Gina that she was looking for cities in the National Geographic section. She did not tell her that she was looking for 'Natural Disasters and Climate Change.' Lacy had hoped to find similar stories on floods. To her amazement, she found plenty of related stories in the more recent issues.

Lacy stepped out of the library. To her surprise, the water had subsided. Usually, floods would stick around for days. It had only been an hour since Lacy walked into the library. The water that was more than knee-deep was now less than ankle deep. She looked around and knew that the water had disappeared into the city drainage basins.

Because of the intensity of the rainstorm, and its duration, much of the city was flooded. What added to this deluge was the frost of the late winter season, which retarded the water flow to the city's drainage. These basins would run on a downslope and channel towards the Atlantic. In this instance, the ice buildup had broken away, allowing the water to break free for the runoff into the ocean.

Lacy thought about this discovery. She was relieved that there was not as much snow throughout the city as in previous winters. There has only been a lot of ice. As she trod through the ankle-deep water to her SUV, she thought about past flood seasons. These downpours came not just on one day. These were rainy seasons. As for the frost, the ice jam formations along the Petitcodiac River have not yet thawed. This is enough to cause more problems if the city were to receive another deluge. Moncton can experience a flash flood no less devastating than its sister city, St. Johns.

What day is today?

On Monday, March 16th, at 8:00 AM, Lacy pounded the snooze button on her alarm. It sat freely on a nightstand by her bed. Lacy came to and knew she should have pressed the cancel. Because she had hit snooze, she knew the annoying alarm would sound again in fifteen minutes. Lacy turned, then tossed, and finally mustered the strength to rise. Waking up that morning was extra challenging because of the late Sunday outing that drained the last bit of energy out of her.

Lacy's Saturday outing with Gina began at the hair salon. There had to be a makeover. What Lacy saw in Gina was a naturally attractive woman in disguise. She wore a bronze-colored ponytail, with loose strands of hair that broke free from the hairline. Gina did not wear any makeup. Lacy could not remember Gina ever wearing anything on her face. She had a well-proportioned nose that was cute. She had full lips, a beautiful facial structure, and the shade of her eyes was a cross between green and hazel. Gina had all this going for her, yet her face was bland, and her clothing was tasteless. Lacy had to do something about Gina.

By the end of her trip to the salon and the shopping mall, Gina went through a total transformation. Her hair was let down and done in wavy curls that dropped over her shirt and covered her chest. Gina loved her hairdo. It was the style of clothing that made her uncomfortable. She was used to the more modest wear that covered every inch of her body except her neck, face, and hands. Lacy wanted her to let loose, which led to the more tightly fitted clothing that revealed more of her figure. Gina used the coolness of March as an excuse to keep her coat on. But Lacy would not allow that, for when they were on the dance floor, the jacket had to come off.

Gina felt naked, knowing that all eyes were on her, especially the wandering eyes of men. Lacy saw a beautiful woman that night. The men in the building saw a bombshell that night. In the washroom mirror, Gina saw a strumpet that night. Out of the many male eyes that were on her that night, few were bold enough to bypass the "Lacy screen" to approach Gina. Lacy, Gina, and others danced into the late hours.

After leaving the dance floor, Lacy and Gina rendezvoused with some of her friends from the city. The conversations went to three in the morning. Lacy was ready to leave. Gina was not. Lacy found out that Gina had drunk a little too much. They taxied their way home. Then there was Sunday evening. Gina wanted to go out again.

Lacy thought, *"What have I created?"*

The two had another outing that Sunday night. It was a wet and rainy weekend. One would think that people would enjoy the comforts of their homes more. They went to a social gathering that Sunday evening with several of Lacy's friends. They had conversations into the late night. They also danced and drank themselves into a stupor. Lacy and Gina Ubered home. By the time they arrived, it was already four in the morning.

Lacy looked at the clock again. The time showed 8:05 AM. She had to ready herself to be at the office for 9:00 AM. After two steps to the washroom, Lacy felt the same migraine she had felt the night before. She had drunk more than she had planned. Lacy and Gina were tipsy. Gina was more of a mess by the time they arrived home that morning.

Lacy climbed into the shower, then went to her walk-in closet, then to the kitchen for whatever she could put together in the space of only ten minutes. After a black coffee and a piece of toast with honey, Lacy slipped her coat on and started her SUV.

Lacy walked into the office at 9:11 AM. The parking lots were full. She was left with no other choice than to find a distant parking lot. After walking four blocks, Lacy walked into the building. It was a busy Monday morning. Everyone who worked at that center was at their station. One of the first faces to greet her on entry was the manager—a strappingly tall black woman with a Trinidadian accent.

"Good morning, Daylia."

"Gyul, Ah see yuh had a real whopping time on yuh las' seven days off."

"Oh, did I ever," Lacy said with irony.

"Yuh, never look at the mirror lately? It's all over yuh."

Lacy became more self-aware. "Do I look that bad?"

"Ah doh wan yuh tink I'm macoing yuh business."

"Oh, Daylia, My life is an open book," Lacy shrugged.

"An open book, ent? Yuh always pull dat off and still look good. Lacy, ah see yuh makin' style."

"Oh, stop it," Lacy replied, playfully batting her hand.

Daylia continued. "We're following up on our Premier's proposal and his hopes to deal with climate change, the carbon tax, and so on."

Lacy rolled her eyes. "I've heard that before. I'm every bit as interested in what he has to say."

"He's at the downtown banquet hall. He's going to hold a press conference after this."

"I'm on it."

Just then, Lacy felt her phone vibrate inside her handbag. She reached in, looked on the screen, and saw Sage's name and image. Lacy slid to the green icon.

"Hello, Sage."

"Hey!"

"How's your first day back at the school?"

"It's okay. I miss those off days, though."

"That was nice."

"How was your first day back to work?"

"It's okay. I feel a busy week ahead for me."

"What are you going to do today?"

"I'm going to look for our premier, Paul Brouder. Remember him? I'm going to ask him about what he wants to do about our climate. Stuff like that."

"That sounds fun."

"So it sounds," Lacy agreed.

"We gotta meet up when you're free. Last week was the first real fun time we've had together. I hope to have more of that."

"I hope so, too. We'll do so when I'm in your area. Or if you're in mine."

Another incoming call alerted Lacy. It was coming from Gina Preston. For Gina's caller ID, Lacy had an image of her taken at the height of last Saturday evening.

"Sage, there's an incoming call. Can I call you later?"

"Yes. I'll listen out for you. Bye."

Lacy ended the call with Sage and answered the one with Gina. "Hey, Gina."

"Why, top of the morning to you, my fair maiden!"

Lacy rechecked the name to see who was calling. "Gina?"

"Yes. How was your drive to the office this morning?"

"Oh, Gina, yes, I got here in one piece, thankfully."

"How is your morning so far?"

"Fantastic. Where are you now?"

"I'm at the library."

"What time did you get in?" asked Lacy.

"7:30. I decided to go in early."

"Wow," said Lacy.

"Let's do it again this weekend,"

Lacy paused. "Um . . . don't you have your work and your writing to do?"

"Oh, that's nothing. By Saturday, I will have knocked everything off of my to-do list."

"Okay. Well, let's. Anyway, my boss is close by. Let's talk Friday if I don't see you before then."

"That's a plan, Lacy. See ya!"

Lacy ended the call and looked around at the faces in the office that already knew she was in demand.

"It's nothing, really, people. Just a couple of close friends—"

Lacy did not finish her sentence before another name appeared on her screen. Lacy looked directly at it. It was from Jennifer Hampton.

"Jennifer Hampton?" Lacy ran that name through her memory bank, and it wasn't registering. She answered. "Hello?"

"Hey, Lacy. It's Jennifer from the Sally Maye. We spoke about destinations."

"Yes, that Jennifer. How are you?"

"I'm great. Let's meet for lunch if you're in the area."

"I'll be around. In fact, I'll be downtown between noon and one o'clock. I hope you can meet me there."

"I'll work my schedule around that."

Lacy ended the call. The moment she looked away from her phone, she noticed all the eyes pinned on her.

"Like, come on, you guys. Don't you all have social lives?"

Martin, one of the observers, responded with jest. "Not really. Most of our social lives are limited to this building."

Lacy braced both hands against her waist and gave Martin a scolding look. "Well, that's too bad, Martin. I can't help it that only fifteen minutes of my waking hours are devoted to this building."

Daylia returned to Lacy. As Lacy turned her attention to Daylia, Martin took his finger and tilted up his nose at Lacy. Daylia saw the gesture but ignored it.

"I want you to see what our new premier is hoping to do. Like yourself, it appears that everyone else wants a piece of Mr. Brouder."

Lacy gave Daylia an uninterested look. "I find that hard to believe. But I'll track Mr. PC. Let's see what he'll do to this great city and its inhabitants."

Daylia started to walk away. "Peter and Van will follow you to the town conference."

Forty minutes later, the camera crew, led by Lacy, parked at the banquet hall. The grounds and roads were still wet from the recent downpour. In some areas, there were high puddles that might take a while before disappearing. After driving around, they found two separate parking spots. Even in this muggy weather, people are not deterred from coming here. Lacy stepped out of her SUV and scanned the lot for more empty spaces. The search soon turned to disappointment. She frowned at the rows of cars that filled the parking slots from the building's entrance to the fences. They soon found a few slots vacant. These could be vacant because of the puddles, which would make it almost impossible to step out of one's vehicle without getting her socks soaked. Lacy thought that filled spots couldn't have been borrowed. Parking in this lot, other than visiting the banquet hall, was prohibited. *Too many locals were inside that banquet hall. It was okay when the former premier, Lorna Kiley, had these meetings. It was worth filling the parking lots and the seats for those meetings. Not Brouder. People have their jobs to go to. There are, by far, more important places to be than to waste one's time at this meeting. How could this man be so popular? What is Brouder going to do? Destroy everything Kiley had worked so hard to build. These people, these progressive conservative supporters were motivated. And for what? The mess Kiley had been so successful at cleaning up? Now she is gone, and an agent of destruction has taken her place. This is what the people voted for. This is what the people wanted. Then this is what the people will get. People on the right celebrated Brouder's win. Many promises were made at his victory speech. Many promises were going to be made at this speech. And, certainly, more promises would be broken.*

Peter and Van followed Lacy through the entrance, past a couple of greeters, past two people guarding the set of doors to the hall, and into the room where an audience sat on rows of chairs. There were no tables, only chairs, these chairs were all facing one direction. They were facing an elevated platform on which a podium was positioned. Other news teams were at the back. At the front, someone stood behind that podium and gave an oration that stirred the crowd. The crowd appeared to love the speech; even more, these people loved what this man said.

"What impressive rhetoric," whispered Lacy to Peter, who stood by her.

The truth was that Peter was not the only one who heard her. Two other attendees with a keen sense of hearing stole glances at Lacy. Lacy caught one staring. She gave the attendee a sardonic stare until he became uncomfortable. He excused himself from his company and exited the hall. Lacy listened on.

"Now for the man you've all came to see . . ."

"You mean this painful repetitious speech is over?" Lacy thought to herself.

"A man who brought Kiley's reign of terror to an end. A man . . ."

"Will you shut up, already, and introduce the man?" Lacy thought.

"Join me, everyone, as we give our premier, the Honorable Paul Brouder, a Moncton welcome."

This intro was followed by a standing ovation and roaring applause by those in attendance. On the rostrum, the orator turned to another man that approached. He was equally as savvy in his appearance. The only difference was that this man appeared more seasoned by age than the other. He looked to be in his mid-fifties. Paul Brouder stepped behind the ambo and spoke.

"Thank you, all, for that warm welcome, and thank you, Vince, for that bombastic introduction."

The crowd laughed.

"I was beginning to wonder when he was going to call me to the stage."

That received some chuckles.

"I'm honored to be here. Even more, I'm honored to represent such a great province and its citizens. It is humbling to know . . ."

"Will you stop it already with this pretend humility?" thought Lacy. *"Ugh! If I could only fast-forward this display of hypocrisy, I could then listen to you talk."*

"I believe in the work of concerned citizens that are tired of being pushed around by their government. You have no say in the important decisions. What matters is that you're present at the conventions; you add your vote and your petitions to the collective. You are to be seen but not heard. This is what our prime minister has been doing to you. This is what my predecessor did to you . . ."

"And you're an exception?" Lacy thought, while filled with

contempt for the speaker. *"They made a mess. Those nasty Liberals. Those little red devils. Now a savior, a man with a soul, has come to right the wrongs of those leftists. You hypocrite!"*

"Look at the size of that carbon tax bill. It was predicted that the rebates going to families will not come within a hundred kilometers of the amount they have been taxed since the bill was first introduced. This is what I'm talking about: a government that says they are out for the interests of Canadian citizens when, in fact, they are not. The big industries are given the wave. These industries that were responsible for the most pollution have been let off scot-free."

The crowd responded with sounds of agreement.

"We need to let our voices be heard. Too long have we allowed Ottawa to muzzle us from speaking. To our Liberal government, we were seen, yet not heard. This is where we make our presence known, and our voices heard. We are going to redirect this obligation to the big energy companies that can afford it. We are going to transport oil from western Canada to eastern Canada, to make the cost for Canadians more affordable."

Lacy cursed Paul Brouder in her thoughts. Lacy cursed Paul Brouder in her thoughts. Her vow to not make a scene kept her from going off on Brouder, there and then.

When the speech was over, and after the Q&A, Brouder opened the floor for reporters. They assembled at the front as the locals dispersed. Peter and Van had their camera ready. Lacy would be sure to get the first question in. She spoke up.

"Mr. Brouder, when our prime minister introduced the carbon tax bill, he did this to counter the changes to our climate and global warming caused by man . . ."

She said 'man' to highlight the people responsible for the climate change in the hearing of the listening audience.

"What do you propose to do about the problem with pollution?"

Paul Brouder smiled. "I understand there is a need for action for the sake of the environment." He stopped and briefly pointed in Lacy's direction. "Let me ask you a question . . ."

"Please. Ask." Lacy replied.

"What day is today?"

Lacy was taken aback by this question. She was perturbed by it.

"I am trying to understand the whole purpose or even the ethic of this question."

Paul said. "It's Monday, March 16th. That wasn't intended to be a trick question. My whole purpose and ethic of this question are to remind people of a promise in the Bible that God will never again destroy the world with a flood."

Lacy interrupted. "With respect, Mr. Brouder, was that a serious answer? I think that was the reason why a secularism bill was passed in Quebec. This is what happens when people are judged based on religion."

"Whether you want to believe it or not," countered the premier, "the danger is not in a global or even a nationwide catastrophe. The danger is in our unnecessary overspending that will bring our nation backward."

"If we do not turn the responsibility back on citizens, will this not plummet our nation backward?"

"I understand the rhetorical question. The responsibility is the citizen's, and not just our government."

Lacy pressed forward. "Lowering the cost of gas will only encourage more spending on fuel. You do know that the inaction of our government could lead to more pollution. And more pollution, in the long term, will be costly for citizens. It is the pollution that has been causing these natural catastrophes. What about a flood, Mr. Brouder?"

More reporters pressed forward with their questions.

"I would love to answer that, but I must let someone else ask a question."

Paul pointed to another reporter. The other reporter asked a question. Then another reporter asked another question. Lacy figured it was time to pack up and leave. She slipped out of the crowd and the building with her team following.

An hour later, Lacy and Jennifer sat across from each other inside of a Vietnamese restaurant. Before, during, and after the meal, they shared stories from the past week, without missing a beat. So much had happened the past seven days. Lacy could not describe the chemistry between the two. She and Jennifer had bonded in a sisterhood that was beyond words. As reporters and journalists, they were kindred spirits. Lacy had this feeling that they knew each other during childhood and had since been disconnected. But this couldn't have been. They'd revealed their ages, and Jennifer was Lacy's junior by a decade. They could not have been erstwhile companions from childhood. Such familiarity and closeness could not have been forged between them with such an age gap.

"Get out of here," Jennifer said playfully. "I cannot believe that you have never once visited Hopewell Rocks."

"I know," Lacy replied. "I've been around far too often to truly get around."

Jennifer looked accusingly at Lacy. "It's the job."

"No, it's not," Lacy replied, making light of the comment.

"Admit it, Lacy, you've been so focused on these politicians that you've never truly stopped to look at your surroundings."

Lacy was pensive for a moment. "You know, Jen, you are right. Sometimes you need a good friend, in the absence of a mirror, to point these out. I've been too preoccupied with work."

"I'm glad you finally agree with me," said Jennifer. "Your job has you traveling a lot. The next time you leave the province, I encourage you to strip down to your bikini, lie on a rock, and enjoy the sun."

"I am not going to be that audacious," Lacy said with eyes widened.

"I'll scratch that one off your bucket list."

"Now you have my bucket list?"

"Right now, I have your bucket list. And I see that it's empty. I'm only filling in the blanks. You and I need to visit Crabbe Mountain during the snowy season."

"Well, that I could do. I'm not a swimmer. But I can do winter activities."

"Then you're on. Until then, we need to plan something. What day is it today?"

After a time well spent at the restaurant, the two parted ways. Before Lacy was able to step into her truck, her phone chimed. She looked at the screen and saw Sage Palmer's name.

"Hey, Sage."

"Hey."

"Are you home?"

"No, a girlfriend and I are at Timmy's."

"How's the weather over there?"

"It's still very wet. I thought we were going to get flooded again."

"I'm sorry that I didn't call Friday. My hands were tied."

"Okay."

"What are you both having?"

"I'm having a chai, and she a latte."

"What's up?"

"You sound happy," Sage observed.

"I sound happy?"

"You're answering my question with a question. You do."

"Oh, I was just coming off my lunch break with Jennifer."

"That lady from the department store?"

"Yes, her."

"You sound like you've been hitting it off."

"Yes. We only met the other day, and we've become good friends."

"Scary."

"Scary? How is that scary?"

"I don't know. You only met that lady last week. I don't think strangers should hit it off so soon."

"Uh, oh."

"What?"

"Sage, are you jealous?"

"No, I'm not jealous. Do I sound jealous?"

"I don't know. You're talking about my friendship with Jennifer, as though it has replaced our friendship."

"No!" Sage protested. "I don't think that."

"Sage," Lacy said in an assuring tone, "you are my special little friend. And no one, no matter how close we become, will take your place in my heart. You have a special place, no matter what."

"Okay." Sage didn't seem very comforted by this. Lacy had to leave it there.

"Sage, I'm about to step into my truck and drive. And you know I can't drive and talk. We'll catch up later?"

"Okay," Sage said downtrodden.

Lacy ended the call and stepped into her SUV.

Where are you?

Later that evening, Lacy was at the bottom of her driveway when she noticed her neighbor also pulling onto her driveway. Gina arrived just in time for another random greeting. The only difference now was that Gina had warmed up to Lacy. The woman that Lacy had gotten so used to seeing as her neighbor was gone. The brush between the two would not be as abbreviated. Gina stepped out of her vehicle, and Lacy gave her a little wave. But Gina would not settle for the passing greeting. She had to park her car and walk over to Lacy.

"Hey, stranger! Strangely, I should call you a stranger."

"Hello, neighbor. And how was your day?"

"Relaxing. Almost too reposing. And how busied was yours, Ms. Pendleton?"

"Well, Ms. Preston, you have an idea what my day has been like."

"I saw the network during my lunch break. It must have been fun debating the premier."

Lacy held her hand out. "I don't know if I would call that debating. I will say that the coming days and months will be challenging because of some of the people that are being elected to office."

Gina's face morphed into an expression of concern. "Then you're going to need much alone time, at least tonight?"

"You've guessed right, Gina. Thank you."

"Maybe we can do something over the weekend."

"Maybe. But no promises. Good night." Lacy turned to go indoors and hoped in her mind that Gina would do the same.

On Wednesday, March 18th, at 2:30 PM, Lacy pulled up at the local library. She had a book to return: *The Last Days of Socrates: Euthyphro, Apology, Crito, Phaedo* by Plato. It was not the first time that Lacy had read this classic. She wanted to revisit the series of discourse between Socrates and some of his opponents, as Plato would retell it, a book that promotes a Socratic way of thinking. Lacy loved reading classics: Locke, Kant, Hume, and others. They were thinkers that made people think. Now that she thought about it, Lacy wanted to be sure that she would not be late with this return.

Then Gina came to mind. The weekend came and went, but Lacy had no time to spare. It'd been more than a week since they had spent any time together. Now that she had pulled up to the library, Gina came to mind. Lacy planned to drop off her book, look for Gina, chat a little, then leave for the office.

Lacy noticed herself becoming more like Gina. Before this, Gina was the one that casually slipped by because she had something to do and somewhere to be. For the past several days, it had been the reverse. Lacy had something to do and somewhere to be, while Gina wanted to stop and chat, so Lacy became scarce. She had been laden by her work and needed the space. Apart from the regular lunchtime meets with her other freelancer friend, Jennifer, Lacy had little time for social engagements.

Lacy went through the set of doors at the entry to return her book at the counter. She greeted the old lady at the desk and strolled through the library in search of Gina.

After an exhaustive search, Lacy concluded that Gina was off. That day, there were other librarians on duty. She decided to stop at one. "Excuse me. Do you know what day Gina will be in?"

The young woman turned to Lacy with a look of recognition. "You're Lacy Pendleton? It's nice to finally meet you. But I'm sorry, Gina quit yesterday."

"She quit?" Lacy's jaw dropped.

"I'm sorry. Tuesday was her last day."

"Do you—" Lacy stopped. She decided not to belabor the question on Gina's whereabouts. "Thank you for the update. And yes, it was nice meeting you."

Lacy dismissed herself and walked out of the library to her parked vehicle. She slipped out her phone and dialed.

"Hello?"

"Gina! Hey, how are you?"

"Hi. I'm fine, Lacy."

"Where are you?"

"I'm with company now. Can I call you later?"

"Sure. You know how to reach me."

"Good. Bye."

Lacy looked down at her phone, and the line was dead. She did not like being brushed aside. Lacy then thought to herself that the same way she had been brushing Gina off, Gina had just brushed her off, in turn. *Lacy was now getting her comeuppance. Now she had to wait to be called, like a politician willingly lending precious time to that waiting reporter. The question now was, "How long would this go on before Lacy found out more about this sudden change in Gina's life."*

Late that evening, Lacy was on her desktop browsing the net. Her eyes were glued to the screen. On the bottom-right corner, the time showed 10:30 PM. She would soon turn in for the night. She heard a car door close outside, and that sound was followed by voices. It sounded like more than one person, and it seemed like causal chatter followed by laughter. This could be neighbors returning home from an outing. Then again, it could be Gina with her company.

This possibility gave Lacy all the reason to leave her desktop to peer through her window. She stopped at the blinds. Slowly, she turned them for visibility. Meanwhile, she listened in on the neighbor's speech. One out of the two voices sounded like Gina. She was not alone. The second voice was a male voice. Lacy peered through the blinds and saw what she heard: two persons walking into the house next door. One of them was Gina. The door closed as soon as they walked in.

Lacy thought about Gina's male companion. That voice sounded familiar. It seemed like a friend of a friend that Gina had just met merely a week ago. Lacy knew the person, but vaguely. If it was who Lacy thought it was, then this was the person who had made some accomplishments in the writing of fiction and non-fiction. Brendan is his name. Lacy could remember overhearing Gina and Brendan's Saturday-night conversation. She missed much of the details, such as the focus of his literary works and genre of fiction.

Lacy put the thought behind her as she returned to her computer.

The next morning, Lacy took what she needed for the day as she stepped out of her house. Gina was on her mind then. Throughout the night, she had been in Lacy's thoughts. Gina hadn't called back since they last spoke. Just maybe, her hands were tied to her work.

Lacy was facing her Rogue when the site of a strange vehicle caught the corner of her eye. It was sitting on Gina's driveway. Gina did not own a black Mercedes, but it was sitting on her driveway. Her Civic was almost there and had to be someone else's. Gina has a visitor. What time did this visitor pull up onto Gina's driveway? This could have been the car door that she had heard the night before. The owner of the Mercedes is still there. Lacy looked down at her watch and saw 9:01 AM. Yet the street was quiet, and the air was eerily still. Gina's blinds were closed, and her house was unusually quiet and still.

Lacy brushed it from her mind as she turned her attention back to her SUV.

Lacy's trips home had been intermittent. One night she pulled up to her driveway and saw Gina's Civic. The Benz she had seen days before was there. After the break of dawn, Lacy saw it still sitting on the driveway. What she saw next shocked her. She saw Brendan. But there was another man as well. He, too, was handsome and appeared to have come with Brendan. *"What is this?"* she thought. Lacy brushed the thought aside. She did not want to jump to conclusions. Then again, to think this overnight stay was out of pure intentions would be naivety at its heights. Otherwise, how could Lacy know? Gina never called. And whenever Lacy called, Gina had been unreachable. Lacy got the picture. All she could do was let Gina be. But how could she? Wasn't Lacy a friend with a genuine concern for her girlfriend? *Girlfriend?* They'd only went out together a few times. Since then, life had taken a toll on their relationship. That "friendship" soon regressed to something that was below mere acquaintances.

That was not what Lacy had wanted, but this is life, and she had grown to accept it. That was what she learned from her father. And this is what she was teaching Sage.

Life is short. People will pursue that which they'd consider of value. What is of value? And what is worth pursuing? Are friendships worth pursuing? Are they of any importance? Are they worth fighting for? Who in this world did Lacy value? Jennifer? They had hit it off since the day they first met. Is Sage, or is Gina in that category?

The following night, Lacy saw Gina's Civic, Brendan's Benz, and another vehicle—a white BMW. Okay, Gina had gained a wealthy clientele for her business as a writer. But at 9:30 PM? Why this late? Her relationship with Brendan—so it appeared—had been more than professional. What was with this other vehicle parked on her driveway? Lacy slept on it.

The next morning, Lacy peeped through her blinds to see who would walk out of Gina's house this time. As expected, the three vehicles were still parked on the driveway. After ten whole minutes, Lacy retired to the kitchen. While she placed bread inside her toaster oven, she heard voices outside. Lacy briskly walked to her window. She wanted to make out the people, and she did. Lacy saw Brendan. What she also saw made her jaw drop. Two women followed Brendan out of Gina's house. They were mature, yet as attractive as Gina. Their clothing appeared slightly crushed, and their hair somewhat unkempt. Gina, who followed them, did not look any better. *"What is going on?"* Lacy thought.

The foursome bade each other farewell as Brendan stepped into his Mercedes, and the women climbed into the BMW. As they pulled out of the driveway, Gina waved, then walked back into her house.

Later that morning, Lacy sat at her desk and dialed Gina. Weeks had gone by since Lacy and Gina had had a good conversation. It was already Friday, March 20th. The line rang five times, and the wait felt like a millennium. After the sixth ring, someone picked up on the other line.

"Hello?"

"Hi, Gina, it's Lacy."

"Hi, Lacy."

Lacy waited for more than "Hi, Lacy," but there was only silence on the line. It was deafening. *How could this woman have become so alienated?* Just by this reply, Lacy could tell that Gina was being inconvenienced by the call.

"It's been some time since we've spoken. How've you been?"

"Good! And you?"

"I'm good. Am I calling at a bad time?"

"It's fine."

"I just had a feeling that I was . . . Where are you?"

"Where am I?"

"Yes. I was at the library a few days ago. I heard that you quit a month ago."

"I did."

"Where are you now?"

"At home, devoting more of my time to my other work."

"That's good. And I trust that it pays."

"It pays me well, thank you."

"Okay, then, that's good. I was wondering . . . I haven't seen you for some time. Are you okay?"

"Oh, I'm fine," Gina replied with bitter sarcasm. "Why are you so inquisitive? Oh, I forgot, it's what you do."

"What has been going on with you? I don't get why you're so choleric."

Gina shot back. "This conversation is over."

"You know what? Fine."

The line was already dead.

Lacy slipped the phone back into its cradle. Unless there was an incoming call, that phone would not be leaving that cradle again, especially after a conversion gone sour. Lacy needed five minutes to register what had just happened. How did it come to this? After knowing Gina for a little while, they had become fast enemies. Was it something Lacy did or did not do? Maybe it was what Lacy said or did not say? Why had Gina suddenly become so offensive?

The phone rang from its cradle. Lacy looked at the phone. It rang three times before she lifted it off its cradle.

"Daily News Team, Lacy Pendleton's line."

"Hey, Auntie!"

"Is that you, Sage?"

"Yes."

"You do know I cannot do personal calls with my business line?" Earlier, Lacy had made a personal call using her business line.

"I called your personal phone several times. I got no answer."

Lacy picked up her phone and noticed that she had it on silent since the night before. "I'm sorry. I didn't turn the sound back on this morning."

"Mom told me you were in the area on Friday. You promised that you'd visit."

"My time there was short. I'm really sorry." Lacy changed the subject in hopes of lightening the mood. "How is the crabby teacher? What's her name . . . Mrs. Siren.?"

"Oh, miserable as ever."

"Good. I see that all is going well in your world."

Sage paused for a moment. "Are things going well in your world?"

"I wish they were. But maybe that's why I still have a job. I got to update the public on the good and the not so good."

"I want to travel with you sometimes."

"How about visiting Staci while she's working? I've never seen you at the news center."

"But I have been. I was there three times. You were never there then."

"Okay. I guess you've one-upped me on that one."

Lacy looked down at her phone and realized that the mute was still on. It lit up. A number and name turned up, one she recognized.

"Sage, could I call you later? I promise you, I'll call back."

Lacy ended the call and stared at the number on her phone. The only difference was that this number had never turned up as an incoming call before. Lacy saw this, and her heart leaped. This was not a leap of joy, but of dread. If she answered, what would she say?

"Dad?"

"Hi, Lacy."

"Uh, what . . . um . . . why are you calling me now?"

"I'm sorry, sweet pea . . ."

Sweet pea? When was the last time Lacy heard this? She was a little girl when he used to call her that.

"Um . . . is everything alright, that you would call me now?"

He chuckled nervously. "No . . . well, yes . . . I'm well."

"Then why are you calling me?"

"I'm sorry that I'm calling you at this time. You've been on my mind a lot. These recent months, I've been doing a lot of soul-searching."

"Dad," Lacy said in her attempt to snap him into reality. "You're retired. Retired people do soul searching. And it's in those moments that they learn that it's too late. They will never again see that opportunity because it is long past. All they have with them is a life of regret: the things they should have done and the people these persons should have acknowledged when they had the chance. Forced retirement is a bummer. It took forced retirement to force you to look yourself in the mirror and learn where you've gone wrong."

He sighed deeply. "I can truly say that I have wronged you. I've wronged you by my neglect."

"And you're calling me to say you're sorry, and to ask for forgiveness?"

"I know this will be hard for you, but yes."

"I don't know if I can do this. You've wronged me. Throughout my childhood and into adulthood, you've treated me like another face in the crowd. And you're expecting me to forgive you?"

Lacy noticed someone walk by her desk. It was one of her co-workers, and she must have heard that last line. *"But what do I care?"* thought Lacy. *"What matters is that my father heard it."*

Lacy continued. "You've had a half-a-century worth of time to build a relationship with me. But the church was much too important for you. You had so many people to reach, and so many people to bless. And the whole time, you had a daughter who was longing to be reached and longing to be blessed. Now you are retired, and you are expecting me to receive you with open arms?"

"I know, Lacy. And I understand your feelings of resentment. You may never trust me again. But I want you to know that I'm sorry."

There was dead silence on the other line.

Lacy's father continued. "I want you to know that you're not the only one that I've wronged. Even more, I've sinned against God. There I was, thinking that I was doing God's bidding. I got carried away in my mission to reach others. What I did not realize was that the greatest mission I had was at home. You're right. I'll never get that opportunity again. But I am confessing to you how wrong I've been. You may never want to speak to me again. I'm calling out of my desperation because I know what God has been trying to show me these years."

Lacy fought to suppress her tears. "What is that? What has he been trying to show you?"

"My daughter . . ."

Lacy could not hold back the dam any longer. The tear ducts burst, and the wellspring of tears began to flow.

Her father continued. "For my neglect, I needed forgiveness. And because Christ died for my sins, I believe that I have been reconciled back to God. I now want to be reconciled with my daughter. But I know I must give you some time. I hope you'll forgive me in the end. Most of all, I hope you'll one day be reconciled with God."

Lacy dried her tears. "I want to go now. I'll think about it."

"I understand, Lacy," her father said with sadness in his voice.

"Thank you,"

Lacy ended the call. What she did not notice was the tall woman that stood behind her. It was Daylia.

"Lacy, ah can hear yuh bawlin' from around the corner. Is everyting alright?"

Lacy hastily dabbed the moisture in her reddened eyes and forced a smile. "Thanks! I'll be fine."

"Eh-heh. Sound like yuh faddah on the line. Who else can make dose eyes red?"

Lacy chuckled, "Daylia, you've got the sharpest hearing."

Daylia nudged her. "Ah got this from years of listenin' fo gossip."

Lacy tilted her head before responding in jest. "Oh, you are good." Daylia laughed, then gently rubbed her back. "In all seriousness, I hope every ting will be alright between yuh and yuh faddah."

"I hope so too."

Lacy believed the road to healing would be long and arduous. There would be many missed opportunities to make up for. Would Bishop Pendleton ever be able to make up for those missed opportunities? The damage was done. That may never be repaired. To do so would mean to go back in time and undo the many days of neglect. Now that would be impossible. But what about others that could have been recipients of the same type of negligence, such as close friends? Sage soon came to mind.

Are you in there?

On the afternoon of Monday, March 23rd, Lacy sat across from Jennifer at a Mediterranean restaurant. Scraps of what they had left clung to their plates. Their glasses were less than a quarter full. One of the women that stood behind the counter wiped empty tables until she got to theirs. She cordially lifted their plates off the table. Jennifer looked up and smiled.

"Thank you."

The woman smiled briefly and turned to Lacy. "Thank you for the work that you do."

"You're most welcome." Lacy returned a smile.

The woman continued. "I, too, believe in saving the environment."

"Thank you for following and for voicing your support," Lacy said. "And be sure to follow us on Twitter."

Lacy turned to Jennifer as the worker walked on.

"You see, Jen, we need more voices to stem the tides of Brouder's madness."

Jennifer said, "You and I know that Brouder is not the only problem in our country."

"Definitely not," said Lacy. "But we gotta start somewhere. And Brouder's politics is a good starting point."

Jennifer looked glum. "I need to say this, Lacy, something must be done. Brouder must be stopped. If we do not, everything our former premier worked for in our province will be lost in our memory."

"I know, Jen. We need to create a petition."

Jennifer spoke with bitter sarcasm. "Here's one: 'By signing this petition, you are asking Ottawa to keep Brouder away from our pockets, and away from the gaslighter."

Lacy smiled at the comment. "I'm amazed at how many people buy into his rhetoric."

Lacy's phone played a ringtone that both Jennifer and she loved.

Jennifer queried. "Who on your list gets Queen Bey singing to her caller ID? That has to be a special someone."

Lacy readied herself to take the call. "It's Sage. And you're right. It's a special ringtone for someone special. Hello, Sage."

"Hi, Lacy."

"How are things back in St. John?"

"Not good. I don't know if you heard, but our city is expecting a lot of water."

"I already know about it. What are you going to do?"

"They're telling people to evacuate the city. Can I come over to where you are?"

"Wow, Sage. I'm going to be—" Lacy stopped and thought for a moment. "When are you coming?"

"Today. I'm taking a Go bus."

"I'll meet you at the train station. Just call me when you're close. And I'll get you."

"Thanks!"

Lacy laid her phone down.

Jennifer said, "What time will you be expecting her?"

"I don't know. Maybe this evening."

"They're now saying that there may be a flood here as well. Your friend may be caught in what she's trying to get away from."

"It may not be as bad here as it will be there."

"Maybe not. Lately, we've been subject to the unpredictable."

"You've got the point there, sister. That's why I never liked doing weather reporting. I did it once. I felt like the fool when the weather did not turn out as predicted."

Jennifer's eyes widened with her jaws agape. I love weather reporting. How could you not?"

"Well, I prefer politics, the thing that ruins relationships," Jennifer laughed.

Lacy continued. "My head has been entirely immersed in the political arena."

Jennifer sat back on her chair and smiled at Lacy. "You know, the irony is that the political has been impinging on the weather."

"That's true," Lacy said. "I'll let you know that Paul Brouder is going to be in our city tomorrow."

"Perfect!"

Lacy gave Jennifer a skeptical look. "Perfect?" "Perfect timing because I hope that meeting is rained out."

The two shared a laugh.

"Either way . . . I am going to plan to be there when he holds that meeting. I have some questions for him."

Later that evening, Lacy and Sage pulled up onto her driveway. It was 8:30 PM, and the lamp posts had already lit up to counter the pitch blackness around them. There was no moon in their sight, and the stars were obscured by the hovering clouds.

Lacy parked the vehicle. She and Sage were in the middle of their girlish chatter. The moment they took the time to breathe, Lacy's instincts kicked in. She was not thinking about it, but it was a part of her to look to her left.

"Oh no. Not again!"

Sage heard the disappointment in her voice. "What's wrong?"

Sage turned and saw what Lacy was peering at. On the neighbor's driveway, a blue Honda Civic, a black Mercedes Benz, and a white BMW.

"What's wrong?" Sage asked again. Lacy shook her head, trying to dismiss what ran through her mind. "Neighbors."

"Why? Are they noisy?" Lacy thought about the innocence

of her question and was deciding on what to tell her. "They are a noisy bunch. Come! Let's go inside."

The two walked indoors. Sage made herself at home as she plopped onto a two-seater. This is a place of comfort. The plush beige leather sofas were soft enough to cause the persons sitting on them to dose off.

Lacy smiled while amused. "I can see you've made yourself at home."

"I've always loved it here. I think I can stay here for days."

"Well, Sage, you are more than a . . ."

Lacy was about to say 'guest,' when she heard a car door close outside. Soon she heard another door close.

Lacy scurried over to the window. She tilted one of the blinds. The moment that she did, the headlights from both BMW and Benz blazed, stealing some of Lacy's visibility. Then both vehicles backed out, leaving the parked Civic alone. Gina's door was already closed when both cars drove away. The tires on the Mercedes screeched the moment the driver hit the accelerator. The driver did not sink it; he stomped on it, causing an afterglow of smoke from the rubber.

Lacy turned her eyes from the scene. She was now deep in thought. Someone is either angry or frustrated. Someone heard the infamous 'No.' Then, with a tinge of anger, the driver left the house, stepped behind his steering wheel, then burst forward in an outward display of reckless abandon.

"*Tonight will be a good night, after all*," Lacy thought.

"What are you looking at?" asked Sage.

"Two cars just pulled out of the driveway. We may get some decent sleep tonight."

Throughout the night, Sage lay with her eyes closed, as the rumbling of thunder was heard. With this, there was a constant beating against the window caused by the downpour. Before she gave herself to sleep, her mind ran on St. John, home, and Mom. She knew Mom had left the area. She would not tell her where she was heading. The mother did not want Sage to worry. It was for the better that she did not know.

All Sage could do was rest, while leaving all worries for the next day. So, she did rest. Unlike St. John, there were no predictions of massive flooding for Moncton. Sage would stay in Moncton until the waters in St. John had dissipated.

In the morning, it continued to rain. Now it rained even more heavily. Sage joined Lacy at the island in her kitchen.

"What are we making this morning?"

"We're making omelets."

"Yay! I was hoping for something more challenging."

"Well, Sage, my dear, I would save most of my energy for the day, for we don't know what it holds."

Sage's face lit up. "You mean that I'm coming with you?"

"You are surely coming," replied Lacy. "It's raining outside. I wonder when this will stop?"

"I'm not sure. Hopefully, at some point this morning. Strange that I haven't looked outside this morning."

"Neither have I," Sage said.

Lacy peered through her kitchen window, and the overview wasn't enough. She walked to her living room window and opened the blinds. Water between four and five centimeters high flowed across the sidewalk. Sage joined her and saw the flooded street.

"It's not as bad as St. John," Sage said, now with concern in her voice.

Lacy massaged her back to give her some reassurance. "Don't worry. It shouldn't be bad."

An hour later, they were on the road. Lacy's Rogue sailed across the roadways and intersections with ease. Since pulling out of the driveway, the rain had lessened its intensity. The outdoors did not look like day. The rolling of thunder echoed across the sky. Sage stared upward, hoping that she would see a few breaks in the clouds above. So far, she had seen none. The angry dark clouds moved across the sky while making no promise that day would come. Sage turned to Lacy.

"Where are we going?" she asked.

"We're going into the city. The premier is also expected to be there."

Sage turned her attention back to the road ahead. It was at that moment that the way into the greater city area was barricaded. Two officers stood by the roadblock. Lacy stopped. One of the officers walked to Lacy's side of the truck. Lacy lowered her window. She held out her badge showing her affiliations and why she's there.

"I'm sorry, ma'am. You cannot pass. A flood broke through the street." "Is there any way that I can get into the city? I'm supposed to meet with my camera crew."

"Can't tell right now. Only look out for roadblocks like this. And do be careful."

Lacy turned her truck around and drove away, merging onto another street. From that street, she turned onto another. Her phone chimed. It was wirelessly connected to her vehicle, so she hit an icon on her steering.

"Hello?"

"Hey, Lacy, it's Jen."

"Hey."

"I have a surprise. You wouldn't believe what I have with me."

"I wouldn't believe it? What do you have with you?"

For a moment, there was dead silence on the line.

"Come to my position: the Main Wheeler King, at the inn south west-east."

Lacy knew where to find her.

Sage did not understand the cryptic language. Lacy would explain it to her as soon as she got off the phone with Jennifer. Jennifer decided to encode her directions, believing that the line could be tapped.

Lacy drove to an inn that sat south of Main, west of Wheeler, and east of King. It was close to the estuary of a smaller river. By the time they got there, the water from that river had swollen, to the point that it took up the entire parking lot. The river rose, and the angry current that led into the ocean began to shift the few remaining cars out of their place. The parking lot looked like it was part of that river, while the hotel sat at the center of this riverbed. Lacy stopped when her truck was deep enough that the water was almost three-feet high.

Sage was wide-eyed, and her heart constricted. As she looked over the vast body of water, she had almost forgotten to breathe. Her fingers clamped onto the side of her seat until the tips grew numb. Like Lacy, Sage never learned how to swim. What makes her plight worse than Lacy's was her perpetual fear of large bodies of water. This phobia's origin was a mystery, even to Sage. She only knew that this fear of drowning had gripped her heart for as far back as she could remember.

Lacy pressed an icon on her steering and dialed the last caller.

"Lacy, I see you. I'm inside the inn. You wouldn't believe what I've found. Pull up to the building."

Lacy turned to Sage, who turned to her with pleading eyes that begged for Lacy not to obey.

Lacy replied. "Are you serious? Do you know the river is now moving your car downstream?"

"Just drive to your right. That way, you're fighting against the current. And stay on your accelerator."

Lacy turned to Sage, who shook her head vigorously.

"I'm really not liking this. It would have been better had I taken a boat over to this inn."

"Who do you have with you?"

"I have Sage with me."

"Please, Lacy, you gotta trust me. I found the cause of this flood."

"Before I go any further, are you alone?" Lacy asked."

I'm here with two friends of mine that work at his hotel. The people have evacuated. It's just us." Lacy grew more suspicious by the moment.

"This must be really important for you to call me with such urgency."

"Oh, it is! This discovery will amaze you. It will change the way we understand these disasters so that we will know what to do in the future."

"Okay, Jen. Back to my drive to the entrance. Are you sure about this?"

"Please. You must trust me, Lacy. There is a shallow part to your right, and it's the hilly part. Drive on that side, then pull as close to the entrance as you can."

Lacy paused and wondered if the effort would be worth it. She had a young passenger with her, and neither of them could swim. Suppose the SUV was to be swept away by the current, it would be the end for them. Lacy tried to make sense of this scenario. She questioned if going through this would lead to a new discovery, or to pure madness.

Lacy placed her hand gently on Sage's trembling lap to still the unease. Then, she sank the gas pedal. Sage screamed. That was the only thing that almost spoiled Lacy's focus. As Jennifer advised, she steered towards her right. She stayed on the pedal. The river, which was almost up to the window, attempted to push her eastward. Sage continued to scream. Tears streamed down her eyes as Lacy stayed on course. Sure enough, the SUV took them to the entrance. Lacy pulled as close to the building as she could and parked. Water was almost to the window. Lacy lowered the windows, and she climbed out. Then she helped Sage out. They both walked through the entrance with water up to their waists. By the time they got in, the deluge was not as deep. The flood did not force them in one direction, because it was still.

Lacy called out. "Jennifer?"

She called out again; there was no answer. Then her phone chimed. She answered.

"Jennifer, where are you?"

"We're down the hall, in room 106."

"We're coming."

Lacy and Sage pushed through the water. By then, there was no electricity. They arrived at 106. Lacy touched the door slowly, then called to the people in the room.

"Jennifer, are you in there?"

"Come in, Lacy."

Lacy opened the door. A man, she had never seen or met before, stood at the doorway to greet them. There was an oddness about him. He looked like his being there could only come with an ulterior motive. By his black gear, he looked like he was dressed for mystery, and for the ominous. He waved Lacy and Sage into the suite. What Lacy saw next startled her. There was another man who had the same dress code and Jennifer. She also wore black. Her hair was in a ponytail. They both stood by a chair. On that chair was their hostage: Paul Brouder. He was bound with arms behind the chair, ankles tied together, and gagged with silver duct tape. The man that stood by Brouder had an automatic pressed against the premier's cranium. Jennifer also had a pistol in her hand.

"Jennifer, what is going on?"

"What many will find out when this flood is over—that their premier has died."

"Jennifer, I'm going to ask you not to do this. This is not the way."

"At first, this was not my action of choice. After considering for a while, I came to this conclusion: a drastic step must be taken if we are going to see real change."

"Jennifer, this is insane. You do not murder politicians just because they're in the wrong. They should rather be voted out."

"Voted out? Lacy, he was voted in by the gullible and unsophisticated among our citizens. They couldn't tell bad policies apart from the destructive and poisonous goals of a misanthrope. This is what should be done."

"Then, how do you plan to do this, Jennifer?"

"Simple . . . my friend, to my left, will put a bullet through Mr. Brouder's brain. Once we have done this, we will untie him, then leave him on this bed with the gun by his side. Either this, or we topple his chair over. Brouder falls into the knee-high water and dies by drowning. Either way, it will look to investigators that Premier Paul Brouder has committed suicide. By then, we will be long gone. It will never be traced to us."

"Um, your car . . ."

"Yes, my car . . . I knew that it would be taken away. Now, that is why my friends came in their motorboat to pick me up."

"After you have killed Brouder, others with the same goals will take his place. Will you kill them too?"

"Good question! I know bad politicians are not hard to come by. Then, we may have to go through this process again."

"Will there be any end to this? And what will you do about us, now that we know what you did?"

"Lacy, either you are with us, or you are not. One thing is certain, neither you nor our young friend will tell the authorities what we did."

Lacy ground her teeth and spoke through them. "Jennifer, if you ever so much as touch a hair on my Sage's head, I will—"

"I know what you would do," interrupted Jennifer. "But I should not be held responsible for what my friends do to her."

Jennifer briefly looked at her fellow captors. The two men drew closer to Lacy and Sage. Lacy stepped in front of Sage to shield her from the approaching men. The men drew their weapons and pointed them at the two women. Jennifer spoke in an audible tone.

"I want you both to witness the death of our soon-to-be former premier." Jennifer ended this exclamation with a laugh.

Lacy pleaded one more time. "Jennifer, please do not do this."

"Sorry, Ms. Pendleton, It's far too late to beg for the former premier's life."

The moment she said this, Jennifer kicked the premier's chest, causing his chair to fall back. He landed into the water with a splash. Both Lacy and Sage shouted, "No!"

Jennifer shouted back. "Yes!"

Meanwhile, Brouder's tied up feet were kicking. Bubbles began to break away to the surface.

Lacy could not tell if this was her gut reaction. Before the men could anticipate her movement, Lacy dashed for the premier. One of the men reached for her, but she had slipped from his grip. Lacy dove where Paul Brouder was, then pulled his head out of the water. Jennifer remained calm, but she had a disappointed look on her face.

"You should not have done that." She then pointed her gun at Sage, who stood helpless. "Now, it's going to be life for a life."

Lacy's hair was wet, yet she was tensed. "You would point a gun at my Sage? I'll tell you the truth, Jennifer, one of us will not leave this building alive."

"Tsk, tsk. I'll tell you the truth, Lacy, that I don't take kindly to threats. You have a choice: put him back, and your Sage will live; attempt to save him, and your Sage will die. What will your choice be?"

Just then, a loud bang that sounded like the toppling of large boxes was heard. This startled the captors. To the group, this could be the effects of the flood, and that the building was about to collapse. Jennifer motioned to one of the men to go see what that was. He obeyed. He walked stealthily out of the suite with his gun trained in the direction of the noise. Jennifer turned her attention back to Lacy and Sage. The other captor grabbed Sage and gripped her tightly by the hair, as Jennifer walked over and pointed her pistol at her.

"I am serious. Put him back or the—"

A bang from a gun was heard, then a splash. This startled the two captors. For them, this was a moment of confusion.

Jennifer turned to her other helper. "Go see what happened to John."

He left the teenager to Jennifer and ran out to join his fellow captor. The moment he turned the corner, "Bang! Splash!" Jennifer's look of confidence suddenly morphed to great concern.

She called out to her friends. "John? Dave?"

"They're dead." Everyone in that suite was startled by the voice and by the presence of a new person. Holding a rifle and pointing it in Jennifer's direction was Gina Preston. Her hair was let down, and she wore a brown checkered button-down.

"Gina!" Lacy shouted, now feeling a slight sense of hope for the first time. Jennifer pulled Sage in front of her and held the gun at her head.

She shouted, "No one move!"

Jennifer didn't notice that while she had Sage in front of her, her hand was by her mouth. Sage bit down on Jennifer's hand. This caused Jennifer to loosen her grip on both Sage and the gun. Sage broke away from Jennifer, as her weapon fell into the water. Lacy saw this and dashed for Jennifer. Gina rushed to Paul Brouder's aid, the moment he fell back into the water. Jennifer went under and lifted the gun. Lacy reached for that hand and grabbed her wrist. The two women wrestled for control of the weapon. One-shot, then a second round tore at the ceiling, as Lacy and Jennifer struggled for possession of the gun. Suddenly, the pistol fell back into the water. Jennifer reached for it. Lacy pounced on her back. Soon, the two women struggled underwater. They lifted their heads for air. At that moment, Jennifer pulled Lacy underwater. Soon, Jennifer gained the upper hand and was on top of Lacy with her hands around her neck. With this advantage, not only would Jennifer squeeze the life out of Lacy but also cause her to drown. Lacy's struggle to free herself from Jennifer's grip was fading. She was losing air and was growing weaker by the second.

Just as Lacy was at the brink of losing all consciousness, Jennifer's grip loosened. Lacy looked through the water and saw Jennifer on top of her. But she was glassy-eyed. Jennifer's eyes were absent. Lacy pushed herself out of the water. The woman that had Lacy at a disadvantage fell sideway and drifted lifelessly into the water.

Puzzled, and wondering what had happened, Lacy looked around. That's when she saw Sage standing over her and her nemesis with Jennifer's gun still trained on its owner. Jennifer lay underwater, looking up at the ceiling, with an absent stare, that was a look of terror.

Lacy stood up, ran, and embraced Sage with all her might. They both looked in Gina and Brouder's direction. Gina freed the captive.

"Gina," Lacy walked towards her. "How did you know we were here?"

"I followed you both," Gina replied. "I found a motorboat with keys in it and followed you. Lacy, I want to apologize for the way I've been treating you. I've done a lot of thinking."

Lacy was bedazzled. "You apologize to me? Gina, no, I owe you an apology. I was wrong. I have not been fair to you. I should be the one on your tail, not the other way around. And here you are on our tail. We would have been dead had it not been for you. Gina, I am so sorry!"

Gina smiled. "We both have a lot of apologizing to do. I don't think our apologizing will ever undo the hurt. I've been thinking about my need for forgiveness, not only from you but also from God. I've done things these past several weeks . . . and I am ashamed of them. I had to break it off with Brendan last night. I feel the weight off, yet I feel so dirty still. I feel God's forgiveness, but I need cleansing."

Lacy stood speechless. "Um, Gina, I am not the preacher-type,

I'll tell you that much. But I think I know someone who could talk with you about that."

The two women embraced and held each other tightly for a while. When they pulled away, they turned to Sage. "Gina," Lacy said, "this is Sage."

Gina smiled. "I've heard so much about you."

Sage said, "Thank you for saving us." The two embraced. Sage continued. "I've been the atheist-type. After this, I think I'll visit a church, maybe Mom's church.

Lacy drew again to Sage. "And Sage, I have not been fair to you, especially. I promise that this will change." The two embraced again.

Lacy turned to Gina. "I'm still wondering how you managed to knock off two armed men before coming to our rescue."

Gina smiled. "I think I got the inspiration from either a Patricia Cornwell or a Kathy Reichs novel. I think I now have my inspiration for my first novel."

Unnoticed by the three women, Paul Brouder stood. He stood patiently, allowing this reunion to take its course. They finally turned to him. He turned to Lacy.

"Lacy, thank you! Thank you, three. I don't think I have the words to express my gratitude. But thank you!" The women did not know how to respond to this.

Lacy spoke out and said, "You're welcome?"

He drew closer and gave them an authentic smile as he held Lacy's hands. He said to the three, "You may never share my political views. Neither do I expect you to share them. I guess this is a good reason for debate. We may never stand shoulder-to-shoulder on our goals. But I'll do all that is in my power to work towards a common goal. Your act of heroism will not go unnoticed."

Lacy, Gina, Sage, and Paul entered the boats, as the rescue team arrived. Premier Brouder would bring this story to Ottawa. Lacy, Gina, and Sage would soon expect to receive medals of honor from the prime minister himself. The clean-up crew arrived at the hotel and retrieved the three bodies, as the waters slowly returned to their place in the rivers and ocean.

Many kilometers west, Lacy, Sage, and Gina traveled in Gina's rented SUV. They drove into St. John in New Brunswick. Lacy stared out the passenger window to see that much of the city experienced the effects of a massive flood. There were thousands of dollars in damages. Despite this, the women saw in the people of the area the resilience that kept them for generations. There were no signs of gloom or despair. The people continued as though life was supposed to come with adversity. This was the kind of spirit that Lacy saw back in Moncton and was what she was seeing in St. John. Even with the higher gas prices, the people of St. John remained the people of St. John. As Gina drove, Lacy scanned the area and saw, on a hill of a cemetery, a man that stood at seven-foot-three in height. He is a presence that she knew all too well. It was Barry Windrop.

Barry was straightening a tombstone. As his eyes were locked with hers, he straightened up. She smiled at him. He then raised one of his hands as a gesture that said, "Hello!"

After allowing her phone to dry, Lacy was finally able to use it. She dialed.

"Hello?"

"Dad? It's Lacy."

"Yes, Lacy." His voice showed that he was excited to hear from her. "Yes, sweet pea."

"Dad, you'll be seeing me soon."

"Yes," he said. "Please come."

"Okay. I'm coming with company. I'm bringing with me two of my dearest friends."

Printed in the United States
By Bookmasters